*Their lives wove a tapestry
of love and hate . . .*

CONRAD. The man who had everything . . . except a sense of honor.

DOROTHEA. The brilliant concert pianist who gave up too much to be Conrad's wife.

KARL. Their son. Heir to his father's iron will, he struggled to fulfill his mother's gentler dreams.

LISL. Karl's sister, who looked for love in his best friend's arms, blind to the threat that darkened their lives.

HIRO. The sensei. His wisdom gives meaning to Karl's battle with himself . . . and with his father.

TATSUO. Heir to a great Japanese empire, torn between the destiny he was born to and the love he cherishes.

THE LAST SUNRISE

"You alternately suffer and rejoice with two fascinating families. The final pages had my heart racing."
—Robert Shea, author of SHIKE

THE LAST SUNRISE

NORMAN CARELIUS and VERNA KIDD

A JOVE BOOK

THE LAST SUNRISE

A Jove Book / published by arrangement with
the authors

PRINTING HISTORY
Jove edition / April 1984

ISBN: 0-515-07530-2

Heartfelt thanks to
Hiro, Beverly, and Andrea,
who made this book possible.

Contents

THE LAST SUNRISE

BOOK ONE
THE BOY

〔 1 〕

Wednesday, August 15, 1923.

A blazing orange sun crept slowly over the horizon, setting fire to the calm waters of the Pacific. The white hull of the *Empress of the Orient* sliced effortlessly through the water, and on this, the sixth day of her voyage from Vancouver to Yokohama, it was apparent she would surpass the speed record of seven days, twenty hours, and sixteen minutes set by her sister ship, the *Empress of Japan*. Accommodations on the new *Empress* were elegant and luxurious; she boasted nine decks, six with open-air promenades which allowed her 1,107 passengers to enjoy the majesty of the vast Pacific. Towering over the ship were two enormous funnels, each bearing the red and white insignia of the Empress Line. Colorful flags neatly strung out at regular intervals between the funnels and masts flew proudly in the ocean breeze.

Conrad Richter stood alone on the top deck, his rigid face shadowed by the rising sun. It could have been a handsome face, with the blond hair above the broad forehead and blue eyes of a startling intensity, but there was an unyielding hardness in the line of his jaw and in the harsh set of his mouth. Mesmerized by the rhythmic sounds of the ocean and the gentle, almost imperceptible sway of the ship, Conrad let his mind wander. He did not often allow himself this pastime, for he considered dreaming a useless waste. His father had been a

3

dreamer, barely eking out an existence on a narrow strip of land near the village of Koenigsberg in Prussia. Conrad realized, long before his father ever did, that the tiny farm would never produce enough to make them rich or even to keep their stomachs full during the grim winters. Along with that realization came disgust for what Conrad considered weakness in his father's character. The dreams faded with the years, and Conrad began to plan his flight from the poverty and futility that had been forced upon him. In the end it was a simple escape. His father collapsed one day in the field and by the time Conrad found him, he was dead, a look of resigned sadness on his face. Conrad buried him alongside his mother's grave on the hillside overlooking the house. Within a month Conrad sold the farm to the first bidder, packed his clothes, and walked away without a backward glance.

His father's world behind him, Conrad ran blindly for the coast of Germany. In Hamburg, filled with the fear of being trapped again and the longing to run even further, he stumbled into the merchant marine. His youth did not present a problem, for he was tall and well muscled—the daily struggle for survival had matured his face and sharpened his instincts.

The transformation from a landlubber to a seaman was simple and almost immediate. Despite the grind of backbreaking labor, he grew accustomed to the sea, and his plans for the future began to crystallize. Determined to wipe out every trace of his dismal past, Conrad drove himself relentlessly toward the ultimate goal of amassing wealth and with it, power, and he vowed never to allow fate or circumstance to interfere with his plans.

After six years, Conrad left the merchant marine and bought two old freighters that had been sitting idle in the naval dockyards at Seattle. Realizing that he could operate more freely and profitably in Canada, he moved the ships to Vancouver, a major seaport situated twenty miles north of the international border. The move proved to be a wise one, for his shipping company grew at an astounding rate, as did his reputation as a shrewd businessman. He was now firmly established in the shipping industry and could be depended upon to fulfill his contracts and complete shipments unerringly. No doubt this was the very reason the Takezawa *zaibatsu*—business empire—had contacted him. He had reached a turning point in his business career; it was time to reinvest his profits and establish a bigger empire.

Conrad heard footsteps behind him and he turned, annoyed at the intrusion.

Karl saw the look of annoyance on his father's face and for a moment he hesitated. At thirteen, he was beginning to show signs of maturity. The muscles in his chest and shoulders were thickening, the soft curls had disappeared from his straw-colored hair, and he walked with the unsteady gait of a youth who was not yet certain of the height he had suddenly acquired. There was an aura of vitality about him, a hint of the strength he would have as a man.

"It's almost breakfast time, Father," he said. Karl's blue eyes held the same startling intensity as Conrad's, and already there was a firm directness in his gaze.

"Did you think I would lose my way?" Conrad asked abruptly.

"No, sir."

"But you had nothing else to do? Well, we arrive in Yokohama tomorrow afternoon. Perhaps I could arrange a tour of the ship's engine room and helmsman's station for you. You should learn all you can about this ship and every other ship you sail on. Your livelihood will depend on it one day."

Instantly, a wide smile appeared on Karl's face. His inherent love of ships and the sea had been nurtured by both parents. His mother had opened the magical doors to the enchanted world of literature as soon as Karl had learned to comprehend a few simple words. She loved reading to him, and he always listened with rapt attention. When Karl learned to read, he surprised even his mother with his insatiable appetite for books. Stevenson's classics, *Treasure Island* and *Kidnapped*, captured his imagination while Kipling's *Captains Courageous* was the essence of all his boyhood dreams. From that time on, thoughts of ships and the sea occupied his mind constantly, and his mother wisely, but often with a heavy heart, encouraged that interest.

"How big are her engines, Father?" he now asked.

"This particular liner has four steam turbines that can pump out twenty thousand horsepower, and even though she weighs twenty-six thousand tons, she still averages twenty-three knots. Speed is very important whether your cargo is lumber, silk, or people. It's a highly competitive business, and any new technology must be incorporated into our ships as soon as possible. It's a hard life in the merchant marine, and only the best survive. The others either sink or end up hauling garbage.''

"What will we be hauling to Japan?"

"I want to set up a contract with the Takezawas to transport their silk and tea to Vancouver and bring back lumber, wheat, coal, iron ore, and whatever the hell else they might want. The Takezawas are very powerful and very wealthy, and I want their business."

The bell sounded for breakfast. They walked quickly to the Veranda Café, where enticing aromas of bacon and freshly baked bread wafted toward them as they entered. Elegant yet pleasantly relaxing, the café was the exclusive realm of the first-class passengers. Graceful rattan furniture, authentically Japanese, blended unobstrusively into the garden setting. Soft green draperies complimented the oak-paneled walls and the cushions of the fan-backed chairs. White linen covered the round tables, and there were green and white checkered napkins at each place setting. Potted plants with luxuriant foliage stood in little groups around the café, some reaching for the ceiling and others spreading their delicate fronds over the muted brown carpet. Exquisite Japanese waitresses attired in traditional kimonos of dazzling spring colors hovered over their guests, daintily filling their plates from silver trays that rested on wooden trolleys. The diners, warmed by the sun that flooded through the windows, lazily drank freshly ground coffee while the soft drone of their voices filled the room.

The Richters chose a table close to the window. Instantly, a tiny Oriental waitress, dressed in yellow kimono, appeared at Conrad's elbow. She filled his cup with steaming coffee and poured water into Karl's glass. Karl stared wide-eyed at her, thinking she looked exactly like the doll his sister kept in a glass case in her bedroom.

The waitress smiled, revealing perfect white teeth. Tilting her head slightly, she said in a musical voice, "Master Karl, you have beautiful eyes. They remind me of a lake near my home in Japan." She turned to Conrad. "And you also, Mr. Richter, but yours remind me of the lake on a stormy day."

Conrad paid little attention to the waitress. At that moment Victoria Forsythe had entered the café, and Conrad watched intently as her party followed their waiter. Close behind her were her husband and an awkward-looking boy in his early teens.

It was obvious that Victoria was one of those emancipated women so much in vogue now. She walked with the easy grace of a trained model, her stride long and sensual, her head erect. Fashionably bobbed hair framed her face and glistened in the morning light. She wore an eggshell-colored dress that flowed smoothly against her skin, accentuating her full breasts and gracefully curved thighs.

"Good morning, Mrs. Forsythe. I must say that you look very beautiful today," Conrad said boldly as they approached his table.

Victoria flushed under his mocking gaze. "Good morning, Mr. Richter. May I introduce my husband, Julius, and our nephew, Vincent. This is Conrad Richter and his son, Karl." She smiled at Karl. "Vincent is spending the summer with us. It won't be long before he takes his place in the family business, and of course Julius is the right man to teach him."

Conrad wondered if the warmth in her voice was sincere. If it wasn't, she was a good actress; her eyes were clear and innocent as she placed her hand on her husband's arm.

Julius Forsythe was short, thin, and extremely energetic. The family business he had inherited, a men's clothing store on St. Laurent Boulevard in Montreal, had been unpretentious but very lucrative. Upon his father's retirement, Julius had sold the store, deposited the sizable profits in a Montreal bank, changed his name, and begun looking for a business more suited to his aristocratic affectations. Armed with quick wits and a strong practical streak, he soon became profitably established in the silk industry. Promptly expanding into fabric mills of his own, Julius was soon producing enough material to meet the demands of many eastern clothing manufacturers. He now lived in an ostentatious mansion filled with "family heirlooms" secretly purchased in England. So thoroughly was he entrenched in his assumed character that had anyone reminded him of his real past, he would have been sincerely shocked. He had a passionate love for objets d'art and considered Victoria to be one of his finest. Although he regarded Richter as a bourgeois commoner with no social standing, he was inexplicably threatened by him and fought the desire to lash out in self-defense.

Conrad also felt an overpowering resentment as he acknowledged Julius's less than polite nod and Vincent's aloof stare. Looking only at Victoria, he said, "Would you like to join us for breakfast?"

Julius stepped quickly in front of Victoria and placed his hand on her elbow. "No, we prefer to be alone, thank you. We have some private matters to discuss."

Delighted at Julius's obvious agitation, Conrad kept his voice low and his eyes on Victoria. "As you wish. I'll look forward, then, to seeing you at the captain's table this evening."

Julius glared at Richter. "I sometimes wonder how a ship's captain chooses his guests; he must pull names out of a hat."

Victoria listened to the carping exchange and again a flush crept into her cheeks. Julius unconsciously straightened his silk tie and brushed imaginary lint from his immaculate blue serge suit; then, steering Vincent and Victoria ahead of him, he started to move away from the table. Before he had taken more than a few steps, Conrad's voice shot out threateningly. "Forsythe."

Julius waited without turning.

In a taunting but audible whisper, Conrad said, "Fuck you."

Julius's shoulders stiffened as though he had been struck squarely in the back; his hands tightened into fists. For a moment Conrad thought he would turn back, but with shoulders still squared, he quickly walked away.

Conrad returned to his breakfast. The waitress, looking like a yellow and green butterfly, refilled his empty coffee cup, and he ate with renewed appetite. His hand was steady as he picked up the cup.

Agitated by the tension, Karl searched for something to say. "That Mrs. Forsythe is sure pretty, isn't she?"

"Yes she is. Too bad her husband is such an ass." Conrad's contemptuous tone closed the subject. "Eat heartily, son. We'll soon be in Japan, and then you'll have to eat rice and raw fish like the Japs do."

"Yuck!" Karl replied with an exaggerated grimace.

Conrad detested raw fish and barely tolerated rice. He patted his slightly spreading middle with disgust and decided that perhaps a Japanese diet was exactly what he needed. He had always been lean and muscular, his body hardened by arduous physical labor, but now the effect of affluence was becoming obvious.

The waitress bowed respectfully as Conrad and Karl left the café. The decks were already crowded with morning sun-bathers sprawled comfortably in deck chairs, some armed with dark glasses and books while others slept off the effects of the previous night's excesses. The more energetic passengers strolled along the promenade decks, taking advantage of their last day aboard the *Empress*. Ladies with lavishly adorned hats and colorful parasols added a festive air to the atmosphere of the liner. Two elderly gentlemen faced each other in motionless concentration across a chessboard, their wax-figurine-like stillness disrupted only by an occasional puff of smoke from identical pipes. Every passenger aboard the *Empress* was pampered, indulged, and amused, and since almost all of them were wealthy enough to be accustomed to being waited upon, they accepted it as part of their innate privilege.

The Richters made their way aft in search of the captain. As they approached the bridge, a muscular seaman politely informed Conrad that passengers were prohibited from the area for their own safety.

"I understand," Conrad said. "However, I would appreciate it if you would inform the captain or first mate that I would like to see him as soon as possible."

"Who shall I say is making the request?"

"Conrad Richter."

The seaman was unimpressed by the name but bounded effortlessly up the stairs to the bridge. In a few moments the first mate, immaculate in a white uniform, came down to meet Conrad.

"Good morning, Mr. Richter. What can I do for you?" He extended his hand to Conrad. The gold buttons on his jacket, polished to a mirror shine, caught and reflected the sun's rays.

"Yes," Conrad answered. "I operate several freighters, but as you know, they are the workhorses of the sea and considerably different from this fine ship. I would like to arrange a tour of the engine room and helmsman's station for my son."

The first mate smiled and turned to Karl. "Maybe I shouldn't show you the *Empress*; you might put us out of

business one day." He disappeared for a few minutes and
returned with another officer whom he introduced as Mr.
O'Neill, the ship's third mate.

"This young man would like to tour the ship, Mr. O'Neill.
Would you please show him what makes her run?"

"Aye, aye, sir." O'Neill motioned for Karl to follow.
"Come with me, son. We'll start with the engine room and
work our way to the bridge."

The next three hours passed quickly for Karl and the third
mate. O'Neill had often conducted tours through the *Empress*
but found it difficult to make boilers and drive shafts sound
interesting to bored passengers. To his surprise, he found Karl
Richter was not only extremely knowledgeable about ships but
also genuinely interested in what he had to show him.

When the tour was over, Karl returned to the empty state-
room and lay down on the huge bed. The room was cool,
scrupulously clean, and oppressively lonely. He turned onto
his stomach and closed his eyes, unwilling to admit even to
himself that he was homesick. He remembered how serious his
mother had looked on the day of their departure. She had
tried hard not to cry when Karl hugged her, but he had felt her
wet cheek against his and pretended not to notice.

Unable to contain his loneliness, Karl left the state-room
and climbed to the upper deck. The ocean was rough, but Karl
enjoyed the brisk wind blowing past his face as he walked
along the open-air promenade. Suddenly his path was
blocked. He looked up and recognized the face of the youth he
had met earlier at breakfast. Vincent Forsythe stood resolutely
in his way, holding the hand of a slender, pale girl.

"Excuse me," Karl said as he attempted to go around them.

The girl tugged gently at Vincent's arm. "Please let him
pass."

Vincent bristled at the thought of their earlier meeting in the
Veranda Café and of the open hostility between his uncle and
Karl's father. "No, I won't let him pass."

The girl's pale color faded even further, and her frightened
eyes widened at the anger in Vincent's voice. "Please," she
begged.

Karl saw the worried look on the girl's face and felt sorry
for her. He moved over deliberately and once more tried to go
around them. Not noticing Vincent's outstretched foot, he

stumbled over it and pitched headlong onto the hard deck. Eyes dark with rage, Karl stood up slowly to face the older boy. Even in his own ears his voice sounded strange. "You stupid, wide-ass son of a bitch!"

Vincent, a head taller and thirty pounds heavier, smiled smugly at Karl's insult. Suddenly, Karl lashed out with a quick right hook which caught Vincent high on the cheekbone, causing him to stumble backward. Someone laughed, and Vincent gave vent to his suppressed fury. Grabbing Karl's hair with his left hand, he pummeled his fist into Karl's face several times before letting go. Karl fell to his knees, blood streaming from his nose. He waited for his head to clear, then lunged at the bigger boy. Karl's punches came from all directions and landed with telling effect. As Vincent attempted to grab hold of Karl's hair once again, Karl planted his knee in Vincent's groin. Vincent crumpled to the deck, the smug look gone, replaced by fear as Karl closed in. There was a dull thud as Karl's boot connected with the older boy's face, forcing several teeth through his lip. A crowd had formed; several passengers screamed. Three crew members finally appeared and quickly dispersed the crowd before taking the bleeding combatants to the sick bay.

Karl lay quietly on the treatment table as a medical officer examined him. His eye was puffed up and a small clump of hair was missing from the right side of his head.

"Well, I guess that's about it." Dr. Climie grinned down at Karl. "From the look of that eye, it must have been a good scrap."

Karl tried to smile. "He asked for it."

The young doctor chuckled. "Yes, the other guy usually does. Other than that bruised eye, which will turn into a dandy shiner, you'll be as good as new in no time. I want you to stay here for a few more minutes so I can check that eye once more before you go." He left the room to join the other medical officer.

"How is your patient, Don?" he asked.

Dr. Ballantyne continued working on Vincent and, without looking up, asked, "Who was this fellow fighting—Jack Dempsey?"

Dr. Climie raised his eyebrows in surprise on seeing Vincent's face. "Can I help with anything?"

"Yeah, check the pupilary response while I suture this lip."

Climie shone the narrow beam of light into Vincent's eyes; they contracted quickly and evenly. "Looks normal. How's the lip?"

"A couple of teeth went right through. He's still a bit groggy—we better contact his parents before discharging him."

In the waiting room, Conrad confronted the two doctors. "I'm Karl's father. What happened? If my son started this damn fight, I'll deal with him right now."

Dr. Climie stepped forward. "Now just relax, Mr. Richter, your son is fine. From what I gather, Karl didn't start the fight. The seaman who brought him here said he was provoked by the other boy. We had to put in a few stitches to close the fellow's lip, but other than that he'll be fine, too. We're keeping them both here a little longer for observation, so please make yourself comfortable."

Conrad sat down heavily in the overstuffed chair. Half-heartedly, he leafed through the latest edition of the *Ladies' Home Journal*, which had obviously been selected to distract and amuse apprehensive visitors. Theda Bara, the alluring vamp of the motion pictures, stared out from the cover. Unaffected by her artificial sensuality, he tossed the magazine aside and stood up impatiently. Annoyance replaced his earlier relief, and he began to pace the floor. Perhaps bringing Karl on this trip had been a mistake.

Suddenly the door burst open and Julius Forsythe stormed through the waiting room, followed by the first mate. As the door slammed behind them, Conrad realized that Karl's opponent had been none other than Forsythe's nephew, and he wondered what had incited the two boys to fight. It was evident from their earlier meeting in the Veranda Café that Vincent was rude and insolent, but if he was anything like his uncle, Conrad doubted he would resort to physical means to win an argument.

Julius stomped from the treatment room, his face scarlet with rage. The first mate attempted to calm him, but Julius shook off his restraining hand and faced Conrad. His small frame was taut with hostility.

"Your son could have killed Vincent! I will expect restitution for this criminal behavior!" His voice was shrill and resounded off the walls with piercing intensity.

Conrad would have enjoyed laughing uproariously; instead

he smiled benignly. "Restitution! Really, Julius, what would you have me do—pay for your nephew's boxing lessons?"

The redness in Julius's face deepened. "You bastard, you rotten Kraut bastard!"

The first mate stepped between them. "Gentlemen, please. I think we should forget about this unfortunate incident until cooler heads prevail." Turning to the doctor, he asked if the boys were ready to be released.

"Yes, they're fine," Dr. Climie replied.

Karl emerged first, his face pale and his eye visibly swelling, but the nurse had combed his hair and straightened his blood-spattered clothing.

Conrad was silent as they returned to the state-room. Once inside, Karl sat quietly, waiting for the reprimand he was sure was forthcoming. "I'm sorry, Father. I didn't want to fight, but I just couldn't help it."

"I can't say that I'm happy you caused such a disturbance. The fight apparently upset several passengers, and I don't think it made the crew very happy either. From what I understand, though, the overfed bastard deserved a thrashing, and I'm glad you gave it to him. But I think you had better stay out of everyone's way for the rest of the voyage. I just don't want any more trouble. I'll have dinner sent up here. Don't look so disappointed; we'll be in Japan tomorrow."

Conrad paused at the mirrored entrance into the huge banquet room and adjusted his perfectly fitted dinner jacket. His tailor had worked frantically to complete the wardrobe he had ordered for the voyage to Japan. Unlike the established rich, whose imperfections in dress could be passed off as eccentricities, Conrad demanded impeccable workmanship and the latest styles fashioned from the finest fabrics. As he stood under the high archway surveying the crowd, he knew that his money had been well spent.

Four enormous chandeliers hung from the ornate domed ceiling, their crystal prisms dancing in the shimmering light. Waiters were already hovering about the assembled guests, filling their delicate long-stemmed glasses with wine.

The maître d'hôtel appeared at Conrad's side. "Sir, the captain awaits your presence at his table. The guests are anxious to begin dinner."

Let them wait, Conrad thought. He knew without a doubt

that the captain would not start without him, for among his duties was keeping his passengers happy, especially the influential ones.

Captain Logan acknowledged Richter's belated arrival with a nod. "Ladies and gentlemen, now that we are all here I would like to introduce our head table guests." He quickly made the introductions, strategically pausing to compliment the ladies. Most of the guests at this particular table were unaccustomed to delays such as had been forced upon them by Richter, and Logan hoped the elegant dinner prepared by his expert chefs would soothe their irritation as well as appease their appetites.

Aware of the cold stares he was receiving, Conrad calmly sipped his wine and studied the guests as they were introduced by the captain. Sitting opposite him were two young Japanese men, obviously students on their way home from university; Conrad wondered what they were being groomed for. Wealthy Japanese families often sent their sons to schools in Europe and America to prepare them for a variety of positions in government, business, and industry. He noted that when they spoke, the young men retained the detestable habit of pronouncing *r*'s as *l*'s and wondered if it was the shape of their mouths or merely their uncompromising nature that prevented them from mastering the English language. Acknowledging their polite bows, he carefully concealed his contempt. Having spent the past two years negotiating with the Japanese, Conrad had learned to eat their revolting food, to listen stoically to their tuneless music, and to acknowledge their enigmatic art. More precisely, he had learned how to camouflage his emotions. Over the rim of his glass he studied the fine cut of their suits and thought, You can exchange your kimonos for expensive suits, but you can't get rid of your fish smell and yellow skin.

"Are you the same Mr. Richter who married the German pianist Dorothea Koenig? My husband and I have traveled extensively, you know, and we had the extreme pleasure of hearing Miss Koenig play at a concert some years ago. Oh, she was delightful!" Jewels bobbed and sparkled on the ample bosom of the matron sitting next to the students. Words poured from her mouth between spoonfuls of soup. "Whatever have you done with her, Mr. Richter? Surely you are not keeping her all to yourself! I understand her father was killed in some monstrous accident . . . he left her a sizable fortune, though . . ."

"You'll have to excuse my wife's impertinence, Mr. Richter
—she loves to talk." Lord Jamison temporarily stopped Lady
Jamison's barrage.

Conrad nodded. "My wife *is* Dorothea Koenig the concert
pianist. She has by her own choice given up her career to raise
our two children. She has not been well since the birth of our
daughter and prefers to stay at home."

"What a pity she could not be with you." Lady Jamison's
high-pitched voice rose above the chatter around the table.
"The sea air seems to perk up one's health; it has done
wonders for mine. Of course, I do love my home in England,
but—"

"My wife is home taking care of our daughter," Conrad interrupted. "However, my son is with me. I think it is very important for parents to spend time with their children and not
leave their training to nannies and governesses."

Lady Jamison colored slightly and her loose jowls quivered.
"But we have a very capable governess; our children are extremely well cared for." She quickly turned her attention to
the succulent roast beef the waiter had placed before her.

Captain Logan listened somewhat nervously to Richter's
curt remarks. Worse, however, were the glances that began to
be exchanged between Richter and Victoria Forsythe. Logan
hoped Mrs. Forsythe's husband would not notice. Any open
display of hostility, particularly so near the end of the voyage,
could be disastrous. Mrs. Forsythe was very beautiful and,
judging by her animated and candid conversation, quite
unrestrained. Her pointed remarks were intelligent and mildly
controversial. Her ability to keep the conversation interesting
and the laughter gay had earned her and her husband a regular
place at the captain's table. Logan was sure Julius had assumed these invitations came because of his auspicious rank in
the business world.

Conrad remained aloof from the chatter, speaking only
when he was addressed directly. He noticed that although
Captain Logan seemed to be entirely at ease, he was instantly
aware of any lull in the conversation and alert to contentious
subjects. Skillfully, he renewed lagging discussions or maneuvered them to safer ground. Trite banalities were sprinkled
with clever witticisms, and the guests, encouraged by the wine
and enjoying the pleasant sensation of mild intoxication, re-

peatedly burst into gales of laughter.

When the volume of the conversation seemed to be at its peak, the lights were dimmed and waiters appeared with the traditional flaming dessert, whose dramatic blue flames emitted the aroma of cherry brandy. For the guests it was an elegant finale to their last dinner aboard the *Empress of the Orient*.

Julius Forsythe was feeling the effects of an exhausting day and of the potent wine. Confused and disoriented, he silently cursed Conrad Richter. It seemed that at every turn he faced those razor-sharp eyes, and to his dismay, he continued to be intimidated by the man. In the past he had enjoyed the covetous admiration in men's eyes as they watched his beautiful Victoria, for he knew that she was his prize and he enjoyed flaunting her. But when Richter looked at her, jealousy suffused Forsythe's mind, and hatred replaced reason.

Victoria gave him a muted warning as he signaled the waiter to refill his wineglass. Forsythe ignored her and emptied the glass; the alcohol seemed to ease the grip of tension in his stomach. In the background he could hear the soft strains of music from the ship's orchestra. As the waiters removed the last of the sumptuous dinner, he felt nauseated and realized he had underestimated the power of the wine. He tried to stand up but his knees buckled, and he supported himself against the table until he felt Victoria's firm hand on his arm.

Conrad watched Victoria as she led her husband from the room. He did not realize how intoxicated Julius was until he saw his clumsy attempt to leave the table. Apparently Victoria had anticipated what would happen and was prepared. She had quietly disengaged her husband from the rest of the dinner guests and before anyone other than Conrad was aware, she had steered him toward the nearest exit. Conrad felt a sense of disappointment as he watched her receding back. Then, at the door, Victoria, still holding her husband upright, turned suddenly and gazed around the ballroom until she found Conrad. When their eyes met, he knew she would be back.

Upon her return, Victoria walked directly to him. Without a word, she stood in front of Conrad until he took her hand and led her to the dance floor. As if in response to his command, the orchestra immediately began to play "Estudiantina," and the dancers melted together. Conrad drew Victoria closer and noticed that she smelled of perfumed soap. He ran his hand up her supple back; she wore very little beneath her dress, and as he felt the softness of her skin, he felt himself harden against her. She gasped softly as he drew her more tightly against him, kissing her neck, where her pulse beat rapidly. Her hand tightened on his back and her body welded to his as they moved with the music.

"I could use a drink," he whispered, his lips against her ear. She nodded in the semidarkness. "So could I."

He guided her through the crowd and out onto the open promenade. "I always travel with a supply of my favorite Scotch. Will you join me in my room?" For an instant she appeared uncertain, and he thought she would refuse.

"Yes," she replied finally. "I would like that. But—your son?"

"We have adjoining state-rooms. He won't disturb us."

They walked slowly along the deck, and Victoria knew Conrad was watching her as the wind molded her dress to the curves of her body. Her skin felt hot in spite of the coolness of the night.

Conrad walked into the room ahead of her and turned on the small table lamp. The door closed firmly behind them, shutting out the music, and as he turned to look at her in the mellow light, she panicked for a moment. Her hand shook as she reached out for the glass he offered. Conrad stood behind her, and she leaned back against him as he caressed her arms and ran his fingers along the nape of her neck, where her hair curled.

When her drink was finished, she turned to face him, feeling powerless under his direct gaze. Conrad held her gently at first, and then, with the intensity of mounting desire, he dug his fingers into the soft flesh of her arms. She moaned as he pushed his tongue between her teeth, and then she met it with hers. She felt his urgent fumbling with the buttons on her dress and trembled as the garment slipped from her shoulders to the floor. She stood before him, the dim light catching the swell of her breasts and playing with the shadows on her slender legs.

"Take off the rest of your clothes." Conrad's voice was urgent, commanding. His breath caught as she dropped her undergarments to the floor, her naked body gleaming as though bathed with delicate oil. He could not remember carrying her to the bed, but he heard his own harsh breathing and could feel the softness of her body under his. Her back arched

and she gasped as he caressed her breasts with his tongue, and
when his tongue moved down her body to the inside of her
thighs, she moaned softly. Her hands sought him out, electrifying him with her light touch, exploring, demanding, and
sending exquisite sparks of desire through his body and into
his throbbing groin. Her body moved rhythmically against
him, and Conrad groaned as he drove himself into her.

His hands crushed her breasts, and she cried out in surprised
pain. She tried to struggle but was helpless beneath his violent
thrusts. Swollen with desire, Conrad continued his relentless
penetration, his arms pinning her down in a viselike grip.

He could taste the blood from her lips where she had bitten
them to keep from crying out. His release came like an explosion; he convulsed with ecstasy and then lay quietly beside her.

Slowly, Victoria moved from the bed. Her body felt weak
and bruised, as though she would never be free of her weariness. Had it not been so painful, she would have laughed,
thinking how eagerly she had sought him only a short time
ago. When she was dressed and had repaired her makeup and
hair, she stood beside the bed and looked down at him.

"Thank you, Mr. Richter, for the drink. This has been an
evening I will not easily forget."

After she had gone, Conrad felt a strange unrest and lay
awake, staring at the ceiling.

Several hours later, in the cool solitude of the early dawn,
father and son stood watching the coastline of Honshu Island
draw closer. Mount Fujiyama, previously obscured by the soft
haze of the morning, now came into spectacular view, its
majestic peak reigning in sunlit splendor over the rest of the
rugged terrain. Midway up the mountains, the clever Japanese
had carved flat ledges into the steep slopes for cultivation, filling every available inch with rice paddies and vegetables.
Warmed by the tropical black current and irrigated by abun-
dant rainfall, the east side of Honshu Island was green and
lush, dotted here and there by neatly lined orange groves. The
Empress steamed past small inlets crowded with fishing boats,
all small and fragile and vying for space among the numerous
little islands and peninsulas that jutted out into the sea. The
rugged coastline, rimmed with tiny villages, slipped gently by.
Squat, diminutive houses, some of which were obscured by
willows and craggy, wind-blown pines, crowded the land-

scape. Soon the tranquility of the fishing villages gave way to the riotous confusion of Yokohama Bay. As if in preparation for the docking of the great liner, the entire harbor was aglow with colorful paper lanterns strung in mass profusion; paper flowers, deceptively real, added a festive touch to the busy seaport.

"If you think this is bad, wait until we try to get through the streets and train stations." Conrad shook his head knowingly. "Crazy Japs love pushing and bumping into each other . . . Christ!"

The *Empress* had broken the old speed record by a full two hours. The powerful tugboats that pulled her into port looked insignificant beside the grand lady, but they were not to be underestimated, for they easily escorted the *Empress* to her mooring. Dozens of smaller craft raced around the huge liner, their colorful flags fluttering in the wind. Blasts of horns shrilled through the air, and geysers of water cascaded from the nozzles of firehoses. It was a carnival atmosphere that greeted the passengers who crowded onto the open decks. The sun shone brightly in a cloudless sky, and the smell of fish and humanity permeated the air.

Karl watched the display with unconcealed delight and wonder. He grinned and waved frantically, forgetting his father's admonitions about the smiling, happy people who waved back at him. His nose had already grown accustomed to the peculiar smells, and he cocked his head to hear the high-pitched music that rose above the noise of the crowd.

The loud blast of a horn announced that the *Empress* was finally coming to rest at her mooring site. With the hawsers in place, the winches began pulling the liner closer and closer to the pier. The gangplanks were lowered, and as the passengers began to disembark, a small orchestra, shrill and tuneless, began playing with great gusto.

Conrad waited quietly until most of the passengers had left the ship. When he spotted Victoria and Julius walking toward the gangplank, he stepped directly into their path. "Good morning, Victoria," he said.

"Good morning, Mr. Richter," Victoria answered quickly.

Conrad's eyes widened with surprise as the wind blew the scarf from her face, revealing an ugly welt on her cheek.

"What happened to you?" Conrad put a restraining hand on her arm and looked accusingly at Julius Forsythe.

The corners of Forsythe's mouth lifted in a part smile, part sneer. "What happens to Victoria is my business, Richter, but accidents do happen, particularly when one stays out too late at night. I strongly suggest that you be on guard as well. Strange things have been known to happen in the Orient, *Herr* Richter." Julius spat out Conrad's name with a perfect German accent, his voice seething with contempt.

Conrad was momentarily caught off guard by the unmistakable threat in Forsythe's voice, and he stood speechless as Julius walked away with Victoria trailing behind him.

"What did he mean by that, Father?" Karl asked.

"Nothing that is of any concern to you," Conrad replied.

When the gangplanks were clear, the Richters made their way down to the waiting Japanese.

[2]

The gangplank swayed gently as the Richters descended. The moment their feet touched the pier, two men emerged from the crowd and greeted the new arrivals with ceremonious bows.

"*Kon-nichi-wa*, Richter-sama. Welcome to Japan." The spokesman was surprisingly tall for a Japanese, his voice low and clear. The two men were similarly attired in what Conrad recognized as street clothes—dark kimonos and sandals.

"Kon-nichi-wa." Conrad carefully returned the hello.

"I am Hitoshi Takezawa, and this is Takeo Kuniba. We have been given the honor of escorting you and your son to my father's home in Tokyo."

Conrad was surprised and then irritated that the elder Takezawa had not come personally to meet him, but instinct warned him that Hitoshi Takezawa probably held a high position in the hierarchy of the zaibatsu.

"I have left instructions that your luggage be taken to the train station," Hitoshi continued. "Please come with me."

He raised his hand. Instantly two jinrickisha runners scuttled forward, their bodies naked to the waist and glistening with perspiration. Hitoshi helped Conrad and Karl into the jinrickisha, where they settled back under the canopy that shielded them from the hot August sun. The heat and oppressive crowds were beginning to penetrate Conrad's composure. Perspiration soaked through his suit, leaving dark stains under his arms and between his shoulders. Hitoshi remained unaf-

fected by the heat and teeming crowds, his face impassive and
unreadable. As he stepped into the jinrickisha, Conrad recognized the graceful movements of a trained athlete and realized
that this man would make a formidable enemy.

At Hitoshi's signal, the runners sped through the crowds
with amazing dexterity and made their way along a narrow
street that ran parallel to the pier. Yokohama was a busy harbor; many ships lined the wharves awaiting cargoes. The
raucous voices of longshoremen could be heard above the clat-
ter of rolling freight wagons and the scream of steam winches;
loading nets and cargoes swung precariously above their
heads. Low wooden buildings and warehouses lined the docks,
their company names boldly displayed on huge banners that
snapped in the brisk wind.

Karl pointed excitedly to several signs that he recognized:
Commonwealth Trading Company; Shanghai and Hong Kong
Bank; and Canadian Pacific Passenger Terminal. It was obvious that many foreign investors had taken a keen interest in
the economic fortunes of this tiny but dynamic nation. Suddenly the runners changed direction and turned into the heart
of the city. The jinrickishas rolled along the narrow streets,
passing a profusion of buildings and shops decorated with
colorful lanterns, paper flowers, flags, and banners that beck-
oned the shoppers who jostled their way along the noisy
streets. The entire thoroughfare was alive with activity—cluttered, overcrowded and strangely alien.

"It smells so different," Karl said, screwing up his nose.

"Something like a huge laundry bag?" Conrad laughed.
"Actually, it's a combination of the food stalls and the
people. Vast amounts of money change hands on these tiny
streets everyday. The Japs are very industrious."

Soon the streets widened. Trees and gardens replaced the
noisy stalls and shops; even the air seemed cooler and fresher.
The wheels of the jinrickisha clattered over an arched wooden
bridge shaded by a cascade of weeping willows. The Richters
stared in silent appreciation at a gracefully turreted wooden
building that seemed to be an extension of the moss-covered
terrain upon which it sat. Flowering shrubs and gracefully
pruned trees blanketed the grounds with color; sunlight filtering through the willows cast a pink hue on the white pillars
that supported the upper levels of the elegant structure. The
only adornment in evidence was a large lantern hanging directly above the entranceway.

After the jinrickisha came to a stop, Hitoshi jumped out nimbly and smiled for the first time. "I can see by your face, Richter-sama, that you are impressed. This is called the Jinko-In, because the architecture resembles one of our famous shrines. But do not be intimidated by its venerable appearance; it is merely a place to eat."

Leaving Takeo behind to deal with the jinrickisha drivers, the small group walked up the cobblestone path and passed through the intricately carved doors into the coolness of the building. They were met by two smiling hostesses, who bowed repeatedly in unison. Conrad guessed that Hitoshi Takezawa's arrival had been expected and that his patronage was held in high regard.

Karl's eyes widened as the girls knelt down to remove his shoes, giggling between bursts of conversation.

"Please do not mind the ladies, Karl. They are intrigued by your leather shoes and by the size of your feet." Hitoshi chuckled at the boy's apparent embarrassment.

With their feet now clad in soft, cloth slippers, they padded along after the ladies, whose wooden *getas* clunked hollowly on the polished floor. A hand-painted paper partition was opened for them, and after several bows they were ushered into a small room furnished only with a low table and silk cushions.

"You are the honored guest, Richter-sama. Please sit here under the *tokonoma*," Hitoshi said, pointing to an alcove where a neatly lettered scroll hung beside a clay pot that contained a single delicate chrysanthemum.

With a grimace, Conrad twisted his long legs under him and tried to find a comfortable position on the silk cushions. He cursed silently.

The paper door slid open and Takeo entered, followed by four waitresses carrying clay pots and hot towels. Chattering and giggling, they held out the steaming towels for the men to use. Karl's face was grave as he tried to copy Hitoshi's example, wiping his face and the back of his neck. The towel was scented with lemon, and he soon felt pleasantly refreshed and cool. The girls disappeared with the soiled towels, then returned almost instantly with trays of fish and vegetables.

Behind them came a young man brandishing a long, gleaming knife. He knelt at the end of the table, where an enormous, ugly fish lay on a worn cutting board. With sure, even strokes, he quickly sliced the fish into paper-thin fillets, which the girls then rolled into tiny balls. After dipping the white morsels in ginger and horseradish, they offered them daintily to their guests. Conrad smiled unconvincingly and forced himself to gulp down the fish as quickly as possible. Karl's eyes watered from the horseradish, but he bravely swallowed the morsels.

Hitoshi laughed as Karl nodded in appreciation. "I am surprised, young Richter-sama, that you like raw fish. Most westerners find it difficult to acquire a taste for it." Turning to Conrad, he added, "Children are far more adaptable than adults."

With the skill of an experienced chef and the flourish of a seasoned actor, the young man diced the vegetables and twirled the knife for his appreciative audience. The mushrooms and beef quickly disappeared under the flashing blade and emerged uniformly sliced. When the job was completed, he stood up and tossed his knife high in the air before jamming it neatly into the sheath that hung from his belt. With a final exaggerated bow, he disappeared, closing the screen quietly behind him.

Karl's mouth watered, and even Conrad watched expectantly as the girls cooked the vegetables and beef on the glowing braziers. They teased Karl, poking him playfully, and flirted with the others while they cooked. Conrad found himself drawn into their playful mood. Although not completely to his liking, the food was at least palatable, and the *sake*, served at precisely the right temperature, helped remove the taste of soy sauce from his tongue. Having convinced the waitress that he was filled to capacity, Conrad leaned back against the wall and watched Karl clean his plate, using his fingers whenever the ivory chopsticks failed to work quickly enough.

Hitoshi shook his head and smiled. "Karl, you have an amazing capacity for food. Our hostesses are delighted with your appetite."

While pretending to be absorbed with the antics of the girls, Conrad studied Hitoshi. Obviously he had received some schooling in America, for his English was impeccable; even the inevitable slurring of the *l*'s and *r*'s was barely noticeable. He had about him an aura of worldliness, but also of reserve, as though he had examined life fully and had come to terms with it. Yet he was inextricably Japanese, subordinate to customs and governed by the pristine traditions of his ancestors. Conrad fervently hoped that all the Takezawa zaibatsu officials would not be as imposing as Hitoshi. He consoled himself with the thought that perhaps they would prove to be as amiable around a conference table as they were around a dinner table. Conrad's thoughts were interrupted by Karl, who, unable to control himself, was doubled over with laughter.

"I can't eat that," he said, pointing to a large mushroom the hostess held between her fingers. Suddenly realizing the reason for Karl's mirth, she blushed prettily and giggled. In a moment, everyone at the table shared Karl's secret. Their laughter filled the room.

"Ah, Karl," Hitoshi said as he wiped the moisture from his eyes, "that is a mushroom—we call it *matsukate*. Although it resembles your most private parts, I assure you it is very delicious." Taking the mushroom from the waitress, he dipped it into a bowl of sauce, then bit into it with obvious delight.

Karl quickly followed Hitoshi's example, carefully placing a mushroom in his mouth and chewing slowly. Conrad watched with disbelief as his son proceeded to devour the elongated fungus.

With dinner finally over, a screen was opened which exposed the garden; cool air scented with flowers drifted into the room. They sat, lazily sipping at tiny cups of *o-cha*—tea—as the sun filtered gently through the willow trees.

"It would be very pleasant to stay here all afternoon, but the train will be leaving for Tokyo very soon," Hitoshi informed the group.

Conrad nodded. In the past, his visits to Japan had been brief and confined only to long, trying meetings in the midst of Yokohama's teeming commercial hub. He had been well aware, however, of Japan's wealth and potential for trade and had resolutely worked toward acquiring what he considered his fair share. He was now very close to realizing that goal by forging an agreement with the Takezawas, who were wealthy and powerful, perhaps beyond his imagination.

The train station was exactly as Conrad remembered it. People still streamed en masse, ruthlessly stampeding into the waiting cars, heedless of the heat and stale air. What amazed Conrad was that they seemed to be enjoying themselves! He steeled himself against the impending onslaught, determined that he would remain unaffected by the crowds. To his astonishment, the jinrickisha sped past the crowd and stopped in front of a closed off area where an empty passenger car stood waiting on the narrow steel rails.

Conrad smiled sardonically. Of course, the Takezawas had a private car, he realized.

Hitoshi Takezawa and the Richters were soon escorted into the car by a uniformed attendant while Takeo was once again left behind to dispose of the runners.

As if reading Conrad's mind, Hitoshi said, "Takeo has been with the zaibatsu for many years. His parents were killed long ago, and since it is of utmost importance for everyone to have a family, he adopted ours and we gratefully accepted him. He is an invaluable associate and a trusted friend."

Conrad's face did not show his true feelings as he thought bitterly, Who do you think you're fooling? You pay him and he runs your errands. Instead, he said, "Trusted friends and employees are certainly an asset to any business."

"Takeo and I attended school together in San Francisco," Hitoshi explained.

"Yes, I gathered that both of you had gone abroad to study. You have an excellent command of English."

Hitoshi smiled. "We became quite Americanized during our five years in California." After a pause, he continued. "Japan has a way of enveloping her people, and even though I returned as a rebellious, undisciplined student, I was quickly brought back to our traditional way of life."

As long as Hitoshi was being expansive, Conrad would continue to ask questions. It was important that he learn as much as possible about the Takezawas. He wondered if Hitoshi had an Achilles heel and, if so whether it would become a lever with which he could move the entire zaibatsu. He studied Hitoshi's tranquil face for a moment, realizing one would have to dig deeply and skillfully to find any such weakness.

"What did you study at university?"

"I majored in business administration and commerce, while Takeo studied engineering. Initially, I was a very reluctant student—I did not want to leave Japan. But it was my duty to obey my father's wishes. Fortunately, he foresaw the benefits of a liberal education. Japan is entering a new era of technology and foreign trade, and we must prepare ourselves—we can no longer depend entirely on our old ways. Although Japan has been self-sufficient for centuries, we must now open our doors to the world."

"I hope I can be of service to you."

"I hope so too, Richter-sama."

Takeo swung easily into the railroad car and sat down beside Karl. Conrad could hear them chatting and laughing as the train pulled out of the station after a few convulsive starts. Smoke stacks were soon visible in the distance, their gray fumes smudging a clear sky. Hitoshi brought them to Conrad's attention.

"This is Kawasaki, one of our rapidly expanding industrial cities. We have just completed the construction of a storage and distribution center and several more are in the planning stages. Approximately one mile north of the city we are building a steel mill; last year our sawmill became operational, and as you know, our silk factories are also located here. Japan is moving rapidly into heavy industry, and the success of our ventures will depend on foreign trade. So you see, Richter-sama, it is important that we establish a stable and mutually beneficial arrangement."

So, they are as anxious for my business as I am for theirs, Conrad thought. Concealing his eagerness, he inquired cautiously, "When do you expect to operate your own ships, Takezawa-sama?"

"That is very difficult to predict at this time. International restrictions and the shortage of steel slow us down considerably. That is something you will have to discuss with my father."

As he watched the unfamiliar landscape rush by, Conrad's shoulders sagged with an unaccustomed weariness. He did not usually tire easily, nor did he often succumb to stress, but today was an exception. He closed his eyes in an effort to calm his whirling thoughts and to enjoy the drowsy aftermath of sake. He resolved to limit his intake in the future. Unlike Scotch, which always steadied his nerves, sake merely dulled them.

"Richter-sama." Hitoshi shook his arm. "We are in Tokyo."

Conrad opened his eyes and sat up as Hitoshi's voice and the noisy confusion of the railroad station ended his sleep. The train lurched several times before coming to a complete stop. A man in a black uniform came aboard. He bowed with reverent formality to Hitoshi, who in turn acknowledged him with a slight inclination of his head. The formal greetings over, the man began waving his hands, and his voice trembled with nervous agitation as he spoke.

Hitoshi replied quietly, attempting to calm him down.

He explained the problem to Conrad. "Our driver says the streets are particularly crowded today, and he narrowly missed having an accident. My father's car is a nineteen twenty-one Haynes, the only one in Japan, and the driver feels very responsible for its constant care. I am sure he would commit *seppuku* if he put a scratch on it."

The driver picked up the luggage and cleared the way through the crowd to the waiting automobile. He shouted curtly at the people who had gathered around the Haynes to examine the lavishly upholstered interior and to run their fingers along its polished body. They quickly stepped back at his sharp command. Hitoshi and Takeo stood smiling as the attendant wiped the fingerprints from the fenders and mirrors with a cloth that he carried for that purpose. The Richters, too, stood back to admire the car's classic beauty. Except for the silver disc wheels, headlights, and hood ornament, the car was entirely black, polished to a spotless sheen. The front doors bore the Takezawa insignia, modest yet conspicuous.

Having satisfied himself that he had removed every trace of dust and all fingerprints from the vehicle, the driver swung open the door for his passengers and bowed as they climbed in. With a final word of reproach to the crowd, who still shuffled around the car, he slid in behind the wheel. The elegant Haynes had been built for loftier frames, and the driver's chin barely cleared the dashboard. However, he had solved this problem long ago. He started the car with one hand while the other deftly slid an embroidered cushion under his legs, elevating him well above the dashboard. Expertly, he guided the car through the crowd and into the narrow streets of Tokyo.

"My father's house is in the Uplands district," Hitoshi said.

The engine purred quietly as the car sped through the convoluted streets of the city. The driver, upon Hitoshi's instructions, avoided the teeming business and market streets, following instead the longer but quieter residential route. Tokyo was a sprawling, vibrant city, and even in the residential district the small wooden houses were interspersed with shops, lavishly decorated and bearing signs painted with inscrutable letters. The streets were alive with people, mostly women and children wearing brightly colored kimonos.

As they left the Ginza district, the gardens of the imperial palace came into view. Fountains, partially obscured by lush, manicured foliage, spewed forth their spray. The palace was embowered in pines and willows, its leaning stone walls surrounded by two moats. Ducks and swans floated languidly in the water, protected by gates and bridges that separated the palace from the frenzied activity of the city. White turrets jutted out past the walls, their symmetry blending gracefully with the huge trees. Even Conrad admired the peaceful tranquility of the royal enclave and the delicate beauty of its architecture. The limousine rolled slowly past the grounds, allowing the Richters time to enjoy its majesty.

"The Emperor moved the capital from Kyoto to Edo in eighteen sixty-seven. At that time he changed the name to Tokyo, which means eastern capital," Hitoshi explained. "The Emperor's son, Taisho, now lives in the palace."

"Is the public allowed to go in?" Conrad asked.

"Only on the emperor's birthday and on January second. The rest of the time it is closely guarded."

The occupants of the limousine were quiet as they proceeded along Hongo-Dori Avenue, a street lined with willows and wisteria. As they neared the Kanda Myojin shrine, a group of near-naked youths, carrying a portable shrine, paraded onto the street, chanting to the rhythmic beat of a gong. Karl twisted in his seat as they drove past the procession. The youths seemed to be bowed under the weight of the gilded shrine, but they continued to chant and weave their way down the street, followed by a group of men whose bodies were vividly tattooed. The smell of incense became overpowering as they passed.

A few minutes later, Hitoshi pointed to a group of impressive gray buildings surrounded by beautifully tended gardens.

"That is Tokyo University. Takeo and I studied here before going to California. It is a great honor to attend this university; the competition for acceptance is very difficult. In fact, it is so fierce that often, those who are not accepted commit seppuku."

A look of disbelief crossed Conrad's face.

"Yes, it is true, Richter-sama. It is considered honorable to die for such a reason. My father is still called upon to teach philosophy to the postgraduate students at the university. His time is very limited, but he is always pleased when he is invited to lecture. I sometimes think he missed his calling—he should have been a teacher. He has a unique way of motivating even the most headstrong and making one face reality with a clear mind and open heart." Hitoshi noted Conrad's questioning look. "I do not mean to make my father sound like a paragon of genius. Actually he is an astute businessman who has been blessed with a poet's heart."

The limousine made a sharp turn and passed under a high wooden arch bearing the insignia of the Takezawa zaibatsu. The car bounced gently along the white stone driveway, the entire semicircle of which was lined with cedars, all uniformly sized.

With practiced ease, the driver stopped smoothly in front of the entranceway to the Takezawa home. The house was large but not grand. Its curved tile roof reached out over broad windows and covered a porch that ran the entire length of the building. Two turrets gracefully outlined the one-story dwelling against the velvet green lawns. In a carefully edged garden across the driveway roses bloomed in a mass of colors. The Richters stood, momentarily hushed by its beauty.

The large doors of the *genkan*—entranceway—swung open, and two women dressed in brick red kimonos stepped out to greet them. The older of the two began chattering in a soft musical voice. Hitoshi put his arm around her affectionately.

"This is my mother, Miyoko, and Yuri, my wife. Please excuse them. Their English is very limited, but they are pleased to have you as their guests."

Conrad felt awkward and wished they would stop their ridiculous bowing. The women led them into the genkan, where their shoes were whisked away and replaced with soft slippers. The genkan opened into the main room, which was completely glassed at one end, affording an unobstructed view of the courtyard and gardens. Emulating the *shibui* tradition of simplicity, the floor was covered by *tatami*—mats—on which stood two wooden tables surrounded by several silk cushions. The customary *tokonoma* contained a scroll depicting a country scene and a violet vase with three delicate shoots of bamboo. Paintings by Sanraku, rich with color, hung on the white walls, and graceful wood carvings of birds stood in silent elegance.

"Come this way," Hitoshi said. "My father is anxiously awaiting your arrival." He opened a sliding paper door and led the Richters into the *dojo*. Scrolls portraying battle scenes hung on the walls along with ornately decorated samurai swords; two long black poles were propped up in the corner of the room.

Karl stared at the swords. He longed to run his fingers against them but stood back reverently.

"This is where my father practices the martial arts," Hitoshi said. "He is a *sensei*, or what you would call a master. He teaches *kendo*, which is an ancient form of the martial arts in which the combatants use heavy oak fighting sticks. He also uses these swords and can cut the eye out of a grasshopper as it jumps through the air." He looked directly at Karl. "They never enter this room when the sensei is home."

In the nearby garden Karl noticed a man dressed in a black kimono sitting cross-legged, erect and very still. Although the voices emanating from the room were loud, the silent figure did not move.

"My father is meditating, as is his daily habit," Hitoshi explained as he led them into the garden. They waited quietly by the moss-covered rocks several yards away. Conrad was surprised at the apparent slightness of the man who was a master of the martial arts.

Without turning, the sensei spoke. His voice was clear and his English, like Hitoshi's, faultless. "Welcome to Japan, Richter-sama. I trust my son has brought you here without too much inconvenience." With hands clasped loosely in front of him, he rose to his feet in a quick, effortless motion, the folds of the black kimono falling to their full length. He faced the new arrivals with a composed smile.

Conrad offered his hand to the elder Takezawa. The hand that clasped his was small, but the knuckles were large and covered with leathery, thick skin.

Karl stepped forward and bowed low. "I am pleased to meet you, Mr. Takezawa." He held out his hand and looked directly into the sensei's dark eyes. The hand clasp felt strange to Karl, as if, without effort, Hiro Takezawa could crush his fingers. But his strength was not a threat, and Karl felt comfortable holding the hand of this remote man whose face and body reflected an inner peace.

"It is a pleasure to meet you both. We have much to discuss, but I hope business matters will not prevent you from enjoying your visit."

Conrad forced himself to laugh and began to assure the

elder Takezawa that their trip had been pleasant thus far.

Hiro Takezawa stood very still as he listened to Conrad. It was not his habit to form opinions prematurely. Richter had an admirable business record, and his shipping company appeared stable and reliable in spite of a few questionable transactions. His instincts, however, warned him to be cautious of Richter. He knew that this man needed the zaibatsu to fulfill personal ambitions, and this, he hoped, would keep him trustworthy. The boy seemed quite unlike his father; his stunning blue eyes were open and friendly.

Karl's curiosity soon overcame his good manners. He stared unabashedly at Hiro and longed to ask how he could see in all directions at once. The narrow dark eyes did not focus on any one place, but seemed to encompass everything without moving. His manner of walking, too, was strange—smooth, unhurried, and feline.

Hiro turned to Conrad. "Your room is ready, Richter-sama. You will no doubt wish to change into something more comfortable. There is still time to relax in the bath before dinner. Please follow Reiko; she will show you to your room and also the way to the bathhouse."

The room where the Takezawas' servant led them was simply furnished. Sleeping mats were rolled up and stored neatly in one corner; Conrad groaned inwardly when he saw them. Their shoes, now cleaned and polished to a glistening sheen, stood outside the sliding door. Two gray kimonos hung from wooden pegs, one garment considerably larger than the other. Calmly, Reiko took the larger one from the peg and held it up to Conrad. He turned and began unbuttoning his coat.

"Father, I think she wants you to take off your clothes." Karl sounded uncomfortable.

Reiko's voice was high-pitched and musical as she rattled away in Japanese. Conrad shook his head and tried to indicate with his hands that he would undress himself. Reiko remained, obviously surprised.

Karl took the kimono from Reiko and handed it to his father. He smiled as he took her tiny hand in his and escorted her through the door. Quickly, they removed their clothes and slid into the kimonos, tying them securely before the insistent Reiko could return.

Karl marched about the room, enjoying the caress of the

smooth fabric around his legs. "I like it, Father. It feels nice."

"Well, I don't. If you ask me, skirts were meant for women."

"Do you think she will come to the bathhouse with us?"

"I'm afraid that is one of their customs. No doubt she does it every day, and I'm sure we don't have anything she hasn't seen before." Conrad laughed as Karl blushed.

The door slid open. *"O-furo ga dekimashita,"* the smiling Reiko said. She motioned for them to follow.

The bathhouse was completely separated from the main building. They followed a narrow rock pathway lined with azalea bushes. It was cool in the garden, and a breeze caught the bottoms of their loose kimonos. As they entered the small changing room, they felt the heat rising up through the rough, wooden floor. Reiko deftly helped them out of their kimonos, oblivious to their discomfort, then led them into the next room. Karl eyed the four large tubs, recessed into the floor, from which steam rose in menacing clouds. An attendant stoked the coals in the braziers situated under the tubs, her face flushed from the heat. Reiko chatted with her as she dropped a round marble of soap into each of their hands. She scooped a dipper of water from the nearest tub and gestured for Karl to soap himself. Karl gasped as the near-scalding water trickled over him. Not taking his eyes off her or the dipper, he lathered carefully. He could not understand exactly what she was saying but guessed that he was being scolded. He quickly ran the soap behind his ears and around his neck as he prepared himself for the next dipper of hot water, which, to his surprise, felt comfortable.

Reiko became quiet as she poured the water over Conrad and waited for him to soap himself. He had the distinct feeling that she was examining his private parts, and to his chagrin he felt himself begin to harden. Quickly, he turned his back to her. As she poured the water over his soapy body, her voice rose for the benefit of the attendant below. When their duties were completed, they retreated from the room, chattering in excited voices and giggling uncontrollably as they closed the door behind them.

Lowering himself gingerly into the water, Conrad threw back his head and laughed uproariously.

"What's so funny?" Karl asked.

Conrad shook his head, reluctant to explain to Karl the

reason for Reiko's incredulous expression.

In a few minutes, Hiro and Hitoshi came in, followed by the now demure attendants. They scrubbed themselves vigorously with soap as Reiko poured dippers of hot water over them. As Hiro turned under the streams of water, Conrad could see several long white scars spanning his back and stretching across his muscled stomach. They were old scars, faded, yet striking evidence of a cruel battle. As Hiro came toward them, he no longer seemed small in stature, for his powerful body was disciplined and fluid. Placing one hand on the edge of the wooden tub, he rose effortlessly into the air and slipped into the water.

"Ah, the *o-furo* is cool today! The attendant must have been lazy. We usually keep it at one hundred thirty degrees. Perhaps it is just as well. You might have found it a little too warm."

Conrad wanted to tell him that they already felt like over-cooked chickens in a pot. "The water is warm enough for us just as it is." He wondered how far the Takezawas would go to make his stay comfortable. He gritted his teeth and forced himself to lie back further in the tub.

Karl rested his head on the rim of the tub, chin barely above the water, eyes closed, and a look of contentment on his face.

"I am glad that you are enjoying your bath, *tomodachi*," Hiro remarked, using the word for friend.

Karl opened his eyes. "I thought we were supposed to scrub ourselves in the tub, but Reiko made sure we were clean before we got in! That is not the way we do it at home."

"Baths are for removing tensions and soothing aching muscles," Hiro answered. "Of course, everyone has his own custom." With that, Hiro sank slowly under the water.

The Richters sat waiting for several minutes. Finally Karl could not contain himself any longer and, turning to Hitoshi, asked urgently, "Aren't you afraid he will drown?"

Hitoshi smiled and shook his head. "No, he is fine. He will come up in another few minutes."

"In a few minutes?"

Five minutes dragged by before Hiro's head appeared above the water.

Karl let out a sigh of relief, his eyes wide with admiration. "How can you breathe under water?" he asked.

"I cannot breathe under water; only fish can do that. Someday, tomodachi, I will teach you to discipline your body in such a manner." Hiro lay back in the water, his thoughts suddenly in a turmoil. Why had he made such a promise to a boy he would never see again?

Hitoshi was the first to leave the bath, and Conrad gratefully followed his example. He felt almost nauseated from the heat, which he was sure had risen well above the intended one hundred and thirty degrees. He felt drained of energy and longed to soothe his tormented skin under an icy shower. He waited impatiently for Hiro and Karl to dry themselves and return to the house.

As Hiro stopped to examine a dwarf cedar, Hitoshi explained that his father had planned the entire garden and personally supervised its constant care. Beyond the pond where they had first seen Hiro stood a small shrine, partially concealed by delicate maples. They walked over the narrow bridge and stood quietly in front of the tiny building.

"This is my favorite place," Hitoshi mused. "Here I can separate myself from the world and become one with nature."

More bullshit, Conrad thought.

Slowly they strolled back to the house, passing through the genkan and into the main room. A small brazier glowed at the end of a long wooden table, and a pot of water steamed above it. Conrad, the honored guest, was seated next to the tokonoma with Karl beside him.

The door opened softly and Yuri, Hitoshi's wife, entered. She padded noiselessly across the room, carrying a tray on which sat four small cups and an earthenware pot. Her graceful hands fluttered daintily as she brewed the tea and stirred the concoction vigorously with a bamboo whisk before serving it. The odor of the herbs and seaweed assaulted Conrad's sensitive nose.

Hiro slurped his tea with gusto, loud aahs of appreciation punctuating each mouthful.

"What is Mr. Takezawa doing?" Karl asked, his mouth close to Conrad's ear.

"I'll explain later," Conrad whispered back, trying to look nonchalant.

Karl sat listening to Hiro. He tried to keep his head lowered over the teacup, but he could not restrain himself. Each time Hiro slurped, he would steal a surreptitious glance from under his bowed head. Finally, with a sigh of resignation and a shrug of his shoulders, he too gave a long, loud slurp; a smile of accomplishment spread across his face and glints of mischief sparkled in his eyes. Conrad choked on a mouthful of tea and turned to reprimand his son. He stopped when he saw Hiro's nod of approval and the look of conspiracy that passed between them.

"Richter-sama, I understand you have a particular liking for Scotch whisky. I would be delighted to offer you some of our finest import," Hiro said.

"Thank you, Takezawa-sama." Conrad nodded, his face brightening. "You are making my stay extremely pleasant. I hope someday to be able to repay your kind hospitality."

Hiro bowed in return. "It is our pleasure. Tonight we will relax and enjoy each other's company. Tomorrow we will show you the Takezawa operations, at least the part with which you will be concerned."

"Hitoshi has already pointed out some of the warehouses and factories in Kawasaki. You have expanded considerably since my last visit to Japan," Conrad remarked.

"You are correct, Richter-sama. We have made advances into heavy industry. But silk is still our major export. Do you know how silk is made?" he asked, directing his question to Karl.

Karl shook his head.

"Silk is made from the cocoons of caterpillars, namely *Bombyx mori*. This illustrious little creature has a very interesting life cycle and with careful nurturing produces the finest silk in the world."

"Mr. Takezawa, silk was discovered by the Chinese, wasn't it?" Karl asked.

"Yes, we cannot take credit for its discovery, but we are very proud that nowhere else in the world will you find a natural fiber more beautiful than Japanese silk. I hope you will come with your father tomorrow, for I think you will be impressed."

"May I, Father?"

"Yes, by all means."

"Mr. Takezawa!" Karl pointed to a boy about his own age standing in the doorway behind Hiro.

It was Hitoshi who turned and motioned for the boy to come in. "This is my son, Tatsuo. Mr. Conrad Richter and his son, Karl."

Tatsuo bowed. "I am very happy to meet you." His ap-.

praising gaze rested on Karl. Karl returned the gaze, still startled by the boy's remarkable resemblance to his grandfather.
In an awkward motion, he offered his hand to Karl in the
traditional western gesture of welcome. Karl grasped it tightly
in his.

"Take our young friend for a walk in the garden," Hiro
suggested. "Perhaps he would like to see our exotic fish?"

"Yes, *Ojī-san.*"

Karl straightened his cramped legs and followed Tatsuo.
"Where did you learn to speak English?"

"I have been studying English in school and also with my
grandfather since my fifth birthday."

"How old are you now?" Karl asked.

"Thirteen."

"I'm thirteen too. Do you always wear a kimono?"

"No, I wear pants to school. It is easier to play baseball in
pants."

"Baseball! Do you play baseball? I thought all you did was
fly kites—that's what the pictures in my book showed."

Tatsuo shook his head and laughed. "I am the captain of
our team. We have not lost a game all year."

"You look just like your grandfather. How did he get those
scars on his back?"

"Ojī-san—my grandfather—will not speak about it, but my
father said that he was beaten with a sword for not obeying the
orders of a *daimyo*—a noble lord. But now a sword can no
longer hurt him. Even if you strike with all your strength, you
cannot cut him. He has much *Ki.*"

"Ki? What's that?"

Tatsuo's face became grave. "I cannot explain it. It takes
much study and concentration. But Oji-san can do it, and I
can too, sometimes. He makes his body like steel by using all
his inner forces."

"Will you take me to the dojo, where your grandfather
practices the martial arts?"

"Yes, but you must promise not to touch anything. My
grandfather is a sensei, a kendo master." Tatsuo's voice rang
with pride and reverence.

In a few moments the boys stood alone in the huge dojo.

"There are his fighting sticks, but he has many more."
Tatsuo pointed to the black oak sticks Karl had seen previously.

Karl stared at the swords displayed against a drapery of

purple silk. The hilts glittered in the semidarkness of the room; gold braids hung from their scabbards. Karl's hand reached out for one of the swords and instantly Tatsuo grabbed his wrist; pain shot through Karl's arm and he sank to the floor.

"Do not touch the swords. My grandfather would kill you." He spoke in a frightened whisper.

Karl gritted his teeth against the pain as he tried to free himself. Enraged, he lunged at Tatsuo. Suddenly the room turned upside down for Karl and he flew through the air. He landed with a dull thud on his back, gasping for breath.

Tears shone in Tatsuo's eyes. "Please, tomodachi, the swords are sacred. Anyone who touches them will die."

Karl's ears were ringing with rage. He caught his breath and lunged at Tatsuo's midriff and again he was in the air. His face reddened with frustration, he turned to stalk his cunning opponent. Tatsuo's pleas fell on deaf ears. Karl's fist shot forward and landed with a sharp crack against Tatsuo's unresisting jaw. Tatsuo did not try to move; his arms hung limply by his sides, and a small trickle of blood ran down the side of his chin. Blindly, Karl raised his fist again, his breath coming in ragged jerks. Suddenly the anger cleared from his eyes, and Tatsuo's sad, resigned face swam before him.

"Ojī-san's swords are sacred. If I let you touch them, you would have to die." Tatsuo wiped the blood from his chin with the sleeve of his kimono as tears welled up in the corners of his eyes.

"You were only trying to protect me!" Slowly Karl lowered his fists. He could not speak and stumbled out into the coolness of the evening.

Tatsuo retreated to the solitude of his room, where he changed his stained kimono and wiped away the last traces of blood from his face. He wished fervently that the fight could have been avoided. If Ojī-san knew, he would be very ashamed. Tatsuo placed himself in the lotus position before an open window. He closed his eyes, and his breathing settled into a slow, imperceptible rythym; his mind was at peace once again.

Karl sat by the bridge in the garden, gazing into the pond.

"Damn, why did I have to hit him? He didn't even try to fight back! I should have left that sword alone."

He felt a hand touch him lightly on the shoulder, and he

looked up into the concerned face of Hiro Takezawa.

"Kon-nichi-wa. Why do you sit alone, looking so sad?"

Karl tried to explain, his eyes swimming with tears. "Do you think Tatsuo will still be my friend?"

"Yes, I guarantee it. Tatsuo will protect and honor your friendship as he did the swords. You see, Karl, the samurai sword is a priceless treasure. It is the spirit of Japan."

"Would you have to kill anyone who touches it?"

"Not you, tomodachi, only those who would bring dishonor upon it. Come now, the hour is late and we have a busy day ahead of us."

They walked side by side toward the house as the moon became visible over the high fence. Karl, intent on imitating Hiro's graceful gait, did not notice the sensei's silent laughter. Inside the house, Hiro opened the door to Tatsuo's room and pointed to a tatami upon which lay a thin white mattress and blanket.

"But I thought . . ."

"Tatsuo was worried about you and asked if you could sleep in his room tonight."

Karl was relieved. "Good night, sir."

"Oyasumi nasai." Hiro touched Karl's blond hair lightly and left.

Karl lay on the thin mattress. He could hear Tatsuo's even breathing.

"Good night," Tatsuo whispered.

"Oyasumi nasai," Karl replied.

In spite of his apprehension about the forthcoming day and the dubious comfort of the tatami and thin mattress, Conrad slept well. In the morning, he returned from the bathhouse, clean-shaven and refreshed, his mind clear and sharp. He reviewed the events of the previous day and felt satisfied that he had impressed the Takezawas, although recalling Hiro's friendliness to Karl as well as his son's admiration of the elder Takezawa, he unconsciously resented their rapport.

He doubted that the zaibatsu would believe he was incorruptible, but he could surely convince them that he would act in their best interests. There was no doubt in Conrad's mind that Hiro Takezawa was the autocratic ruler of the family, and it was his confidence that would have to be gained. Although presented as the passive philosopher with a poet's heart, Hiro would exercise his authority with ruthless finality, of that Conrad was chillingly certain. He did not yet know the organizational structure of the zaibatsu, but when their couriers had made contact with the Richter Shipping Line, there were intimations that it was controlled by four executive heads, one of whom was Hiro Takezawa. The prospect of facing all four of these business titans dented his self-assurance slightly, but not enough to erode his spirits or determination.

The house was beginning to stir—its paper walls and parchment doors did not leave much for the imagination. He could hear soft murmurings and the shuffle of footsteps in the hallway. Conrad buttoned his immaculate gray suit and adjusted the celluloid collar and blue tie. He had considered replacing the ludicrous slippers with his own leather shoes but decided to persevere until they left the house. There was a soft knock on the door, then Reiko, with a series of animated hand gestures, indicated that breakfast was ready. Conrad took a deep breath; the day had begun.

Karl felt a gentle nudge on his uncovered shoulder. He peered at the solemn face of Tatsuo through sleepy eyes.

"I am sorry to wake you, but your father will be leaving soon."

As Karl's eyes cleared, he noticed the bruise on Tatsuo's chin. He sighed. "I'm sorry about the fight. I guess you were just protecting me."

"I have forgotten about it, but you do have a good punch." Tatsuo rubbed his chin gingerly.

"Yeah, but if you hadn't let me, I would never have connected. How do you move so fast? And your grip—it felt like a vise. Your arms are only half the size of mine!"

"Maybe its because Oji-san has taught me how to use all my strength. He does not approve of fighting, but says it is very important to keep your body in good condition."

"Do you know how to arm wrestle?" Karl asked.

"What is that?"

Carefully, Karl explained the procedure and merits of arm wrestling to his friend. He purposely avoided mentioning that he was the undisputed champion of his class. Confident that his title would remain intact against Tatsuo, he lay down on the floor opposite his opponent, prepared to demonstrate his prowess and tenacity. With arms raised and hands tightly clasped, they lay face to face.

"When I say ready, you try to push my hand down to the floor," Karl said.

Tatsuo nodded.

"Ready? Go . . ."

Grimacing, Karl pushed with all his power against Tatsuo's lean but unmoving arm. Tatsuo's face looked blank as he stared at their clasped hands. Karl's arm quivered, but his concentrated effort was useless; Tatsuo's arm remained rigid. In desperation, Karl tried with both hands to pull Tatsuo's arm down. Still it did not move.

"Your arm is like steel! I can't budge it."

Expression returned to Tatsuo's face, and he smiled sheepishly. "What did you say?"

"I said your arm must be made of steel. I can't budge it!"

Tatsuo shrugged. "I just use my Ki."

"How do you do that?"

His attempts at an explanation only deepened Karl's confusion. Finally, Tatsuo said helplessly, "I cannot explain it. You will have to ask my grandfather."

After they had dressed and rolled up their bedding, the boys raced to the dining area. Breakfast was already in progress as they entered the room. They bowed in unison before approaching the table, where Miyoko was preparing omelettes and broiled fish to be served with rice cakes.

Hiro welcomed them. "I am glad that you two have reconciled your differences. I have a feeling that your years together will be many and your friendship will grow."

The black Haynes was waiting for them, with the driver energetically polishing the already glistening hood. Hitoshi and Conrad eased into the back seat while Tatsuo and Karl raced into the front, where they knew the visibility would be better. Hiro stood beside the car for a moment, breathing deeply and savoring the sweet scent of roses that permeated the morning air. The sun, now well above the top of the high fence, promised a warm, cloudless day. The cool ocean breezes that usually blew in from the bay would be ineffectual today.

Hiro spoke to the driver, who immediately appeared crestfallen but dutifully stepped around the car and opened the driver's door for him. "I think I will drive today; I do not want to lose my confidence that I can handle the car," Hiro said.

The sullen driver closed the door behind Hiro, then gently removed the fingerprints with his cloth. As they drove off, the rear-view mirror reflected the boyish animation on Hiro's face, an expression that Conrad found to be entirely contradictory to his seemingly staid, reflective personality. It lent purity as well as adolescent mischievousness to his usually disciplined countenance. He drove the car carefully, acutely aware of his responsibility as a driver, but with a certain degree of daring, as though, at the slightest encouragement, he would roar through the streets at breakneck speed.

Hitoshi appeared relaxed and unconcerned, apparently certain of his father's driving skills. The car seemed to pick up speed at each corner, and Conrad found himself wishing for the return of their fastidious chauffeur with his pillow and polishing cloth. Before his concern could reach uncomfortable proportions, they entered the clamorous business section of Tokyo, where Hiro slowed down with obvious reluctance.

"Our offices are just east of the railroad station, in the Marunouchi district. We will be there soon."

The car came to an abrupt halt in front of a three-story stone building bearing the now familiar Takezawa emblem. Unlike the other buildings along Nihonbashi Street, it was without decoration except for the emblem, yet it was unmistakably the finest and most auspicious building of all. Tatsuo and Karl were the first to step out into the brilliant sunshine.

"Be back in fifteen minutes," Hitoshi called after the boys' quickly receding heads. Conrad appeared hesitant. "Do not be concerned, Richter-sama. Tatsuo is very familiar with this street."

As Conrad was ushered into the front office, he knew expense had not been spared in its construction or decoration. Wooden floors were polished to a burnished sheen, furniture was efficient and aesthetically pleasing, wall and drapery colors were subdued and blended unobtrusively into their opulent surroundings. A large mural depicting a restful landscape covered one wall; several carvings of birds in flight stood on white pedestals about the room. The industrious hum of activity ceased as the three men entered the office. Each worker stood up and bowed respectfully as the Takezawas passed by.

"Our executive offices are on the top floor," Hitoshi explained.

Conrad, who had anticipated a long flight of stairs, was surprised when Hiro led them to an elevator with an elaborately worked metal door. It took them quickly and silently to the top floor and opened onto a carpeted hallway. The door opposite the elevator was ajar. Hiro opened it wide, allowing Hitoshi and Conrad to enter. It was a large room, bare almost to the point of austerity; it reminded Conrad of his own office. He hated distractions of any kind, and clearly the occupants of this office were of the same opinion.

An elderly Japanese gentleman dressed in a black kimono rose slowly and walked around a huge desk to greet them. Trying not to stare at the man, Conrad could not remember ever seeing anyone so thin. His bones seemed to be held together by parchment-thin skin. His high, wide forehead was further heightened by a complete lack of hair, but his eyes were keenly observant. Conrad felt those eyes look directly through him.

Shozo Takezawa did not smile, but slowly his dark eyes lost their penetrating stare. Conrad guessed that he had been temporarily accepted by the ancient patriarch of the zaibatsu.

Shozo spoke to Hiro in Japanese.

"My uncle is pleased to meet you," Hiro said. "He trusts that after you have familiarized yourself with our operations, you will be prepared to negotiate a contract with us."

Conrad spoke in an even voice. "I am pleased to meet him, and I look forward to doing business with the zaibatsu."

An older, slightly heavier version of Hiro entered the room, and in spite of advancing age, his bearing was lithe. He, too, bore the Takezawa mark of intelligence—shrewd, observant eyes beneath a high, wide forehead. Conrad recognized a tone of respect in Hiro's voice as he introduced his brother, Koji.

Koji's English was halting but intelligible. "I trust my brother has made your visit pleasant."

Conrad was acutely aware that he was being scrutinized. "Very pleasant, thank you, Takezawa-sama."

"We have examined your company's records and are satisfied with our findings. My brother will show you our factories and mills, after which we will expect to receive your decision as to whether or not you are prepared to do business with us."

"I will do all I can to accommodate you," Conrad answered quickly.

"Are you prepared to expand your fleet?" Koji asked.

"Of course, if I have a definite contract."

"I can assure you that once the Takezawas have made a

contract, we do not break it," Koji replied sharply.

"What if my company fails to meet your expectations?"

"You will not fail."

Conrad felt his stomach muscles tighten, and for the first time in his life he found himself questioning his own decision. But his lips formed a determined line. This was what he had strived toward for so long, and now it was finally within his grasp. "No, I will not fail," he said.

As they emerged from the Takezawa headquarters, Conrad noticed that the sun had kept its early morning promise; the air was warm and humid. Karl and Tatsuo sat waiting in the Haynes, their faces flushed with exertion.

"You two look as though you have been to the top of Mount Fujiyama and back. I hope you have not expended all your energy, for we still have a long way to go." Hiro tousled their hair playfully.

Even with the windows open, the air in the car was stifling. They followed a road that ran along the waterfront, carefully avoiding foot traffic, jinrickishas, wagons, and the occasional car. Gradually, the congestion began to lessen as they left Tokyo; the air cooled and the smell of the ocean became predominant. In the distance, Conrad could see stacks against the skyline, tall and black, belching smoke in giant puffs. As they drew closer to Kawasaki, he recognized the acrid smell of oil, the telltale yellowing foliage and scarred countryside that follows on the heels of intense industrialization.

Conrad was staggered by the extent of the Takezawa empire. He had anticipated their involvement in sawmills and silk factories, but he was totally unprepared for the degree to which the zaibatsu controlled the economy of the country. The major portion of Kawasaki's industrial center was under their control. Vast piles of iron ore lay waiting to be absorbed into the steel mills; lumber stacked in neat rows surrounded the sawmills, and the small but efficient factories were visible proof of industrial vitality. What they lacked in mechanization, they made up for with manpower. He was certain that he had seen only part of their operation—no doubt, there were others that were not open to foreign scrutiny. Although they had avoided touring certain factories and assembly lines, Conrad's discerning eyes recognized stock piles of defensive weaponry behind high wire fences.

The road leading to the outskirts of Kawasaki was dusty and

rutted. In the middle of a huge orchard, Hiro stopped the car and stepped out; the others followed.

"The silk factory will be our last stop for today," Hiro said. "Since the bulk of our exports will be raw silk, I would like to familiarize you with its manufacture from these mulberry fields to the finished product that will fill your ships." Hiro leaned against the car, now gray with dust. He shielded his eyes from the afternoon sun and gazed silently at the sea of green foliage that surrounded them.

Hiro explained the importance of providing a coarse, dry soil. "The quality of the mulberry leaf will determine the type of silk produced by the caterpillars."

They wound their way to a long wooden building at the far end of the orchard. It was well lighted, immaculately clean, and lined with long wooden benches occupied by women wearing bright kimonos. Hiro picked up a tray covered by a layer of white cheesecloth. "In this section we grow the silkworms. Notice the tiny white eggs that the moths have laid—it is called silk seed. They are very small, so look carefully. One hundred of these weigh but a single gram!"

As they proceeded further into the building, Conrad mopped his forehead with a damp handkerchief. Hitoshi inspected an oversize thermometer on the wall. "It is exactly seventy-five degrees; hatching should take place very soon."

"This is the incubation area," Hiro explained. "The temperature is started at sixty-five degrees and is raised two degrees each day until it reaches seventy-five degrees, at which point hatching takes place. The ladies then cover the cheesecloth with finely chopped mulberry leaves. The larvae will wiggle through and start feeding on the leaves." Hiro pointed to a stack of shallow trays that almost reached the ceiling. "The larvae grow quickly and are ready to eat whole leaves within three or four days. They are black when newly hatched and then turn a cream color as they grow to their full size of about three inches." Hiro pulled a tray from its frame and passed it to Karl and Tatsuo. He took two wriggling larvae from the tray and handed them to Karl, who watched them twist and dance in his palm.

"I don't see any silk," Karl said. "Where is it?"

"Do not be so impatient, tomodachi, I will show you." Hiro continued the tour. "In about six weeks the larvae are ready to spin a cocoon, and fortunately we do not have to guess when they are ready. They announce the time by raising the forepart of their bodies and slowly waving from side to side."

"Hey, Karl, like this." Tatsuo stood on the tips of his toes and swung from side to side.

"I do not think you will ever pass for a silkworm, my son," Hitoshi laughed. "You are far too clumsy and you do not eat enough." He hugged the boy affectionately, holding his slight frame tightly against him.

"Now here is where the larvae begin their work." Hiro pointed to trays containing small compartments. "There is one larva in each compartment, and in three days it will have spun the cocoon."

Conrad ran his finger lightly over the smooth cocoon as he listened to Hiro.

"In another week the larva will turn into a pupa, and at this point we must kill it before it destroys the cocoon."

"It seems like such an involved process. Is there any way to speed it up to increase the volume?" Conrad asked.

"The work is painstaking, but the results are always gratifying. We produce the finest silk in the world, and we will not lower the standards of quality for the sake of quantity. It is because of this very quality that we receive high prices for our goods. Let me assure you, Richter-sama, this is a very profitable operation."

"I have no doubt, Takezawa-sama, that all your operations are very profitable."

Hiro nodded in agreement. "To show you just how painstaking the production of silk is, let me give you an example. From one ounce of eggs we hatch about thirty thousand silkworms. These worms will eat one ton of mulberry leaves and will eventually produce approximately one hundred and thirty pounds of fresh cocoons from which we can manufacture only twelve pounds of reeled silk."

In the next building, the Richters were shown how the cocoons are reeled and the threads twisted together, the number of which determines the thickness of thread produced. Hiro concluded his commentary. "We can boil the gum, or sericin, from the silk and weave it into fabric or we can pack the raw silk into these small bundles—we call them books. They are packed into bales, each weighing one hundred and thirty-three pounds."

"And that is where you come in, Richter-sama," Hitoshi

continued. "Your ships will carry our silk to the markets in North America. We also need the ships to bring in raw materials for our factories. Are you interested?"

Conrad nodded without hesitation, fighting to control his elation. "Yes, I am interested."

The drive back to the Tokyo office passed quickly. The boys, dusty and tired, dozed in the front seat while the men sat quietly, each immersed in his own thoughts. Conrad tried to estimate the potential of these new shipping contracts. He had assured the Takezawas that he would expand his fleet, and he mentally calculated the expense. When the Haynes stopped in front of the Takezawa building, Hiro gently pulled the ears of the two sleepy boys. "After you two lazy cats have shaken the sleep from your eyes, you can amuse yourselves by visiting my friend Yasuda-san at his glass factory. Tell him I sent you, and I am sure he will entertain you while he creates his masterpieces. We have some business to complete, but we will not be long." The boys nodded their drowsy assent.

Their arrival had been anticipated—Shozo and Koji Takezawa were waiting. Koji indicated the empty chairs to Hitoshi and Conrad. Hiro sat behind his heavy oak desk. During the interval of silence that followed, Hiro inspected the folders that lay in front of him. "Richter-sama, you have indicated an interest in putting your ships at our disposal," he said finally.

"Yes, in whatever capacity you may need them."

Without looking up, Hiro asked, "How many ships do you have at the present time?"

"Eight freighters, seven thousand gross tons each; in the next month or so, I will have three more." Conrad sensed that he was being interrogated and inwardly resented it. He was certain that the Takezawas already knew all there was to know about his shipping company, and quite possibly about his personal life.

"What condition are they in, and what types of cargoes can they handle?" Hiro continued.

"All my ships are less than fifteen years old and are in excellent condition. They have triple expansion reciprocating engines and run on coal. The newer ships will have oil-raised steam. When fully loaded, they average ten knots on the open seas, and as far as cargo is concerned, I can handle all types except for bulk liquids like oil."

Hiro reached into the top drawer of his desk and removed a

recent edition of *Lloyd's Register of Shipping*, a thick black volume containing pertinent data on all vessels over one hundred tons. Conrad recognized it instantly.

The bastard, Conrad thought. He was just testing me! He watched as Hiro ran his fingers along the cover without opening the volume, a subtle display that the zaibatsu was not to be trifled with. Conrad accepted the warning, but his gaze did not waver, even as perspiration shone on his forehead.

Hiro continued. "Richter-sama, you are probably wondering why we do not build and use our own ships."

"Yes, that question has crossed my mind. Your operation is certainly large enough to include shipbuilding."

"There are several reasons. There has been a severe shortage of ships since the Great War, and as you probably know, shipbuilding in Japan has been limited by the terms of the Washington Conference. Primarily, we would like you to carry silk, tea, and a few sundry cargoes to Vancouver on a regular basis, but you must also be ready to make emergency shipments at very short notice. Because of drastic fluctuations in the silk market, we must be assured of your readiness."

Hitoshi poured sake into tiny shot glasses and served his father first.

Conrad carefully sipped his sake, wary of its intoxicating powers. "You have my word on it."

Hiro studied Richter's face intently before continuing. "The zaibatsu would like to avoid the conference system and its brokers. By working together, we can eliminate many variables to our mutual benefit . . ."

Conrad leaned back in his chair, waves of relief flooding through him. He, too, had objected strongly to the restrictions imposed on him by the shipping brokers at Lloyds and the Baltic Tavern in London. Until this moment he had had no recourse but to accept their authority—now all that would change.

"The zaibatsu will send Hitoshi and two assistants to Vancouver to act as forwarding agents. Hitoshi will secure various cargoes which you will bring back to Japan."

"What will these cargoes consist of?" Conrad asked.

Hiro opened a large file on his desk and carefully scanned the neat rows of characters. "These will vary, but the bulk of the shipments will consist of wheat and lumber. Whenever it is economically feasible, Hitoshi will purchase certain raw materials we require for our factories—namely, lead, zinc spelter, iron ore, coal, and chemicals. Our reports show that you have access to certain shore facilities and ground transport. Can you elaborate on this?''

"I have the use of several wharves and warehouses on the Vancouver waterfront, along with shorecranes and other equipment for moving cargo. The longshoremen's group and the railroad companies have been very cooperative in the past and I'm sure that our operations will continue to run smoothly."

Koji translated the conversation for Shozo. The fading afternoon light glinted on his smooth head as he nodded at Koji's words. Conrad was left completely out of the conversation; he listened without understanding as their voices changed inflection and volume. Finally Shozo rose, bowed slightly, and left the room.

Hiro folded his hands deliberately in front of him and measured Conrad unswervingly with his gaze. "It appears that your shipping company meets our current requirements. We would like to have the exclusive use of your ships. The zaibatsu will cover your operational expenses plus give you four percent of the value of the cargoes handled during the year. Our mutual success will depend a great deal on timing and reliability. Can you operate under these conditions?''

Four percent far exceeded Conrad's expectations. He had anticipated difficult negotiations with grinding hours of see-saw concessions and contract revisions, but in fact he had only been exposed to a brief interrogation. "Yes, the rules are fair and so is your offer. Will you send the necessary documents for my lawyer to finalize?''

A penetrating silence filled the room. Hiro rose from his chair and drew himself up with quiet dignity. "There will be no contract other than our oral agreement. Ink can be washed away, but a man's word must always be upheld.''

Conrad's initial reaction was one of disbelief. "An oral contract of this magnitude—impossible!'' Hiro waited, his mouth set in a firm line. Finally, Conrad said, "It is done, Takezawa-sama. The first ship will arrive in Yokohama in less than two weeks.''

"Takeo will give you a preliminary schedule of shipments before you leave Japan. My son and his family will proceed to Vancouver within a month to set up their office. He will keep you informed as to our requirements and forthcoming shipments; you can depend on him to clear up any difficulties that might arise."

Conrad shook hands with Hiro and Hitoshi. "Takezawa-sama, I trust our association will be a long and profitable one."

"I have no doubt that it will be," Hiro answered.

Karl and Tatsuo were sitting on the curb, their heads bent together in earnest conversation. When the Takezawas and Conrad emerged from the building, Karl jumped up, unable to contain his excitement.

"Father, look at what the glassblower gave us!" Both boys held up their treasures—tiny glass monkeys, no larger than a man's thumb, but perfect in every detail.

Hiro smiled. "I see my friend has been kind to you. But your stomachs must be sticking to your backbones by now. Come, it is time we filled them again."

Tatsuo grinned at his grandfather. "Your friend is very generous. He shared some tea and rice cakes with us. If we had stayed longer, we would look like him." Tatsuo puffed up his cheeks and folded his hands around an imaginary rotund middle as he waddled to and fro.

"Ah yes," Hiro said in mock concern. "My friend has a weakness for food. But, my two gluttons, Tatsuo's grandmother will be most unhappy. One of her greatest joys is to see the men of her household eat heartily. I was depending on you to gladden her heart with your appetites." He twisted his face into a caricature of a tragic Kabuki actor as he proceeded to imitate Miyoko's impending display of disappointment. Karl and Tatsuo howled with laughter.

Conrad was amazed at the mercurial change in Hiro, from shrewd industrialist to whimsical clown. He had never known the Japanese to be so demonstrative and unrestrained; he recalled Hitoshi's earlier observation about his father: perhaps a poet's heart did beat under that imperious exterior.

As they left the Marunouchi district and its conveyor-belt traffic, Hitoshi observed the sky. "Tonight will be excellent for moon viewing."

"Perhaps we can reserve tomorrow night for moon viewing." Hiro suggested. "I have advised the mistress of the Oriental Tea Garden that we will be having dinner there tonight. I hope I have not taken too much liberty, Richter-sama."

As usual, Conrad's mind and body sang with vitality after

strained negotiations. "No, not at all. It will be very pleasant to relax and to be entertained." Images of white-faced geishas with Victoria Forsythe's sensual body flashed before his eyes, and he tensed with anticipation.

Hitoshi smiled knowingly. "I think you will find the geishas at the Oriental Tea Garden beautiful and talented, but the food may seem strange to you."

Feeling magnanimous, Conrad placed his hand on Hitoshi's shoulder. "My friend, I place my fate in your able hands."

From the front seat, Hiro listened to the good-natured conversation, then shuddered inexplicably as a cold shiver coursed down his back.

As the Haynes pulled up alongside the door of the Takezawa residence, the chauffeur greeted them. He opened the car doors, and his disapproving eyes scrutinized the dusty, neglected limousine.

"The mulberry fields were particularly dry today, my friend," Hiro said apologetically.

Dusk was settling comfortably over the city as the three men emerged from the house, bathed and refreshed. Three jinrickishas, each with a colored paper lantern swinging from its shaft, waited in the driveway. The moon, hanging precariously over the tops of the mountains, seemed to follow them as they rolled noiselessly on air-filled tires into the heart of the city. Conrad had forgotten about the magical quality that Tokyo assumed at night, no longer alien and intimidating but garishly exciting.

The Oriental Tea Garden was surrounded by a high wooden wall covered with wisteria. Dimly lit lanterns, each a tiny replica of a shrine, outlined the entranceway, where a guard stood with folded arms. His face, loose-jowled and fierce, softened into a grotesque smile as Hiro spoke to him. He bowed low before stepping aside, allowing the runners to pull up to the front door.

A manservant met them, bowing repeatedly until they had crossed the threshhold. He then removed their shoes and replaced them with soft felt slippers before leading them into a large room that was divided into cubicles by delicately painted paper panels. As expected, there were no chairs, only individual tables, a few inches high, with braziers beside them.

Conrad hid his annoyance as he arranged himself on the matting; his knees ached as he folded his long legs under him.

The panels slid open, revealing three geishas, who knelt with their foreheads touching the floor, their kimonos shimmering in the soft light. Conrad watched in fascination as they rose, fluttering gracefully before settling in beside the men; their delicately provocative scent filled the room.

"Your geisha's name is Yuko," Hiro said. "Are you pleased with her?"

Conrad was noncommittal as he watched the doll-like figure light the brazier. He wished that she was not so tiny, for he towered two heads above her.

Yuko had been expertly trained, and although quite young, she displayed remarkable talent. Her prime purpose in life was to please her patrons, and tonight she had been engaged by the illustrious Takezawas to do just that—entertain their business associate, who was obviously a man of distinction. When she raised her eyes to meet his, her heart beat rapidly and she forced herself to smile. The Takezawas were honored patrons; her mistress had warned her to do her very best and then perhaps the gods would smile on her.

Yuko watched Conrad, noting the stern face beneath the shock of blond hair. As she settled beside him, careful to let her knee rest against his, she sensed his withdrawal. He would be a challenge, but she would soon enjoy his response to her subtle ministrations. She fanned the brazier with sure, delicate movements, aware of his cool blue eyes on her. Taking his large hands in hers, she held them over the warmth of the brazier, stroking the palms sensuously with the tips of her fingers. As she removed his coat and tie, her hands lingered on his arm and she could feel him relax. You are not ready yet for games, my giant lamb, but you will be soon enough, she thought.

When the food arrived, she fed him tiny morsels of delicately spiced vegetables and fish. Gradually the sake began to take its effect, and he responded to her fleeting caresses and flirtations. Desire sparked in his eyes, and as she leaned seductively against him, she heard him catch his breath and attempt to hold her to him. She avoided him playfully, so as not to suggest rejection, and gazed at him with disconcerting devotion. Yuko was aware that his breath had quickened and that he was physically aroused—it was now time to entertain from a distance. She signaled to the other geishas, and they took turns singing and dancing, each movement purposeful, modest yet exquisitely seductive. The games were next, silly childish games invented to please the man as well as the boy in every patron—all seemingly innocent except for the subtle hint of eroticism.

Conrad responded just as Yuko had expected. She laughed at his unrestrained enjoyment and gently wiped the perspiration from his face. She blushed and feigned shock when Conrad noticed her looking at the evidence of his desire and hid demurely behind her fan.

"Richter-sama, I can see that you are pleased with Yuko. At present she does not have a patron; you may stay with her for the rest of the night if you wish," Hiro said.

Without taking his eyes from Yuko, Conrad nodded.

One of the geishas knelt beside Hiro and whispered quietly in his ear. Hiro raised his eyebrows slightly in surprise. He said to Conrad, "There is someone outside who has a message for you, an urgent message!"

"A message for me?"

"Do you know a Victoria Forsythe? The message is from her."

"Yes, I know Victoria Forsythe." Conrad stood up quickly and followed the girl into the garden. The door closed behind him, shutting out the light and sounds of the geisha house.

He called out into the darkness. "Is someone here?"

A shadow moved in the silence and then a voice called out behind him, grating and urgent. "Mr. Richter, we have Victoria Forsythe."

Conrad turned, his senses spinning. "Victoria? Where is she?"

Two men stepped into the dim light.

"Come with us. We will show you," the grating voice commanded.

Conrad stepped back in protest and surprise. Strong arms suddenly grabbed him, propelling him through the garden and into the alley behind the tea house.

"Wait! Let go of me! Where is Victoria? Who the hell are you?"

A sharp pain seared through him as his arms were twisted and pinned tightly behind his back. He struggled helplessly against the incredible strength of the man who held him. The other assailant pulled a long narrow knife from his coat and held it with a menacing smile against Conrad's exposed throat.

The man's face was distorted in the dim light, his breath vile.

"She is not here, but we have something for you from her husband."

Conrad felt the knife being pushed slowly and steadily against his throat until the skin broke; blood trickled down the blade. Conrad's face was etched with horror. His low cry was stifled into a gurgle by the continued pressure of the knife.

"Mr. Forsythe wants to remind you to be careful. Strange accidents happen in the Orient," the man said as he tightened his grip on Conrad's arms, almost forcing them from their sockets.

Conrad gasped and, with strength reinforced by fear, wrenched his aching arms free. The man holding the knife moved with lightning speed and thrust his pointed fingers deep into the pit of Conrad's stomach. Pain stabbed through to his spine and he sank to the ground; the night echoed with the sound of his agonized gasps. With a vacuous smile, the knife-wielding assailant twisted Conrad's shirt, ripping the thin fabric.

"Are you still listening, pig?" His rasping voice was thick with insolence. The knife pierced the skin above Conrad's navel and slowly sliced an oozing gash up his chest. Blood dripped freely onto his pants and shoes. For an instant, Conrad stared in horrified disbelief until fear again intensified his strength. He tore his arms free and bolted into the darkness, but his escape was short-lived. A foot connected with his groin and he sank to the ground, pain searing through his body.

The alley felt hard and rough against Conrad's cheek; his eyes focused with difficulty on the small pebbles that lay in front of him. He writhed uncontrollably and slowly forced himself to sit up, fighting the spasms of nausea. A hand gripped his hair and brought him to a kneeling position; the face, only a few inches from his, was dark and threatening.

"Mr. Forsythe does not want to see you again. You make him very upset . . . understand?"

Conrad nodded mutely.

"I asked if you understand?"

"Yes," Conrad whispered hoarsely. "I won't see him again, I swear it. Please don't kill me."

The bloodstained blade slid past Conrad's teeth and rested on his retracted tongue.

"Mr. Forsythe does not like the way you talk to him. Understand?"

Conrad tried to pull away, but the hand held him and the knife slid further into his mouth. Vomit rose into his throat and spilled out as the blade cut slowly. Blood trickled down his chin in a warm stream. His mind screamed for mercy, not death. Please, God, not death!

Suddenly a voice cut through the night; the words were unintelligible to Conrad, but the tone was commanding. Relief flooded through him as the knife left his mouth and the grip on his hair was released. His blurred vision focused on the outline of Hiro Takezawa, who was walking toward them. His steps were slow but deliberate, his hands held low by his sides. The man with the knife braced himself.

"This is not your affair, Takezawa. Leave now, before it is too late."

Hiro ignored the warning and moved closer, his gaze not wavering from the two men who stood beside Conrad.

"It is already too late for you," Hiro said. His voice was low, dangerously threatening.

Fear registered on the faces of the two men, and without warning, the man with the knife lunged forward. Instantly Hiro's sword flashed in the moonlight, swung in a glistening arc, and snapped back into its scabbard. The assailant's hand, severed perfectly at the wrist, fell to the ground, still clutching the knife in its warm but lifeless fingers. The man gasped in disbelief and horror as blood gushed from the stump, then screaming with terror, he squeezed the end with his remaining hand.

The man's accomplice stood motionless, unable to move. His eyes darted from the severed hand to the empty space where Hiro's sword had arced. Slowly, as if in a dream, he stumbled back.

"Stop!" Hiro commanded. "You have brought dishonor upon the Takezawas by your vicious attack. This is unforgivable."

The man cowered, pleading for mercy as Hiro walked toward him. Beads of perspiration covered his face and his eyes widened with fear.

"Please do not cut off my hand, Takezawa-sama. We did not know he was your guest." He cringed in anticipated horror and fell to his knees.

"Get up, you coward, before I cut you in half!"

Slowly the man rose, stumbling backward against the wall. He held up his hands in a final desperate plea for mercy.

"Please, Takezawa-sama," he whispered.

Hiro grasped the outstretched hand. The sound of cracking bones and joints preceded the agonized cries of pain as he began applying steadily increasing pressure. Still his grip tightened until blood spurted from engorged fingertips. The man sank to the ground, his hand limp and bloody.

"Pick up your friend and leave. Should I see you again, I will take your lives."

As if in a trance, the man retrieved the dismembered hand and staggered as he helped his stunned accomplice; together they disappeared into the darkness of the narrow street.

Hiro studied the bloodied face of Conrad as he sat immobilized, eyes riveted on the pool of blood where the severed hand had been. He tried to speak to Hiro but could only moan. He rose unsteadily to his feet, allowing Hiro to support him. The moon spun crazily in an empty sky and the earth seemed to vanish beneath him; he sank into the darkness.

Karl's persistent voice coaxed Conrad from the depths of heavy sleep. He opened his eyes hesitantly. His mind was confused; he remembered only the terrible fear. Conrad tried to speak to Karl, but his tongue filled his mouth and the words were slurred and unintelligible. He braced himself with his hand and tried to sit up, squinting painfully at the sunlight that poured in through an open window. As memory came flooding back, a sharp pain gripped his stomach and he fell back on his pillow.

"Do not try to talk or move, Richter-sama." Hiro sat cross-legged by the foot of Conrad's tatami, an open book on his lap. "Our physician has advised that you remain in bed until tomorrow. By then the swelling will have gone down and your wounds will not be quite so painful. If your head feels light, it is because he has given you some medicine to ease the pain. He will be back later today. In the meantime, he has left this for you to drink."

With Karl's help, Conrad sat up. The hot liquid smelled vile and tasted even worse.

"Father, is it true that two men attacked you in the dark? Mr. Takezawa said that one of them had a knife and that you did not have a weapon to fight back with."

Conrad tried to avoid Karl's eyes. He could not bring himself to tell him that it was Hiro who had inflicted the damage on the thugs and had saved his life. Rage boiled up inside him and he clenched his fists under the thin blankets. I'll get you, Forsythe, he promised silently. But I won't hire anyone to do the job. . . . When I'm finished, you'll cut your own throat. He closed his eyes as the potion began to take effect, erasing the smug face of Julius Forsythe from his mind. In moments he drifted into a dreamless sleep.

Karl stared down at him with concern.

"Do not worry, tomodachi. The drink has put him to sleep and the healing herbs will work their wonders. It is an ancient Chinese remedy developed for the emperor and kept secret for many generations. The Chinese claim it restores youth to aging bodies and heals wounds."

"Will my father be well enough to travel soon?"

"Yes. His wounds are painful and ugly but not serious."

"Takezawa-sama, did my father fight well?"

Hiro was silent for a moment. "Come, my young friend, the garden is cool at this time of the day. It is the best place to rest and to gain peace of mind."

"You have not answered my question!"

Hiro placed his hands on Karl's shoulders and bent down so that their eyes were level. "Your father's wounds were avenged and his honor was protected. Now, sit here beside me and I will teach you how to still a troubled spirit."

As they sat under the sweeping branches of the elm, insects hummed and water splashed from an unseen waterfall.

"Tell me what you hear, Karl."

Karl bent over his folded legs, hiding his face in the palms of his hands while he tried to concentrate.

"No, Karl, you must sit up straight in order to hear the sounds around you. If you bend over in that manner, they might pass you by. Close your eyes and let your mind walk through the garden."

Karl straightened his back and raised his head. "I can hear the bugs and I can hear a waterfall, but I don't remember seeing one."

"What do you think it looks like?"

"The water does not make as much noise as White Falls at home, but I think it is as tall as your house, and the pool at the bottom must be deep enough for me to swim in." Suddenly his eyes opened. "But that can't be! I don't see any mountains or waterfalls in this garden."

"But, tomodachi, you can see them in your mind's eye and that is sufficient. Close your eyes again and listen . . . can you not feel the coolness of the water and see the white spray of the falls?''

Karl nodded slowly, and a smile appeared on his face. "Yes, I think I can.''

"Keep your eyes closed," Hiro continued, "and let your mind stay in this quiet place by the waterfall.''

"The pool is deep enough to swim in," Karl said after some time had passed. He opened his eyes and smiled at Hiro.

"You have a Japanese soul, my friend," Hiro told the boy. "You are one with nature. If you could see the falls with your eyes, you might be disappointed, but your imagination allows them to appear exactly the way you want, and that makes your heart happy.''

In one fluid movement, Hiro rose to his feet and motioned Karl to follow him along a narrow path to a section of the garden secluded by graceful wisteria and shaded by tall pines.

"The pine trees which you see here are almost two hundred years old and were transplanted from my grandfather's garden many years ago. They have lent their beauty to three generations of Takezawas, and I had hoped they would continue to grace the lives of my grandchildren. But that is not to be. It has been decided that my son and his family will move to your country, and I must abide by this decision.''

"Do not be sad, Mr. Takezawa. You will be able to visit them, and they will visit you.''

"Yes, but still my heart is heavy. Although Tatsuo does not say very much, I know he is troubled about leaving Japan and moving to a strange country where the people and customs will not be familiar to him.''

"I understand," Karl said softly.

"I would like you to be Tatsuo's friend when he arrives in Canada. Help him when he needs it, shield him from unkindness—for he has always been surrounded by love—and teach him the ways of your country.''

Karl did not reply for a few moments, but his brilliant eyes studied Hiro's face. "I don't know if I can do all you ask, Mr. Takezawa, but I promise I will try my very best and that I will always be Tatsuo's friend.''

Hiro laid his hand on Karl's head. "Thank you, Karl. You have made me very happy. Let this remain a secret between us.''

Karl's face was solemn. "I wish you were coming to Canada with Tatsuo.''

"My place is here in Japan, but then we cannot foresee the future. Now come with me—I have something for you that will seal our pact."

Silently they walked to the house, acutely aware of the bond that now existed between them. Hiro opened a concealed door in the dojo and carefully removed two ivory figurines of samurai warriors. He held them out for Karl to examine.

"Many years ago, my father saved the life of a samurai and they became lifelong friends. Before the warrior died, he gave these two figurines to my father. He had carved them himself from ivory to symbolize their friendship, inlaying the tiny swords with gold to represent the purity of their devotion to each other. It is my priviledge to give one of them to you, Karl."

Karl was incredulous. He gently ran his finger over the intricately carved figure and touched the fierce scowling face and the sharp edge of the gold sword. "I wish I had something to give you."

"You have already given me something," Hiro replied softly.

Under the care of the Takezawas, Conrad recuperated rapidly; the wounds were healing well and the swelling in his tongue receded. He lay back on his tatami, enjoying the skillful attention of the servants, while he formulated plans for the eventual destruction of Julius Forsythe. Conrad had requested that he be left alone during the day, and even Karl stayed away, returning only when summoned. Conrad was astonished and then curious when Karl displayed the ivory figurine, recognizing immediately the fine artistry and the worth of the intricately carved warrior. He wondered why Hiro had given Karl such a valuable gift and whether he expected something in return.

Within three days, Conrad was well enough to travel. He had booked passage on the *Ossinian*, a sturdy tramp that had logged many miles. Though not in the same class as the elegant *Empress*, her limited passenger facilities were comfortable. Hiro drove the Richters to the waterfront, accompanied by Hitoshi and Tatsuo.

"Thank you for your hospitality and care," Conrad said politely.

"I guarantee your next visit to Japan will be more pleasant," Hiro promised.

Silently, Karl shook hands with each of the Takezawas, his smile belying his sadness. When the ship's horn sounded, he turned and marched up the gangplank ahead of Conrad. He wanted to look back one more time but dared not, for he was sure his emotions would be evident. Only when the *Ossinian* had cast off did he look back and wave.

On the way to Tokyo, Hiro suddenly stopped the car and relinquished the wheel to Hitoshi. "It has been a trying week, and I would like to rest."

An uneasy feeling gripped Hiro, and a strange voice seemed to shout from the depths of some dark abyss. His body trembled in an attempt to ward off the inimical force that threatened to overcome him. Hiro did not speak for the next two hours and became oblivious to the motion of the car and to the passing countryside. Turning his total energy and consciousness inward, he struggled to enter the depths from which the voice came. Beads of perspiration formed on his face, and his gaze grew fixed as the voices became louder. His face twisted as dull rumblings pounded at his ears and a vision flashed before him. The earth twisted and split; cries of anguish tore at his soul—then silence. The bloodstained face of Conrad Richter smiled and faded.

Hiro lay back on the seat in total exhaustion. His eyes remained closed until they arrived at the Takezawa estate. Then Hitoshi helped his father from the car and led him slowly through the garden to the shrine, where he knelt in silent prayer. In the pond, shaded serenely by the lofty branches of the elm, fish darted wildly as a noiseless tremor traveled through the water.

❲ 3 ❳

An oppressive pall lingered over the Takezawa home. After the terrifying premonition, Hiro sat in the garden beside the shrine throughout the afternoon and into the night. He refused all food and drink and totally ignored Miyoko's chastising. During the night a light rain began to fall, soaking his clothes and hair with its chilly wetness; still he sat unmoving. At first he had tried to dismiss the vision as an ugly nightmare, but when morning finally came, he knew with certainty that the premonition had been real. He prayed again before returning to the house.

Hitoshi met his father at the door, concern showing on his face, but Hiro raised his hand to stop the question that his son was about to ask. Hitoshi knew his father well enough not to pursue the matter.

"At least come in and change your wet clothes. Yuri has tea ready for you."

"I will be there shortly." Hiro touched Hitoshi's shoulder reassuringly before entering the bedroom and sliding the door shut behind him. Then, as if every movement was an extreme effort, he slowly removed the wet clothes and slipped into a dry kimono, appreciating its familiar warmth against his cold skin. He gazed longingly at the tatami that lay unfurled where Miyoko had placed it, but he knew his weariness would not be assuaged by sleep. Carefully, he rolled up the mat and stored it behind the sliding door; this simple, mundane task forced his mind back to reality. Hiro opened a window and took several deep breaths. The smell of honeysuckle filled his nostrils with its cloying sweetness. Insects droned beneath the window and a bluebird, balancing precariously on a willow branch, scolded its silent mate. The tension began to leave his body; the ravaged voices were temporarily stilled. He heard a gentle knock on the door.

"Ojī-san, Ojī-san!"

"Come in, Tatsuo."

The door opened partially, and Tatsuo peered in. "Oji-san, are you not feeling well? We have been waiting for you. Please, will you come now?" Tatsuo searched his grandfather's face for reassurance. "Why do you look so tired?"

Hiro held the boy at arms' length and looked directly into his dark brown eyes. "Tatsuo, will you do something for your ojī-san?" Tatsuo nodded obediently. "Stay close to the house for the next few days. Do not venture outside the wooden fence."

"But why, Ojī-san? I like—"

"Please do not ask questions, Tatsuo. Only do as I ask."

"Yes, Ojī-san."

Together they walked down the hall and into the main room of the house, where breakfast was already under way. The murmur of conversation stopped abruptly when they entered. Although Hiro's face was now etched with deep lines of weariness and devoid of its usual mirth, he appeared serenely composed. Only Miyoko noticed the resignation behind his outward composure, and her hand trembled slightly as she poured the steaming tea. She avoided meeting her husband's eyes in an effort to hide her own apprehension—today his face looked the same as it had many years ago, when their infant son, afflicted with influenza, had struggled desperately for life.

"You are all worried, and I am sorry for the distress I have caused you. I have been given a glimpse into the future, but it was very obscure. I am not yet able to interpret it completely. Please bear with me for a few days; when it becomes clear in my mind, I will tell you about it. In the meantime, I would like you to carry on with your daily activities as you have been doing. Your departure for Canada is only a few days away."

A protest began to take shape on Hitoshi's lips, but he stopped abruptly for his father's decisions could never be questioned. "I will not ask any questions, Father, but please do me the favor of staying home today. I am sure Uncle Shozo and Koji will understand. I plan to review the latest reports from Kawasaki, and perhaps if you are rested by this evening, you could assess them with me and give me your opinions.''

Hiro nodded in approval, but his eyes did not register their usual intense interest. ''Yes, I will be pleased to examine them with you.'' He emitted a barely audible sigh. ''But now I will just sit in the garden for a while. Come, Tatsuo, keep your tired ojī-san company.''

Hiro patted Miyoko's hand gently before leaving, and she smiled, grateful for his attempt to reassure her. She desperately wanted to cling to her husband and to share his burdens, but she sat in silence, only her eyes following him as he left the room. She would wait; when he was ready, he would tell her.

Hiro sat on a bench under the maple tree, watching Tatsuo whittle a block of wood with an ivory-handled knife. ''What are you carving?''

''A bird for Obā-san. It will remind her of me.''

''I do not think she will need reminding. She will miss you very much. We will both miss you.''

''Will you come to visit us?'' Tatsuo asked.

''Yes, we will come often.''

''I shall be very lonely without you, Ojī-san.''

''Ah, Tatsuo, do not look so unhappy. This will be an exciting adventure for you. Imagine—a new country, new friends, and a new school. And Karl will be there. He will prevent you from being lonely. I only hope you will find enough time to write to us.''

Tatsuo's face brightened. ''I am looking forward to seeing Karl again. We made many plans before he left. Do you think he will be at the dock to meet us?''

''I am absolutely certain that he will be there.'' Karl's solemn face flashed before Hiro's eyes. ''Let him help you to learn the customs of his country, but do not forget your Japanese heritage. Train your body as well as your mind, as I have taught you.''

The sun beat down mercilessly, but the garden remained cool and peaceful with a gentle breeze rippling the water in the pond and rustling the leaves. Tatsuo, his head cradled on his arms and his bare legs stretched out on the soft grass, fell asleep before the sun had passed its meridian height. Hiro, too, soon slept, his chin resting lightly on his chest. They slept dreamlessly while the sun wheeled across the sky, until Hiro felt something shake him. He was instantly awake and alert, his eyes squinting against the sun but finding nothing amiss. The garden was quiet, almost too quiet. He stood up, waiting, until Tatsuo's voice broke his concentration.

"Oji-san, why are you standing there? Is something wrong?"

"Something woke me." Hiro hesitated, looked around the garden and, then said, "Perhaps it was a dream."

"You look strange, Oji-san. Are you sure it was only a dream?"

"No, I am not sure, but it has passed now. Please fetch my tools. The garden looks somewhat neglected."

For the rest of the day Hiro gave the shrubs and flowers his most diligent attention, stopping only when Tatsuo required answers to his endless questions or when Miyoko tempted him with delicacies from the kitchen. When Hitoshi arrived home, his arms laden with the inevitable files, Hiro knew he would have to summon all his resources to push the uneasiness from his mind and concentrate on Hitoshi's reports.

He was proud of Hitoshi, proud of his son's dedication to the zaibatsu and his devotion to his family. He possessed a brilliant mind, and in a few years, when experience had sharpened his intellect, Hitoshi would become a director of the zaibatsu. When the decision had been made to establish an office in Canada, it was inevitable that his son would be chosen to direct it. Hiro realized the decisions of the Takezawa executive were irrefutable. Even so, he hoped that somehow their decision could be revoked and Hitoshi would be permitted to remain in Japan. He watched Hitoshi approaching, his steps heavy from weariness but his face alight with enthusiasm.

"Father, we received word today that the first of Richter's ships, the *Prometheus*, will arrive in Yokohama next week. Apparently it is one of his finest. It seems that Richter is putting his best foot forward." Hitoshi turned to his son. "Tatsuo, do you think you will be able to endure two weeks aboard the *Prometheus*?" Before Tatsuo could answer, Hitoshi turned and walked toward the house, wiping his moist forehead. "The Ginza was unbearably hot today—I feel as if I have been in the bath with my clothes on. By the way, Father, I have brought the files home for your inspection." With that he disappeared into the genkan.

"Father must be very preoccupied. He did not even wait for my answer," Tatsuo said sadly.

"Your father has many things to take care of before you leave for Canada. I will try to answer your questions."

"Have you ever been on a ship, Oji-san?"

"Only on fishing boats, never on a large ship like the *Prometheus*."

"Do you think I will be seasick?"

Hiro ruffled his grandson's hair. "Do not worry. Your mother has already taken the necessary precautions to prevent such occurrences. She has special herbs which she will brew up for you should you feel sick. They are guaranteed to cure you immediately."

"Do they taste like the other herbs that Obā-san makes me drink? Bah, I would rather be sick." Tatsuo grasped his neck with both hands and let his tongue loll out of his mouth while his eyes rolled back. Feigning death, he collapsed into a heap on the ground.

For the first time in two days, Hiro laughed. "Tatsuo, if I did not fear a severe reprimand from your grandmother, I would give you away to the Kabuki theater."

Tatsuo sniffed the air as the aroma of pungent sauces escaped through an open window. "Ah, I smell food. I am starved! Do you think they have started supper without us?"

"Without calling the hungriest member of the family? I should say not!"

After dinner the Takezawas sat around the table savoring a final cup of tea while Yuri listed the items they would have to purchase before leaving Japan. Aware that Hitoshi was becoming impatient, she hurried through her growing list of absolute necessities. "I cannot go to Canada, dear husband, without these things. Forgive me for encroaching on your busy schedule, but they are very important. You yourself told me these items are not available outside Japan." She looked beseechingly at her husband.

"Yes, yes, of course you will have them." Irritation began to edge his voice. "Tomorrow I will take you shopping myself." He waved his hand. "Now please, my father and I have matters of great importance to discuss."

Yuri bowed and left the room without a word. She realized it was not the time for household discussions.

"Take a look at these," Hitoshi said as he spread the papers on the table. He had prepared exhaustive reports on the requirements of the zaibatsu, and based on these reports, he had drawn up detailed shipping schedules and quotas for the needed raw materials. Soon they were completely absorbed, Hiro's turmoil temporarily forgotten.

"Do you think Richter can meet these schedules?" Hitoshi asked.

"You must see that he does," the elder Takezawa answered.

"What will we do if he cannot?"

"We would modify our schedules until an alternate plan could be implemented. But I do not think we need concern ourselves about Mr. Richter. He answers to the smell of money—he will serve us well as long as we continue to fill his pockets.

Hitoshi yawned widely and arched his back to ease the dull ache that lingered between his shoulders. "I have exhausted all my energy today. If I am to take Yuri to the city tomorrow, I had better get some rest before it is too late. Judging from the length of her list, I will be tested to the limits of my endurance, but I suppose I should indulge her. This is a trying time for her—she does not say much, but I know she is terrified to leave Japan. She is planning to take as much of it with her as she can." The corners of his eyes crinkled with amusement as he opened his hands in a gesture of condescension.

"I think Yuri has great strength of character. Do not underestimate her, my son."

Hitoshi sighed. "I remember the first time I saw her. I thought you and Mother had lost your minds completely when you chose her to be my wife. She was as timid as a mouse—she almost crawled under the tatami when I looked at her."

"Small wonder! You insisted on wearing those ridiculous western clothes that matched the black scowl on your face. Had I not warned her beforehand, she probably would have *bolted* under the tatami."

"What do you mean—warned her?"

"I told her what you were really like—gentle, intelligent, generous, devoted, and so on. She loved you even before she met you."

Hitoshi laughed. "Honorable Father, you never cease to amaze me. Did she actually believe you?"

A trace of the old humor sparkled in Hiro's eyes. "I was very convincing. And you must admit that we made an excellent choice."

"Yes, that is true," Hitoshi said seriously. "But enough of this—we must get to bed, Father. I am concerned—it is not like you to be so preoccupied and weary."

"Yes, I am weary. Good night, my son."

The evening was oppressively hot and sultry. Sleep was difficult for the members of the Takezawa household; they twisted in the sticky dampness of their mats. Occasionally a soft groan could be heard as they tried to find a cool place for their feet and heads. At three o'clock in the morning a violent wind began to blow, slapping the shutters noisily and sending a deluge of rain into the house. Just before dawn, the storm finally vented its last burst of fury.

In the morning Hitoshi opened the shutters and gazed at the rainswept garden. He did not notice the unusual stillness, nor did he wonder about the sudden departure of the birds that had arrived earlier in noisy flocks to feed on the seeds that Miyoko had left for them. After a scanty breakfast, Hitoshi and Yuri left for the city, long before Tatsuo even knew they were gone. He would surely have objected to having been left behind.

By eleven o'clock, Tatsuo was busy packing his belongings and was about to tie up a box containing his most valued treasures when Hiro knocked at his door.

"May I come in, grandson?"

Tatsuo looked up eagerly. "Oji-san, please help me tie up this box. I hope I have packed everything. They will allow me to take these boxes, won't they?" he asked, suddenly concerned.

"I am sure they will. The *Prometheus* is a large ship. But before you tie that box, please come with me. I have a few things you might want to take with you."

Hiro led the way to the dojo, where he opened a sliding door, revealing a large wooden chest inlaid with ivory and gold. Tatsuo had seen the chest before; his heart raced as he tried to control his anticipation. Hiro pulled the chest from its hiding place and opened the lock with a heavy brass key. "Now you may look inside."

Slowly, Tatsuo released the catch and the lid swung up easily and quietly. He knelt and peered inside. "Oji-san, it is beautiful."

A large leatherbound book and a samurai sword lay on a drape of brilliant red silk. The scabbard felt cool, and Tatsuo noticed the tiny insignia that flashed on the gold inlaid hilt.

His slender hand trembled slightly from the weight of the sword, but when he freed it from the scabbard, it seemed to become an extension of his hand. He swung the blade cautiously, cutting the air with precise, even strokes. Its symmetry and perfect balance pleased him as he fought an imaginary foe.

"That sword," Hiro said gravely, "is one of five, and it has been in our family for over two hundred years. It is a symbol of the honor exemplified by your ancestors. It belongs to you now, and you must accept the responsibility that accompanies this treasure. This sword has always belonged to men who have had the courage to live and die by their principles."

Tatsuo ran his fingers lightly along the razor-sharp edge. "Has it ever been used to commit seppuku?"

"Yes, once. Your great uncle, in a violent fit of rage, once killed a man he thought had dishonored him. He later learned he had killed the wrong man; he was very ashamed and proceeded to atone for his grave error. He committed seppuku, and I acted as his second, using this very sword."

"Did he regain his honor?" Tatsuo asked, wide-eyed.

"When he drove the knife into his side and drew it across his stomach, I watched carefully for any sign of pain on his face, but there was none. When he plunged it in again and forced it up until his bowels spilled out, he actually smiled. Yes, he regained his honor!"

"Were you sad, Ojī-san?"

"I missed him very much, but I was happy for him as well." Hiro picked up the leatherbound book from the chest. "Your great uncle's death is recorded here."

Tatsuo took the book from his grandfather, and as he opened the cover, he recognized his grandfather's strong but beautiful handwriting.

Hiro smiled almost shyly. "This book contains the history of the Takezawas. I have also included my own philosophy, the practice of the martial arts and *zazen*—meditation. As you can see, Tatsuo, the book is only half-filled. It will be your duty to continue this work for the benefit of your children and for their children after them." Tatsuo nodded respectfully and promised to comply with these wishes. Hiro continued. "I hope you will study these pages carefully, for they are your heritage and will help mold your future. Turn to the inside cover and read aloud what I have written there."

Tatsuo turned the parchment pages until he found the inscription. " 'To my grandson, Tatsuo. September 1, 1923. Strive for perfection, become strong, but maintain a gentle heart. Know yourself so that you will be at peace with your soul, and always seek truth and wisdom for only then will you become one with the universe.' " Tatsuo's eyes swam with tears, but his voice was even and sure. "I will protect and cherish these treasures with my life, Ojī-san."

"Look further into the chest."

Tatsuo carefully replaced the sword in its scabbard and reached into the chest. He removed a thick cotton *keiko-gi*, that lay neatly folded under the red silk. Quickly he took off his *yukata*—kimono—and slipped into the new white training robe.

"Did Obā-san stitch this for me?" he asked proudly.

"Yes, but your mother embroidered the Takezawa insignia."

Tatsuo drew his slender form up as tall as he could, folded his arms, and stood with legs apart, scowling fiercely at his grandfather.

Spurious fear appeared on Hiro's face. "Aha, the robe seems to have given you formidable powers," he laughed.

The scowl disappeared, and Tatsuo hugged his grandfather with childlike exuberance and affection. "Thank you, Ojī-san."

"You still have not looked deeply enough into the chest."

"You mean there is more?" His hand searched the chest until he felt a small pouch. Even before opening the bag he was aware of its contents. "I knew it," he shouted. "My favorite—ginger candy! There is enough here to last all the way to Canada." With that he popped a piece into his mouth and offered the bag to his grandfather.

As Hiro reached out to share the treats, the floor began to shake violently, as if some giant creature had awakened beneath the house and was now seeking its freedom. Hiro's face became transfixed with horror. It was in that instant that he realized the implication of his premonitions—*earthquake!*

The lid of the chest slammed shut and for a moment the chest sat motionless. Then it slid across the room, ripping through the paper wall. Miyoko screamed as the heavy chest careened part her. With arms outstretched, she stumbled as the house shifted and heaved. The great polished timbers that held the roof began to grind and splinter; the floor lurched. Like a barge on an angry ocean, the entire house began to sway. Pictures crashed to the floor, furniture from adjoining rooms cut through the flimsy walls of the dojo, heavy statues and priceless treasures became lethal weapons as the force of the earthquake shook them from their lodgings.

Hiro winced with pain as a roof timber struck him on the shoulder. Holding tightly to each other, the three crawled as quickly as they could toward the doorway. A splinter of glass grazed Tatsuo's cheek, and blood spurted from the wound. Strengthened by desperation, Hiro pulled Tatsuo and Miyoko to the relative safety of the garden, as far away from the house as possible. They watched in horrified fascination as the ground heaved and swallowed up the south end of the house. Then, as suddenly as it had started, all was still. The quake had lasted only four minutes, but it seemed like four hours. They stood silently, surveying the awesome destruction as the dust settled upon the debris around them. In the distance, smoke rose in thick billows over the city, blocking out the copper-colored sun.

Miyoko began to sob hysterically. "Hitoshi and Yuri—they are in the city!"

Gently, Hiro disengaged her hands. "We will find them." Hiro felt as if he had emerged from a nightmare only to find himself thrust headlong into another. Quickly he removed the debris from the car, which had escaped unscathed except for minor dents and scratches. A thick tree had fallen across the road. He removed it, his mind bent only on locating Hitoshi and Yuri. Hiro prayed silently for their safety. The chauffeur materialized from behind the still-intact portion of the house, his face streaked with dirt and blood.

"It is over," Hiro said. "Stay here where you will be safe, but watch out for fires. That is the worst danger now. I am going into the city to search for my son."

"Let me come with you, Takezawa-sama. I will help you search," the chauffeur pleaded.

"No, stay here and take care of Reiko and the other servants. I will take Tatsuo and Miyoko with me."

Hiro sighed with relief when the car started. Tatsuo helped his grandmother into the front seat, and she clung tightly to him as Hiro eased the Haynes through the debris that littered the road. The streets were cracked and in places impassable, so that frequent detours were necessary. They stared in disbelief at the devastation around them.

It was silent now, as though the end of the world had finally come. Mere fragments of buildings remained, shattered evidence of a once busy residential area. Sacred shrines were flattened, their lonely pillars standing like monuments to a happier time. The extent of the catastrophe became more apparent as they neared the city center. Much of what remained standing was now in flames; people ran blindly while the wind fanned the smoldering fires into flaming infernos. Hiro could drive no further—the streets were littered with twisted, broken buildings and mutilated bodies. They would have to walk.

When they stepped out of the car, the smoke burned their noses and throats, and the intensity of the heat became almost unbearable. They covered their faces with the sleeves of their kimonos and pushed on as if led by unseen hands. The fires spread quickly; frail wooden structures dissolved in the flames. Oil drums began exploding at the refinery, sending giant fireballs into the sky. The shock waves came seconds later, almost lifting them from the ground. The acrid smell of burnt flesh and hair filled their nostrils; cries of anguish and pain rang in their ears. A small child ran toward them, his hair and clothing in flames and his mouth open in a scream of terror and agony. Hiro snuffed out the fire with his kimono and handed the child back to his weeping mother. Angry, blistering welts were beginning to appear on the small body; Miyoko touched the mother's face in sympathy.

"We cannot go on," Hiro said. "We will have to wait until the fires die down."

Miyoko's voice was an anguished wail. "They will die unless we find them."

Hiro shook her gently. "My dearest heart, I feel as you do, but to walk into that inferno would mean certain death for us. Pray for the wind and fire to subside so that we may carry on."

Within three hours much of the city had been consumed by fire, and only then did the flames begin to die out.

"Come, I think it is safe to go on," Hiro said gently.

Holding hands for reassurance and safety, they continued their gruesome search, numbed by the appalling destruction around them, yet they pushed on through the glowing nightmare. Smoke rose from the charred remains of homes, stores, and office buildings; shattered glass was strewn along the streets, where wooden structures had exploded from the intense heat. The remains of metal furniture, clay pots, stoves, pipes, and cleverly designed wrought-iron ornaments lay twisted and broken among the debris, grotesque reminders of an industrious city.

Within the hour they reached the Marunouchi district. Hiro was surprised to see that most of it was still intact. Other than a few ravaged exceptions, the steel and concrete buildings had withstood the shock of the earthquake and devastating fires. The interior of the Takezawa building was in shambles, but the structure itself was intact. It had been built to withstand severe shocks.

Tatsuo stumbled on tired feet and his thin face was gray and still. Miyoko tried desperately to stifle her sobs, but tears ran unchecked down her smoke-stained face. Unlike most Japanese women, she had only one child on whom she had lavished all her motherly affection. Hitoshi had given purpose to her life.

"Takezawa-sama . . . wait!"

Hiro did not recognize the urgent voice or the wretched, charred figure who shuffled wearily after them.

"Please, Takezawa-sama, do not go any further."

Only then did Hiro recognize the face of his friend Yasuda, the glassblower. "It is you! I am glad to see you are unharmed. We are looking for our son and his wife."

"I pray they were not on the grounds of the Army Clothing Store. A terrible holocaust has occurred there. Thousands of people were roasted alive. They had gathered on the open square for protection, believing the fire would pass them by, but the wind changed and the flames bore down on them. Their clothing and possessions caught fire and they burned—they all burned! It is too horrible to see—please do not go any further."

Hiro could feel Miyoko collapse against him. "We have no choice, my friend. We must find them." The glassblower shook his head as they walked on.

A bright red paper lantern that had somehow escaped the fire blew forlornly down the empty street, making a hollow rasping sound as it tumbled after them. Without warning, the direction of the wind changed, blowing smoke and dust into their faces. With it came the smell of burnt flesh; the stench was overpowering.

Nothing could have prepared them for the grotesque scene that surrounded the Army Clothing Store. The grounds, as large as a military parade square, were covered by a blanket of burned and shriveled bodies. The Takezawas stood motionless, unable to believe what they were witnessing. Thousands of people, the clothes burned from their bodies, some with bones protruding from their melted flesh, clutched tightly to their possessions, which were now welded to them forever. For several minutes they stood in stunned silence, trying to reject the terrifying possibility that their loved ones could be part of the blanket of lifeless humanity.

Miyoko's voice was a hoarse whisper. "He is here, our son is here. Tatsuo, you must wait here."

Tatsuo did not hear her, but he stayed rooted to the spot, frozen with horror. Miyoko and Hiro walked carefully over the charred remains. The bodies lay so closely together that they were unable to avoid stepping on them. They cringed each time their feet touched the burned, slippery flesh, but they did not have to search long. Hitoshi and Yuri lay together. Hitoshi's body was burned almost beyond recognition; Yuri was only slightly burned but had obviously suffocated, and even in death her face was contorted with pain. Hitoshi had tried to protect her with his own body but had not been able to save her; she had died clinging to him.

Covering her face, Miyoko fell to her knees beside the two bodies, her sobs now only thin wails of grief. Hiro emitted a ragged sigh as his face crumpled with emotion; he too sank to the ground. Gently, he tried to console Miyoko but she did not hear him. It was then that they noticed Tatsuo. He stood behind them, his gaze transfixed on the two charred bodies that lay at his feet. Hiro tried to gather Tatsuo in his arms, but the boy stood straight and unyielding.

"They are dead," Tatsuo said, his voice flat and cold. "Just like the others—all dead."

Hiro stood in front of his grandson and gently held him by the shoulders. "Tatsuo, although they have gone from us, death is not the end. For them it is another beginning."

Tatuso's glazed eyes measured the grim scene around him. His thin body trembled, but his mouth remained set. "I understand," he said in a barely audible voice. He knelt down beside Miyoko and closed his mind to the cries of grief of those who continued to search desperately through the remains.

A uniformed man, brisk and authoritative, came forward and spoke to Hiro. "There will be a mass burial here tomorrow. If you have family here, give me their names so that—"

"No!" Hiro's voice was vehement. "We will take our children home."

"It would be much simpler if you allow . . ."

This time Hiro's direct stare cut him short. The man shrugged his shoulders before turning to speak to a distraught man holding the body of a small child.

Leaving Tatsuo and Miyoko beside the bodies, Hiro made his way toward Nihonbashi Street and the Takezawa building. The streets were filled with dazed, wary people, tightly clutching what was left of their belongings. He was not surprised to see that the debris had been cleared from the first floor of the building and that it had been turned into a makeshift hospital for the injured and a place to bring the dead. The once glistening floor was strewn with bodies; those beyond help were covered with white shrouds.

News of his own loss had preceded Hiro; sympathetic eyes met his. Offers of help were instantaneous, and Hiro accepted them gratefully. He retraced his footsteps back to the square, where Miyoko and Tatsuo waited. With infinite care the bodies were separated and, under Hiro's supervision, wrapped in smooth white silk.

"My car is only a short distance from here," Hiro said after the gruesome task had been completed.

Their progress was slow. Smoke hung in dismal clouds and heat still emanated from the smoldering ruins. They walked slowly through the rubble, picking their way among the fissures that criss-crossed the streets. The Haynes was gone; a wide crevasse running the entire length of the street had apparently claimed it.

"It is of no importance," Hiro said. "We will continue on foot."

By the time they reached the Takezawa estate, evening had fallen. In the distance, the sky still glowed, illuminated by the unyielding fires that cast their eerie specter over the silent house. Although more than half the house lay in ruins, it presented a welcome sight, and the exhausted group collapsed on the steps. The servants knew without asking what lay concealed within the silk shrouds.

"Will you prepare the bodies for burial, my husband?" Miyoko whispered.

Hiro looked past her at the rising moon and nodded. "I will not rest until the task is done." He touched her smoke-stained face. "We will bury them beside the shrine—it was Hitoshi's favorite place."

As he wrapped the bodies, Hiro felt his strength wane; his hands tremble as anger and grief welled up inside him. He clenched his fists in despair. Hitoshi was his only child—he had prayed for many grandchildren, but now these hopes were gone forever. The wretched agony of his loss crushed Hiro, and the tears finally came, spilling unheeded onto the silk shrouds that covered the bodies. He wept silently and alone until he was exhausted; then he began to pray. Slowly, strength returned to his aching body, and a path through the darkness became clear. The teachings of his old masters came to mind once again: life is fragile and impermanent, but it is this very impermanence that makes it so precious. He rose, giving thanks for Tatsuo's life, and began to prepare the bodies for burial.

After washing the bodies carefully, he dressed them as best he could in the white garments Miyoko had provided and covered their faces with translucent silk. He constructed two coffins from the dark burnished wood that had once lined a wall of his dojo. The insides of the caskets were covered with soft tatami mats laid carefully over pallets of rice straw. Finally, he placed the bodies inside the caskets and carried them to the tiny shrine in the garden. When dawn seeped through the smoke-filled sky, Hiro sensed they were at peace; their flesh, unlike his own, would no longer suffer. He placed a handful of copper coins in each of the caskets to ensure their safe journey across the Sanzu River.

Without turning, he felt Miyoko's presence. She had not slept; her face was composed, but she seemed to have shrunk in stature. Her kimono was deathly white, and as she came toward him, Hiro's throat constricted—she was brave yet so vulnerable.

"They will need these," she said softly.

Hiro recognized Yuri's precious *samisen*, a treasure from her childhood. Without speaking, they both remembered the first time they had heard Yuri play the stringed instrument and how appalled they had been at her inability to carry a tune. But gradually they had become accustomed to her soft monotone and eventually enjoyed the soothing, tuneless quality of the samisen.

Miyoko placed the instrument at Yuri's feet. She moved to
her son's coffin, where she placed a small book, his favorite
and probably the only one he still read since finishing school.
It contained the Buddhist prayers that he had learned while
visiting a remote mountain temple as a young man. So absorbed had he become in the world of business that he did not
allow himself time to read for enjoyment except for his prayer
book.

"Stay here and comfort Tatsuo when he comes," Hiro said
gently. "I will summon the priest."

A summer wind wafted billows of smoke about them as they
stood silently around the mounded graves. The priest, austere
in his black robes, repeated prayers while the Takezawas said
their farewells.

The directors gathered behind closed doors to discuss the
events that had taken place.

"Our zaibatsu has suffered great losses," Hiro's brother,
Koji, said, his forehead lined with concern. "Our couriers inform us that Yokohama has been completely leveled and that
which was not destroyed by the earthquake was consumed by
fire. Tidal waves have smashed villages along Tokyo Bay and
washed them into the sea."

"There is no time to waste on pity or regret," Shozo said in
his rasping voice. "We will begin to rebuild immediately.
Business must go on as usual."

Hiro marveled at his uncle's stoic practicality. If one could
pinpoint the reason for Shozo's success, it would have to be
his dauntless spirit, his ability to function in the face of overwhelming adversity.

Hiro placed a hand on his uncle's thin shoulder before
speaking. "Please give me a few days to straighten out my
household. We have already begun repairs. I will report to you
as soon as my home is habitable. In the meantime, please keep
me informed of the progress."

"Do not mourn too long, nephew. Life must go on."
Shozo's dark, discerning eyes had seen beyond Hiro's composed exterior and into his grieving heart.

For some the nightmare of the earthquake would linger forever, for others it would fade quickly, but the task of rebuild-
ing had to be faced by everyone. The restoration program
began even before the smell of smoke had disappeared from

the air and the ashes had grown cold. The dead were buried, some in mass graves, like those who had perished on the grounds of the Army Clothing Store. Thirty-two thousand people had died there. Their blackened bodies were not removed; rather, they were cremated where they had died and their ashes were used to strengthen the concrete that formed the commemorative monument erected in their memory.

With unequaled enthusiasm and energy, the stalwart survivors began to reconstruct their homes and businesses. Streets were cleared and made passable, rubble was pushed aside and buried, while plans for a new city began to take shape on the drawing boards. Inured to hardship, the people quickly recovered their indomitable spirit, working together to establish a new life. It was not uncommon to see the injured with bandaged limbs working alongside the able-bodied survivors. Slowly the cities and villages were resurrected, business was resumed, and smiles reappeared on determined faces.

Within three days the Takezawa estate was restored, certainly not to its former elegance, but at least to the point where it could be lived in. Employees of the zaibatsu had been dispatched and soon arrived laden with tools and materials. They began replacing broken beams, torn and splintered walls, shattered windows and heaved-up floors. They salvaged what could be reused, discarded what was damaged beyond repair, filled the gaping holes in the earth, and replaced uprooted shrubbery and plants. When their work was completed, they left as quickly as they had arrived and a hollow silence settled over the household.

Miyoko studied her grandson's pale, pinched face with concern. "Tatsuo, please eat something," she begged.

"I am not hungry, Obā-san."

"But you look so thin; you must eat."

Tatsuo shook his head and said nothing. Miyoko tried to tempt him with morsels from her own plate, as she had done when he was very young, but he choked when he tried to swallow them. On the seventh day after the death of his parents, he stood by their graves in stony silence as though he too wished to retreat from the world. Commemorative prayers were recited in their honor, but he did not even hear them.

Hiro planned to return to work on the morning of the eighth day. He awoke early and began to exercise, preparing himself as he had always done, hesitantly at first and then with renewed vigor until his muscles ached and his breath came in gasps. Finally, he meditated in the garden until the sun came over the horizon to open the day.

The chauffeur met him at the door, a look of excited pleasure on his face. "Takezawa-sama, I took the liberty of sending the jinrickisha driver back to the city. I have a surprise for you." Proudly he pointed to a well-maintained Chandler touring car parked at the edge of the driveway. "Someone abandoned it near the British embassy. I assured them you would be happy to buy it should the owner return. I gave them your name and address."

Hiro's face was stern. "You certainly did take liberties!" He walked slowly around the car, peering under the hood and running his fingers along the upholstery. "Well, let us try it out." A smile played at the corners of his mouth as he slid into the car.

The driver, his chin smugly elevated, drove carefully to the Takezawa headquarters while Hiro surveyed the destruction wrought by the Kanto earthquake. When they reached the Marunouchi district, he noted how minimal the damage had been here in contrast to the other areas. Many of the steel and concrete buildings had remained intact. The Imperial Hotel, designed by the American Frank Lloyd Wright, was already open for business. It had been built on floating footings in the loose soil and had escaped the disaster unscathed. The streets were buzzing with activity, and although evidence of the recent disaster was still present, business was being carried on as usual.

The Takezawa building had been converted back to business offices again. As Hiro entered, he noticed several empty chairs and the polite, subdued greetings of his employees. His reply was equally solemn. Perhaps later he would speak to them individually and offer his condolences, but not yet. He would have to face his first day at work without Hitoshi, and he needed all his strength.

Reports began arriving almost before he was seated. Interesting! Hiro thought as he quickly scanned the headlines of a newspaper. The *Prometheus* had stopped in Hong Kong to pick up emergency medical supplies and had just arrived in Yokohama. Its cargo holds had been cleaned and converted into a temporary medical treatment area.

So, Mr. Richter is not only a shrewd businessman, but he hopes to gain the respect of the Japanese people even before he has begun to do business with us, Hiro mused. In the face of the recent tragedy, there were many acts of heroism and mercy, but for a newspaper to print such a full-scale article about the *Prometheus* . . . Hiro wondered if Conrad had bribed someone to write the story.

Richter was soon forgotten in the deluge of work that fell on Hiro's shoulders. He was acutely aware of Hitoshi's absence, but by the end of the week, he learned that he could cope more easily if he buried himself in his work. The days stretched into weeks, as though time had begun only after the quake. Because of its immense wealth and size, the zaibatsu recovered quickly. A giant self-contained entity, it altered its course and continued to operate by transferring orders from damaged mills and factories to those that were still intact. The recent disaster represented a serious inconvenience to the zaibatsu rather than a major setback; its investments were widely distributed, and the citadels of its wealth remained unassailable.

The boardroom was quiet as Hiro, Koji, and Shozo studied the reports submitted by their engineers and accountants. Shozo tapped his head with his fingertip as he read the figures. There was a discreet knock on the door.

"Come in," Koji barked.

The door opened quickly and a sallow-faced young man peered in and motioned to Hiro. "Takezawa-sama, your driver is outside. He has an urgent message for you."

Hiro was on his feet instantly. He bowed politely to Koji and Shozo, and ran after the retreating figure of the young man. The driver held the car door open as Hiro approached.

"It is your grandson! He has collapsed!"

The journey home seemed to take hours. "Please hurry!" Hiro urged repeatedly. When they finally arrived, Hiro ran to Tatsuo's room.

"I am afraid he will die," Miyoko cried.

Hiro bent over his grandson and studied him intently for a moment. Gently, he ran his fingers along Tatsuo's cheek and forehead. "No, he will not die. He is not feverish, and his breathing is strong and even. I think he has finally succumbed to exhaustion; sleep is the best thing for him now."

"Are you sure he will not die? He seems so still, and he is deathly pale."

"Please do not worry. His spirit is suffering more than his body."

Anxiously, Miyoko followed Hiro into the garden.

"My dear wife, I know you are very concerned, but I would like you to go about your household chores as usual. He is our only grandchild, and I will watch over him very carefully."

Tatsuo slept through the day without moving. By evening Hiro knew what he must do. "I will take Tatsuo to the ocean tonight," he informed Miyoko. "We will return in the morning."

"I do not doubt your reasons, my husband, but do you think he is strong enough to spend the night outside?"

"Yes. But even if he were not, I would have no other choice."

Hiro gently roused Tatsuo, guiding his feet. Miyoko tied the sash around his kimono, then draped a heavy blanket around his shoulders before Hiro led him to the car.

"Where are we going, Oji-san?"

Hiro did not reply. Tatsuo sat silently as they drove along the dimly lit streets. When they finally stopped, Hiro turned to Tatsuo and spoke quietly. "We are here."

The smell of the ocean was all around them, and they could hear the waves crashing with relentless persistence against the shore. The moon hung like a jewel in a sky that glowed with stars. They stood mesmerized by the sight and sound of the thundering waves, mindless of the cool sand on their bare feet.

Hiro's voice was tender but firm. "Sit here and wait for my return. Keep your mind free and do not force thoughts." He waited while Tatsuo positioned himself.

The tone of his grandfather's voice discouraged the questions Tatsuo wanted to ask. He yearned to call after his grandfather when he heard the footsteps melt away into the night. He knew he had been brought here for a purpose and sat down dutifully, as he had been trained. He did not force thoughts, but his mind raced wildly; images of charred bodies flashed before him. He saw his mother's laughing face before it was transformed into a mask of death. His ears echoed with the screams of children and the gurgles of men approaching death, their faces changing into those of his parents as the fire engulfed them, consuming their flesh and choking the air from their lungs.

He opened his eyes to dispel the nightmare and stared into the night. Once again he shut his mind and allowed the sound of the crashing waves to fill his senses. The wind touched his face, elusive but real. He began to pray until his heart rose above the walls of his self-created prison; the sadness that had constricted his heart left and was washed away in the resounding waves. The hours passed, and he wondered if this was what it felt like to die and to be awakened to eternal life— floating endlessly through time as if on the waves of the ocean, propelled only by the wind.

A gull shrieked in the distance. Tatsuo suddenly became aware of the ache in his body and the prickly cramps in his legs. The desire to stand up and stretch almost overpowered him, but he knew from experience that one must never assuage the desires of the body during meditation. Soon his thoughts quieted again and all became gray and still; his body no longer existed. His mind was suddenly free; his spirit soared and reached out further and further. Perhaps because his young mind had been trained from early childhood, or perhaps because this was the quintessential moment of his own being, he grasped in that brief instant of time what it takes most people a lifetime to experience—that the present life on earth is but a feeting moment within eternity, that physical death is not an end but rather another beginning, that life has no meaning by itself but only in relation to the whole universe; everything is of the same root and ever-present, and it is all in harmony.

Tatsuo felt warmth on his face. His shoulders sagged under the weight of the heavy blanket, and pain trickled down his back and into his throbbing legs. He knew it was morning, for he could sense the sun's brilliance through his closed eyelids. He raised his face to receive the full warmth of the dawn, then slowly he opened his eyes. He cringed sharply against the brilliant stab of color and forced himself to gaze fully at the sun as it rose over the horizon. The intense light stung his eyes and they teared in defense. Gulls, silhouetted against the sky, soared and fell, their shrill cries shattering the early morning stillness. Gracefully, they skimmed the sunlit waters and then, riding an updraft, they soared heavenward on extended white wings. Tatsuo's spirits flew with them, his discomfort forgotten. Strong arms lifted him to his feet and supported him until the flow of blood brought new life to his numb limbs. He stretched, reaching for the sky, and dug his toes into the cool white sand.

"How do you feel?" Hiro asked.

"I am fine. The gulls sound happy." He pointed to the

multitude of swirling birds and smiled broadly.

Hiro's sigh of relief was long and audible. He, too, had sat through the night, keeping a silent vigil over Tatsuo while seeking solace in prayer. As they stood together, bathed in the warm sunlight, Hiro's voice rose over the sound of the waves:

> " 'How black the night without its stars.
>   Gulls are happy
>   In the morning sun.' "

Tatsuo's smile was radiant as they walked slowly toward the waiting car.

The wounds inflicted by the Kanto earthquake were healing rapidly. The *Prometheus* was no longer needed to house the victims of the catastrophe, and she stood empty, awaiting cargo. Within a week she was joined by a second Richter ship, which dwarfed the small fishing boats crowding the harbor. Like the workhorses they were, the ships settled comfortably under the weight of the bales of silk and tea that were crammed into the depths of their dark holds. Their cargoes would be worth ten million yen—a trial run for Richter.

Conrad had informed Hiro by cablegram that arrangements for the silk and tea had already been made. After arriving in Vancouver, the shipments would be dispatched by rail to Montreal and New York, where buyers were waiting eagerly. Japanese silk was in constant demand by every couturier in both countries, regardless of the price, and now there were rumors that Japan would be producing silks to which had been added a toughening fiber, making the fabric suitable for men's suits. The price would be exorbitant, but clothing manufacturers were already clamoring to place their orders.

Of equal importance were the cargoes that the *Prometheus* and her sister ships would be bringing back to Japan, especially timber and logs to reconstruct the devastated cities and villages. Richter had already been advised of Hitoshi's death, and this meant that for the time being Richter would be totally responsible for arranging the return shipments. Sealed orders containing explicit instructions for the completion of these shipments would be delivered to Richter on the *Prometheus*.

Shozo was uneasy about this arrangement. "You realize, Hiro, that we have no assurance that Richter will carry out his promises now that we have no one in Vancouver to protect our interests."

"You worry needlessly, Uncle. Richter is intent on building a dynasty, and we are providing him the means by which he can achieve this. By safeguarding his own interests, he must protect ours as well."

"In addition to this," Koji added, "I am sure that Richter-sama is aware that we could swallow him in one gulp should he step out of line."

Shozo's eyes remained veiled, and Hiro sensed his lingering uncertainty. Finally, he spoke. "Time will tell, but it is probable that other arrangements will have to be implemented at some future time."

Hiro and Koji looked up with questioning eyes, but Shozo did not elaborate. "The *Prometheus* is due to sail within two days, and a sister ship will follow soon after," Shozo continued. "Please deliver these orders to her captain as soon as you can, Hiro."

"I have made arrangements to attend to that matter tomorrow morning. I am taking Tatsuo with me. He has never been on board a large ship, and for that matter," Hiro added with a glint in his eyes, "neither have I."

Shozo regarded him for an instant before speaking. "Perhaps it would be wise if you both took careful note of the ship. Our success will depend largely on these seagoing vessels." He emitted his breath in a long sigh. "Unfortunately, I am too old for such adventures, so it will be up to you to follow them through." He held up his hand to stop their polite protests. "I wish it were not so, but I have reached the twilight of my life. However, that does not include my mind," he added sharply.

Had protocol allowed it, Hiro would have enjoyed a deep chuckle, but one did not laugh at a venerable uncle. He had no doubt whatsoever that Shozo's mind would remain alert for many more years.

The piers at Yokohama were almost inaccessible, shore-cranes and derricks whirred industriously and freight wagons clacked purposefully as longshoremen sweated in the warm autumn sun. The harbor had changed following the disaster, but the activity, resembling a discordant beehive, was now even more intensified. As Hiro and Tatsuo walked toward the *Prometheus*, they were greeted frequently, at times with polite nods but more often with respectful bows. Hiro did not find this recognition surprising, and acknowledged it with a slight but courteous inclination of the head. For many decades the Takezawas had maintained a prestigious position in Japan. Hiro did not overrate this fame, nor did he particularly relish it, preferring instead to remain anonymous.

The *Prometheus* was impressively large and, judging by her scrubbed appearance, considerably newer than her sister ship. As they walked up the gangplank, Hiro thought that in spite of her sturdy appearance, she was a beautiful ship.

A bilious seaman leaned over the railing and bellowed at the visitors. "Hey, hold it right there, you two. No one's allowed on board. We're casting off soon."

"I am Hiro Takezawa. I have orders for your captain. Please inform him that I am here."

Fuck me . . . it's Takezawa himself, thought the seaman as his eyebrows shot up in surprise.

The crew had been thoroughly briefed by Richter before sailing. The Takezawa deal was the biggest shipping contract ever handled by the company, and Richter's instructions about every detail were to be followed to the letter. The Takezawas were to receive nothing less than red carpet treatment, and Richter had not minced words as he explained what would happen should anyone disobey his orders. The seaman stared down at Hiro, unable to reconcile this small Oriental with the legendary samurai who had reportedly saved Richter's life. The little bastard didn't look strong enough to lift a sword let alone hack someone's hand off with it.

"Tell your captain that I am here." Hiro's voice rang with authority.

The seaman reacted instantly. "Yes, sir!"

Hiro reached the deck and waited quietly, ignoring the inquisitive stares of several seamen. In a few moments the captain approached with his hand extended.

"Welcome aboard, Mr. Takezawa. I have been expecting you."

Hiro gripped the captain's hand firmly as they exchanged greetings. "I am pleased to meet you, Captain Horvath. This is my grandson, Tatsuo."

The captain could no longer contain himself. "I am amazed at your command of English." His broad face was openly sincere.

Hiro smiled. "Actually, I not only speak it, I have on occasion taught English at Keio University. Does that surprise you?"

After a pause, the captain answered, "Yes . . . it does. You look so . . . well . . . Japanese! You caught me off guard. I expected you to arrive with an interpreter."

Hiro removed the sealed white envelope from his kimono and handed it to the Captain. "These are directives for Mr. Richter. Please be sure they are delivered as soon as you arrive in Vancouver. Any delay could be costly."

"I will attend to it, sir." Captain Horvath could not put his finger on it, but something about Hiro Takezawa commanded his respect. His appearance was not formidable; his manner, though abrupt by western standards, was courteous, and yet he seemed to emit an aura of uncompromising strength.

Hiro bowed formally to the captain, and Tatsuo quickly followed suit. Taken by surprise, the captain removed his hat with a flourish, exposing his white scalp, and bowed awkwardly in return. His expression was thoughtful as he watched his strange visitors descend the gangplank.

Tatsuo's face was animated with excitment, straining to absorb the multitude of sights and sounds that the waterfront offered. Finally his carefully restrained curiosity bubbled forth. "Oji-san, what are they loading there? Is that going to Canada, too? Do you think I will be able to work on a ship someday?"

Before Hiro could stop him, Tatsuo collided abruptly with a muscular seaman, who swung around quickly, a menacing sneer on his thick mouth. "Watch where you're going, rice cake, or I'll kick your ass."

"My grandson is sorry. It was an accident," Hiro said quickly.

"Let 'im speak for hisself, Jappo, or I'll kick both your asses." He was not a tall man, but his broad shoulders gave him the appearance of greater height. His red hair, oiled to control its unruliness, gleamed in the afternoon sun and several aged tattoos were stretched across his upper arms. Tatsuo stood speechless until Hiro stepped in front of him.

"We are sorry for the accident, but your language disturbs me."

"Well, ain't that just too fucking bad. Whatcha gonna do about it, Jappo?" He stretched his neck so that his face was inches from Hiro's nose.

Hiro shook his head in disbelief. "Your manners are truly

lacking. Come, Tatsuo, we do not have time to waste here.''

A vacuous smile appeared on the man's flushed face, and he winked at the small crowd that had gathered. He lifted his boot and aimed it with full force at Hiro's receding back. Hiro anticipated the attack and shifted his body slightly, causing the boot to miss and the man to pitch forward, off balance.

"Tricky little bastard, ain't you!" He swung his fist at Hiro's face, missing as Hiro moved back to avoid the blow. The crowd laughed and someone shouted, "Kick his ass, Slivchak." He spat from the corner of his mouth and folded both hands into thick fists.

Hiro appeared calm in spite of his annoyance. "Please . . . I do not wish to harm you."

Enraged and humiliated now, Slivchak grabbed Tatsuo, spun him around and kicked him on his buttocks. Hiro helped Tatsuo to his feet and turned to face Slivchak, his eyes narrowed into slits of wrath.

The crowd immediately sensed the change and backed away; the fight now had the smell of blood, and they stood like vultures, waiting.

Slivchak hesitated, then rushed full force into Hiro with his head and shoulders. This time Hiro did not move. Pain reeled in Slivchak's head as he connected with the iron wall that was Hiro's stomach. He sprang back, fear and disbelief mingled on his face.

Hiro spoke deliberately and slowly. "Rudeness is sometimes the result of ignorance and can be overlooked, but attacking children cannot be excused. Remember this as your bones are healing." Before Slivchak could move, Hiro swung his foot with lightning speed. The sound of breaking bones accompanied Slivchak's scream of pain; a jagged bone protruded through the knee of his pants. The crowd gazed in horror as the leg bent sickeningly backward. Slivchak crumpled to the ground in a merciful faint. Hiro straightened his kimono and tightened the sash; the crowd formed a wide path as Hiro and Tatsuo walked away.

As they left Yokohama, dark clouds loomed overhead, heavy with the promise of rain, and the air grew damp and chilly. In Tokyo, the dampness changed to an insidious drizzle. The mountains disappeared behind the oncoming storm, visible only when bolts of lightning ripped through the sky. By the time they had arrived home, the drizzle had become a torrential rain, intensified by cold winds blowing off the ocean.

For days it continued without relief. People ventured out only when absolutely necessary. The rest of the time they barricaded themselves within the security of their homes and pitied those unfortunates who had nowhere to shelter. A depressing fog covered the city, through which only the brightest lights flickered. October drew to a close; still there was no respite from the rain. What was left of summer gardens lay flat in surrender to the relentless wetness.

Toward the end of the third week, a meeting was held in the boardroom of the Takezawa building; all senior officials were required to attend. The gravity of the occasion was enhanced by the appearance of Shozo's brother, Hidetoshi, now semiretired because of ill health. Although younger than Shozo by a full decade, he appeared older and thinner. His face was lined with premature age and pain, but his eyes, like Shozo's, were bright with intelligence.

"You have by now surmised the purpose of our meeting, which is to find a replacement for Hitoshi," Shozo announced. "His death is a terrible loss to us all. However, in spite of this tragedy, we cannot lose sight of our goals, which include expansion into western markets." He waited while everyone murmured in agreement.

Koji interjected, "I have seriously considered this expansion, and it is evident that we cannot implement our programs without a representative in western Canada; it is too hazardous."

Hidetoshi spoke for the first time. "It has been my task to choose this representative." Except for the familiar pounding of the rain on the tiled roof, the room was silent.

"Because of the great distance between Japan and Canada, we have to keep the blood ties strong. This narrows the choice to family members."

All eyes rested on Hidetoshi. Even Hiro felt an uncomfortable chill.

"Shozo has seen many seasons go by and is not able to travel," Hidetoshi continued, "and I am too ill. Koji's talents do not lie in public relations. That leaves only you, Hiro. You will be our representative."

Hiro stood up slowly, unable to believe what he had just heard. "That is not possible! My life is here in Japan."

"My dear nephew," Shozo said, his voice firm but edged

with sadness, "we have no choice. You know as well as anyone the importance of that position and also that you are the
only one left to fill it. The circumstances are unavoidable. The
decision is final. Please be ready to leave in two weeks."

Hiro yearned to shout out his refusal, but he spoke quietly.
"I am aware that the decision is irrevocable, and I will
comply, but I cannot go until the final commemorative serv-
ices for my son and daughter-in-law have been observed. Nor
will I leave until my brother agrees to move into my home to
care for the graves of my children."

"Your wishes will be followed precisely," Shozo said. Koji
nodded without hesitation; the bond between him and Hiro
had always been strong.

Long after everyone had left, Hiro remained in the silent
boardroom, reconciling himself to the decision of the zaibatsu. To sever the ties of five decades in his beloved homeland
would be difficult, and Hiro felt the agony of the imminent
separation.

The night before their departure Hiro did not sleep. Instead,
he sat in the garden beside the pine trees, feeling the presence
of his ancestors. He would not say farewell, for he would take
Japan with him in his heart and impart it into the foreign soil
that would be his new home.

It will be difficult, he thought, but I will survive and we will
be happy.

[4]

The forward deck of the S.S. *Hudson* was deserted except for Hiro, Miyoko, and Tatsuo. It was early morning, but already the gulls followed the ship as she steamed out of Tokyo Bay; Mount Fujiyama shone in the distance.

"Ojī-san, are you sure my trunks are safely aboard?" Tatsuo asked.

"Yes, you saw them being loaded."

"But I did not see the wooden chest which you gave me—the one with the sword and my keiko-gi."

"I took care of that one personally," Hiro reassured him.

They stood silently, watching the graceful gulls soaring on the wind.

"Will the mornings be as beautiful in Canada, Ojī-san?"

"Yes, they will."

"But did you not say Japan is the land of the rising sun?"

Hiro smiled but did not look at Tatsuo. "I have no doubt the rising sun will be almost as beautiful, and those gulls," he said, pointing to the birds, "they will follow." He turned to face the wind, a solitary tear glistening on his cheek.

On the day before their scheduled arrival in Vancouver, Hiro retrieved the trunk containing their new clothing. "I think perhaps we should accustom ourselves to wearing western clothes."

While Hiro struggled with the strange garments, Tatsuo quickly put on gray flannel trousers and a stiffly starched

89

shirt. "This is how it is done, Ojī-san. I watched Karl do it."
He tugged at the collar where it scraped his neck with unfamiliar stiffness. "But I think I prefer my old clothes."

Hiro gravely buttoned his shirt and tucked it into his
trousers before studying himself in the mirror. Behind him,
Miyoko hid her face in her hands and giggled.

"You do not fill those clothes very well, honorable husband," she said between suppressed bursts of soft laughter.

Hiro scowled in the mirror at himself and then at Miyoko.
The clothes were ill-fitting—the sleeves of the shirt were too
long, almost covering his hands, the pants bagged at the seat,
and the cuffs fell in deep folds around his ankles. He tried
pulling the pants higher around his waist, but they still folded
neatly at his feet. The clothing had been made for Hitoshi,
who had been taller but not as heavily muscled as Hiro.

Miyoko pulled at his shirtsleeve. "Take them off and I will
try to alter them."

With a sigh, Hiro removed the clothing and slipped back
into his familiar kimono. "I am not a vain man," he said, eyeing himself in the mirror, "but my own clothes are far more
becoming and certainly more comfortable. I will not wear
those ridiculous, wretched suits of armor."

"But Ojī-san, I thought you said we must adapt to the ways
of our new country! Does this not include dressing as they
do?"

Hiro looked at Tatsuo in the mirror before he answered.
"Yes, Tatsuo, it means dressing as they do. Your grandfather
was just being obstinate." He passed the discarded garments
to Miyoko. "Please adjust them for me as best you can and I
will wear them." He felt a wave of regret that fate would send
him to a strange, cheerless country devoid of shrines and
gardens and populated with people who could not appreciate
the beauty of a haiku or the freedom of a cool, flowing
kimono.

"You look like a stranger in those clothes, my husband,"
Miyoko observed sadly. "Not at all like a samurai."

Hiro's sensitive heart constricted with sympathy for his
wife. She had always been obedient to his wishes, seldom re-
buking him for any of his decisions. With the gracious simplicity of a gentle woman, she had made his life happy and
full. He reached out and lifted Miyoko's chin with his fingers
so that he could look into her eyes. She smiled tremulously.

"I will make you a promise, Miyoko—and you, Tatsuo. We

will find a home in Vancouver, one with large trees, and we will build a shrine with a garden around it. In the evening we will wear our kimonos and view the moon as we have always done. The same moon that shines in Japan will shine there too, and one day we will return to Japan and be comforted in our old age by all that is familiar and dear to us.''

Miyoko's face brightened, but her eyes still shone with tears. She knew her husband well, perhaps too well, for despite his brave, resolute words, she sensed his innermost feelings. She knew they would probably never return to Japan, and she quickly looked down at her sewing to hide the hopeless feeling her eyes might reveal.

When the alterations were completed, Hiro's clothing fit better but it was still uncomfortable, binding him in the most unlikely places so that even his breathing was restricted. But he had made a promise to his family and he meant to keep it.

Tatsuo carefully studied his grandfather from every angle and then nodded with approval. "You look fine, Oji-san. There is only one thing wrong." He pointed to Hiro's bare feet. "You must wear shoes and stockings. They will pinch your toes at first, but you will become used to them, just as I have. See . . . watch this." Tatsuo jumped up and down a few times, then took several giant steps across the length of the cabin. Then, to further illustrate his adaptability, he leaped into the air and clicked his heels together, much to the delight of his attentive grandparents.

Hiro pulled on the stockings and pushed his feet into the shoes. He grimaced as he laced them up snugly, obeying Tatsuo's careful instructions. The shoes, black and shining, squeaked with newness as he walked slowly around the cabin. If he felt any discomfort, he concealed it well. He scowled at himself again in the mirror and announced he was ready for their arrival in Vancouver.

By noon of the seventeenth day, land was sighted, and the ship's crew prepared for docking. As the *Hudson* steamed through the Straits of Juan de Fuca, the rugged majestic beauty of the mountains with their lush vegetation was clearly visible even through the mist and low-lying fog. A light drizzle fell on the unheeding Takezawas, who stood huddled together on the flying bridge. The channels grew narrower as they passed by the Gulf Islands, forcing the freighter to move along at quarter speed.

The helmsman caught Hiro's attention and pointed to a tiny

settlement in the distance. "That's Steveston—mostly populated by Japanese fishermen. They have their own canning
plant and hospital too. Just north of there lies Vancouver."

Tatsuo's face was flushed with excitement. "Will Karl be
there to meet us when we land, Ojī-san?"

"Yes, I am sure he will be."

The sea had turned gray and choppy as the *Hudson* approached Prospect Point, and the waves rose to meet the rain.
Gulls swooped down over the ship, and in the distance Vancouver Harbor came into view. A squat, powerful tugboat signaled her approach with a hollow blast of her whistle. Deftly
she led the *Hudson* through the First Narrows. Although
many ships lined the harbor, one of the biggest in North
America, the piers were quiet on this afternoon. There were no
colorful flags, no ear-shattering horns, only an occasional
blast from a disrespectful tugboat. The scream of winches
broke the silence as the *Hudson* was pulled tight against the
pier and the hawsers secured.

Suddenly Tatsuo began waving frantically, his voice pitched
high with excitement. "There he is! I can see Karl."

On the pier below, a figure in a navy suit waved enthusi-
astically with both arms. A slim, dark-haired woman stood
beside him, occasionally lifting her hand to wave, and even
from a distance Hiro recognized her beauty. A girl in a bright
red coat held on to her arm. Conrad Richter stood several
paces behind them.

As the gangplank was lowered, Karl's booming voice could
be heard above the noise of the machinery. "Tatsuo! Tatsuo!
There he is, Mother!"

"Yes, I see him, son," Dorothea replied. "At least wait
until the gangplank is in place."

Conrad's admonitions for restraint went unheeded. Karl
raced up the gangplank that had not yet touched the pier.
Tatsuo, still awkward in his leather shoes, walked down to
meet him, and like two mischievous bear cubs, they tussled
precariously on the narrow walkway. Between excited questions and loud whoops, Karl pulled Tatsuo back toward his
mother and sister.

"This is my friend, Tatsuo Takezawa," he announced
proudly.

"I am pleased to meet you, Mrs. Richter," Tatsuo said
solemnly. He smiled at the girl.

Dorothea looked down at the slight figure and into the quiet dark eyes. Pulling Tatsuo into the circle of her arms, she placed a gentle kiss on his cheek.

Gusts of wind drove the dampness through Conrad's heavy coat as he paced restlessly through the pools of water that had formed on the pier. He detested waiting and would have preferred to send his chauffeur to pick up the Takezawas, but he dared not risk offending them.

Christ! How far were they going to carry this charade of a grand welcome? he wondered as he watched Karl and Dorothea hover around Tatsuo. Yet he realized it was not a charade—their joy and smiles of delight were sincere. Karl had talked so much about the Takezawas since his return from Japan that his mother and sister, Lisl, were soon caught up in his excitement. The suggestion that the Takezawas stay at the Richter estate until they were settled in their own home had been Dorothea's. Initially Conrad favored the idea, feeling it would be an excellent way to ensure their gratitude, but his reservations grew steadily until he was sure that he had made a serious mistake. He now cursed himself for having agreed.

Hiro appeared more drawn and pale than Karl remembered, and he looked very uncomfortable in his shapeless suit. Miyoko, too, seemed thin and subdued.

"Have your grandparents been ill?" There was concern in Karl's voice.

"No, but Obā-san has been very sad, and my grandfather is not a sailor. He has been seasick for most of the voyage," Tatsuo answered.

It shows, Conrad thought as he guided Dorothea by the elbow toward Hiro and Miyoko. "Mr. Takezawa, I am pleased to see you again. I trust you have had a pleasant journey," Conrad said through an artificial smile. "This is my wife, Dorothea, and our daughter, Lisl."

"I am honored to meet you, Mrs. Richter, and you, Lisl." He bowed low before taking their hands in his. "May I present my wife, Miyoko."

Eleven-year-old Lisl curtseyed. The two ladies stared at each other for a moment, then embraced shyly.

"I am pleased to meet you, Miyoko. Karl has told me so much about you and your country. I hope that you will like Canada and that you will consider our home as your own," Dorothea said. To her own surprise, she instinctively reached out to the Takezawas. Was it the sadness she saw in their eyes, or could it be the aura of strength that surrounded Hiro?

Conrad stepped forward. "I have two cars waiting. Your luggage and crates will be delivered later today. Let's get the hell out of this rain. I'm drenched to the skin." He led them to the end of the pier, where two sleek black cars were parked. "They are not as elegant as your Haynes, Takezawa-sama, but they are exceptional nonetheless."

Hiro carefully examined the identical cars. "Cadillacs, model sixty-three, are they not?"

"Why, yes! How did you know?" Conrad asked with surprise.

"Cars are a hobby with me, or perhaps a passion. At one time I was content just to drive them, but my son aroused my interest in their mechanics and design as well. His dream was to enlist the zaibatsu in building a car of our own," Hiro added wistfully. "Perhaps if you are interested I could show you some of his drawings.

Considering the idea too far removed to be of any practical value, Conrad merely raised his eyebrows quizzically. He knocked on the window of the first car to awaken his sleeping driver, who stirred a little, then buried his chin further into his coat; the peak of his hat rested on his nose, shielding his eyes from the world.

"Son of a bitch!" Conrad muttered through clenched teeth. The window rattled from the intensity of his second knock, and the driver sat up with a start.

"Get out," Conrad shouted.

The driver immediately opened the door and jumped out. "Sorry, sir. I must have dozed off for a minute." He avoided looking at Conrad and fastened his gaze on the third button of his employer's coat.

"Help the ladies into the car, William, and follow me to Drachenschlucht. I will be taking a different route home today, so make sure you stay close behind, otherwise you might get lost."

The driver flushed noticeably but remained silent as he helped his shivering passengers into the spacious back seat. Hiro joined Conrad in the other car. With Conrad in the lead, they left the City Wharf and turned east on Water Street, where the traffic was heavy in spite of the downpour. Unconcerned by either the traffic or the now-blinding rain, Conrad maintained a steady speed, swerving occasionally to avoid other vehicles.

"The car handles very well," Hiro observed.

Conrad nodded proudly. "As you can see, there are miles of railroad track all around the waterfront and False Creek. This is one of the busiest seaports in North America." He pointed to the warehouses and grain elevators that were now visible along the shoreline.

"I am impressed," Hiro said quietly. "The harbor is larger than I expected, but where are all the people?"

Conrad chuckled derisively. "Hiding from the rain, no doubt, but they're here all right, one hundred and eighty thousand of them. Vancouver is growing fast, too damn fast to suit me." He slowed down to accommodate a streetcar that had stopped to discharge its passengers while Hiro stared curiously at a triangular-shaped hotel at the foot of Alexander Street.

Conrad pointed to the waterfront again. "You will be visiting this area often in the near future. As you can see, the shore facilities are excellent and the grain elevators are filled to capacity as usual. It's been a boom year for wheat; ships are even going through the Panama Canal en route to Europe." Conrad accelerated and sped down Hastings Street; the rear car followed at precisely the same speed. "We're going into Chinatown now," Conrad explained. "The Chinese have a very active community here with several thousand residents. Many of them came with the railroad years ago. They work like slaves and don't expect too much money."

Hiro chose to ignore the last remark and studied the passing storefronts with interest. "This is a most fascinating city."

"Your zaibatsu will prosper here, Takezawa-sama. Once you're settled, I'll show you my warehouses and introduce you to some of our suppliers. They will be anxious to do business with you, I'm sure."

As they sped over the Granville Street Bridge, which spanned False Creek, the rain stopped abruptly. Behind them, black clouds lingered threateningly over the city, but ahead the sky had cleared and the sun thrust brilliant pink and orange rays high above the horizon.

Spellbound by the spectacular sunset, Hiro sat motionless while Conrad was looking at him expectantly. "I am sorry. I was completely engrossed by the beautiful sunset. Is it often this spectacular?"

"Yes, I suppose so, but I wanted you to take a look at the factories and sawmills below us."

Hiro gazed down at the cluster of buildings as they drove over the bridge. Most of them had obviously closed for the day, and only a few people could be seen scurrying about. How little there was here to remind him of his beloved Japan, where people and activity were ever present.

"We'll soon be at Drachenschlucht—it's only a few more miles," Conrad continued. "The Shaughnessy district was developed by the railroad about fifteen years ago. Unlike much of Vancouver, all the homes are situated on spacious lots, where we can maintain our privacy." He hesitated. There was no point in telling Hiro about the unspoken rule forbidding Orientals and blacks from purchasing property in the area. The only way they were allowed in was as domestic help or gardeners. Which was exactly as it should be, he thought.

"What is the meaning of Drachenschlucht?" Hiro asked as his tongue rolled with difficulty over the harsh word.

"It is the name of my estate. It means 'throat of the dragon.'"

Hiro smiled and thought, how appropriate.

Conrad turned onto a tree-lined avenue. The oak and maple trees were almost bare, with only an occasional leaf clinging bravely to stark branches.

"This is Angus Drive; Drachenschlucht is just around the next corner," Conrad announced.

Hiro recognized the estate even before the cars entered its circular stone driveway. The house was an extension of Conrad Richter. It sat ostentatiously behind a stone wall which was further heightened by the wrought-iron railing that was cemented into the stone. The house was a three-story structure, supported on both sides of its stone stairway by four Doric pillars and flanked by two marble dragons with bared teeth. To lessen the frightening effect of their rapacious faces, some gentle hand had trained an ivy to grow lushly over their bodies and brutal, gaping mouths. The decorative windows facing the street were narrow, allowing only thin shafts of light into the high-ceilinged rooms.

Before the cars had come to a full stop, two huge Great Danes bounded down the steps, barking their loud welcome. They had recognized the cars and wagged their tails eagerly as their barking increased to a near howl. Conrad was out of the car instantly.

"Harras, Prinz—quiet, damn you!"

Ignoring the command, the dogs raced past him toward Karl and Lisl, who embraced them and laughed with delight as they licked their faces and pushed them with their cold, wet noses.

"Okay, okay . . . calm down. Tatsuo, come and meet my two friends; they won't bite you," Karl said as he scratched the tops of their massive heads.

Tatsuo patted their heads cautiously and was immediately rewarded with several wet licks. "I have never seen such huge dogs in all my life!"

"They're strong, too," Karl boasted. "They used to carry Lisl and me on their backs."

Tatsuo backed away as the dogs rushed toward Dorothea, who had just stepped out of the car. She spoke to them sternly, but her soft voice had no effect. They continued to bound back and forth between her and the children until Conrad's voice boomed out again. This time the dogs, sensing Conrad's anger, walked over to Karl and sat by his feet. Only then did Miyoko alight from the car, still watching the Great Danes suspiciously.

Dorothea held out her hand to Miyoko. "Come, they won't hurt you. They're big and clumsy but friendly."

"And they're also useless," Conrad growled. "I bought them when they were pups and intended to train them as guard dogs, but Karl ruined them. You have to be stern with them so they know who's boss. I was away too often and couldn't train them properly—now they're useless freeloaders."

Hiro knelt down beside the car and stared at the dogs. They became instantly alert and cocked their heads at a curious angle, their eyes riveted on Hiro. Everyone became silent as they watched the strange wordless communication between them. He whispered to the huge dogs, and they came to rigid attention; even their tails formed a straight line. Hiro then nodded and the dogs came to him, sitting dutifully on either side of him. He spoke softly to them in Japanese; the huge animals responded with low throaty growls but did not move from their crouched position at his feet.

"They are very intelligent and responsive, Richter-sama. They merely require some direction. Perhaps I could help Karl train them."

Amazed, Conrad stared at the dogs. "You're welcome to try, but please speak to them in English. Otherwise you will inherit them permanently."

There was a burst of relieved laughter as they started up the steps toward the house. The wide wooden door, on which rested a heavy brass knocker molded in the shape of a dragon's head, opened to reveal a tall, gray-haired woman with an ageless face. She stood with her arms folded tightly over a sparse bosom. Her hair was neatly braided into a bun at the back of her head, and when she smiled, her eyes disappeared into a series of wrinkles.

"Mrs. Lange, I would like you to meet your houseguests," Dorothea said. "This is Hiro Takezawa, his wife, Miyoko, and their grandson, Tatsuo."

There was a soft lilt to Mrs. Lange's voice and the hint of a German accent. "Come with me, and I will show you to your rooms. Dinner is nearly ready."

Mrs. Lange did not walk, she bustled, and the Takezawas nearly ran to keep up with her. They passed a blur of huge vases with chrysanthemums in the hallway, an elaborate chandelier, and then they climbed an endless stairway with a carved bannister and plush Indian rugs. Nothing registered firmly in their minds except the feeling of unfamiliarity, of large uncomfortable furniture, of cold rooms with high ceilings and mirrors that reflected their uncertain faces.

"Your grandson will share this room with Karl. Mrs. Richter thought that would be the best arrangement. You and Mrs. Takezawa will have the blue bedroom at the end of the hall. Each room has its own bath. I trust you will find them suitable." Her heels clicked efficiently on the oak floors as she scurried along, opening doors as she talked. Then she left them.

Miyoko hesitated at the threshold of their room, her hands clutched tightly together in the sleeves of her kimono. Her eyes slowly surveyed the room, and a hesitant smile appeared. "It is much too large for us, my husband. An entire family could fit in here comfortably."

Tentatively, they explored the room, warming their hands at the fire that crackled in the fireplace and testing the stuffed rocker by the bed. There was a separate dressing room with a huge gaping closet and a mirrored wall. They stared at the high bed complete with stepping stool and canopy and shook their heads in dismay.

"I do not belong here," Miyoko sobbed. "Everything is so strange—I will surely fail as a wife. Oh, my husband, what will you do with me?"

"First of all, you will wash the tears from your face, for they do not become you. Then we will have dinner with the Richters. Later, when you have had a chance to rest, we will make our own plans—about the house we will have, a school for Tatsuo, and the fine job you will do in making a comfortable home for us. You are needed here. Tatsuo and I would be lost without you."

Dorothea had anticipated the Takezawas' preference for their own familiar food and surprised them with a dinner consisting of a variety of lightly cooked vegetables and baked cod served with lemon slices. The Takezawas found the meal palatable and satisfying. They were amazed at the amount of food Karl consumed but noticed that Mrs. Lange did not pass the fish to Conrad.

When the meal was over, Hiro leaned back in his chair to enjoy his tea. "Mrs. Richter, your son has told me that you are an accomplished pianist."

Dorothea colored slightly. "It was my life for many years."

"You still play, of course?"

Dorothea did not look at Conrad but could feel his eyes on her. "Only for my family and friends," she replied carefully.

"But you are a concert pianist!"

"I used to be, but not anymore, I'm afraid."

Conrad spoke. "After the children were born, we decided that Dorothea's place was at home rather than running all around the world for other people's enjoyment."

Hiro sensed the undercurrent of anger in Conrad's voice and caught the hint of sadness in Dorothea's eyes. It is a subject best left for another time, he thought.

Tatsuo did not feel the charge of emotion in the room and allowed his curiosity to surface. "Please, Mrs. Richter, will you play for us?"

Dorothea looked at the imploring eyes and answered without hesitation. "Of course. It would be a pleasure. Bring your coffee or tea and come into the parlor."

When everyone was settled comfortably around her, Dorothea started to play. Her fingers danced easily over the keyboard, and the room reverberated with haunting and beautiful melodies, captivating her small audience. Hiro leaned back on the sofa and closed his eyes, and soon a look of contentment came over his face. Lisl crept up beside him, and before long she curled herself comfortably into the circle of his arm. An hour passed, and still the enraptured audience did not stir. Tatsuo's eyes seldom left Dorothea's slender form as her music created colorful images and moods in his receptive mind. At times his eyes were filled with unshed tears, soon displaced by sparks of joy as the melody changed. Part of Dorothea's success as a concert pianist had been her ability to touch the soul of her audience, and Tatsuo was no exception. Even Conrad appeared relaxed, and the grim lines around his mouth eased. Finally, when she announced the end of her recital, everyone sighed with regret until she promised they could have another performance the next evening.

"You have made our first day in Canada a memorable one, Mrs. Richter," Hiro said.

Tatsuo did not say anything; he couldn't. It had been a magical time for him, listening to the heart-stirring music, watching the exquisite beauty of Karl's mother and the soft breathing of the fairylike girl who slept in his grandfather's arms. Earlier Tatsuo had caught himself staring at Lisl; she was unlike anyone he had ever seen. Her blond hair hung in heavy silken curls around her shoulders, and her skin was so fair it was almost transparent. She had looked at him with open curiosity, and when she smiled, Tatsuo could not help but smile too.

When Hiro and Miyoko entered their room for the evening, they discovered that someone had turned down the bed for them, stoked the fire, and drawn the draperies. Their luggage lay neatly stacked in one corner, unopened. Exhausted, they sank onto the soft bed.

"I feel as though I am suffocating in a giant bean cake," Hiro complained.

"My bones are beginning to ache; I cannot sleep on this," Miyoko whispered. She tossed and turned, trying to find a comfortable position. Finally, she sat up and threw off the heavy quilt. "This will not do!"

"What are you going to do?" Hiro asked.

"You will see." Miyoko walked over to the window and pulled open the heavy draperies, allowing the soft moonlight to illuminate the room. She removed a heavy blanket from the foot of the bed and spread it over the thick carpet. The quilt and the pillows came next. Hiro chuckled as they lay on their newly made bed; soon they slept with the moon shining down on them and the branches of a nearby pine tree whispering in the wind.

• • •

At precisely eight o'clock the next morning, the loud barking of Harras and Prinz heralded the arrival of two flatbed trucks in the driveway.

"Your crates have arrived, Takezawa-sama," Conrad observed. He was out the door before the trucks had come to a complete stop; Hiro was close behind.

A heavy, barrel-chested man with a cigar in his mouth and a hat set precariously on the back of his head jumped out of the lead truck. "Sorry we couldn't get these here last night, Mr. Richter. They're so damn heavy we couldn't budge them; had to bring in a couple of extra guys to help us load up. Where do you want them?"

Conrad motioned to Hiro. "I have allocated some space for them in my warehouse. You can direct the men as to which crates you wish to keep here and which you would like to store."

Hiro jumped nimbly onto the deck of the truck. The stocky driver raised his eyebrows. "Hey, how'd you do that?"

Hiro pointed to five crates marked with strange characters and bound with steel bands. "I would like to keep these here, if you don't mind, Richter-sama. The others can be stored at your warehouse. I will not need them until I have purchased a house."

"Those are heavy bastards," the driver said, cursing under his breath. "Well, we might as well get started—ain't got all day."

With the aid of ropes and dollies, the crates were moved one by one into the basement. When the task had been completed and the trucks were gone, Conrad turned to Hiro. "What have you got in those crates?"

"Gold," Hiro replied.

"Gold! Good God, you didn't ask for guards or anything?" Conrad almost shouted.

"I did not want to attract attention," Hiro said calmly.

"Who the hell cares about attracting attention? What if someone had hijacked the truck?"

"The best way to hide something is to keep it in the open."

"Say what you will, I'm going to put some armed guards around here until you get that gold into a bank vault."

"As you wish, Richter-sama."

After Conrad had left for the office, Dorothea took the Takezawas to the sun-room, where Mrs. Lange served a leisurely lunch. Only their laughter and the excited chatter of the two boys and Lisl interrupted the stillness of the lazy fall day. Hesitantly, Miyoko told Dorothea in her uncertain English about the garden they had left behind, the age of the old sculptured trees, the roses destroyed by the earthquake, and the new graves beside the shrine. Hiro related their plans for building a new life in Canada and revealed to Dorothea his apprehension about Tatsuo's future.

"I would like Tatsuo to adapt to the ways of this country, but at the same time, I do not want him to forsake the customs of his ancestors."

After listening to him, Dorothea sighed. "And I do not want my children to suffer the disappointments that I have been faced with. I wish they could view the world forever as they do now—exciting and full of promise."

"That is the wish of many. Students of Zen strive toward this very goal all their lives, to return to the source and to see the world as it really is—new and exciting and, as you say, full of promise. It is my deep hope that Tatsuo will continue to seek wisdom and understanding as long as he has breath."

"Just as you have, Mr. Takezawa?"

Hiro looked at her for a moment. "Yes."

On the morning of their second day in Vancouver, Hiro was awakened by the distant barking of Harras and Prinz. He was surprised to see that sunlight knifed through the narrow windows; it was not often that he missed a sunrise. The house was still. He dressed quietly, wincing as he tried to push his feet into the stiff leather shoes. "What a curse these miserable things are!" He pushed them aside and slipped into his favorite *zori*. As he walked soundlessly past Tatsuo's door, it opened.

"Oji-san, I have been waiting for you," Tatsuo whispered. "The sun is almost up!"

"*O hayo*, Tatsuo-san. We have not missed it altogether. If we hurry, we can still extend our apologies." Hiro chuckled softly.

They stole noiselessly out the back door and into the garden. The dogs, jumping and barking with excitement, welcomed them. Hiro issued a sharp command, and the dogs stood rigid with ears and tails pointed.

"Are you ready to be greeted by these great beasts, Tatsuo?"

Tatsuo moved from his hiding place behind his grandfather. Hiro gave another command, and the dogs leaped forward, licking Tatsuo's face and knocking him over in their exuberance.

"That is the second time your face has been washed this morning. Your grandmother will be very pleased with you."

Tatsuo giggled as he struggled playfully with the dogs. Obedient to Hiro's command, they quieted instantly and walked submissively at his heels through the garden, their breath clouding the crisp air.

"What day is this, Ojī-san?"

"November twenty-seventh. It is time we found a school for you. It has been too long since you have sat in a classroom."

Tatsuo nodded as he patted the dogs. "Yes, I am ready to go back to school. Will it be very different here?"

"Yes, it will be. When your father left Japan to study, he found it strange at first."

"Did he like it?"

"Yes, after a time, just as you will."

They walked in silence, each lost in his own thoughts, but enjoying their closeness. As they neared the house, the dogs stopped abruptly and whined; a few moments later Karl and Dorothea came out to meet them.

"Good morning. I see that you are both early risers like my son and me," Dorothea observed. "What are your plans for today?"

"We must find a place to live and a school for Tatsuo."

"Of course, but first—breakfast," Dorothea said.

Conrad joined them in the dining room. "The city is growing fast, and I don't think you'll have any trouble finding a suitable home. I will give you a map and show you where to look."

"I will help Mr. Takezawa. I think I know just what they are looking for," Dorothea suggested cheerfully.

Conrad stared at her coldly.

Dorothea ignored the silent warning, confident that he would not show displeasure in front of these particular guests. "I would like to take them to Stanley Park, too. It is so beautiful at this time of the year."

"Oh, Mother, can we go today?" Lisl asked, assuming her most beseeching expression.

"Only if our guests are interested and can spare the time."

"They're interested—aren't you, Tatsuo?" Lisl flashed him a brilliant smile, and Tatsuo nodded, wondering how anyone could ever refuse Lisl.

"We can pass through the park on the way to the office," Conrad consented. "I want to show Mr. Takezawa our office and shore facilities." The subject was now closed, and he turned to Hiro. "Your silk shipment will be on the train tomorrow."

"Has it been insured?" Hiro asked, although he already knew the answer.

"Yes, for three million, as directed by your head office."

By the time the driver had brought the two cars around to the front of the house, Karl and Tatsuo were restless and Lisl was almost in tears as her mother's patience began to wane. Dorothea forced herself to relax, thinking that it had been many months since the entire family had gone on an outing together. Only she knew just how volatile Conrad could be, yet today she was happy and felt more comfortable in his presence than she had for a long time. Perhaps it was because of the Takezawas. She felt protective of them, especially the thin-faced Tatsuo, whose spirit shone clearly in his dark eyes. Yet it was she who needed protection. But from what? Her brow furrowed slightly. Yes, Conrad could still hurt her superficially, but he could no longer intimidate her as he once did.

Dorothea knew now that other than her children, her father was the only person she had truly loved and who had loved her in return. Her mother, a shadowy figure, ill as far back as Dorothea could remember, had died many years ago. She had not significantly affected Dorothea's life; it was her father who had showered her with affection, encouraged her musical career, and organized her life. It was he who also chose her tutors, her escorts, and her concert appearances. They were happy together and skipped from country to country, leaving the memory of her music behind them. And then suddenly, when she was twenty-four, he had died, and she was left defenseless. Alone, frightened, and wealthy, she was approached by every philanderer and second-rate patron of the musical arts.

Then she met Conrad—self-assured, ambitious, resourceful, and spuriously charming. When he asked her to marry him, she accepted without hesitation. How blind she had been, how naïve and vulnerable. Fully expecting him to take over where her father had left off, she was stunned to discover that he had a single-minded purpose in life which had nothing to do with her music. Although he had allowed her to continue making concert appearances, she traveled alone, and even these were curtailed when she became pregnant with Karl. Soon after, her performances were confined to an empty parlor and eventually to Karl and Lisl, who had an inherent love for music but no real talent.

Dorothea now realized that it wasn't Conrad that she feared or the threat of losing material security, but rather the emptiness that seemed to engulf her. It was disconcerting to drift aimlessly with no real purpose in life. But now, with the arrival of the Takezawas, perhaps her life would take on a new meaning; she felt needed by them and even loved—she could see that in Tatsuo's eyes.

The ride through the city was pleasant. The morning was clear and crisp. Cotton white clouds trailed across the sky. Cyclists peddled happily along the narrow roads in the park, where huge Douglas fir and cedars, their trunks encased in ivy, towered above them. Lush green ferns, looking like misplaced denizens from some tropical garden, grew between the trees.

Conrad and Hiro traveled alone, as they had the day before. Hiro breathed deeply, enjoying the salt air. "How different the ocean looks today. When we arrived it was gray and now —endlessly blue. It has a personality of its own!"

Upon reaching the recreation area near Brocton Point, the second car pulled in behind them, and before the engines were turned off, the children were out of the car and racing toward the water.

"Mr. Takezawa and I will carry on, Dorothea. Spend the day if you like; we will probably not be back until supper."

The office of the Richter Shipping Line was housed in a two-story stone building on the corner of Cordova and Abbott streets, two blocks from the waterfront. It was a practical structure, simple and without embellishment. The front office was occupied by Patricia Harley, Conrad's secretary and receptionist. He had hired her several years ago, recognizing the intelligence and ambition behind her plain, unadorned face.

It was also impossible to overlook Patricia's other physical attributes. At one time she had been ashamed to be seen with her flat-chested classmates; no matter what she wore to conceal her breasts, they remained very conspicuous. Now she did not try to hide them. Her clothes were smart and serviceable and she wore them with a singular flair. Patricia had been married once, unhappily, and had no intention of falling into that trap again.

During the time she had worked for Conrad, she had slept with him occasionally, but there was no commitment on her part or on his. She allowed him into her bed only at her convenience and made no demands upon him. The extras she received, such as gifts of jewelry, expensive but tasteful, would no doubt stop should their relationship change. At times when she felt a twinge of loneliness, Patricia wondered what would happen if she were to put pressure on Conrad; but like many secretaries, she knew her employer well and for this reason preferred to keep their relationship on a neutral basis. During office hours she remained formal and businesslike.

"Why, Mr. Richter! I didn't expect you in today." Patricia smiled, revealing slightly crooked teeth.

"Hello, Patricia. I wanted to show Mr. Takezawa our facilities and see if we can find an office for him. Mr. Takezawa, this is my secretary, Patricia Harley."

Hiro bowed formally. "I am pleased to meet you, Miss Harley."

Her eyes flickered with surprise at his perfect English. "I, too, am pleased to meet you, Mr. Takezawa." There was a tone of genuine pleasure in her voice. Up to now, Hiro Takezawa had been just a name on correspondence from Japan. Even though he was considerably less imposing than she had expected, she had learned long ago not to judge men by their appearance. She turned to Conrad. "Mr. Richter, I have a list of calls for you on my desk and also your appointments for Monday morning. Would you care to look at them now?"

"I won't have time today. Keep them for Monday." Conrad was confident that she would have screened all his calls and appointments very thoroughly, and had there been any that required immediate attention, she would have said so.

"Mr. Richter, it just occurred to me that the top floor of this building will be vacant soon," Patricia said. "Perhaps Mr. Takezawa would find it suitable for his needs."

At a loss for words, Conrad hesitated momentarily. Although he had never discussed the matter with her, he was angry that Patricia didn't know how he felt about mixing too closely with the Japanese. He recovered quickly and nodded to Hiro. "Yes, of course. I had forgotten. Perhaps we can look it over a little later."

Conrad led Hiro to his private office at the rear of the building. There were several chairs around a large desk, a lounge against one wall, and a small partition that partially concealed a well-stocked bar. Photographs of his freighters hung in a neat row on the opposite wall. From the filing cabinet, Conrad produced a book containing detailed records of his shipping contracts for the last few years. Hiro nodded in approval as he studied the book, but his face was expressionless. Conrad then showed him a list of companies and suppliers who were eager to trade with the zaibatsu, some of whom had already submitted their bids and proposals.

Hiro rubbed his eyes with his thumb and forefinger. "I have much to learn, Richter-sama. Selecting lumber is very different from raising silkworms. Perhaps we should look at the office space upstairs while we are still here."

The rooms were spacious and the large windows afforded an excellent view of the harbor and city. Hiro walked with measured steps from room to room, imagining comfortable but practical furniture filling the emptiness and walls enhanced by paintings and sculpture and perhaps even a tokonoma. There would be no need to drape the windows; he would let the sunlight pour in.

"Yes, this will be adequate for my needs, and the location is particularly advantageous." Although Hiro was not aware of it, there was a ring of authority in his voice. "Please arrange for my occupancy of these offices as soon as possible."

The commanding tone did not go unnoticed by Conrad. "I will have Miss Harley look into it." He turned quickly to avoid Hiro's discerning eyes, afraid that he would guess his true feelings.

Hiro gazed out the window at the ships that dotted the busy harbor. The waterfront and ocean seemed remotely familiar, but it was not Japan. Before too long this will be home for Tatsuo, he thought, but will it ever be my home? Will I always feel like an intruder here? He heard Conrad's heavy footsteps.

"You're in luck. Old man Wilson says you can have this space if you can meet his payments."

"Old man Wilson?"

Conrad chuckled. "Actually his name is Cyrus Wilson. He's a tough old bird and cantankerous as hell. Just be prepared to sign a lease with all sorts of rules and regulations."

"I do not think that will be necessary."

"I think you will have to bend a little this time," Conrad said dryly.

Hiro followed Conrad into the street, and as they drove away, he wondered if Conrad would mind him walking over his head while occupying the upstairs offices. "I will need a secretary. Do you think it is possible to find one who can write in English and Japanese?"

Conrad shrugged. "I am sure there are some in Steveston, but they seldom venture beyond their own district."

Conrad was relieved that Hiro had been impressed with what he had seen so far of the company's facilities. There was a comfortable silence in the car as they returned to Drachenschlucht.

"Richter-sama, would you show me where your children go to school?"

"School! Yes of course, but shouldn't we get that gold safely into the bank before we go looking at schools?"

"The gold will remain long after you and I are past caring, but Tatsuo will not—his education is more important. Do not worry, I will relieve you of that burden soon."

Conrad's eyes narrowed as he laughed aloud. "I was just thinking how I could relieve you of that burden myself."

Hiro laughed too, but his voice had a deadly undertone. "It would weigh very heavily around your neck."

They stopped in front of a group of neat wooden buildings on King Edward Drive. "This is where Lisl goes to school. It is a girl's academy. Most of the girls live in the dormitories, but Lisl comes home every day."

Hiro nodded in approval. "Yes, at that young and vulnerable age it is best for her to be at home."

"That is questionable," Conrad said. "Actually, I tried to convince her to stay during the week and come home on weekends and holidays, but she was very rebellious and refused to study or even eat. She became quite ill and we had no alternative but to allow her to commute back and forth every day. Dorothea has given the children far too much freedom. At times they are incorrigible."

How strange, Hiro thought. In Japan children were treasured.

On Cartier Street, Conrad pointed to a red brick and stone building situated in a huge open field. "This is Karl's school —St. John's College. It's operated by the Christian Brothers of Ireland. They're heavy on sports, but they also have strict academic standards."

"Do they accept non-Catholic children?"

The implication of his question suddenly struck Conrad. "As far as I know, they don't have any particular restrictions. Are you considering this school for Tatsuo?"

"Perhaps, but I will not make my final decision until I have spoken with the headmaster."

Conrad hoped the headmaster would have enough sense to send Hiro to the Japanese community at Steveston.

[5]

The front door of Drachenschlucht slammed loudly as Karl and Tatsuo raced to the waiting car. Hiro walked out behind them, glancing at the armed guard who stood at the entrance of the driveway. The leather satchel felt heavy in Hiro's hand, and he placed it carefully into the car before getting in. The driver seemed pleased to be with the Takezawas, and he talked freely, giving his commentary on the elegant homes as they drove by.

"The school looks different today," Hiro said as the car came to a stop in front of St. John's College. Boys of every age filled the grounds, some engaged in games, others standing in small groups, laughing and jostling each other. Activity ceased as the Takezawas approached the main entrance. There was a nudge and a few whispers, but most of the boys just stared, their inquisitive gaze following the strangers to the door.

"That's Father O'Brien's office," Karl said, pointing to a doorway at the end of a long hall. He punched Tatsuo playfully on the arm. "Good luck. I'll see you later."

Tatsuo's heart thudded in his chest, but he took a deep breath and smiled bravely at his grandfather.

In answer to Hiro's soft rap, a voice sharp with authority commanded, "Come in, come in!"

Father O'Brien stood with his back to the door. He was absorbed in a row of books, his eyes and fingers searching through the titles. "Sit down, I'll just be a minute."

Hiro and Tatsuo remained standing while they studied the headmaster of St. John's College. He was tall by any standard, but to Tatsuo he seemed like a giant. In reality he stood six feet, four inches, his head topped with a shock of tightly curled red hair. His shoulders were stooped slightly, as though the black habit he wore weighed them down.

"Aha, here it is." He turned around as he leafed through the book, still not looking up at his visitors. His forehead was furrowed in concentration; his mouth was firm, but the lines around it revealed a sense of humor; the nose was long and flared at the nostrils. The features fitted together to form the lean, intelligent face of a man well into his fifties.

"Now, what can I do—" He stopped in midsentence and stared at the two individuals in front of him. Twenty years of teaching had insulated him against the unexpected, but the sight of the two dark heads bent in a deep bow came as a complete surprise.

"Good morning, Father O'Brien. I am Hiro Takezawa, and this is my grandson, Tatsuo. I wish to inquire about enrolling him in your school."

Father O'Brien quickly regained his composure and indicated the two chairs in front of his cluttered desk. "I am pleased to meet you."

Hiro read the title of the book in the priest's hand. "Are you interested in Greek philosophy?"

Father O'Brien put the book down on the desk. "Yes, Aristotle is my favorite.

Hiro appeared thoughtful. "I, too, have studied his doctrine of the mean, but it is sometimes difficult to apply it to all men. What is moderation for some is not for others."

Father O'Brien looked surprised. "You have read his works?"

"Only portions of it. I have lectured at Keio University, but we dealt mainly with the philosophy of Zen."

"Keio University? Then you are not residents of Vancouver?"

"No, we have just moved here from Tokyo. The Takezawa zaibatsu will be setting up an office here."

"The Takezawa zaibatsu! I spent some time in Yokohama a few years ago, at a Christian mission, and I recall hearing of your zaibatsu."

"We have expanded considerably over the past few years.

We are now involved in foreign trade as well.''

Tatsuo listened impatiently while the men talked at length on a variety of subjects. Finally, Father O'Brien asked, "Why are you considering this particular school for your grandson?"

"My associate, Conrad Richter, has a son attending this school, and from what I have seen, I think the college would be ideal for Tatsuo."

Father O'Brien realized that the school's enrollment did not include Orientals, nor had any ever applied. He hesitated now, fearing the reaction of the other students and perhaps even of the teachers. Could this thin-faced lad with the serious eyes survive in their midst? "You understand that this school is run by a religious order."

"Yes, I am aware of that, and I am also aware that your standards are very high." Hiro removed a neatly folded paper from his breast pocket and handed it to Father O'Brien. "Here is a transcript of Tatsuo's school record. It has been translated into English."

Father O'Brien removed a pair of glasses from his desk and placed them midway on his nose. They appeared awkward, almost comical, as though a mischievous boy had drawn them on his face. Unconsciously, he rubbed the end of his long nose with his finger as he read the transcript. The lad was undoubtedly bright and probably an exceptional student.

"Tatsuo's father . . . where is he now?"

"My son and his wife both died in the Kanto earthquake in September. Tatsuo was his only child and is my only grandchild."

"That is most unfortunate." Father O'Brien pretended to study the transcript again as he assessed the situation. Tatsuo would undoubtedly be an asset to the school, except for one thing—he was Japanese! He wondered how the board of trustees would react. Would they object and try to override his decision? No . . . he would never concede to their prejudices and must not even consider them; he couldn't live with that. "Is there any reason why Tatsuo could not start today?"

"None at all," Hiro answered quickly.

"Will I be in the same class with Karl?" Tatsuo asked.

Father O'Brien walked around the desk to where Tatsuo sat stiffly. "We will give you an achievement test, my boy, to find out exactly where you stand in our system. I suspect you might be a little behind Karl right now, but I see no reason why you cannot catch up."

Tatsuo grinned, and his eyes sparkled with pleasure. "I promise that I will work hard."

Father O'Brien held out his hand, and although he towered above Hiro, he felt the strength and determination in the handclasp and returned it with reassurance.

"I will return at four o'clock to pick you and Karl up," Hiro said. He touched Tatsuo lightly on the head, and with a formal bow to Father O'Brien, he left the office on soundless, aching feet. The stiff leather shoes he wore were unbearable.

"Where to, Mr. Takezawa?" the driver asked as he held the door for Hiro.

"The Federal Bank. Do you know where it is?"

"Sure do. That's where Mr. Richter deals."

Although it was not quite nine o'clock, the streets were busy on this Monday morning. People hurried along with their chins buried in their coats and their backs bent against the wind that reddened their cheeks in the sudden chill. Intent upon reaching their destinations, they made no contact with each other. There were no smiles of recognition and no brushing of shoulders as in the busy streets of Tokyo. The spirit was meant to be happy, Hiro thought, not lost and joyless as these people appear to be.

"Here it is, sir," the driver said. "Would you like me to wait?"

"Yes, if you do not mind. I may be in there for quite some time."

"That's okay . . . take as much time as you like."

Hiro picked up his worn leather case and stepped onto the busy sidewalk, noticing the classical stone pillars that lined the entranceway of the bank. As he walked toward the door, the window washer caught Hiro's reflection in the sparkling glass and turned to stare at him. Customers emerging from the bank also turned as they passed the awkwardly dressed Oriental. A uniformed attendant opened the door and concealed his surprise behind a trained smile.

The central area of the bank was large, surrounded by marble counters and glass wickets; it looked more like a crypt than a bank. Six elaborate chandeliers hung from the high domed ceiling, their images reflected in the dark polished floor. As if awed by the immensity of the bank, people talked in hushed tones, but their voices carried easily across the sterile coolness.

Hiro approached a woman standing behind the marble counter. "I would like to establish two accounts with your bank. My company has been in contact with your manager, Mr. Dalzell."

The woman peered down at him through thick glasses and smiled cheerfully. "Mr. Dalzell isn't in right now but his assistant, Mr. Fenton, will look after you. He's right over there." She pointed to a man who sat behind an oversized desk. He was impeccably groomed. His hair, gleaming from a recent application of tonic, was parted precisely in the middle.

"Thank you." Hiro shifted the heavy leather case to his other hand and proceeded in the direction of Mr. Fenton.

The young assistant sat behind the fortress of his desk, reviewing the financial statement of the Breckenridge Hardware Company, a now floundering company which had become a thorn in his side. Damnit—how dare these idiots apply for another loan? he thought. As he read the list of expenditures, he made bold red marks beside the figures he felt were contrived or suspicious. His anger increased, for it was he who had recommended and approved the loan and now the bank would surely lose money. He resolved to be more careful in the future when dealing with upstart companies.

It was at this point that he looked up and saw Hiro walking toward him. He studied the Oriental's ill-fitting suit and unsightly leather satchel. The man is obviously lost, he thought, and resumed his analysis of the financial statements.

Hiro placed the heavy case on Fenton's immaculate desk and stood waiting to be acknowledged. For a moment Fenton stared at the case and then carefully laid down his pen and folded his hands. Not quite masking his annoyance, he asked, "What can I do for you?"

Hiro noted the pinched, angry face, but his eyes did not waver. "I would like to establish two accounts with your bank —one for business purposes and the other for my personal use."

"Will there be foreign currency involved?"

"Yes, some."

"I see." Fenton's eyes kept straying back to the ugly leather case and to Hiro's suit. He adjusted his tie, which always seemed too tight when he was in an uncomfortable situation. "What is the name?"

"Hiro Takezawa."

Fenton cleared his throat and, recalling his resolution to be more discriminating, squared his shoulders and leaned back in his chair. "I really think, Mr. Takehara, that your needs would best be served by another bank specializing in your particular currency. Perhaps you could try the Bank of Canada, near Pender and Main—that's in Chinatown." He smiled in an attempt to be polite. "I am sure you will find them to be very obliging."

Such rudeness would never occur in Japan, at least not to any member of the zaibatsu, Hiro thought. In another time and place, Fenton would have been disciplined and perhaps even killed for his lack of respect. Summoning the self-discipline and tolerance that he had acquired over the years, Hiro removed the heavy satchel from the desk, leaving a faint mark, which Fenton eyed with unconcealed annoyance.

"The name is Takezawa, not Takehara," Hiro announced crisply before he left.

Takezawa? The name was vaguely familiar, and Fenton felt uneasy as he watched Hiro move across the polished floor. He wished he could recall where he had heard the name and that he could forget the menacing look in the Oriental's eyes.

As he had promised, the driver was waiting patiently beside the car. "Are you ready to go home, sir?"

"No, I did not have much success with the Federal Bank. It seems that they do not want my business. Do you know where the Bank of Canada is on Pender Street?"

"Didn't want your business! They must be bloody well off or stupid. Well, hop in, I'll have you there in no time."

As they drove along the busy streets, Hiro wondered how the zaibatsu would react when they learned that he did not intend to do business with the Federal Bank as he had been instructed. They did not usually approve of such deviations; however, the change was unavoidable.

"This is it, Mr. Takezawa, the Bank of Canada. Not as fancy as the Federal but their money is the same color."

"Please wait for me," Hiro said. He gripped the leather bag tightly until his knuckles whitened. It was not a large bank or as old and prestigious as the Federal, but it had a solid appearance and it hummed with activity. There was no doorman. Many of the customers were Orientals, which reminded Hiro of the Hong Kong-Shanghai Bank on Silk Street in Yokohama. The interior was brightly lit, and the once shiny floor was already scuffed from the day's traffic.

"Can I help you?" an inquiring voice asked.

Hiro turned. "Yes. I would like to speak to your manager. Unfortunately, I do not have an appointment, but I will wait."

"That won't be necessary. Please come with me," the sprightly teller said. Her speech, like her walk, was quick and efficient. She stopped outside a door marked R.P. Gingras, Manager, and raised her hand to knock. "Excuse me, but what is your name?"

"Hiro Takezawa."

She knocked on the door with sharp insistence before opening it. "Mr. Gingras, there is a Mr. Takezawa to see you."

Gingras offered Hiro a chair. "Please be seated, Mr. Takezawa," he said while he shuffled several sheets of paper into a neat pile on his desk. "Damn mail always gets ahead of me."

Hiro watched, bemused. Although in his early forties, Gingras was already showing signs of premature aging; two chins rested on his collar, and his gray hair had receded noticeably. Shaggy eyebrows bristled over his glasses, and the permanent crease above his nose suggested that his vision was strained in spite of the thick lenses. When he leaned back in his chair, his double-breasted suit did not quite hide the spreading midriff, but his smile was genuine.

Hiro relaxed his grip on the leather case and settled back into the chair. "I represent the Takezawa zaibatsu of Japan, and I would like to establish two accounts with your bank—business and personal. Mr. Fenton of the Federal Bank suggested that I see you."

Gingras raised his shaggy eyebrows in surprise. "Business must be good over there if they're sending us customers."

"Mr. Fenton felt that this bank would be more suitable to my needs. Apparently you are more willing to handle foreign currency."

Gingras nodded knowingly. "Well, we would be happy to have your business, Mr. Takezawa. We have no reservations about handling foreign currencies."

"The zaibatsu has contracted the Richter Steamship Line to export silk from Japan and to import Canadian raw materials —mainly lumber, wheat, and ore. Foreign currency will be involved, and there may be times when I will have to be covered by an overdraft, however at the present time that seems unlikely. Please understand that there will be very large sums of money involved and I must be assured there will be no delays during these transactions."

Gingras listened intently, nodding his head periodically. "I know of Mr. Richter." There was a flicker of concern in his eyes. "Your zaibatsu has investigated him?"

"Yes, thoroughly."

"Well then, it will be a pleasure to handle your accounts, Mr. Takezawa. I will have the necessary documents prepared. I assume that you will be the only one to have power of attorney over these accounts."

"Yes, that is correct."

"Now, about this overdraft. You understand that I will need some form of security to guarantee repayment until your credit is established with our bank."

"Of course." Hiro opened the heavy satchel and removed several large bundles of crisp new Japanese currency. "I am not certain about the exchange rate, but I have fifty million yen that I would like to deposit."

Gingras did not try to conceal his surprise; he opened his fountain pen and quickly wrote some figures on a pad before speaking. "That's roughly one hundred and seventy thousand dollars—a very substantial beginning, Mr. Takezawa."

"That can be deposited in my personal account. The business account will be considerably larger, and the major portion of my assets will be deposited there." He lifted the leather case and placed it on Gingras's desk, then removed a gold bar that was stamped with the Takezawa insignia.

Gingras was speechless.

Hiro smiled and removed a second bar, equally bright and stamped with the same insignia. "These are twenty-four-carat gold."

Gingras's eyes glistened as he ran his fingers lightly over the bars. "They are beautiful!"

"It is strange the effect gold has on men, almost hypnotic."

Gingras looked at Hiro and nodded. "Wealth is power, and gold has always been its ageless emissary."

"I have one hundred and fifty of these bars," Hiro said. "I would like you to keep them in your vault and use them to establish the necessary accounts."

"One hundred and fifty of them! That's over a ton of gold!" Gingras said incredulously.

"Over two tons, actually. Each bar weighs thirty-five pounds. I would like to convert some of them into cash."

"Certainly, Mr. Takezawa, but that might take a day or two. Let's see, gold is at $20.66 per ounce." Again the pen quickly scratched figures on the pad. "Christ, that's $1,735,440. When will you deliver the rest of the gold?"

"Tomorrow morning. Sell fifty bars and leave the remaining hundred in your vault. I must have some cash available very soon."

Gingras cleared his throat. "Under what name do you wish to head up the business account?"

"Our branch office here will be known as Pacific Far Eastern Trading."

Gingras's hand shook slightly as he printed the name boldly on his scratch pad. "The forms will be ready for your signature in the morning—sooner if you like."

Both men stood up to shake hands. "This has been a fortunate day for our bank, Mr. Takezawa. I hope we will be able to serve you well. And now I think we should have a glass of sherry; we don't often get customers who deposit two million dollars in one lump sum."

Hiro chuckled. "I would be honored to drink with you, but I do not know what sherry is."

Gingras produced a crystal decanter and two glasses from a mirrored cabinet in the corner of the office. "May this mark the beginning of a long and prosperous association for us."

"I have no doubt that it will, Mr. Gingras."

They both downed the sweet liquor in one gulp, each expressing his enjoyment with audible appreciation. A few minutes later, Gingras escorted Hiro to the door and quickly called a meeting of his senior staff. The meeting was brief, the orders precise, and by noon Hiro Takezawa and Pacific Far Eastern Trading had become established on the ledgers.

Upon his return from lunch, Mr. Gingras found a note on his desk advising him that Mr. Hugh Dalzell from the Federal Bank had called. Gingras was thoughtful for a moment. For some unknown reason they had sent Mr. Takezawa to his bank—obviously an error on their part, for they would never knowingly forfeit an account of that size. Most likely they were unaware of what Hiro Takezawa represented; but their loss was his gain. He smiled at the thought.

Gingras was still smiling when he returned the call. A well-modulated British voice answered. "Mr. Gingras. Yes, I'll put you right through."

The initial greeting was followed by an exchange of customary platitudes sugared with politeness. "No, she's fine now, just a slight cold." His mind wandered. Yes, Hugh; no, Hugh; up your ass, Hugh . . .

It was several minutes before Dalzell finally came to the purpose of the call. "Just as a point of interest, Robert, did a Mr. Takezawa come in to see you today? I had an appointment with him this morning, but I missed it and my assistant apparently sent him over to you."

"Yes, Hugh, he was here, and he'll be back tomorrow to sign some papers."

After a lengthy pause, Dalzell answered, "I see. Did he give you any indication as to his banking requirements?"

"Yes, he certainly did, and I would like to thank you for sending him over to us. He said something about your bank not wanting to handle foreign currency." Gingras could not resist adding the barb.

The tightness in Dalzell's voice was now very evident. "Yes, well, it seems there was some sort of misunderstanding. Thanks for returning my call, Robert. We must keep in touch." There was a sharp metallic click as Dalzell hung up.

At the Federal Bank, Hugh Dalzell sat pensively in his decorated office and stared out the window. He seldom showed emotion, for he had learned over the years that a successful banker must always maintain complete control of his feelings, at least outwardly—and he had an ulcer to prove he could do just that. Unconsciously, he rubbed the painful spot on his stomach before reaching for the medication that helped to relieve his discomfort. He swallowed the thick milky liquid and straightened his jacket before instructing his secretary to send for Fenton.

"You wanted to see me, sir?"

"Yes, Fenton. Come in." Dalzell's eyes were icy. "Did a Japanese gentleman come in to see me this morning?"

"Yes, sir." Fenton's own stomach gave an uncomfortable lurch. "He looked like an unmade bed and I . . . aah . . . thought that the Federal could do without his type. Business with them is very limited . . . just involves a lot of extra paper work." He stopped, realizing that he was sputtering nervously.

"Do you have any idea who he was?" Dalzell asked.

"He said his name was Takehara or something like that."

"His name is Hiro Takezawa," Dalzell corrected. "Have you ever heard of the Takezawa zaibatsu of Japan?"

"Yes, I . . . I think so." Fenton could not prevent himself from stammering.

"Well, I will refresh your memory. It is the most influential and richest company in Japan, and if you will recall, they were in contact with us several months ago. I am not sure of the exact figures, Fenton, but I expect that his initial deposit was over a million dollars, and do you know where he put it? Yes, just where you told him to—in the Bank of Canada. Because of your petty little prejudices, we lost his account."

Fenton sank uneasily into the chair behind him.

"Now, Fenton, if you were in my position, what would you do?"

He swallowed before answering, "I guess I would approach Mr. Takezawa and try to get him to reconsider."

"Out of the question! He's Japanese, and you would never get a second chance to insult him. Try again."

"Well, I suppose that I would reprimand the person who lost the account.

Despite his resolve, Dalzell completely lost his temper. "Reprimand, eh? In many ways, Fenton, you are a genius. You put figures together on paper and analyze companies as easily as a kid packs a mud pie. But when it comes to people, you are a colossal failure. The real assets in our business are people." Dalzell's teeth clenched as he rubbed his stomach. His voice was a little quieter now. "Many years ago, a shoeshine boy named J. P. Fulton came into this bank. He had only a few dollars at that time, but our manager treated him with the same courtesy and respect that other customers would receive. He owns the Fulton Shoe Company now and has stores all across the country. Do you know where he still does his banking?"

Fenton nodded; he knew the account very well.

"Does that tell you something, Fenton? Had you suggested that I fire you and throw you out the door, I would have thought there was still hope for you, but you didn't. You haven't learned a damn thing. You're finished here, Fenton.

You've got ten minutes to get out, and don't bother cleaning your desk. I'll have your belongings forwarded to you."

Fenton remained seated for a moment, unable to think beyond the fact that he had just been fired. Finally, he stood up slowly and walked out of the office, across the polished floor and into the street.

"Good afternoon, Miss Harley," Hiro said as he entered Conrad's office.

"Hello, Mr. Takezawa. Mr. Wilson is already here. They are expecting you."

Hiro walked into the rear office, where he was greeted by Conrad. "Come in. I would like you to meet Cyrus Wilson."

A large cigar hung from Wilson's lips; his voice had a gravelly edge. "Just call me Cyrus—never could stand that formal stuff. What did you say your name was?"

"Hiro Takezawa," Hiro said as they shook hands.

"Hero, eh?" A laugh rumbled from somewhere deep in his throat. "Well, you don't look like no hero that I've ever seen, but then neither do I." His face became even more creased as he laughed.

Hiro responded to the old man's laughter and felt the tension of the morning leave his body. "Well, since neither of us is a hero, let us just be friends." He searched his empty pockets. "I have just deposited over a million dollars in the bank, but I do not have a penny left to buy you a cup of tea."

Cyrus slapped his knee with a sinewy hand and growled with laughter. "How about that! Is that how you made your millions—filching nickels from old buggers like me?" He laughed again at his own joke. "Well, come on, Heeero, this one is on me."

The transporting of the gold to the Bank of Canada proceeded according to schedule in spite of Conrad's mounting apprehension. Once safely secured inside the thick steel vault, the gold bars were stacked and catalogued, and even Hiro was relieved when the task had been completed. Next on his agenda —a check to Cyrus Wilson for $1750, rent paid in full for the balance of 1923 and all of 1924.

What had Cyrus said to him? "As soon as I receive the check, consider the matter closed." Apparently Cyrus had gauged him (an expression Hiro appreciated) by his own standards, and Hiro had measured up to them. A written lease was unnecessary between them; a spoken agreement would suffice. In Hiro's eyes, Cyrus also measured up. It was comforting to know that, even on the other side of the world, men such as Cyrus existed. There was no doubt in his mind that he would ever have to change his opinion, and that, too, was a comfort.

In the days that followed, Cyrus became a frequent visitor at Hiro's new office, arriving unannounced and bringing with him colorful stories of people and events in the past as well as the latest gossip about successful and insolvent business ventures, all of which proved to be accurate. Cyrus seemed to have a direct pipeline into people's lives without being obtrusive, perhaps because he was sincerely interested in people and also because he would often lend his assistance. To Hiro, Cyrus was invaluable. He quickly became a trusted and comfortable friend, but more important, Cyrus provided insight into an unfamiliar society and facilitated Hiro's orientation into the labyrinth of the western world. He was grateful, soaking up Cyrus's stories like a dry sponge, learning, understanding, and slowly adjusting.

The activity in Hiro's office gained momentum as the days flew by. Spurred on by the eager demands of the zaibatsu, Hiro worked long hours until the proposals, selections, orders, and shipping schedules slowly began to fall into place like pieces in a giant jigsaw puzzle. Surprisingly, Hiro found that he did not tire from the intensity of the demands made upon him but rather was invigorated by it; as the work load increased so did his energy. He learned quickly and with enthusiasm. His inveterate business sense spanned the chasm of continents and soon earned him the unqualified respect of his business associates. Those who arrived with a condescending air were surprised by Hiro's expertise and left feeling a little sheepish and extremely deferential. He always negotiated fairly but firmly with the suppliers, backing up his proposals with sound commitments, and thus received the same treatment in return. Money, of course, was the driving force behind each decision, and Hiro, aware of this, used the zaibatsu's resources with subtle skill and shrewdness. He was an astute businessman, as people quickly discovered, but he was also a perceptive judge of character, and that gave him a distinct edge in each transaction.

It was still early in the afternoon when Hiro studied the

figures submitted by the Royal City Planing Mill. It was of utmost importance that he consider every possibility before placing the first lumber order for the zaibatsu. The Royal City Planing Mill seemed willing to cooperate in every way and would work around the schedules of the Richter Shipping Line. However, he would make his final decision that afternoon after a meeting with the sales representative from a competitor, the Blondel Lumber Company.

Richard Blondel, his gray hair combed into perfect waves on his aristocratic head, arrived in Hiro's office precisely ten minutes late for his appointment. Still puffing from the climb up the stairs, he seated himself stiffly on the settee in front of Hiro's desk and glanced derisively at Hiro's sparsely furnished office before opening his briefcase.

"Now, Mr. Takezawa, I have here a complete list of our prices as you have requested." There was a trace of affectation in his voice.

Hiro ignored the list for a moment as he poured tea from an earthenware pot into two matching porcelain cups. He offered the fragrant green liquid to Blondel. Blondel stared at the cup with its thick plain sides and returned to his papers without tasting the tea.

"You realize, of course, Mr. Takezawa," he said in a patronizing voice, "that our company has been in business for over twenty-five years."

Hiro sipped his steaming tea for a moment without comment, then replied. "I will make careful note of that, Mr. Blondel."

"And we cannot take unnecessary risks. You, as a businessman, can understand that."

"I'm not sure I know what you mean, Mr. Blondel."

"Well, I will come right to the point, sir. We have a policy —a stringent one, perhaps—that we deal only with established buyers, and since you are new in the area, we must insist that you pay for your orders in advance."

"Yes, Pacific Far Eastern Trading is a new company," Hiro said flatly.

"We are aware that you have overseas affiliations. Our foreign markets are limited, as we have felt that our local markets are far more stable."

"You are not interested in expanding?" Hiro asked, baiting Blondel.

The man looked horrified. "Oh no, Mr. Takezawa, don't misunderstand me. We are very interested in expanding, but we . . . uhh . . . feel that we must be careful. There are some negative feelings about . . . ah . . ." He flushed in discomfort.

"No, I did not know about any negative feeling, Mr. Blondel. Are you sure that they are not merely confined to your company?"

"I was generalizing, Mr. Takezawa. We would be very pleased to do business with you, but as representative for my company, I must take everything into consideration. You are requesting an enormous amount of lumber."

"I understand your reservations, Mr. Blondel, and I can appreciate them. One cannot be too careful when it comes to choosing clients."

"I'm glad that you understand, Mr. Takezawa."

"Your delight is premature. I cannot understand why a company as established as yours would allow itself the luxury —or should I say, the misfortune—of prejudice. I will not take up any more of your time, but before you go, Mr. Blondel, let me put your mind at ease. The Takezawa zaibatsu, of which I am a principal member, has been established for well over two hundred years. Let me also assure you that we would be quite capable of prepaying any order you provided for us." Hiro swallowed his distaste and added, "In fact, we are quite capable of purchasing your entire company."

The condescending air disappeared from Blondel's face, replaced by incredulity. "We must have proof of your financial security," he replied meekly.

"That will not be necessary, Mr. Blondel. I do not feel your company will be able to meet our requirements." Hiro walked quickly to the door and opened it. "Good day, Mr. Blondel. Thank you for your time."

Blondel stuffed his papers back into the briefcase and rose to leave, carefully avoiding Hiro's piercing gaze. "I could leave the figures in case you change your mind."

"I will not change my mind."

Richard Blondel stood in the hallway after the door had closed behind him, feeling deflated and irrevocably dismissed. Behind the door, Hiro dipped his pen and with a firm, even stroke signed his name to an order from the Royal City Planing Mill.

Hiro's calendar indicated one more appointment for the

day, and he anticipated this one with pleasure. He was to be honored with a visit from the Japanese consul general in Canada. Consul General Suyama, a descendant of an honorable samurai family, was the author of several volumes of Japanese history, a devout patron of the arts, and a respected statesman. At precisely the stated time the two men met.

"Welcome, Suyama-sama. I am honored to have you in my place of business," Hiro said as he bowed.

Consul General Suyama returned an equally low bow. "I am honored to be here, Takezawa-sama."

With the formalities over, they soon relaxed and chatted as they drank sake. Suyama's discerning eyes detected Hiro's sorrow as they discussed the Kanto earthquake.

"My heart aches at the devastation and tragedy suffered by our country. I have received reports that we are recuperating quickly as always, however," the consul solemnly remarked.

"Yes," Hiro replied. "Reconstruction began almost immediately in spite of the terrible losses endured by our people. It was not uncommon to see workers with bandaged limbs repairing their homes and marketplaces."

"One could not expect less of the Japanese," Suyama said.

"They now desperately require lumber and steel to rebuild."

"Is that why the zaibatsu has established an office here in Canada?"

"That is part of the reason. In addition, the zaibatsu is expanding its enterprises and requires vast amounts of raw materials," Hiro explained.

"The steel your zaibatsu will be producing is a source of concern to me. As you are no doubt aware, Japan is expanding its military, and I foresee grave consequences," the consul said sadly.

"Let me assure you, sir, that it is not my intention to aid the military. However, we cannot totally ignore the inclinations of the Diet," he said, referring to Japan's parliament.

The consul's intelligent face was intense with concern. Both men were fiercely loyal to their country. They also recognized the dilemma Japan would face should it ever become necessary to defend or expand its territory.

"You are alone here in the office?" Suyama asked finally.

"Yes, but I desperately need a secretary, and I have been unable to find one."

"Perhaps I can be of some help."

Hiro's expression brightened. "I would be most grateful. You see, I need someone who is well versed in both English and Japanese and who is capable of managing my office."

"I have someone in mind, an extremely capable young lady, but she comes from a strict Japanese home. Unfortunately, her father has some old-fashioned ideas which are very difficult for her to accept, particularly since she has spent most of her life in Canada."

"Perhaps I could speak to both her and her father," Hiro offered hopefully.

"Yes, I think that would be the answer. Her father is a prosperous fisherman and does not think his daughter should have to work outside her home but of course, she does not share his view. She is very clever and ambitious and feels that she is wasting her life in her mother's kitchen. I suspect her father is hoping she will marry soon, but again, she will have no part of that. As you can see, it is a difficult situation," Suyama said.

"I do not wish to add to her father's problems by asking her to work for me," Hiro said firmly.

"The problem is already there, Takezawa-sama. You might be able to provide the answer to their problem. The young lady is a childhood friend of my daughter's, and I am naturally concerned for her welfare. Because of the restrictions placed on her life, she is very unhappy and consequently so is her family. We are part of a changing world. We cannot adhere to the old ways forever, particularly here in Canada."

"Yes, I am becoming more and more aware of that. I marvel at how quickly my grandson is adjusting, but at the same time I am saddened. I do not want him to abandon or forget the ways of our ancestors."

"With you instructing him, he will not forget. Perhaps you will allow the new to meld with the old. Life is transformation, and change is inevitable. We cannot stop it."

"You are very wise, sir. I wish I could share your firm convictions about change. You have been away from Japan for a number of years now, have you not?"

"In my heart I have never left Japan, and I have not changed my views dramatically, but I have accepted new ones." He smiled apologetically. "Does that sound ambiguous?"

"No, please go on." Hiro poured another cup of sake for

the consul general and settled back in his chair.

Suyama's voice had a pleasant ring. "Life means giving and taking, exchange and transformation. It is not taking complete possession of anything, but rather taking part in everything that comes in touch with us. We are transformed by what we accept, and we transform what we have accepted by assimilating it. He who opposes this process of transformation will die the slow death of rigidity."

Hiro nodded, slowly digesting the consul general's words. "I agree with you," he replied. "But there are some things that I will not change—we cannot bend like a willow in the wind. Discipline must also be a part of our lives."

"You are right, Takezawa-sama. Stability must definitely be a part of our transformation. Were it not so, we would be nothing, mere heaps of unmolded clay."

And so they talked at length, grateful for each other's company. It was with reluctance that the consul general prepared to leave Hiro's company.

"I trust this will be the first of many visits, Takezawa-sama. I would be honored if you and your family would come to my home very soon."

"It will be our pleasure. By the way, what is the young lady's name?"

"Maiko Sakamoto. Her father's name is Michi. If I am successful in convincing him to allow his daughter to work for you, I will ask them to come to your office within the next few days. Thank you for your gracious hospitality."

They exchanged respectful bows and Hiro escorted the consul general to the door. In the last glow of daylight, Hiro returned to his desk and sat for a long time, immersed in the thoughts that had been planted by Suyama.

Early the next morning the anticipated telephone call came.

"Good morning, Mr. Takezawa." The voice was low-pitched but resonant. "My name is Maiko Sakamoto. Consul General Suyama has kindly suggested that I call you. Would it be possible for you to see me today?" The words were clearly enunciated with the clarity acquired when English is learned as a second language and not spoken often enough to be affected by the slur of colloquialisms.

"Certainly, Miss Sakamoto. Please feel free to come at any time this morning."

"I will be there before ten." There was a short pause. "Mr.

Takezawa, my father will be coming with me. I hope you will understand."

"Please do not be concerned. Your father is most welcome."

Maiko Sakamoto was very much like her father, tiny, with smooth olive skin and eyes shining with youthful vitality and intelligence. But despite the spirit glistening in her eyes her face was gravely intense, and her hands were clasped tightly to hide their nervous trembling. She stood politely behind her father as he made the introductions.

"I am Michi Sakamoto and this is my daughter, Maiko."

"I am Hiro Takezawa. I am honored to meet you both."

"Consul General Suyama has told me that you are of the Takezawa zaibatsu. It is indeed our honor to meet you." Both father and daughter bowed several times.

Michi Sakamoto had arrived in Canada penniless, ambitious, and with only a smattering of English that he had learned by listening to the seamen on the docks in Japan. In the years that followed, he had purchased a small fishing boat and made enough money to send for his wife and small daughter. His ambition served him well, and before long he had acquired several more fishing boats and a respectable home as well as two more daughters. Maiko was his youngest and also his favorite. When she was sixteen, the reluctant Maiko was sent to her uncle's home in Tokyo to complete her last years of schooling and to develop the graceful manner of a Japanese lady. She had returned with all the attributes that Michi had hoped for, but she was still her father's daughter; she had a mind of her own and she intended to use it.

"Maiko is seeking a position as a secretary. I would be honored if you would consider my daughter for the position."

"Please come in and sit down." Hiro indicated the two chairs by his desk. He would have preferred to talk directly to Maiko, but instinct warned him that he must abide by their customs, so he looked at Michi as he spoke.

"I need someone who is fluent in both Japanese and English, someone who can attend to the stenographic duties in my office and," he spread his hands in a helpless gesture, "look after a Japanese businessman who is not yet familiar with the ways of this country."

Maiko spoke for the first time. Her voice was surprisingly low, softer than it had been on the telephone. "I have not had much experience, Mr. Takezawa, but I would like to have the opportunity to prove that I can fill the position. I am fluent in Japanese and English." There was a sudden hint of humor in her face. "I can even play the samisen if you wish."

"You may be called upon to do just that," Hiro replied. Some of the tension left Maiko's face as they laughed, and her hands relaxed. Again Hiro addressed Michi. "I would be very pleased if you were to allow your daughter to work for me."

Michi looked directly at Hiro. "I would prefer that my daughter did not work, but as you can see she is a very determined young lady. If she is to work for anyone, I would prefer that it be with you, honorable Takezawa-sama."

"Thank you, Sakamoto-sama."

Michi extended a gnarled hand to Hiro, a hand that had seen many years of hard work. "I expect my daughter to work diligently, and I trust that you will take good care of her." He patted his daughter lightly on the shoulder and left the office.

"Where would you like me to start, Mr. Takezawa?" Maiko asked.

"You may start by organizing my filing cabinets, and then I have some correspondence that is long overdue."

"Mr. Takezawa?"

"Yes, Miss Sakamoto."

"Do you suppose you could call me Maiko?"

"Of course." He was rewarded by a wide smile.

Although the days began to assume a patterned routine for Hiro, with early morning practice sessions, meditation, work, supervision of Tatsuo's studies, and finally sleep, he became increasingly restless. He needed a home of his own, the reassuring presence of a simple orderly household, the solitude of a garden—a home that would provide the tranquil security he longed for. Only in Dorothea's sun-room did he feel relaxed; the rest of the house began to close in on him tighter and tighter. Miyoko grew quieter with each passing day, and watching her, Hiro knew that he could not wait any longer.

At dinner, he announced his plans to the Richters. "Tomorrow I will look for a home for my family," he explained. "We are very grateful for your hospitality, but the time has come to find a place of our own."

"I will make a list of the real estate agencies that could help you," Conrad said quickly.

"That would be very helpful." Hiro turned to Dorothea.

"Earlier, you offered to help us look. Are you still willing?"

"I will be sorry to see you go," Dorothea said with a sigh, "but I will help you."

As they rose to leave the table, Dorothea said in a quiet voice, "I noticed today that the stone house on Matthews Avenue is still up for sale. The grounds look a little neglected, but the house itself is well cared for."

"You mean the Sommerville home?" Conrad asked.

"Yes, that's the one. It's only a few blocks from here."

"I don't think that house would be suitable." Conrad's voice held a note of warning detectable only to Dorothea.

"Is it being sold privately?" Hiro asked.

"No, I believe the sign said Rand Brothers Real Estate is handling the sale." Dorothea avoided Conrad's darkening eyes.

"I recall seeing the house," Hiro said thoughtfully. "Perhaps I will call them in the morning."

Behind the tightly closed door of their bedroom, Conrad confronted Dorothea angrily. "You goddamn idiot. Why did you even suggest the Sommerville estate? Christ, it's only two blocks from here!"

With her back to Conrad, Dorothea slowly undid the long row of buttons on her green silk dress. She felt drained of energy, and the thought of another angry confrontation with Conrad was more than she could bear. She was too tired even for tears.

"You are wasting their time, Dorothea. No one will sell them a home in this area."

"We shall see about that," Dorothea answered quietly as she hung up her dress.

In three short steps Conrad was across the room. He grabbed her savagely by the shoulders and spun her around. She could feel his hot breath on her face as his words came out from between his clenched teeth.

"I am warning you, Dorothea. Don't push the issue! I don't want them for neighbors, and neither does anyone else in Shaughnessy."

Dorothea did not flinch as Conrad's fingers dug into her shoulders. "Not everyone thinks as you do. *I* want them for neighbors." For an instant Conrad simply stared at her. Dorothea returned the stare. The thought crossed her mind that he might strike her, but she did not waver. What did it

matter? She was too tired to care. As if reading the indifference in her face, Conrad flung her away from him. She stumbled backward and fell awkwardly onto the bed. Conrad stood
above her as she buried her face in the blankets.

"I will not allow them to buy a house in Shaughnessy! Remember that."

Dorothea raised her head from the bed, her voice a harsh
whisper. "You wouldn't dare stop the sale!"

"I wouldn't dare? We shall see about that."

Mr. Rand of the real estate company was waiting for them
when Hiro, Miyoko, and Dorothea arrived at the Sommerville
estate. He approached Dorothea with his hand outstretched.
"Mrs. Richter?"

"Yes, I'm Mrs. Richter," Dorothea answered, taking his
hand. "You are Mr. Rand, I presume?"

"Yes. From our telephone conversation this morning I
understand that you are not interested in the house for yourself."

"No, I'm not. Let me introduce Mr. and Mrs. Takezawa.
The house is for them."

Rand acknowledged Hiro and Miyoko with a slight tip of
his hat. He fidgeted nervously with the book he was holding.
"Oh, I see. I'll . . ."

"Please show us the house, Mr. Rand," Dorothea said
curtly.

"Certainly." His manner again reverted to that of a practiced salesman—polite, informative, and condescending.

"The house has been empty for a few weeks, but as you can
see everything is in good order. When Mr. Sommerville died,
the family was undecided as to what to do with the house,
until recently, that is. It's an extremely well constructed home.
I'm sure you will be delighted with it." His voice droned on as
if he had rehearsed the speech.

The house stood well back on a two-acre plot of land, partially obscured from the street by large, carefully shaped trees.
A stone and iron fence ran only along the front of the property; the rest of the grounds were separated from the neighboring properties by low shrubbery. A black wrought-iron gate
opened onto a long cobblestone driveway, lined with delicate
silver birches, which wound its way up to a large courtyard in
front of the house, circled a small fountain, and then con-

tinued on to the outbuildings at the far end of the property.
The house was a one-story structure, long and rambling, built
for the convenience of Mr. Sommerville, who had been
severely crippled. It was also a durable structure with broad
windows in the thick stone walls. One side of the house was
covered by English ivy, which the recent frost had turned into
a brillant array of fall colors.

They entered the house through a massive oak door adorned
with an ancient brass latch still glistening from many
polishings. Rand led them into a spacious foyer whose parquet
floor reflected the warmth of the morning sun. The rooms
were devoid of furniture, and their footsteps sounded hollow
as Dorothea and the Takezawas followed Rand through the
house, but with the sunlight streaming through the windows,
each room seemed welcoming.

Hiro mentally measured the rooms. They were large, but,
except for the main living room, not large enough to seem
cold. He looked about that room in consternation.

"Too large for you, Hiro?" Dorothea asked.

"It must be at least eight tatami mats," Hiro said, shaking
his head.

"Eight tatami mats? I don't understand." Dorothea's forehead furrowed.

Hiro laughed apologetically. "I will explain. In Japan we
measure the size of a room by the number of tatami mats it
will accommodate. Each mat is eighty-four centimeters by one
hundred and seventy-four centimeters. I am afraid my eye is
still trained to measure in that manner."

"The house has a basement," Rand interrupted, "and central heating. Of course, the fireplaces all work. The garage is
separate from the house, and there is also a small guest
room."

"Is there a sun-room?" Miyoko asked shyly.

It was the first time Miyoko had spoken since the tour
began, and Rand looked at her with surprise, as if not quite
believing her musical voice.

"A sun-room? I don't think so . . . though there is a room I
forgot about. Come with me," he said briskly. He opened a
door at the end of the hall and ushered them into a room that
was obviously designed as a retreat, a quiet bower apart from
the rest of the house. They stood gazing with pleasure at the
bookshelves that lined two walls, the well-used stone fireplace,

but most of all, at the huge window that stretched the length of the wall opposite the fireplace. Directly in front of the window was a small sitting area completely enclosed by a balustrade. To reach the sunlit enclosure one had to climb three stairs and swing open a tiny carved gate. The window looked out onto the expanse of lawns and fruit trees.

Hiro gently directed Miyoko up the stairs and through the small swinging gate, and they stood side by side gazing out the window. Dorothea watched them thoughtfully and knew they belonged here. She could already picture Hiro's books lining the empty shelves and Miyoko pouring tea while a fire crackled in the fireplace and snow fell beyond their window.

Hiro turned to Rand, who was waiting patiently by the open door. "You have been very accommodating, Mr. Rand. I will call you in the morning."

Rand looked dubious for a moment, then with a slight shrug of his shoulders, replied, "Certainly, Mr. Takezawa. You realize, of course, that this house is selling for seventy-four thousand dollars." His tone indicated his guess that the house was far more than the Takezawas could afford. But then again, one could never be too sure.

"No, I did not know that, Mr. Rand. But I will take it into consideration."

As Rand drove away from the house, he glanced at his watch impatiently; he was late for his next appointment. He had found the Takezawas disconcerting, and he perspired in spite of the cool November air. He had been in the business long enough to be able to detect those who could afford fine homes, but Takezawa was an enigma. He looked like a street vendor, yet up close he had the smell of wealth, and when he spoke it was as though he was accustomed to issuing orders and having them obeyed. Strange man, he thought. *I wonder how this neighborhood would like having a Jap in their midst?* He accelerated rapidly and weaved through the traffic—he abhorred being late for appointments.

It was well past the dinner hour when Conrad arrived home and found his family and the Takezawas listening to Dorothea play the piano. The music reflected her mood—she could not help feeling despondent. She knew without being told that Hiro had decided to purchase the Sommerville estate and would soon be leaving Drachenschlucht.

Behind her, she heard Conrad ask Hiro whether he had been

successful in finding a house, and she tensed in preparation for the tirade she was sure would follow.

"Yes, I have found a house," Hiro answered.

"Where?"

"I have decided to purchase the Sommerville estate. I will complete the transaction tomorrow morning with Mr. Rand."

Hiro did not miss the look that Conrad shot at Dorothea—it was an angry warning, and Dorothea quickly turned back to the piano. Her trembling hands struck a discordant note, but she recovered and carried on.

Conrad downed his Scotch in one gulp, his knuckles turning white as he gripped the glass. A few moments later he excused himself and strode out of the room.

As if to drown out his receding footsteps, Dorothea increased the tempo of her music until Hiro rose and placed a hand lightly on her shoulder. "Have we caused you unnecessary anguish, my dear?"

Dorothea leaned her forehead against the coolness of the piano for a moment and then looked at Hiro, her gray eyes clear.

"Conrad and I are worlds apart even though we live in the same house. Please pay no heed to his anger."

"But he is angry that we have decided to buy the Sommerville home."

"He will get over it."

"Can we be of any help?"

"You already have helped, probably more than you realize. Please do not trouble yourself. I am only sad that you will be leaving my home."

"But we will not be far away," Hiro reminded her.

"Yes, and for that I am truly grateful. Now let's try to dispel the gloom with some happy songs." Her fingers flew over the keys, and the music, like a child's mirthful laughter, reverberated through the house.

It was late when Conrad reached Harold Rand's home. He rang the doorbell and heard its tuneless peel resound through the silent house. A light shone immediately in an upstairs window and then he heard footsteps. The door opened a mere crack through which Rand peered out.

"Mr. Richter!" he said, opening the door wider. "What on earth are you doing here at this time of night?"

"I want to speak to you, Harold."

"Of course. Come in."

Rand, in bedroom slippers and a robe that did nothing to hide a body that had settled into a shapeless bulk from overindulgence, led Conrad into a small study. He flicked on the light and squinted against its brightness as he seated himself behind his desk.

"Now, Mr. Richter, what is it that you want?"

"The Sommerville home—you showed it to Hiro Takezawa today."

"That's right."

"Well, he has decided to buy it, but I don't want you to sell it to him."

"Why, Mr. Richter, I can't refuse to sell it to him. That wouldn't be ethical," Rand protested.

"Goddamnit, Rand, you and I both know that you aren't the least bit concerned about ethics. You're in this business only to make money, so cut the bullshit!"

Rand shifted uncomfortably under Conrad's gaze, and his indignant look quickly disappeared. "Well, I stand to make a damn good commission on this deal," he said defensively.

Conrad leaned over the desk so that his face was only inches away, and he thumped his finger on Rand's fleshy chest. "Look, Rand, I know all about the shady deals you've made and I can easily dredge up a few more—enough to make your life pretty miserable. But I'll be kind to you and make you a deal. I will pay the commission you would have made on the sale, and later you can sell it to someone else and make another commission."

Rand narrowed his eyes. "I want it in cash," he said quickly.

The next morning, Harold Rand arrived at his office later than usual. He showed evidence of having spent a restless night, but his smile exuded its usual cheerful confidence.

"Any messages for me?" he asked his secretary.

"No, but Mr. Takezawa is waiting in your office."

"Oh!" His smile drooped a little. "Well, I might as well get it over with." He continued smiling as he entered the office.

"Good morning, Mr. Takezawa," he said brightly.

"Good morning, Mr. Rand."

"I suppose you have come about the Sommerville house? I'm sorry to say, Mr. Takezawa, that the house has already been sold. However, we have others that I'm sure will be equally suitable. I can show them to you this morning if you like." He searched frantically from pocket to pocket for his pipe and then through the pile of papers on his desk.

"That is very strange," Hiro said. "I drove by this morning and the FOR SALE sign is still on it."

"We haven't had time to remove it yet. The man who bought it has been looking at it for some time and yesterday he finally decided to make an offer." Avoiding Hiro's eyes, he leafed nervously through a binder with listings of other available houses. "Ah, here we are. I have some fine homes listed here, Mr. Takezawa . . . now let me see. Yes, here is one that I'm sure you will approve of." Rand wished he could find his pipe.

Hiro's voice was razor-sharp. "How much was offered for the Sommerville home, Mr. Rand?"

"Why, Mr. Takezawa, I'm afraid that is confidential information," he said indignantly.

"How much was offered for the Sommerville home, Mr. Rand?" Hiro repeated.

"Seventy-four thousand."

"Seventy-four thousand. That is not a very realistic price, Mr. Rand."

Rand looked at Hiro for the first time and said defensively, "It's worth every penny. It's just that not too many people can afford to pay that price."

Hiro's smile was benign. "What I meant, Mr. Rand, is that I think the house is worth more. I am willing to pay one hundred thousand dollars for it."

Rand's mouth gaped. "Well . . . perhaps I can persuade the other client to reconsider, since you are so anxious to have the house." The owners of the house certainly didn't have to know Mr. Takezawa had bettered their asking price by twenty-six thousand dollars. The money would go directly into his own pocket, plus the healthy commission from the seventy-four thousand they were asking. He would have to arrange to have them sign the papers separately, so he could juggle the figures.

"I will speak to the other buyer and advise you as soon as I can, Mr. Takezawa."

"No, that will not do, Mr. Rand. Contact him now. I will wait in the outer office." Hiro knew that Rand was being dishonest; he had guessed the man was lying the instant he told him the house had been sold. Perhaps he had been bribed by Conrad; Hiro did not know, nor did he care. The Sommerville house felt like home, as if he belonged there, and the garden promised to be more than he had hoped for. The joyful look on Miyoko's face when she had seen the little sun-room had convinced Hiro that they must have the house.

Behind the closed door of his office Rand pounded the desk with frustration, cursing Richter for his interference and desperately searching for a means to evade Richter and his threats. In the end he gave up, lifted the phone, and asked for Richter's number.

"Richter," he said without any preliminaries, "Takezawa is here and has offered one hundred thousand dollars for the Sommerville estate. He knows that it hasn't been sold."

"I don't care what he knows," Conrad shouted. "I don't want that house sold to him for any price."

"Well, I can't just contrive a buyer," Rand whined. "Can he really come up with that kind of money?"

"Of course he can, you bloody idiot."

"Well then, I'm just going to have to sell it to him unless you can come up with a better offer."

"Rand, you bastard," Conrad yelled into the phone.

"What can I do? He's sitting outside waiting for an answer. Christ, how am I going to turn down one hundred thousand dollars? And besides that, he knows I haven't got another buyer. He'll go straight to the Sommervilles and buy it anyway."

Conrad had difficulty controlling his rage, and Rand held the phone away from his ear as the words hissed through the earpiece. "I don't care how the hell you do it, Rand, but I don't want the house sold to him. Take care of it, or I'll take care of you." There was a sharp click as Conrad hung up.

With difficulty, Rand opened the office door and summoned Hiro back into his office. "It looks as though the other buyer won't reconsider, Mr. Takezawa. I'm sorry." Mercifully, he had located his pipe and bit down on the end as hard as he could. Perspiration had marked the front of his shirt and his sparse hair parted and drooped over his ears.

"Has the other buyer increased his offer to match mine, Mr. Rand?" Hiro asked quietly.

Rand hesitated. "No . . . no he hasn't, as a matter of fact.

The house was listed for seventy-four thousand, and we are obliged to accept that figure.'' He lit his pipe with a trembling hand.

Hiro moved his chair closer and folded his leathery hands on top of the papers littering Rand's desk.

"Mr. Rand," Hiro said, then paused for emphasis. "The house will be mine because there are no other offers on it. It is obvious that you are being threatened by someone who does not want me in the Shaughnessy district, and I am sorry that you are caught in the middle. However, I think that is partly your own doing. If you do not accept my offer, I will contact the owners personally and inform them of your reluctance to sell their property. If you like, I can pursue the matter even further and find out who is threatening you and deal with them also. However, I do not think that will be necessary. I know I can count on you to pass along the message that I have the means to protect my interests as well as those of my associates—namely you, Mr. Rand. If you have any doubt about that ability, I will be happy to give you a demonstration.'' Or you can ask Mr. Richter. He will be able to verify the effectiveness of my methods. He has benefited from them in the past.''

Rand choked on the bitter juices that trickled onto his tongue from the pipe. "Mr. Richter!" he sputtered. "But he . . .'' He stopped in midsentence, suddenly aware that a solution had been reached. Instinct told him that the Japanese man who sat with his powerful hands resting quietly on his desk did not make idle promises. Takezawa would not permit Richter to carry out his threats.

"I'll take your offer to the Sommervilles this morning. I am sure they will be more than happy to accept. Perhaps you could do something for me, Mr. Takezawa.'' Hiro nodded. "Please inform Mr. Richter that you used his name as a reference and that I was impressed by your relationship with him.''

Hiro looked at him directly until Rand felt a tremor run up his spine. "I will tell him, Mr. Rand. I will deliver the money to you as soon as the papers are ready.''

Rand did not move until Hiro had left the office. As the door closed behind him, he sank into his chair with relief.

Maiko was at her desk when Hiro entered his office. "Mr.

Richter would like to see you, Mr. Takezawa. He is with a representative from the Prairie Wheat Pool, and they are anxious to speak to you.''

"I am expecting a call from a Mr. Rand. If the call comes while I am downstairs, please direct it to me in Mr. Richter's office.''

"Yes, Mr. Takezawa.''

"I will get right to the point Mr. Takezawa,'' Conrad said as soon as the introductions were completed. "The Prairie Wheat Pool is anxious to sell wheat to Japan on a regular basis. I have assured them that several of my ships could easily be converted to handle these shipments.''

"We are just as anxious to have your wheat as you are to sell it,'' Hiro replied.

"Fine,'' the representative said, smiling broadly. "Then we can discuss prices and shipping schedules.''

There was a soft knock on the door and Conrad, irritated by the interruption, answered gruffly.

Patricia stepped into the office. "Mr. Takezawa, there is a call for you from Mr. Rand. He says that it is urgent. You can take it on Mr. Richter's phone if you like.''

"Thank you, Patricia,'' Hiro said as he lifted the receiver.

Conrad could only hear Hiro's replies, but he guessed what had transpired and he gripped the armrests of his chair.

Hiro replaced the phone with a smile and announced innocently, "My offer on the Sommerville estate has been accepted. The papers will be ready for my signature tomorrow morning, and we can have immediate occupancy. Apparently someone tried to block the sale, but Mr. Rand chose to ignore it when I informed him that I was capable of protecting my interests. I gave him your name as a reference, Richter-sama. I hope that you do not mind.''

The message behind Hiro's words was unmistakable, and Conrad failed to dispel the image that rose up before him: the agonized face of a man whose dismembered hand lay in a pool of blood at his feet. "No, I don't mind,'' he said weakly.

For the rest of the meeting he spoke only when questioned, and when Hiro and the representative finally left, Conrad remained seated, staring fixedly out the window while blood pounded in his temples.

●   ●   ●

Shortly before moving into the Sommerville estate, Hiro suddenly realized that he would no longer have Richter's Cadillac at his disposal and, consequently, no means of transportation. He combed the car lots but could not find a vehicle that even remotely resembled his old Haynes. On the fourth day, Hiro came upon a Super Six Studebaker Speedster in a showroom near the center of the city; it was displayed on a low pedestal in resplendent elegance. He looked at it through the window for a full ten minutes, trying to convince himself that he should have a more practical automobile. Finally he went inside to examine it more closely. The soft white top was down, folded and buttoned neatly over the back of the maroon body, exposing the luxurious white leather upholstery. It was trimmed with wide chrome strips that extended the length of the car and merged with the smoothly rounded bumpers. In the contour of the polished hubcap Hiro could see a salesman slowly approaching, his hands stuffed into the pockets of his pin-striped pants.

"Beauty, isn't she?" the salesman asked casually.

"Yes, very beautiful," Hiro agreed.

"We get a lot of people looking at this job." He wet the tip of his handkerchief with his tongue and removed a black smudge from the side of the whitewall tire.

"I am sure you do. May I see the motor, please?"

"Certainly," the salesman said. "I never get tired of showing off this baby. She's been here three weeks and we've had more people looking at her than the new barmaid at Jigg's place."

Hiro leaned over the engine. "I see it has six cylinders."

"That's right, and she goes like the wind."

"Up to eighty miles an hour, I understand."

"You've seen one like this before?" the salesman asked, surprised.

"No, but I have read about it."

"Yes, well, that's about all most of us can do—just read and look. Are you interested in buying a car or just looking?"

"I am interested in buying a car," Hiro answered.

"If you'll come with me, I'll show you some of our regular-priced models. I've got a couple of used cars in fine condition too."

"May I have more information on this speedster?"

The salesman felt a twinge of exasperation. It was nearing

lunchtime; he had skipped breakfast, and this farmer was obviously killing time.

"There're some brochures over there." He pointed to a nearby desk. "Help yourself. When you're ready, come into my office and I'll show you the models in the back." He started in the direction of his office.

"I will take this one," Hiro said quietly.

The salesman turned slowly, his expression uncertain. "What did you say?"

"I will take this one," Hiro repeated. "How much does it cost?"

"Twenty . . . twenty-three hundred," he sputtered.

"Will you accept a personal check?"

With eyes wide and unblinking, the salesman nodded. "I would have to verify it with the bank first—company rules."

"Certainly. I deal with the Bank of Canada on Pender Street. Ask for Mr. Gingras. My name is Hiro Takezawa."

"Hiro Takezawa. I'll be right back," he said, and disappeared into his office, leaving Hiro reading the small brochure. He asked for the number almost reluctantly, certain that the bank would deny any knowledge of the Oriental in baggy pants let alone guarantee his check for twenty-three hundred dollars.

Oh well, he thought, it won't be the first time I've done this and been disappointed. He'll probably be gone even before I get off the telephone.

"Mr. Gingras, I hope I'm not wasting your time. This is Jim Sloan from Western Motors. Do you know a Hiro Takezawa?"

"Hiro Takezawa? Yes, I do."

"You do?"

"You sound surprised."

"As a matter of fact, I am. Can he cover a check for twenty-three hundred dollars? He wants to buy a Studebaker speedster," he said cautiously.

Gingras chuckled at first and then burst into loud hearty guffaws.

"I figured so," Sloan said ruefully. "Damn these guys and their games. I should have known better than to waste my time and yours. The guy looks like he couldn't afford a hubcap."

"Mr. Sloan, you're dead wrong," said Gingras, his laughter dying out. "Not only can Mr. Takezawa afford to buy that speedster, he could buy your entire car lot out of petty cash.''

Sloan replaced the telephone lightly in its cradle and reached for a sales contract. Through his office door window he could see Hiro leaning against the Studebaker, waiting patiently. He watched him for a moment, then shrugged his shoulders and began filling in the details of the contract.

"You never know," he said aloud. "You just never know!"

The move into the Sommerville estate was relatively simple. With the help of Cyrus Wilson they had their trunks and crates removed from storage and delivered to the estate. The furniture they had brought with them from Japan scarcely completely filled two rooms, but Hiro's books filled the shelves in the sun-room, and Miyoko lovingly decorated the wall beside the large window. With Dorothea's help, she made draperies from heavy damask which they found in one of the crates that had been packed by Yuri. The fabric, the color of rich cream and embroidered by clever hands, hung in lustrous folds, shutting out the cold December nights. It was Karl who laid the first fire for them in the fireplace.

In December, a light snowfall covered the ground and then disappeared almost as quickly, leaving behind a cold wet slush. With the windows opened wide, Hiro and Tatsuo exercised each morning until their keiko-gis were soaked with perspiration and their breath came out in white puffs. Occasionally, Karl would join them, and under Hiro's watchful eye he would struggle for the perfection Hiro demanded.

Conrad's irritation grew as Karl spent more and more time at the Sommerville estate. "He's beginning to talk like the Takezawa kid," he shouted at Dorothea. "I won't allow that. And why are you serving this goddamn white fish?"

"The fish is for Karl. He thinks it will give him strength. Mrs. Lange has cooked a leg of lamb for you," Dorothea answered.

"How much time are you and the children spending over there while I'm away?" Conrad's voice was a tight growl. Mrs. Lange, who had just placed the roast beside his elbow, retreated hastily to the kitchen.

Dorothea's head remained bent over her plate.

"I asked you a question, Dorothea. Answer me!" Conrad demanded abruptly.

"My days are very long with the children at school. I enjoy Miyoko's company."

"What the hell do you have in common with her anyway? She can hardly speak English."

"Actually, she has learned to speak it quite well. She has been instructing me in the art of flower arranging."

"So I've noticed," Conrad said derisively, eyeing the simple centerpiece on the table. "And what about Karl and Lisl?"

"Karl and Tasuo attend the same school, and they are good friends. It's only natural that they would spend time together. They often include Lisl in their activities."

Her appetite gone, Dorothea picked silently at her food.

Classes were dismissed for the Christmas holidays and whoops of excited laughter rang through the halls of St. John's College.

"Will your grandfather be home tonight?" Karl asked Tatsuo as they walked home.

"Tonight I am sure he will be home early. Obā-san is preparing *anago*. It is his very favorite dish and mine too."

"What is anago?"

"Conger eel."

Karl grimaced and shrugged his shoulders.

Tatsuo grinned mischievously. "You have eaten it at our house several times. You just did not know what it was. If I remember correctly, you liked it and had several helpings. Why did you ask about Ojī-san?"

"I would like to ask him if he will accept me as his pupil."

"I will tell him to expect you," Tatsuo said, relieved that Karl had finally decided to make the request.

The sky was brilliant with stars that night, and the fresh snow crunched under Karl's boots. Apprehension knotted his stomach, and Tatsuo's warnings ran through his mind. "Do not ask him to teach you to fight." Martial arts . . . Zen . . . Shizen Ryu Kempo . . . meditation. The meaningless words whirled inside him and he swallowed nervously. When he reached the house, he saw Hiro's Studebaker in the driveway, covered with a layer of snow. He scooped some off the shiny hood and moistened his mouth with it.

Tatsuo met him at the door. "Grandfather is expecting you. He is in the dojo."

Karl nodded wordlessly and walked in the direction of the training hall.

"Karl," Tatsuo said to his retreating back, "we saved you some anago."

"Thanks," Karl said without turning.

The door to the dojo was ajar, and Karl stepped in. The large room was illuminated only by the glow of flickering candles that sat on a low table. There was no other furniture. A tatami mat was spread at each end of the table. Hiro sat on one of them and indicated that the other was for Karl.

"Sit down, tomodachi."

Karl knelt down on the mat, his heart pounding in his chest.

"I am glad to see you again," Hiro said in a low voice. "What is the purpose of your visit?" The glow of the candles gave his face a strange texture.

Karl took a deep breath before answering. Instinctively, he knew that a great deal depended on his reply. "I want to become your pupil, Takezawa-sama, and I would like you to be my sensei."

Hiro poured tea into a tiny porcelain cup and offered it to Karl. "Why?" he asked simply.

"I want to learn your ways. I want to be able to control my body and mind the way you do."

"For what purpose?"

Karl's voice caught in his dry throat as he tried to answer. "At first I thought I would just like to be able to fight like Tatsuo and be as strong as you, but I know now that there is more. I don't know if I can explain it, but I want to be brave —but in the right way—and I want to be able to understand things better, like you and Tatsuo."

After a long silence, Hiro said, "You have chosen a most difficult path to travel. Only a few complete the journey. You must dedicate several hours each day to your training. This will include time for meditation and introspection. Do you think you can afford this time and still do your duty to your parents and your studies?"

"Yes," Karl answered with conviction.

"You will only have time for six hours of sleep each day."

"It will be enough. And I will not neglect my other duties. I do not know about my father, but I know my mother will be pleased."

"Yes, I think your mother will be happy. She is very close to my heart, just as you are. This dojo will be like a second home to you—sometimes you must even sleep here. It will be your duty to keep it clean at all times."

Karl nodded, swallowing a lump that had formed in his throat.

"For the first few months, you will run every morning for half an hour. You will soon be able to cover five or six miles in that time. You will return here to exercise and strengthen your body. Perhaps by spring we can start with a few basic moves of Shizen Ryu Kempo." Hiro observed the boy's face closely for any sign of displeasure at the schedule he had outlined. There was none.

"During this time," he continued, "I will also teach you how to still your mind and to control your thoughts. Only then will you be your own master and truly free. This takes most men many years to achieve, but it is a worthwhile quest. The practice of Zen is a means to achieve harmony within oneself and with the universe. It is a necessary part of martial arts training. As you train your body you must also teach your mind. You must understand your nature and become its master."

Karl stared at the flickering candles, which were almost completely burned down. "I do not understand all that you are saying, but I will work hard. I promise."

"In time you will understand, and you will become master of yourself. That is the noblest of all victories. And then you will know true harmony and peace. It is our quest, and the journey is our way of life."

The dojo was silent except for the sputtering of the dying candles. When the last candle had flickered out, Hiro said in the darkness, "Welcome, my young friend. Your journey starts here, and tonight you have taken the first step. You may go now."

In the darkness Karl could only see the outline of Hiro's form. There was nothing more to say. He walked out quietly and closed the door behind him.

Hiro decided to close the offices of Pacific Far Eastern Trading during the Christmas season. He needed a few days to relax and prepare for the approaching new year. Maiko was pleased when he announced his plans. She bowed in the traditional Japanese manner and said, "I hope you enjoy a well-deserved rest."

"Thank you, Maiko, I hope you do too. Thank you for the fine job you have done for me."

Maiko smiled, coloring slightly. "It is a pleasure working for you, Mr. Takezawa. I have left the completed orders for the coal shipments on my desk, along with the year-end reports for the zaibatsu. They will be ready for mailing after you have signed them."

"I will look after them, Maiko."

"Before you leave, there is a Mr. Fenton waiting to see you.

"Mr. Fenton? I do not recall that name."

"He said that you would know him when you saw him."

"Send him in."

Hiro recognized Fenton immediately; his clothes were different, his face was thinner, but he was unmistakably the assistant from the Federal Bank.

"Come in, Mr. Fenton," Hiro said politely without rising from his chair.

"Mr. Takezawa, thank you for seeing me. I am sorry to barge in on you, but I felt if I made an appointment you might not agree to see me, and I could not have blamed you for that."

"Why did you want to see me?" Hiro asked stiffly.

"First of all, Mr. Takezawa, I would like to apologize for my behavior on the day you came to see me. I have learned a great deal about myself since that day. Perhaps it is a little late, but I would still like to say it: welcome to Canada. I hope you will be happy here and that you will prosper in your new venture." He extended his hand to Hiro.

Without hesitation, Hiro took his hand and shook it firmly.

"I am not with the bank anymore," Fenton continued. "I've been working on the tugboats."

"You are not with the bank?"

"I was fired," Fenton said flatly.

"Not because of me, I hope?"

"Indirectly, yes. But actually, I deserved to be fired. It was my own stupidity that lost me my job. When I finally realized a few things about myself, my conscience began to bother me. That is why I had to come and see you."

"I admire your courage, Mr. Fenton. Thank you for coming. Are you happy in your new job?"

"No, my heart is still in the business world. That is what I enjoy most, and that is what I have been trained to do. But working on the boats has been good for me. I've discovered muscles I never knew I had."

"Tell me, Mr. Fenton, why did you turn me away from your bank?"

"I feel very foolish telling you about it now, Mr. Takezawa."

"Please, I would like to know."

"Well," Fenton began, "to start with, my morning had not gone well, and when you came in I was angry with myself and with the world. But most of all I was guilty of . . ." He stumbled, groping for words. "I was guilty of prejudice, for which I am ashamed. What added to it, I think, was that ugly satchel you were carrying. When you dropped it on my clean desk, I . . . uh . . . well." He shrugged uncomfortably.

"Please continue—you have earned the right," Hiro encouraged.

"Along with the satchel, I guess I objected to your ill-fitting clothes. At that time you just seemed out of place in that gold and marble bank. I apologize for my ignorance."

Hiro stared down at his suit. It was the same one he had worn to the Federal Bank, the same one Miyoko had altered for him on the S.S. *Hudson*. Now, after many cleanings, it was even more shapeless and threadbare.

"Is it that bad?" Hiro's voice was low. Fenton nodded meekly.

Hiro stood up and walked around the desk to stand in front of Fenton. He looked down at his clothes with chagrin. "You mean to say that I do not look like a representative of the largest zaibatsu in Japan?"

Again Fenton shook his head, but this time quite emphatically.

"What would you suggest I do?"

"I would suggest that you find the best tailor in town."

"I do not know any," Hiro said simply.

"I will find one for you if you like."

Hiro walked back to his chair and sat down, his expression thoughtful. "Mr. Fenton, would you consider changing jobs?"

"What do you mean?"

"I need an assistant in this office. The work load is becoming too heavy for me to handle. Would you consider working for me? I would pay you the same wages you received at the bank."

Fenton's mouth dropped open, and for a moment he was speechless. "I most certainly would, Mr. Takezawa. When would you like me to start?"

"Right now. You can begin by helping me buy a decent pair of pants."

Fenton's reply was a broad grin.

[6]

Karl's throat felt raw and his harsh, labored breath escaped in white billows while beads of perspiration rolled down his forehead. Still he ran, determined to complete the five-mile course within the allotted thirty minutes. He tried to ignore the pain by counting his steps as his feet crunched through the light snow; he could not stop now—the sensei would be waiting. His steps faltered until he saw the Takezawa estate, then, spurred on by the thought that he was almost there, his exhausted body tapped every reserve of energy and he raced toward the house. He collapsed on the front steps, completely drained; phlegm rose into his throat, and he was surprised to see the snow stained red by the mucus he spit out. As his breathing eased, he leaned forward, resting his elbows on his knees while his head drooped between his legs.

Behind him Hiro spoke. "O hayo, Karl-san. You are becoming faster—or perhaps you have taken a shorter route?"

Karl turned to face the master, perspiration still beaded on his forehead. "Good morning, sensei. No, I didn't take a shorter route, but I tried to run faster . . . I almost didn't make it."

"After running so hard, it would be better for you to continue walking until your heart and breathing have slowed down."

Karl nodded. "I know, but my legs just wouldn't carry me any further. I will try to do that tomorrow."

Sympathy shone in Hiro's eyes as he placed his hand on

Karl's shoulder, but his voice was firm. "Come, we must proceed to the dojo."

Karl stood up wearily and groaned. "My stomach hurts and so does my . . ." He stopped suddenly, ashamed for having shown weakness.

"It hurts because you are trying hard, and that is good—I am proud of you."

In the dojo, Tatsuo was already practicing thrusts against a padded punching board that snapped noisily with each blow. Karl watched with envy, mentally copying Tatsuo's moves while Hiro explained the mechanics of the powerful thrusts.

"He is practicing the long thrust and the hook thrust. They are called *gyaku-zuki* and *kagi-zuki*. You, too, will be doing this in several months."

Karl longed to ask for the chance to try now, to show Hiro that he, too, could move with machinelike precision. Hiro read his mind before he could voice the request.

"It appears easy, but it will take many months to achieve adeptness at the punching board. You are not yet ready." Hiro led him to the far end of the dojo and handed him a well-worn straw broom. Karl took the broom and looked questioningly at the sensei.

"The dojo must always be clean, and you will help to keep it so. Tools such as this old straw broom have brought much pleasure to Zen masters and students alike."

Karl began to sweep the already spotless floor and tried to understand how anyone could derive pleasure from household chores.

Hiro smiled knowingly. "When you are finished, Karl, we will begin our conditioning exercises."

The broom felt awkward in his hands; the dojo was much larger than it looked, but Karl knew that he must obey without question. Slowly he worked toward Tatsuo, whose white keiko-gi was damp from exertion. Tatsuo stopped his exercises when Karl reached him.

"I hope you cannot find any dust, for I have already swept the dojo this morning and Ojī-san swept it last night," Tatsuo explained.

"And I am doing it again? But, why?"

"It is part of our training," Tatsuo replied matter-of-factly, and turned to resume his attack on the punching board.

Hiro watched from the corner of his eye and thought, One

day, tomodachi, you will find great satisfaction in simple tasks such as the one you are doing now. He was pleased with Karl, pleased by his persistence and often surprised by the results. Was it his imagination or had Karl's face matured in the short time he had been training? Hiro recalled his feeling when they had first talked in the garden in Tokyo, sensing even then that their paths were destined to run together. In retrospect, he realized how accurate those feelings had been.

"I am finished, sensei."

"Good. But before we begin, I would like you to have something." He handed Karl a package neatly wrapped in brown paper and tied securely with woven string. The paper dropped to the floor, and Karl removed a white training costume.

"A keiko-gi!" he breathed. "Thank you!"

"The white belt indicates that you are in the initial stages of your training. As you advance, the color of your belt will change accordingly."

The canvas fabric felt rough against Karl's skin, but his face glowed with pride as he secured the belt around his waist. His initials were embroidered with fine black thread on the upper-right-hand portion of the keiko-gi. He ran his fingers over the smooth lettering.

"That is Tatsuo's design but Miyoko's clever needlework."

With his head held high and his shouders squared, Karl walked to the center of the dojo and turned. "Now I am ready to begin my exercises."

The moves appeared simple and were executed effortlessly by Hiro and Tatsuo, but Karl groaned with frustration when he attempted to imitate them.

"Keep trying, Karl," Hiro ordered. Again he demonstrated the moves, and Karl forced his weary body to obey. He stretched until he thought his muscles and tendons would tear apart.

"Do not expect to accomplish everything in one day. With discipline and training, your body will learn to react quickly to your commands."

Hiro stood with his feet slightly apart and bent over, touching his knees with his forehead. He repeated the exercise in rapid succession, indicating to his two students that they should repeat the procedure.

The muscles in Karl's heavy legs stretched reluctantly as he bent over, barely reaching the floor with his groping finger-tips. His forehead was still several inches away from his knees, and a groan escaped as the tendons in his legs responded like overwound violin strings. He straightened and bobbed again, but his head still did not meet his knees. Before Karl could catch his breath, Hiro was lying on his stomach, his thick back muscles flexing and knotting as he began his push-ups, first on his fingertips and then on his knuckles. To his surprise, Karl found he was capable of doing push-ups easily, his thick arms and heavy chest muscles proving their strength. After a brief rest and more stretching, they were back on the floor until Karl's breath came in quick gasps and his arms collapsed under him.

"Soon these exercises will be easier, but you must persevere. The pain will eventually disappear," Hiro assured him.

"But you and Tatsuo do it so easily, sensei. Tatsuo is just skin and bones compared to me, and yet he leaves me in the dust."

Hiro's eyes sparkled with laughter and a smile played at the corners of his mouth. "That is one reason why Tatsuo wears a brown belt while yours is white. He has gone through the same agonies that you are now experiencing, just as I have—and every pupil and master before you. Do not look so dejected, my young friend. The journey is arduous but rewarding."

Karl nodded in agreement as the perspiration trickled down his back with an uncomfortable coolness.

"Soon you will begin practicing basic movements like the straight punch and the straight kick."

Karl's face brightened instantly.

"But," Hiro continued, "you must remember that the study of martial arts is a spiritual exercise as well as a physical one. As difficult as the physical exercises may seem to you, they will seem effortless in comparison to the mental discipline that you must cultivate. You must strive toward *jishu-zammai*—self-mastery."

Karl stared intently at Hiro's face in an effort to understand his words. Up to this point in his life, he had not experienced any real difficulties or obstacles. His marks in school were always in the top ten percent, and he achieved these honors easily. He possessed a quick mind and assimilated knowledge readily. He read voraciously, a habit acquired from his mother very early in life, and this gave him a wide scope of knowledge well beyond his years. He had always been a big boy, standing well above the other children; his size and strength carried him easily through all the physical activities he participated in such as football, soccer, baseball, and boxing. Karl was aggressive when provoked, but his quick temper often proved to be an asset rather than a detriment. Now as he stared at Hiro, concentrating on each word, he suddenly realized that he would have to exert all his energy to achieve even a portion of Hiro's expectations of him. The physical training had tested him to the limit, and now he was being told that the mental discipline would be even more difficult. For the first time in his life, he began to doubt his abilities, and he experienced the strange fear of inadequacy.

Hiro recognized the apprehension in Karl's brilliant eyes, but he also sensed the determination of his spirit. He would be an excellent pupil. "There is much to learn, Karl, but you have a lifetime to understand fully—to reach *satori*. We will proceed slowly, one step at a time. A thousand-mile journey begins with one step."

Karl tightened the belt on his keiko-gi and nodded. "My mother says that too."

"As usual, we will end the practice with meditation," Hiro announced.

Tatsuo spread out three spotless tatami mats and cushions. Even though Karl was into his second week of instruction, the position for zazen was extremely difficult for him to assume. His thick legs refused to bend easily into the lotus position, which involved folding his feet onto his thighs and tucking them in close to his stomach. Instantly, his legs began to ache. Through his discomfort he could hear Hiro's voice.

"Karl, what is this position called?"

"The *kekka fuza*, sensei."

"Good. And what is the purpose of this position?"

Karl longed to say that it was for the infliction of pain. "In order to control the mind, we must discipline the body. Breathing must come from the stomach and diaphragm."

"Correct. Breathing must be controlled from the *tanden*." Hiro pointed to the lower part of his sculptured abdomen. "When you practice zazen properly, pressure is exerted into this region and a certain stillness fills your body. It is this stillness of the body that engenders stillness of the mind."

A stifled groan escaped from Karl as his aching legs slipped out of the lotus position. He glanced at Hiro, fully expecting a sharp rebuke. There was no anger in Hiro's face. He sat immobile, patiently waiting for Karl to resume his position. After a moment he reached behind him and passed a small cushion to the boy.

"Perhaps this will help you."

"I would rather not," Karl said, his voice ringing with determination as he struggled to hold his legs in place.

"It is quite permissible to use the cushion. Many Zen masters use one all their lives."

Reluctantly, Karl accepted the cushion and placed it beneath him. This time he was able to pull his legs in tightly and straighten his back. The pain in his legs lessened.

"In time this position will become very natural for you. In fact, any other will probably seem uncomfortable, including sitting in a chair.

Karl was dubious, but he agreed, determined not to allow the cramps to disrupt his concentration. The cushion, he discovered, had only transferred the discomfort from his legs to his back. Was it possible that his body would ever become accustomed to this?

"Now, Karl," Hiro continued, "try to still your body. Hold your hands on your lap with the thumbs together and your palms up . . . bend your head slightly downward." Hiro paused while Karl readjusted himself. "Now use only the tanden. Breathe in slowly as you count to seven . . . hold your breath now until you count to three . . . and slowly exhale as you count to ten. Do not expel all the air in your lungs . . . stop for the count of three, and now repeat the entire process."

As Hiro counted, Karl eased his breath in and out until a rhythmic pattern developed. Suddenly the counting stopped and Karl's breathing became irregular and labored. Finally, he gasped for air. "I'm sorry, sensei . . . I lost count."

"It does not matter. We will begin again. Ready? One, two three, four, five . . ." The counting continued and stopped, again and again. Karl persevered through two counts before gasping for air. Finally, after several attempts, a comfortable rhythmic pattern emerged; Karl forgot the discomfort in his back as his mind followed Hiro's calm voice.

"That is enough for today, tomodachi. You have done well."

Karl looked up with relief. What began as a smile ended as a grimace. His legs felt like blocks of wood when he tried to straighten them, and then a multitude of needles shot through them. He groaned and arched his back, grinning sheepishly at Hiro.

"I think I will have to crawl home."

Hiro rose to his feet effortlessly. "That only indicates that you have followed my instructions."

Karl struggled to his feet and walked around the dojo until the muscles in his legs felt as though they belonged to him again. Slowly he removed his keiko-gi and hung it carefully on the peg beside the door. He had never felt so weary in all his life; his hands trembled as he buttoned his shirt. Hiro helped him on with his coat, reminding him that today was Christmas.

Karl's face lit up. "I almost forgot! Can you believe I worked so hard that I forgot it was Christmas?"

"I believe it," Hiro said knowingly.

"I have to hurry—Lisl is waiting for me. Don't forget that you are coming to our house for dinner."

"We will be there," Hiro assured him.

He trudged up the steps and into the warm house, where he found Lisl waiting at the door, just as expected.

"Karl's here!" she chanted. "Please hurry. I can't wait one minute longer. Father isn't home, but he has a surprise for you, and I know what it is."

Karl stopped at the word *surprise*, but Lisl continued to skip on ahead of him.

"Surprise? What kind of surprise?" Karl called after her.

Lisl spun around and covered her mouth with her hand to suppress her giggles. "I'm not going to tell you."

"Why not?"

"Because then it won't be a surprise, and anyway, Mother made me promise."

"That's right," Dorothea's voice sounded behind them. "And don't you break that promise, young lady."

"How long do I have to wait, Mother?" Karl asked.

"Your father won't be home today. His business wasn't finished in Seattle, and he felt he should stay until it was. However, he said to tell you the surprise will be worth waiting for."

Karl's curiosity was quickly forgotten in the flurry of excitement as both he and Lisl began opening the numerous gifts heaped under the glittering Scotch pine. The warmth of the room and the exuberence of Karl and Lisl brought a flush of color to Dorothea's pallid cheeks. She sat on the floor with her children, enjoying their delight and expressing her own as they opened the brightly wrapped packages. Dorothea admired the colorful silk scarf Karl had given her. Memories of Christmases long past flooded through her mind. She remembered coming down the stairs on a Christmas morning long ago, wearing a new dress, and her father watching with surprised, loving eyes, saying, "What happened to the little girl who helped me decorate the tree last night?" And now she was asking the same thing about her own son—what happened to the little boy who drove the entire household mad with his antics? Who was this familiar stranger who sat quietly at her feet? Had she missed the transition, or had it been so subtle as to go unnoticed? She smiled at the furrows of concentration on his face, the uncooperative cowlick in his blond hair, and the slant of his broadening shoulders. He had lost weight, but certainly not because he was eating less; his appetite had doubled, as Mrs. Lange had confirmed. No, it was undoubtedly the training—the strenuous five-mile run each morning and the hours spent practicing with the sensei, a new word for her.

Lisl, too, appeared older. Her hair, tied with a blue ribbon, hung in soft curls on her shoulders. Above a long, slender neck, the contours of her face had become more defined; dark lashes fringed blue-flecked eyes, and when she smiled a dimple appeared in both cheeks. She was tall for her age, no longer awkward, and Dorothea knew with certainty that one day she would be a very beautiful woman.

Lisl sat now with her legs folded under her, absorbed in a dice and number game with Karl; furrows of concentration wrinkled her forehead. When the doorbell rang, she glanced up expectantly.

"That will be the Takezawas. I want to see the look on their faces when they see the tree."

Dorothea opened the door. "I'm so glad you've come," she said, welcoming them.

"We are honored that you have invited us to celebrate your holy day," Hiro said after the traditional bow.

"We could hardly wait." Dorothea hugged each of them. "Come into the sun-room. We want you to see the Christmas tree."

Dorothea escorted them into the room and then stood back with Lisl and Karl to watch the Takezawas' reaction; they were not disappointed. Tatsuo gasped with delight and then, with his black eyes reflecting the multicolored lights, he walked slowly around the tree, stopping to examine the ornaments closely. "Look, Obā-san, this one has a small piano inside it," he exclaimed.

"Here, let me show you something, Tatsuo," Dorothea said. Carefully, she turned over the miniature ornament and wound the tiny key at the bottom. When she replaced it, the miniature piano turned around and around and played a tinkling melody.

"A very dear friend of my father's made it for me when I was about your age. Look at this one," she said, pointing to a silver bell with a tiny blue cradle inside. "He made this one for Karl when he was born, and this one was for Lisl." She let Tatsuo hold the silver bell with a pink cradle inside it.

"Many of the decorations on this tree came from my family. Traditionally, the German people are craftsmen, and so many of our ornaments are handmade for special occasions."

"Perhaps, like the Japanese, they are somewhat sentimental," Hiro said.

"Some are, others are not—unfortunately," Dorothea replied cryptically. "Now, please sit down—Lisl cannot wait much longer to hand out the gifts."

Lisl passed Tatsuo's gift to him first. "I hope you will like this. We looked all over until we found the one we thought you would like best." She colored slightly when Tatsuo smiled at her; there seemed to be something in his smile that was reserved just for her. She suddenly felt uncomfortable and turned away while he opened the parcel. A look of pleasure came across his face when he removed a gold fountain pen. Gently, he removed the cap and examined the pen.

"It is so beautiful . . . a perfect gift. I will use it to write in the special book Oji-san gave me before we left Japan."

"Lisl made the final choice," Karl said. "She seemed to know the one you would like."

Tatsuo looked at Lisl, but she was carefully examining the name tag on another parcel, her hair covering the deepening flush on her face. Lisl was pleased that Tatsuo liked the present, and the hint of tears in his eyes did not go unnoticed. Except for Karl, she had never paid much attention to boys, but

Tatsuo was different. She was happy when he came to the house even though he spent most of his time with her mother. But the tears and the warm smile—surely they were meant only for her.

Miyoko opened her gift carefully and removed a soft velvet dressing gown, the color of summer sky. Gently she stroked the smooth fabric, her face reflecting gratitude and surprise.

"Thank you. It is very beautiful," she said softly. "You made it yourself?"

Dorothea nodded. "Lisl helped."

Hiro emitted a loud sigh as he pushed his feet into the slippers he received. They were made of soft cowhide, lined with combed sheep's wool, warm and soft. He ventured a few careful steps and then, satisfied with the perfect fit, marched from one end of the room to the other.

"My well-worn zori cannot match these for comfort. Would you mind if I wore them to dinner?"

"Not at all," Dorothea said with a smile.

Dinner was the traditional roast turkey with all the usual accompaniments: dressing, cranberry sauce, an array of steaming vegetables, and a Christmas plum pudding brought to the table wreathed in a spectacular blue flame. The evening ended with Dorothea once again sitting at the piano, her voice blending with Karl's and Lisl's as they entertained the Takezawas with Christmas carols.

As they reluctantly walked to the door that night, Hiro's face was solemn. "My dear friends, you have made this a memorable day for us. We shall treasure our gifts and the memory of this time we have spent with you."

"I cannot remember when I have enjoyed Christmas more," Dorothea said with conviction. "You have made it a memorable day for us too." After the door closed behind them, she pulled Karl and Lisl close to her to ward off the loneliness that threatened to engulf her.

Christmas was quickly forgotten by Karl, who was once again completely absorbed in his training under Hiro's tutelage. The five-mile run was as hard now as it had been when he first started. Each morning he tried to break his record time of forty minutes; the ultimate goal of thirty minutes seemed as remote as it had been on the first day. Only the pain and frustration had lessened slightly. The stretching exercises remained no less difficult; his arms and pectorals ached and quivered from exertion, and occasionally tears threatened as Hiro pushed him mercilessly.

"Your body is pliable and resilient, Karl—capable of meeting more demands than you think possible."

"It is hopeless," he would answer through clenched teeth. "I cannot do any more."

"Try once more!" Hiro commanded sharply.

Then, just before the breaking point, Hiro would say gently, "It is time for meditation." They would walk about the dojo to loosen up first. "You can push your body relentlessly each day, but you must lead the mind quietly along new paths in your search for the Ox."

Karl had heard Hiro mention the Ox several times before, and he struggled to keep his curiosity in check.

"In due time, Karl, you will understand. For the moment, I want you to concentrate only on what I have taught you to this point." Before Karl could ask more questions, Hiro said, "I see that you are able to sit more easily in the kekka fuza. Curve your back a little more. Push the tanden forward and your buttocks backward." Hiro could feel the hard muscles in Karl's stomach and back as he firmly pushed him closer to the desired position. "There, that is better. Does that not feel more comfortable?"

"Yes, I think so."

"Good, now we can begin with the breathing."

Karl closed his eyes and bent his head in preparation. Hiro studied the intense face. Karl had made rapid progress in the short time he had been training, and even though the boy felt the extreme demands to be beyond his ability, it would not be long before he would begin reaching those seemingly unattainable goals. But how long would Karl remain on the journey toward Zen maturity, the arduous path to *samadhi*, the ultimate concentration? Hiro knew he would have to guide him carefully, slowly, just as he had done with Tatsuo. But Tatsuo had been easy to train, to mold, and to direct. His training had begun almost as soon as he was able to comprehend his surroundings. Hiro had seen to that by including the inquisitive youngster in his own training sessions as often as he could. But Karl was beginning at a time when many of the patterns of his life were already established. He listened to Karl attempt to regulate his breathing, only to lose the rhythm again and again. Softly, Hiro counted for him until the rhythm became evident, the breathing even; Karl's face became still.

Slowly everything receded for Karl; the ache in his legs disappeared, and a peacefulness began to fill his mind. He felt strange and removed; Hiro's voice was only barely perceptible somewhere in the distance. As soon as he was aware of his peaceful state, feelings and noise came rushing back. He gasped for air.

"I'm sorry, sensei . . . I lost count again."

Hiro smiled. "Do not be disappointed. You have done very well today. You may not realize it, but you sat here for a full nine minutes, counting by yourself. I am proud of you."

"But that doesn't seem possible!"

Hiro nodded with approval. "The practice session is over for today, but before you go, please get some hot water and soap. Dust has settled on the walls and they must be wiped clean."

Karl silenced a groan as he looked at the spotless white walls. The purpose of the washing was not to clean the walls, but to teach discipline and appreciation for work . . . Tatsuo had told him that. He longed to object, to tell Hiro that he would rather batter the punching board or run with Harras and Prinz, anything but wash walls. But the cloth was waiting for him by the door and Hiro was already sweeping the floor, an expression of peaceful satisfaction on his face. Karl heard a tuneless whistle behind him and turned to see Tatsuo, the sleeves of his keiko-gi rolled up as he swished a wet cloth over the end wall. Silently, Karl gathered up his pail and cloth and joined Tatsuo, his wet keiko-gi sticking uncomfortably to his back.

If this is discipline, he thought, then I will never learn. He wrung the water from the cloth and began copying Tatsuo's circular strokes. Before long he had joined Tatsuo in a tuneless whistle, his discomfort and damp keiko-gi forgotten and the white walls seemed brighter from his efforts.

"You and Tatsuo have done an excellent job," Hiro said as Karl emptied the bucket. "We work well together."

"In harmony, sensei?" Karl asked.

"Yes, in harmony," Hiro replied.

When school resumed after the long holiday, Karl adjusted his training schedule to fit around his study periods. It was difficult at first, and he found his head drooping with weariness shortly after supper, but he soon became accustomed to the rigorous program. With each passing day, he became stronger, more disciplined, and his mind more alert. His efforts began to show in his school work, with marked improvement in every subject. His reading habits suffered initially because his time was limited but eventually his speed increased, and out of necessity he found he could read almost twice as fast and comprehend more readily. This, along with his innate curiosity and insatiable appetite for knowledge, placed him well above his classmates and in step with Tatsuo, who progressed even more rapidly.

At the end of January, Conrad finally arrived home, over a month late. It was early Saturday morning, and expecting everyone at Drachenschlucht to be asleep, Conrad was startled when he met Karl at the front door. Behind Karl, the dogs growled an uncertain welcome.

"Father! We didn't know when to expect you."

"That's what happens when a business expands. There was much to attend to."

"I'm glad you're back," Karl said politely.

"You've grown." Conrad tapped him lightly on the shoulder, noticing how hard it felt.

Karl wanted to say that he had missed him, but the words stuck in his throat. Instead he turned and started out the door.

"Where are you off to so early in the morning, Karl?"

"I run five miles every morning, Father, and then I practice in the dojo for an hour with Mr. Takezawa and Tatsuo."

Conrad's expression hardened. "What do you practice?"

"I'm just conditioning my body right now, but soon I will start training in the martial arts."

"I can see that you have not heeded my advice about the Takezawas, have you?"

Karl's face clouded over. He did not answer his father.

"I'm too tired to discuss it now, but we will talk later."

"Yes, Father."

As Karl descended the porch steps, Conrad called after him. "Karl, I have something for you if you're interested."

The tension in Karl's face lessened, but his eyes still remained distant. "Is that the surprise Mother told me about?"

"I think you will be pleased. We'll take a look at it later."

With a quick wave of his hand, Karl disappeared down the

street. Conrad stood at the door, listening to the receding footsteps crunching evenly through the snow.

Dorothea met him in the hallway. "Conrad! I didn't expect you home today."

Conrad removed his coat and flung it on the chair. "The business has grown so much in the past few months . . . it's unfortunate Karl isn't older. I could use him."

"Yes, I'm sure you could," Dorothea said.

Conrad looked up quickly, searching for signs of sarcasm. Dorothea's face remained smooth and expressionless, the way she willed it to be.

"You're too thin, Dorothea, and pale. I suppose you're still picking at those half-cooked vegetables of yours. Now that I'm home, maybe you'll eat some good red meat. Tell Mrs. Lange to cook up some thick steaks for dinner."

"You look tired," said Dorothea quietly.

"I am."

"The children missed you at Christmas."

"I'll make it up to them. Where's Lisl? I bought her the finest doll I could find."

"She's still in her room. Take the doll up to her and surprise her."

"Speaking of surprises, I want to show Karl his as soon as I shower and change my clothes."

"I'll tell him as soon as he returns."

"You're still condoning his association with the Takezawas, aren't you?"

"They are fine people, Conrad. I have no reason to discourage his friendship with them."

Conrad's face was instantly tight with anger, and his blue eyes sparkled dangerously. "Well, the boat I've bought for him is bound to distract him."

"He's very dedicated to his training, and I doubt that anything will distract him."

"We shall see about that!"

"Conrad, please don't try to stop him from carrying on with his training."

"I told you, I don't want those goddamn Japs influencing my son's thinking."

"But it's a good influence. Karl has matured immeasurably," Dorothea explained.

"He's just growing up. His maturity has nothing to do with

Hiro Takezawa," Conrad retorted. "Just make sure the boy is ready to go with me by noon."

Dorothea stood watching Conrad ascend the stairs, then, with a sigh, she made her way to the kitchen to give Mrs. Lange her instructions. She gagged at the thought of the dripping steak she would have to force herself to eat; recently, even vegetables had lost their appeal.

By noon, Karl was ready to accompany his father. "Mother said we're going to the docks."

"That's right. You'll need a warm coat."

"Did you buy a new ship?"

"Still impatient as ever, aren't you? Well this is a surprise, and you'll just have to wait until we get there."

The sharp wind off the ocean whipped a thin layer of snow into their faces. They walked quickly to a tightly packed group of boats huddled against the wooden pier, rocking in the choppy waves that beat against their hulls. Admiring the boats, Karl lagged behind his father. He looked up to see Conrad jump nimbly onto the deck of a blue and white vessel secured to a group of pilings. The paint was obviously new, the deck was spotless, and the dials were polished to a mirrored gleam.

"Do you like this one, Karl?" Conrad asked.

"She's a beauty. Was she a fishing boat at one time?" Karl asked as he looked her over carefully.

"Yes, but there's not much left of her former self."

Karl walked slowly around the boat, examining the small white lifeboat hanging at the stern, the two silver foghorns and spotlight on the top of the wheelhouse, and finally the newly constructed living quarters. He imagined himself poised behind the wheel. "Do you think we can take her out?" he asked cautiously.

Conrad untied the ropes and pushed off with his powerful legs. "Yes, I think you should have the opportunity to learn how to operate your own boat. One day you'll have a whole fleet to run for us."

For an instant Karl was stunned. "You mean this is my boat? This is my surprise?"

Conrad nodded. "She's all yours. I picked her up in Seattle and had her refitted and painted. She's still called the *Cathy B*—it's bad luck to change the name of a ship—but everything else is new.

The engine started readily, and in a few moments Conrad steered the *Cathy B* carefully through the close line of boats and out of the small harbor. The waves rose higher as soon as they were in the open water, but the boat pushed through easily and headed toward the First Narrows, and then to the open sea at three-quarter speed.

"This boat was built for people who make their living on the sea, Karl. She's thirty-six feet long, and with her new diesel engine, you could probably take her across the Pacific if you wanted to. There's a new compass and a ship-to-shore radio as well."

"She's perfect, Father."

"Take the wheel, Karl. Head north toward Howe Sound and then circle around Bowen Island."

The knuckles on Karl's hands turned white as he gripped the wheel. At his father's suggestion, he tried some turning maneuvers, altering the speed to get a feel for the boat; the *Cathy B* responded quickly and effortlessly.

"Straighten her out, Karl, and then head by the lighthouse on Point Atkinson. When we get back, I want you to study the charts of these waters and all the navigational markers. You'll have to learn how to read them properly."

Karl nodded, not taking his eyes off the water ahead.

"The cabin sleeps eight and the galley is well equipped," Conrad continued. "The fuel tanks are large enough to power several weeks of steady cruising. After you learn to operate her, you can take a couple of friends for a cruise."

"I'd like to take Tatsuo."

"He wasn't the friend I had in mind," Conrad said sharply.

Karl's hands tightened on the wheel, and he held back the words that threatened to spill out. The *Cathy B* was like a dream come true—a boat of his own. Excitement had swelled inside him until his father burst the bubble. Why couldn't he take Tatsuo with him? He would rather not go if Tatsuo couldn't come, but how could he tell his father that? Suddenly a thought occurred to him. Perhaps by summer his father would be gone again on another one of his extended business trips, and then he would be free to take Tatsuo aboard the *Cathy B* as often as he wanted. With boyish optimism, he grinned and increased the speed of the sturdy boat, steering her through the channel.

"Don't be overconfident, Karl—you've got a lot to learn yet. One day you'll be part of the Richter Shipping Line.

Learn as much as you can now about ships and what holds our business together. I don't want you to go into it blindly, like I did. And don't waste time on the Japanese hocus-pocus."

"How old were you when you went to sea, Father?"

"Not much older than you are now."

Karl had never heard his father speak of his childhood or his years at sea, and he turned to look at him with interest.

"It won't be long before you'll be working on our freighters," Conrad mused almost to himself. "It's not easy work." For the next hour they talked comfortably as Karl put the *Cathy B* through her paces. When they approached Coal Harbor, Karl gave the wheel to his father.

Conrad eased the boat alongside the dock. "Before next summer, I want you to know every last nut and fitting on this boat. Don't plan on too many other activities; I don't think you'll have time for much else."

Thoughtfully, Karl ran his fingers over the polished mahogany interior. The boat was not a gift, it was a bribe. He realized that now. But it was his boat, and although the initial excitement had disappeared, much of the joy of ownership remained. The *Cathy B* belonged to him, and she was undoubtedly the most beautiful boat in the world. Somehow he would find time to learn all about her and still not give up his training. He remembered the night in the dimly lit dojo and the promise he had made to Hiro and to himself, a promise that he would never break. He would not abandon his training, and he would not give up his quest to be the master of his own nature.

After the cabin door was locked and the ropes secured, Conrad dropped the keys into Karl's hand. "She's all yours, Karl. Take care of her."

"Thank you, Father. I will."

The streets were glistening from the melting snow and lights were coming on as they drove home to Drachenschlucht. Father and son sat now in an uneasy silence.

I've been away too long, Conrad thought. The boy is like a stranger to me. He glanced over at the youthful face, closed and unreadable under the artificial lights of the city.

"I'm glad you like the boat, Karl. Not many boys your age own a boat like that one."

"I didn't think I ever would, either."

"Well, I have plans for you."

After a few moments, Karl said, "I know, Father."

On Sunday morning, before the sun was even near the horizon, Karl was out running along the five-mile route that he hoped to conquer within the allotted thirty minutes. All else forgotten—push harder, make those legs move faster, push, run. If nothing else, he had learned to concentrate, to think of nothing but the task at hand. Whenever his mind wavered, he lost time and his goal became more elusive, but when he concentrated, his legs moved faster. When he came to the last corner, he focused all his energy and sprinted toward the distant figure waiting patiently on the steps of the Takezawa home. When he reached the finish line, he slowed down to an easy trot and circled the driveway several times before resting on the stairs. Perspiration trickled down his forehead, but his breathing was even. He took several deep breaths and then smiled up at Hiro.

"You're getting faster, Karl," Hiro said.

"But not fast enough."

"Did you see your father before you left?"

"No, he wasn't up."

Hiro studied Karl for a moment. He placed a firm hand on his shoulder and said gently, "Then we had better not waste time." He led the way to the dojo, where Tatsuo was already punching and kicking the padded practice board with balanced precision. As usual, his eyes never left the board and his forehead was moist with perspiration.

Following Hiro's direction, Karl began his exercises, stretching his muscles further than ever before, feeling newfound strength surge through him. Soon his keiko-gi became drenched and still he continued, enjoying the power of his own momentum. When his muscles finally began to ache, he assumed the full lotus position and waited quietly, breathing deeply and evenly, until Hiro sat down in front of him.

"Today, Karl, I do not want you to count. Just leave your mind empty. Try to feel the emptiness, touch it."

Karl closed his eyes and struggled to quiet his reeling mind. "It's very difficult to do."

"Breathe deeply," Hiro instructed, "and with each breath fill your mind with the sound of nothing, of *mu*. Say it to yourself—mu. Stretch it out with each breath until it fills your lungs, your tanden, and your spirit."

Karl drew in his breath, concentrating on the strange word

until his mind became quiet, dark; he felt as if he were floating and turning slowly. Time ceased to exist, there was only silence and the soothing caress of nothingness until he felt a hand on his shoulder drawing him back to the dojo. Karl opened his eyes with difficulty.

"What happened? Was I asleep?" He stared at Hiro questioningly.

"You did not sleep, but you did free your mind for a precious instant. Continue to meditate at home every day, and when you are ready I will show you the next step. Proceed carefully and only do what I have shown you."

"Yes, sensei."

After Karl had left, Tatsuo asked solemnly, "Do you think he found the Ox today, Oji-san?"

Hiro shook his head and smiled. "No, but I think he glimpsed the tail, and now he will seek even harder. Help him when you can, Tatsuo. Answer his questions."

The next morning Hiro dressed apprehensively. The new suit made by the tailor that Fenton had found lay on the chair waiting for him. He suppressed his desire to hang it back in the closet and to put on his comfortable, familiar old clothes. He recalled Fenton's words as the tailor measured him.

"Mr. Takezawa, in this suit you will be a new man."

He did not want to be a new man. A wave of homesickness for the craggy shores of Japan and for the familiar faces of his family and old friends washed over him.

The pants of the suit were snug but not uncomfortable, the vest followed the contours of his powerful chest, and the jacket fell perfectly from his tapered shoulders. He knotted the tie carefully and placed a watch into the small vest pocket, then fastened the gold chain to the appropriate loop. Hiro glanced at himself in the mirror. He did look different! "Yes, that is much better." He squared his shoulders and walked quickly to the dining room.

"Eat your breakfast, Tatsuo. You will be late for school," Miyoko chided as she hovered over him.

"Oba-san, you worry too much. I have never been late yet." His voice was teasing with underlying love.

When Hiro entered the room, Tatsuo's spoon clanged against the table and fell to the floor.

"What is wrong? Do I frighten you that much?"

"Ojī-san!" Tatsuo breathed. "You look like Emperor Taisho. Where did you get those clothes?"

"Mr. Fenton took me to a tailor and this is the result."

"You look very elegant, my husband," Miyoko said.

Maiko was busy at her desk when Hiro arrived at the office. She noted his new clothes with approval before presenting him with the schedule for the day.

"Before you begin, Mr. Takezawa, Mr. Richter would like to see you. He said that he would wait for you in his office."

"Thank you, Maiko. Is Mr. Fenton in yet?"

"Yes, he was here before me this morning. He hasn't taken his nose out of those reports since I arrived."

"Good! Tell him I will be back shortly."

Patricia pointed to Conrad's closed door. "Go right in, Mr. Takezawa. He's expecting you."

Hiro knocked at the door and walked in.

Conrad stood up and welcomed him with an outstretched hand. "I see you've made some changes while I was away." he said, noticing Hiro's new suit. Without waiting for a reply, he handed Hiro three glossy photographs. "These are the three ships I told you about. I will be taking possession of them in a few weeks. One of them is oil-fired, which should be quite an improvement."

"Oil-fired?"

"They are far more efficient, although the initial cost is considerably more than the coal burners. Fueling is far easier, and we can operate with a smaller crew."

"They look like fine vessels," Hiro said, examining the photographs.

"I've arranged for Captain Angus Taylor to take command of this one," Conrad said, pointing to the oil-fired ship. "He's the best skipper I have. He was a little reluctant to leave the S.S. *Hudson*, but I assured him he could have her back if he didn't feel comfortable with the new one. I doubt very much he'll want her back after he's sailed on the new ship."

"You have chosen the right man," Hiro agreed. On the voyage to Vancouver he had had plenty of opportunity to witness Captain Taylor's skill and easy air of authority.

"Have there been any new developments during my absence?" Conrad asked.

"Everything is progressing well. Except for a few minor delays, the shipments have all arrived on schedule. The zaibatsu is pleased. I will notify them about the addition of the three new ships. I am sure they will be anxious to make use of them as soon as possible.''

"Miss Harley has informed me that you have hired an assistant, a former employee of the Federal Bank, I understand.''

"Yes, his name is Patrick Fenton.''

"Has he had experience in the shipping business?''

"No, but he is intelligent and I have faith in his ability to learn quickly. I have already been able to delegate some of my work to him.''

"Isn't he awfully young?''

"Perhaps, but in the last few months he has been forced to mature quickly.'' Hiro stood up to leave. "I would like to thank you for the kindness afforded to my grandson,'' he added. "Karl has invited him to go cruising aboard his new boat and has assured me that you are willing to teach him the rudiments of boating. I am grateful, for I am not a sailor.''

Before Conrad could react, Hiro was gone. Karl had deliberately disobeyed him, and Conrad seethed with anger. He would not allow his son to maneuver him like this ever again; Karl would have to be disciplined.

Patrick Fenton settled into the affairs of Pacific Far Eastern Trading easily and completely. His sixth sense for figures had become an immeasurable asset to Hiro and the zaibatsu. Because of his intense interest and growing loyalty to Hiro, Patrick learned quickly, and as his world expanded, so did his tolerance and understanding of people. A mutual respect developed between Hiro and Patrick, one which allowed them to share ideas, experiences, and even dreams. They did this periodically over a glass of sake or a cup of the bitter green tea that Hiro drank every afternoon. Patrick barely tolerated the rank, steaming liquid, preferring his familiar black coffee laced with sugar. Often Cyrus Wilson joined them, interjecting his ribald stories into serious discussions. They both welcomed his frequent visits.

The weeks turned into months, and before long, winter was only a memory, replaced by the warm spring sunshine and refreshing ocean winds. Patrick encouraged Hiro to shorten his long hours at the office, to leave to him the mundane routines of checking shipments, answering correspondence, and the myriad tasks that needed attention each day. Hiro objected at first, but gradually, as the sun became warmer, his longing to work in the garden increased, and he conceded to working shorter hours. Patrick scoffed at Hiro's concern about his own peaked appearance, claiming that he had always been thin and pale, a trait he had inherited from his mother. But it was true that he often spent his weekends in the office, pouring over shipping contracts, and since much of the correspondence from the zaibatsu was in Japanese, he began studying that too.

Maiko assisted him in his studies, often staying late to help him. Women had always intimidated Patrick, but he was relaxed with the graceful, soft-spoken Maiko. Her gentle yet spirited manner intrigued him, for she represented neither the rigid women of his childhood nor the giggling featherbrained girls he had attempted to get to know in his early years. She remained slightly reserved with Patrick, and only on occasion would she burst into laughter at his strained attempts to speak Japanese. Patrick doubted whether he would ever be proficient in Japanese, but he did hope that he would learn enough to be able to decipher the correspondence from the Tokyo office.

Maiko assured him that he was doing very well. "At least you will be able to order a cup of coffee when you go to Japan."

"You mean I won't have to drink that terrible green soup you call tea?"

"If you promise not to tell," Maiko whispered, "I will make a confession."

Patrick shook his head solemnly, sparks of laughter glinting in his eyes.

"I cannot stand tea either. It took me so long to learn the proper way to conduct a tea ceremony that I became saturated with tea! I only pretend to like it because all honorable Japanese ladies drink tea. I much prefer coffee."

Patrick let out a loud whoop of laughter and slapped the desk with the palm of his hand. "No wonder you are always too busy to have tea with Mr. Takezawa."

When the sun had melted the frost and softened the soil, Hiro hired six gardeners and two carpenters to reshape the grounds around his home. The garden was the embodiment of a dream, a quiet retreat that would shield him from the outside world. For it he carefully chose special rocks from the neighboring mountains; one particularly large stone which he found by the ocean had to be cut into several smaller pieces and later reassembled. Some rocks were partially buried to give them a rooted effect for strength, while others were meticulously arranged into groups and patterns of beautiful simplicity. The shrubs and trees came next, chosen for their graceful foliage and color, and were carefully transplanted under the watchful eye of the master. Tall cedars surrounded the entire garden, shielding it from intruders. Feathery spruce trees lined a pebbled path which led to an oval-shaped pond, while a miniature red maple spread its delicate branches over a partially concealed waterfall. A shrine was erected in one corner of the garden, and Miyoko planted roses and flowering shrubbery on either side of it. A giant oak grew close to the house, and Hiro instructed the carpenters to build benches around its base. A honeysuckle that had encased one side of the house was trimmed and rejuvenated along with the English ivy that grew over the front. The results of all this labor pleased Hiro, for it reminded him of the garden he had left behind in Japan and yet it possessed its own unique personality. It was aesthetically pleasing, as he had intended it to be, and charming to even the most discriminate gardener, but most of all it evoked a feeling of tranquility. As the garden grew and changed color, it became more beautiful in its symmetry, and finally, when birds and small animals began to make it their home, Hiro's dream was complete.

[7]

"You're not eating this morning?" Conrad asked.

"No, I'm not hungry." Dorothea stirred her coffee listlessly.

"What's the matter with you? You look pale, washed-out."

Before Dorothea could reply, the door opened and Karl walked in. His shirt, ringed with perspiration, stuck to him, and his hair was dark with wetness. There was a smudge of dirt under his left cheek where he had wiped away the drops.

"Where the hell have you been?" Conrad demanded. "You're late for breakfast again."

"I've been out running. Sorry. I didn't mean to interrupt. I thought Mother was alone."

"You're not interrupting, Karl," Dorothea said. "Go and clean up. Breakfast is still warm enough to be edible." She indicated the covered warming trays on the sideboard.

Karl grinned and winked at Dorothea before closing the door behind him, but he noticed her pallor and the dark circles under her eyes. His forehead creased with concern as he bounded up the stairs three at a time, and the uneasiness stayed with him through the pelting shower. As he struggled into his clothes, he wondered if his mother was ill. Illness and dying were remote to him, something he rarely thought about; in fact, the only time he ever considered the matter was when Tatsuo mentioned his parents or when the priests discussed death at school. As if to remind him he was still hungry, his stomach rumbled and the thought of food temporarily dispelled the worry from his mind. He ran a brush quickly through his wet hair before hurrying downstairs.

Conrad watched his son wolf down the food, unaware he was being observed. Karl's hands had become broad and his knuckles prominent; his wrists had thickened, and blond hair covered his arms. His face, too, had lost its softness, with obvious signs of maturity showing on his chin and upper lip.

He'll need a razor soon, Conrad thought, and new shirts. The seams were cutting into his shoulders.

"How much do you weigh, Karl?"

Karl looked up from his breakfast, surprised. "About a hundred and fifty. I've been running quite a bit, so I haven't gained too much. Why?"

"I just wondered. You've grown."

"I guess the exercises I've been doing have added a few muscles."

"You're still at that?"

Karl shifted uneasily in his chair. "Yes, but I've kept up with my schoolwork, too."

"Your mother informs me of that constantly," Conrad replied derisively without looking at Dorothea. "Have you had time to study the navigational charts I gave you?"

"Yes, I've gone over them pretty thoroughly, and there are only a couple of things I haven't figured out yet. I've studied the engine, too, and I think I can handle the maintenance myself."

"Well then, I guess it's time for a trial run. We'll take the *Cathy B* over to Salt Spring Island and Victoria next week. Make sure she's fueled up and ready to go." Conrad dropped his napkin on the table and strode from the room.

Karl looked at Dorothea. "I've made other plans for the weekend."

"I think you should cancel them, Karl. This boat is very important to your father."

"Don't I know that! I guess it wouldn't be wise to ask Tatsuo to come along this time, would it?"

"No, Karl, not this time." Sensing his disappointment, she added, "There will be other times."

Karl looked down at his empty plate and nodded, then a smile began to spread across his face. "The *Cathy B* is a beauty, Mother. Next summer you'll have to come on a cruise with us. She cuts through the water like a dream!" His eyes shone.

"I'm looking forward to it, Karl, but it's been a long time since I've been on a boat."

"I promise you'll love it. Tatsuo and I have great plans for the *Cathy B.*"

"Mr. Takezawa has invited me to see his garden today. Would you walk over there with me?" Dorothea asked.

Karl stood up solemnly and with an exaggerated flourish removed an imaginary hat and bowed low. "My dear, it will be a pleasure to escort such a beautiful lady."

Dorothea carried on the game and curtsied equally low. "You are so kind, sir. Please fetch me my cloak."

"Can I come too?" Lisl stood in the doorway, her long hair gleaming from a recent brushing and her eyes wide with anticipation.

"I said I would escort a beautiful lady, not a witch," Karl said, his face still serious but a smile hovering at the corners of his mouth.

"Oh shut up, Karl! You're not exactly Prince Charming."

"But Tatsuo is, isn't he, little sister?" Karl teased, the smile finally breaking.

Lisl flashed a menacing look. "That's none of your business!"

The garden was cool and peaceful. Except for the sunlight slanting through the trees, the world was forgotten within the perimeter of cedars that surrounded the garden. Lisl, Dorothea, and Hiro walked slowly along the winding pathways while Karl and Tatsuo stretched out on the grass under a giant oak tree. There were no flowers to provide a blaze of color, only rocks, moss, shrubs, trees, and water. Each object seemed to flow one into the other, yet each displayed a beauty of its own according to its shape, size, placement, and color. Even the wood in the tiny bridge spanning the pond was left in its natural state, its graceful arch partially hidden by a budding maple tree. Beneath the bridge, water rippled over rocks whose crevices were already softened by thick green moss. Beyond the bridge stood the shrine, set within an an enclosure of flowering shrubs.

"I feel as though I am in another world, like the one I lived in as a small child . . . picnics in the forest by narrow streams and treks in alpine meadows. You have transformed this garden into . . . into . . ."—Dorothea searched for the right word—". . . you have transformed this garden into a symphony."

"Your eyes see one thing, but your spirit feels something else. That is why it reminds you of forests and meadows. I wanted to capture the shibui spirit of the Zen masters. I see by your reaction that I was successful." Hiro looked pleased.

Even the naturally exuberant Lisl was subdued by the peacefulness of the garden. "Who would have thought that rocks could be so beautiful or that you could have a garden without flowers," she exclaimed with wonderment.

The Japanese people believe rocks are symbols of the beauty and grandeur of nature. Their beauty lies in their naturalness," Hiro said.

"More reflections of shibui spirit?" Dorothea asked.

Hiro nodded and led them along a pebbled path to an area concealed from the rest of the garden by sloping lawns and shrubbery interspaced by pines. Here the master's hand was most certainly evident. It was a dry landscape garden, twenty-five feet long and fifteen feet wide, covered by white sand and carefully raked into distinct flowing patterns. Around the outer edge was a walkway of dark flat stones; inside, on the combed sand, were strategically placed islandlike rocks.

"Look carefully," Hiro said. "How many rocks do you see?"

Dorothea counted the rocks. "I can see eleven."

"But, Mother, I only see nine," Lisl said with surprise.

"Now let us move to a different vantage point," Hiro instructed.

"But of course! Now I see only nine,"

"And I can see twelve from here," Lisl called.

"Actually there are fifteen rocks," Hiro explained. "But they are arranged in such a way that some always remain hidden from any vantage point. This garden is yet another gift from the ancient Zen teachers. It represents the mysteries of life."

Dorothea walked around the perimeter slowly, her face thoughtful as she struggled to understand the complexities of the landscape.

"Do not force yourself to understand the meaning, just enjoy its beauty. Listen carefully and it will speak to you."

"My dear and wise friend, I have so much to learn," Dorothea admitted.

"Just as we all do," Hiro agreed. "As we learn about the mysteries of life, these rocks will change because we change, and they will grow as we grow. I would be honored if you would come here often even while we are away.''

"You are going away?'' Dorothea was suddenly frightened.

"Yes, we are going to Japan for the Bon Festival and to visit the graves of Hitoshi and Yuri. It is the Festival of the Dead. They are said to return to earth during this season, and it is customary to decorate their graves for the occasion.''

"Every year?''

"No, only the first year and then after three years, seven years, and finally thirteen years. We do this to commemorate their lives as well as their deaths.''

"Of course you must go, but I will be sad when you and Miyoko leave. I will miss you all.'' Dorothea's throat constricted as she looked across the expanse of garden toward the oak tree where Karl and Tatsuo lay. "You have become part of my family.''

"As you and your children have become part of my family,'' Hiro replied. He put his hand on Lisl's shoulder and pulled her against him.

They retraced their steps toward the house, where Miyoko had tea and rice cakes waiting. When they passed the shrine, Dorothea stopped and ran her fingers over the ornate carvings. She looked at Hiro with an apologetic expression.

"God is very real to me. Ever since Karl began practicing and meditating with you, I have read a great deal about Zen teachings and the Buddhist faith, but I am lost. I admire the principles and ideals, but the Christian faith is very deeply embedded within me and I find it hard to accept anything else.''

"One may study for a lifetime without ever reconciling the western and eastern faiths, but that does not mean they are not both correct. After much searching, I began to understand each religion as a way or path. Some are better, quicker, more sublime, while others demand great courage and self-discipline. But they all share one thing—the way we conduct our lives is perhaps the most important aspect of any religion.''

Dorothea watched Hiro's peaceful composed face. "You seem so unafraid, as though the world's problems never touch you.''

"It is not that I am untouched by the world—it affects me very deeply. It is only that I try to discipline myself to practice the noble truths that Buddha taught: self-control, humility. generosity, mercy, and love. Sometimes even I, who have lived long and practiced the Buddhist faith all my life, find these ideals difficult to live up to. But Buddha also taught that even the humblest of men can eventually find the truth and ultimate salvation. It is these truths that I am imparting to Karl and Tatsuo through our practice of the martial arts and Zen meditation. When we finally learn these truths, we will be in harmony with the world."

"I am surprised how readily Karl has accepted your teachings," Dorothea said.

"I do not teach him what to believe, only how to live in harmony and to strive for perfection. I have not discussed creation or God with Karl, but I feel that he has already given it a great deal of thought, just as Tatsuo has."

"It must be very difficult for Tatsuo to understand the Christian teachings at school," Dorothea said, compassion in her eyes.

"I think the hardest thing for Tatsuo was to reconcile the divisions in the western faith, to think in terms of absolute truth or total error, to divide all things into good and evil. He has been taught that all men are fundamentally good, and the Christian faith teaches that all men are sinners and damned unless they are saved by faith. This is very alien to him." Hiro knelt down and straightened a branch on a new shrub, propping it up with the dark soil.

"From the moment Karl returned from Japan, I knew a special bond had formed between him and Tatsuo. I found it hard to believe a friendship could develop so quickly between two boys from opposite sides of the world," Dorothea mused.

"It is not so strange, really. Tatsuo was taught the Buddha nature, and he recognized it instinctively in Karl. Spiritually, everyone is equal—every race, color, nationality—they are of no importance. Everyone has a Buddha nature." Hiro was thoughtful for a moment and then added, "Perhaps this idealistic philosophy might have worn thin for both of them when problems began to arise, but you see, they are so secure in each other's friendship, the world does not seem to affect them.

Dorothea stopped and turned to Hiro. "Promise me that you will continue teaching them, and I will tell them all I know and feel about my Christian faith. They will perceive the differences themselves and find their own course."

"You have my promise," Hiro replied without hesitation.

Lisl had become tired of their conversation and had gone to join the boys. Dorothea could hear her laughing in the distance. Karl and Tatsuo were attempting handstands and failing, mainly because they were trying to do them with a soccer ball held between their knees. Lisl's laughter spurred them on.

"You will wear yourself out," Tatsuo said. "Oji-san said that we have a long session ahead of us today."

"Hey, pal, I never get tired. I'm as strong as a horse. Just look at these muscles." Karl stood up and assumed a Herculean pose.

"You are not going to use those muscles today; you are going to use the thick muscle between your ears," Tatsuo said from his prone position on the ground.

Lisl lay beside him, one slender leg casually against his. Tatsuo tried to ignore her, but the scent of her hair and the teasing glint in her eyes gave him an odd feeling in the pit of his stomach. He noticed how narrow her waist had become, and how her sweater rose when she took a deep breath.

"Didn't you know?" Lisl taunted. "Karl has been practicing thrusts and kicks against imaginary enemies so hard that his pea-brain has been shaken loose."

Karl feigned a lunge at her; she squealed and moved closer to Tatsuo for protection. She could feel Tatsuo's warm breath on her cheek, and when she looked at him, her heart suddenly began to beat faster. "I think I better go find Mother."

Tatsuo helped Lisl to her feet, and his hand lingered on hers. He knew that his face was becoming flushed and hoped Karl wouldn't notice.

In the dojo, both boys undressed and carefully folded their clothing.

Tatsuo shook his head as he looked at Karl's penis with unabashed interest. "How come yours is so big?"

Karl laughed. "It's a family trait. Also, I know the secret to make it grow."

"Secret! What secret?"

Karl's face became serious as he whispered, "Well, every morning you have to pull it twenty-four times and at night you have to pull it twenty-six times."

"Would that work for me?" Tatsuo asked, suppressing a smile.

"Sure it would," Karl said solemnly. "But you have to be very careful to do it exactly twenty-four times in the morning and twenty-six times at night, otherwise it will become long and skinny." He ducked as a shoe sailed past his head.

"Bring your cushions to the garden!" Hiro commanded. He wore a long black robe tied at the waist with a silver cord. In his hand was a kendo fighting stick. To Karl, the sensei looked unfamiliar, but Tatsuo followed him calmly to the dry landscape garden.

Hiro tapped the stone walkway with his stick. "Sit here, Karl. Tatsuo, please sit here." He indicated a spot for Tatsuo several yards away. After they had assumed the kekka fuza position, he continued, "Now study the rocks and let your minds and bodies relax before we begin." He waited until both boys were quiet.

"If you are to become masters of the Shizen Ryu Kempo, you must seek not only physical discipline and perfection, but spiritual as well." Again he paused.

Karl became restless and lifted his head to ease the discomfort. Instantly Hiro's oak stick thudded loudly on the rocks behind him.

"No movement! Breathe properly as you have been taught. Think of nothing except your breathing. Sit forward, Karl, and exert more pressure on your tanden. Tatsuo, sit forward a little more!" His penetrating voice forced them to concentrate.

Karl adjusted his position on the cushion, and soon his breathing became controlled and even. The minutes passed slowly and stretched into hours. The air became cooler, the garden fell silent; time was meaningless. Karl felt bathed in a soft light, aware only that he was hovering in a state previously unknown to him. Eventually the sky, dark now, came into focus, and the shadowed rocks became visible. He heard Hiro's soft footsteps behind him and then the heavy crash of his stick. Karl tried to resume the even breathing, but his eyes burned, his body ached with stiffness, and the sound of a nearby cricket hammered in his ears. He tried to shut his mind to the shrill persistence of the insect as it reverberated in the hollowness of his senses. Again the stick crashed down behind him and his body jumped involuntarily.

"Remember, Karl, people do not lack strength, they merely lack will," the sensei admonished in a more familiar voice.

Karl's legs were numb; pain from his back reached forward

into his stomach, and his head felt detached from the rest of his body. He struggled to still his mind, concentrating on the words Hiro was softly repeating.

"Abiding nowhere, let your mind work."

The peaceful mood Karl had felt earlier did not return; the pain became more intense, and tears of wretched frustration threatened in his eyes. The sharp clapping of hands seared the stillness, and he saw the sensei standing directly in front of him.

"You may stand up now." From the sound of his voice, Karl knew he was pleased. When he tried to stand, his legs buckled and he moaned softly as he fell. Tatsuo rushed forward to help, but Hiro's raised oak stick stopped him short, and Tatsuo looked down helplessly.

"He will get up himself, or he will not get up at all!"

Karl felt awkward as he struggled to his feet, pushing himself up with his hands before straightening his legs. His knees wobbled, but he clenched his teeth until he could stand upright. He looked up at Hiro, his eyes shining in the evening dusk.

"You did well, tomodachi," Hiro said in a voice that sounded like the deep chords of a piano.

"I saw a light in the darkness," Karl whispered. "I felt nothing and yet there was something . . . warm, floating . . . as if I was no longer in this garden. But the cricket,"—he looked around blankly, "the noise from the cricket nearly broke my eardrums and I couldn't get that feeling back again."

Hiro touched him lightly with his stick. "Do not let the sound of a tiny cricket defeat you. Come, it is late. I will drive you home."

"Late? What time is it?" Karl asked, suddenly aware that it was dark.

"It is ten o'clock. We have been here for almost eight hours," Tatsuo replied.

"You have had a unique and beautiful experience, Karl," Hiro added. "I have the feeling, tomodachi, that tonight you have seen the Ox."

In the darkness, Karl smiled with new understanding.

On the drive back to Drachenschlucht, Karl leaned back against the seat of the sleek Studebaker. "I would like to try again, soon, before I forget."

"You will not forget," Hiro assured him. "You went on a

very special journey today, one that you do not yet fully understand, but you will soon. You freed your mind and traveled where few others have gone. I believe you have experienced what the masters call pure existence. You have had a glimpse of your true nature.''

"But I want to learn to control that feeling!"

"Do not be impatient. The journey has just begun for you. We will spend many hours in meditation.''

"O ya sumi nasai," Karl said as he climbed from the car.

"Good night, Karl. Sleep well." There was a look of tenderness on the disciplined face of the master.

The balmy spring days lengthened with the approach of summer. The Richter freighters, fulfilling the demands of the zaibatsu, crossed the Pacific with regularity, their holds filled to capacity. The officials of the zaibatsu were more than satisfied with their arrangement, as was Conrad Richter, and both parties prospered.

One evening as Karl and Tatsuo kicked a soccer ball back and forth, Karl announced, "I can handle the *Cathy B* well enough to take it out on my own now. Let's go for a cruise before you leave for Japan."

"We will be leaving on July nineteenth. Grandfather made the final arrangements. We'll be away for four weeks."

The ball ricocheted unheeded off Karl's leg as he looked inquiringly at Tatsuo. "Hey, you don't look very happy! Don't you want to go to Japan?"

Tatsuo shrugged. "Sure I want to go." He threw the ball with driving force against the ground and watched it bounce high into the air. "But there is nothing in Japan for me now . . . graves, lost friends. This is my home now."

"Well, you're not going there to stay, so what are you worrying about?"

"I don't know. It is just that every once in a while my grandfather reminds me of my duties to the zaibatsu."

"So what? Wouldn't you like to be rich?" Karl looked at Tatsuo and instantly regretted his flippancy.

"In Japan, I would be expected to think like a man and to shoulder the responsibilities of a man, even now. I guess I am afraid of what I might have to do for them." He tucked the ball under his arm and tackled Karl, but he wasn't quite quick enough. Karl stepped aside and Tatsuo flew by him, hitting the ground with a thud. They rolled and tumbled, yelling with contrived pain until the anxious barking and interference of the dogs stopped them. They lay with heaving chests on the grass, their faces averted from the wet, affectionate tongues of Harras and Prinz.

"Grandfather has a surprise for you, but you will have to wait until tomorrow morning," Tatsuo announced.

"Tell me now. I hate waiting!"

"I think you will be at our house very early tomorrow morning. Patience is not one of your virtues."

The next morning Karl arrived at the courtyard of the Takezawa residence thirty-five minutes ahead of schedule.

"You are early this morning, Karl," Hiro remarked.

Karl continued walking to slow his breathing and stole a glance at Tatsuo's grinning face. Karl returned the knowing smile and followed Hiro into the dojo.

"You are doing well," Hiro said after Karl had completed the stretching and exercise routine. "Today you will practice something new." Hiro removed a white belt from a nearby shelf and placed it in Karl's hands. Tatsuo stood behind Hiro —his friend's surprised expression had been worth waiting for.

"For the next year," Hiro continued, "you will wear the advanced white belt. You must now strive even harder for physical and spiritual discipline, for when you have mastered these, you will be better enabled to exemplify the three primary virtues of the samurai—valor, wisdom, and benevolence." Hiro spoke softly, but his voice echoed in the dojo. "The stance is very important. It is the starting point for all your movements." Hiro demonstrated the proper position of the feet and hands; his fists were clenched and tucked up tightly next to his ribs. The starting position, *saisan dachi*, was not unfamiliar to Karl, and he assumed it easily.

"The stance is an expression of the warrior's state of mind. It must be correct at all times, for it shows the opponent that you are mentally prepared. Now, without moving your head, tell me what you see."

Karl stared straight ahead. "I see the wall and the sword hanging on the wall."

"Do you see me or Tatsuo? Can you see the wall behind you?"

"No, I can only see the wall in front of me and the sword."

"You must become conscious of everything around you," Hiro instructed.

"But how can I see what is behind me if I do not turn my head?"

"Think carefully, Karl. Do not focus on any one object. Your eyes must be like those of a hawk in flight. Keep all your senses alert."

"Is this how you can tell when someone is approaching without turning around, sensei?" Karl asked.

"Yes, this practice is called *happomoku*. Someday it may save your life."

"Do you think I will ever master it?" Karl was doubtful.

"Only if you continue to practice conscientiously."

Karl remembered the day he had first met the sensei. He had been sitting by a small pond, his back to them as they approached. He remembered his surprise when Hiro, without turning around, had said, "Welcome to Japan, Richter-sama." There were no eyes in the back of his head, there were no mirrors or magic tricks, only happomoku, a skill Karl resolved to learn.

During the next two weeks, Karl concentrated on perfecting the basic thrusts and kicks. He learned to make a tight fist that would not be susceptible to injury, to twist it inward on contact, and to strike at the opponent's weak points. He learned to synchronize his blows, to pull one arm back to its starting position while the other arm drove forward. Hiro reminded him to extend the proper salutation to his opponent before and after each practice session.

"Why must I bow?" Karl asked. "Isn't the opponent my enemy?"

"That may be true, but still you must always show respect. To do less might make you overconfident, and this could be dangerous."

Karl learned the names of the thrusts and kicks, embedding them in his mind until he reacted almost simultaneously to Hiro's commands.

"*Kihon-zuki!*" Karl responded instantly with a basic thrust, snapping the practice board back effortlessly.

"*Jun-zuki! Gyaku-zuki!*" Karl attacked the board with a short thrust followed by a series of long thrusts.

After a grueling session at the practice board, Hiro lit a candle and placed it on a table while Karl watched with curiosity.

"When you have perfected your speed and balance, you should be able to extinquish this candle. The velocity of your blows above the candle will create a vacuum, and the flame will die." Hiro called Tatsuo to demonstrate.

He gave the command and Tatsuo's fists merged into a blur of motion; the candle sputtered and went out. Hiro relit it and once more gave the command, this time to Karl. Karl's efforts seemed feeble. The flame wavered, grew smaller, then flared up again in spite of Karl's intense efforts. He tried until he was gasping for breath.

"Stop," Hiro said gently. "You will succeed with practice. Watch carefully now as Tatsuo and I enact a simple battle. Remember—strength, speed, and balance."

Tatsuo adjusted his belt and bowed formally to the sensei. Hiro gave a sharp command. Their blows were delivered with lightning speed and deadly accuracy; Karl watched with intense fascination. It was several seconds before he realized their attack was merely a demonstration, the blows stopping just short of their mark. They were exhibiting skills Karl knew would take him years to master—precisely balanced form combined with accuracy and incredible power. Their moves appeared effortless, yet Karl knew that one slight error in judgment would cause serious injury. When they finished, they stepped back and bowed once more, and it was only then that Karl realized that he was still holding his breath.

Karl built himself a padded punching board so that he could practice at home, and the sound of him driving his fists into it soon became familiar to the household. His feet, which had grown faster than the rest of his body, prevented him from achieving the fluid grace that Tatsuo had demonstrated, but he was relentless in his efforts and gradually acquired speed and agility. He repeated Hiro's words over and over in his mind as he drove his feet and fists against the resilient board. "You must flow like water, gracefully and naturally."

Karl cursed his feet as he struggled with the straight step and the crossover, and when Hiro added the open step and the side step, he stumbled repeatedly. Karl practiced the moves over and over again in front of the mirror, shouting the strange names as he guided his feet carefully through each motion.

"*Sashikomi-ashi*—straight step. *Sashikae-ashi*—crossover step. *Renoji-dachi*—open step. *Chidori-ashi*—side step . . ."
Determined to overcome his clumsiness, he worked until he

was exhausted, and his slow, hard-earned progress spurred him on. The road work which had been such a trial became easier as the summer progressed. He found he could cover the five miles well within the alloted thirty minutes. His legs were much stronger, and he no longer gasped for breath when he paced himself. Occasionally, when he felt an abundance of early morning energy, he would run with a sense of exhilaration, willing himself to move faster and faster, enjoying the extra speed he could muster. At the completion of these runs he was left with burning lungs and aching legs, but his spirit would soar, and he would grin at Hiro through the perspiration that ran from his forehead.

Hiro, realizing the discipline required to carry on with such a rigorous program, marveled at Karl's determination. In the beginning, he had expected Karl to grow weary of the schedule, but Karl continued to practice faithfully.

Life was not easy for those who set straight and narrow courses for themselves, Hiro thought. He had recognized that same unwavering dedication in his own son, but in Karl, he sensed a spirit that would always fight to be free, a spirit that would survive and flourish in spite of all the restrictions the world inflicted. Karl was young yet, his role in life uncharted; perhaps he would never be cruelly tested. But somehow Hiro knew Karl would seek the ultimate test for himself and would emerge the victor or die trying.

Conrad was waiting for him when Karl reached Drachenschlucht. "You're late!" he snapped. "Do you expect Mrs. Lange to cook according to your schedule?"

"I'm sorry, Father. I had an extra long practice session today. The Takezawas are leaving for Japan soon and—"

"Good riddance. Maybe now you will stay home once in a while," Conrad interrupted.

"It's something I have to do, Father, whether the Takezawas are here or not," Karl said quietly.

"Goddamnit, they have filled your head with garbage. What in hell do you need that bloody nonsense for, anyway?" Conrad's voice became louder. "What are you doing about your schoolwork, and what about those navigational charts I gave you? I suppose you've forgotten about them!"

"No, I haven't. My studies come first—that was part of the bargain I made with Mr. Takezawa before I started practicing the martial arts." He stared at Conrad's polished shoes.

"Look at me when you address me, Karl!" Conrad commanded.

"Yes, Father."

"There's more to life than grunting and sweating and building muscles. It's about time you started thinking about your future. You're almost a man, but you're still wasting your time with childish games." Conrad's mouth began to twitch. "Don't expect to have everything handed to you on a silver platter, at least not by me."

Anger was knotting Karl's stomach, and his fists clenched. "I don't expect anything from you."

Conrad stood still for a full ten seconds. "Why, you ungrateful little whelp . . . I'm going to teach you some respect the same way I learned it. Get downstairs. Now!" He gave Karl a shove that sent him sprawling.

Dorothea came out of the dining room. "Please, Conrad," she gasped. "Let it be."

"Shut up, Dorothea! We've been allowing this to go on for too long."

Dorothea heard them descend the stairs as she leaned against the heavy closed door. She could not hear Karl, but Conrad's angry voice blasted through the door.

"Take off your shirt!" Conrad ordered, removing the belt from his pants. Karl stood still, his arms rigid by his sides, his fists clenched.

"I said take off your shirt!" Conrad folded the end of the belt around his hand and snapped it several times as Karl slowly removed his shirt.

"Turn around!" The belt cut through the air, then cracked harshly as it met Karl's naked back. An ugly red welt appeared instantly. Karl clenched his teeth as the belt repeatedly cut across his back. Welt after welt became visible, and still Conrad continued.

Suddenly Karl turned and faced Conrad. The belt stopped in midair. "That's enough, Father!"

Conrad was breathless, and his hand trembled as he lowered the belt slowly to his side. Surprise touched with fear assailed him as he looked into the coldness of his son's eyes. As if hypnotized, he watched Karl slip his shirt back on and walk slowly up the stairs.

When he reached the top, Karl turned. "Good night, Father. I hope you sleep well."

Dorothea followed Karl into his room. "Take off your

shirt, son, and lay down." She gasped when Karl removed his shirt. "Oh God, oh God, what has he done to you?"

"It's all right, Mother, it will heal, but I promise you, he will never strike me again."

Karl spent a sleepless night, the salve his mother had applied to his back only dulling the pain. When he heard his father leave the house early in the morning, he pulled himself out of bed and dressed silently. His back felt raw and he contemplated leaving his shirt off while he ran, but he could not risk someone seeing him—the questions would be difficult to answer. He swore to himself as he pulled the shirt carefully over his head and crept down the hall on his worn shoes.

"Where are you going, Karl? It's only five o'clock!" Lisl whispered through a narrow crack in her bedroom door.

"Go back to bed. It's too early for you to be up. I'm just going for my run."

"Karl, are you all right?"

"Yes."

"Did it hurt, Karl?"

"Did what hurt?"

"You know. I heard Mother crying last night, so I went to her room and she told me."

"Well, it's over, and it won't happen again, ever."

"Karl, if you run away, promise you'll take me with you."

"I promise. Now go back to bed."

The streets were empty. Karl took several deep breaths of the cool damp air and started to run, pacing himself, but the memory of the beating tore at him. He began to push himself harder and harder until his whole being concentrated only on the running. But the perspiration burned as it ran down his back, and he thought of a book he had read about mutinous sailors who were flogged for their misdeeds, sometimes to death. Well, his back hurt, but he was not going to die from the pain.

"Good morning, tomodachi. You are early again." Hiro was waiting in his usual place.

"Good morning, sensei. You are early too. I thought I would be here before you today."

Hiro's gaze was scrutinizing. "You are moving with difficulty! Did you exert yourself too much yesterday?"

"Just a little." Karl could not look at Hiro. "I . . . uh . . . had an accident."

"Accident? Where?"

"I slid down the basement stairs on my back and bruised it a little."

"May I see? Have you had it attended to?"

"No, please . . . it's okay. Just bruised. Mother put some salve on it."

"Perhaps I should take a look at it."

Karl shook his head with determination. "Could we start our exercises now?" Karl's voice sounded strange even to his own ears. The emotions he had held so firmly in check since his father had ordered him down the stairs were now very near the surface, and there was an uncomfortable burning sensation in his throat. He looked away quickly as the tears stung his eyes. To have shown this emotion last night before his father would have been unthinkable; he would have rather slit his own throat. To show it to his mother would have been too unkind. But the sensei—he would understand. Yet he could not bring himself to tell Hiro that his father had flogged him. He could not put into words what he felt sure Hiro had already guessed. When he finally looked at Hiro, there was a gentleness that he had never seen before, and he knew Hiro understood.

"Go to the dojo, Karl, and change. I will be there shortly."

"Yes, sensei."

Hiro sat on the bench under the oak tree. The boy had been beaten, he was sure of that, and by Conrad, of course—who else? He could do nothing short of confronting Conrad, but what would that solve other than to make matters worse for Karl? Lisl and Dorothea must be considered as well. What would Conrad do to them if he were angered? Hiro sighed. Karl was nearly a man and would not be subjected to Conrad's irrational behavior much longer.

He rose slowly and walked to the dojo, where Karl and Tatsuo were already waiting.

"We will have a short practice session today and spend the extra time in meditation. (Perhaps today one of you will ride the Ox home.) This will be my last opportunity to instruct you before we leave for Japan." Hiro avoided looking directly at Karl. "While we are away, Karl, I would like you to continue practicing what I have taught you."

The *Empress of Japan* sailed on schedule. Good weather followed the liner all the way to Japan, allowing her to cut through the water at an even speed of twenty-four knots, yet for Hiro the voyage seemed endless. His stomach revolted against the pitch and roll of the ship and his appetite waned until finally, on the sixth day, it disappeared entirely.

"You will arrive in Japan looking like a wraith," Miyoko chided.

"One or two days' fasting never hurt anyone; in fact, it is quite beneficial," Hiro countered unconvincingly.

"We will be in Japan in two days, my husband. You do not have long to wait. Now, please eat something!"

"Your gentle spirit is only exceeded by your stubbornness," Hiro said as he sipped his tea.

On the eighth day, the familiar snowy peak of Mount Fujiyama came into view. Miyoko stood on the open deck of the *Empress* with Hiro and her grandson and wept openly.

"We are almost home," Hiro said, patting her hand gently.

Miyoko looked at him through her tears. "I am so happy."

Tatsuo stared silently at the splendid panorama. Home? Where was home? Less than a year ago Canada had only been a place on the map, but now it had become part of him. He wondered about his old friends—would they seem like strangers? He remembered his feelings the day he had sailed from Japan on the S.S. *Hudson*, the desperate mixture of sadness and excitement. I should be excited now, he thought, but he could only feel a sense of insecurity, as if he had just awakened from a vaguely familiar dream. But when the *Empress* entered Tokyo Bay and Yokohama drew near, Tatsuo's heart began to race. It was exactly the same as when he had left: clamorous with noise and color, vibrant with flags and paper lanterns strung endlessly from one mooring to the next, with music and people shouting and laughing. Hundreds of boats filled the harbor. No staid reservedness here, no formal gatherings of somber faces. He smiled and understood his grandmother's tears. Hiro's brother, Koji, pushed his way through the crowd to meet them. He was smiling. "Welcome home. It has been a long year."

"It is good to be back," Hiro replied.

Their limousine, bearing the zaibatsu crest, moved slowly through the congested streets along the harbor and into the country.

"Our factories are in full operation again," Koji informed them.

"Your reports show the zaibatsu has realized tremendous profits in the past several months."

"Largely because of the manufacturing made possible by raw materials we have been importing from Canada. Your efforts have already shown results, but our needs unfortunately still exceed the supply. The zaibatsu, too, is changing now that we have more contact with the Diet. Some even say that we control the Diet," Koji added.

Hiro felt uneasy, the same uneasiness he had experienced when he first learned of the military's renewed expansionist policies.

Koji had solemn and profound dedication to Japan and had always been sympathetic toward the military. He had served bravely in the Japanese navy under Admiral Togo on the flagship *Mikasa* when they had defeated the Russians. When Prime Minister Hara Kei was assassinated in 1921 and accusing fingers were pointed at the military, Koji had been livid with anger. Hiro was never sure whether his brother had been defending their innocence or their right to commit murder. A peaceful existense in a turbulent world was a difficult state to maintain, but the agonies of war were, in Hiro's opinion, never justifiable. He knew Koji did not share the same philosophy, and this had always been a source of contention between them. He did not ask the questions that were forming in his mind; there would be time enough for that. Now he only wanted to enjoy the familiar countryside around him, to listen to Tatsuo and Koji and watch the joy on Miyoko's face.

Tokyo was almost completely restored. "I am amazed so much has been done!" Hiro remarked. "If I had not witnessed the destruction myself, I would not believe it had ever happened."

His former home had been completely reconstructed, the gardens replanted, and all evidence of the devatation completely removed. Everything was just as it had been before the earthquake, and for one eerie moment Hiro expected Hitoshi to come striding from the house in his usual brisk manner.

Hiro turned to Koji. "Thank you."

Koji nodded. "I am honored that you are pleased with my efforts."

"The shrine and the graves?"

"They have received special attention. I will leave you now to visit them privately with Miyoko and Tatsuo."

The population of Tokyo swelled as the time approached for the Festival of the Dead, and the entire city shone with elaborate lanterns made especially for the occasion. The lanterns in the Takezawa house and on the grounds were brighter than ever before—the spirits would easily find their way. A sumptuous feast was prepared for the entire family and their guests; later a portion of it would be offered to the spirits of the deceased.

Tatsuo felt strangely alienated from the world around him. When the guests began to arrive, he retreated to his old room and sat quietly on his tatami while his mind whirled with confusion.

When he heard the knock on his door, he knew who was there. "Come in, Ojī-san." He tried to smile at Hiro.

"Why are you sitting in here all alone?"

"I am sorry, Ojī-san, if I have caused you concern. I know I should be celebrating and that I should be happy to be with my family and friends again, but I feel so strange in there. They have all changed. I hardly recognized them."

"You have not given them a chance."

"I tried, Ojī-san, but my father and mother are dead and everyone is having a party!" Tatsuo cried.

"Tatsuo! Have you forgotten the ways of your ancestors so soon? They are not celebrating their death, they are commemorating their life on earth and the continuation of their spiritual life."

"No, I have not forgotten," Tatsuo said, sighing. "It is just that somehow I do not feel that I belong here anymore."

"Your roots are here, Tatsuo. You are an intrinsic part of Japan and a descendant of a very ancient and honorable samurai family. It is your duty to welcome our family members and guests who have come to celebrate the festival with us."

"You are right, Ojī-san. I will come," Tatsuo replied firmly.

The lines in Hiro's face deepened with compassion. He grasped Tatsuo by the shoulders and looked into his eyes. "Do you remember in the book I gave you, the writings of the priest Kenko?"

Tatsuo nodded, for he had read the passage several times.

Hiro recited the poem. " 'Were we to live forever, then indeed would men not feel the pity of things. Truly the beauty of life is its uncertainty.' "

"It is easy to say the words but hard to apply them. I will try, Ojī-san, I promise."

On the final day of the festival, Tatsuo helped prepare the traditional floats for the *Toro-nagashi*; in the evening, miniature floats were taken to the Yodo River, their candles were lit, and then, along with thousands of others, they were set free to drift down the river, guiding the spirits back to their world. With dry eyes, Tatsuo stood apart from the others, watching his own small vessel being carried away until it was lost in the maze of tiny flickering lights. Hiro came and stood beside him without speaking until the last float disappeared into the darkness.

The Marunouchi district had nearly doubled in size during Hiro's absense. Like mushrooms, buildings had sprouted in every direction. The area had not grown according to any ultimate plan—construction merely occurred where there was space—and yet there was order in the final outcome. An aura of excitement permeated the district, a dynamic, industrious excitement fed by the intense energy of the men who occupied it.

"The members of the board are looking forward to meeting with you again," Koji informed Hiro as they approached the Takezawa building on Nihonbashi Street. Although not the largest, it was still the most imposing and impressive structure in the district; a recent face-lift had added to its elegance. "Shozo will be there as well. He spends even more time at home now but continues to participate actively in the affairs of the zaibatsu."

"I have always felt Shozo's judgment and business sense to be uncanny," Hiro replied. "The zaibatsu needs him."

The door opened, and the attendant smiled broadly and bowed. "Welcome back, Takezawa-sama. It is an honor and a pleasure to see you again."

"Thank you."

Familiar people smiled at Hiro and murmured their welcome as he passed through the outer office toward the elevator.

The members of the board were already assembled, and Shozo, who sat at the head of the table, rose slowly and embraced Hiro. There was a shuffle of chairs as the rest of the members stood up and bowed deferentially. Hiro questioned the presence of several unfamiliar faces until Shozo, in his patient, grating voice, explained that the zaibatsu, because of the huge influence of its far-reaching business empire, could no longer be administered entirely by the family nucleus.

"I am aware of that. Certainly the complexity of the organization demands that we have expert opinions before final decisions are made. However, I find it difficult to understand why you would have two naval officers present at a board meeting."

"I will answer that for you," Koji interjected. Hiro felt both officers scrutinizing him coldly, and his uneasiness returned. "Several weeks ago," Koji continued, "we received a directive from you advising the zaibatsu that it would be advantageous for us to build our own freighters to supplement those we are contracting from the Richter Shipping Line."

"Yes, I recall the directive very well. My assistant, Mr. Fenton, supported this with conclusive figures." In the background, the officers shifted uncomfortably.

"I have the figures right here," Shozo said. "Please continue, Koji."

"Although the figures support your proposal, we have no alternative but to turn it down at this time."

"For what reason?"

"It is our concern for Japan that has prompted this decision," Koji said flatly. "Because of the encompassing nature of the zaibatsu, we have been granted considerable influence in the Diet, and because of this influence we also assume enormous responsibility for the welfare of our country." Koji made a gesture of appeal with his hands, but his voice was firm. "There is a new feeling in Japan, and we must give consideration to the military."

Hiro felt himself stiffen. He opened his mouth for an angry retort, but Koji raised his hand. "Let me finish. We are all working toward the same goals. Although we may approach them in different ways, we are nonetheless fighting toward the same end. The two officers present can, perhaps, elaborate further on this, but our common aim is to build Japan's naval and ground strength so that we can protect our shores and our people."

Hiro stared at Koji in disbelief. "Protect our shores and our people from what?" Slowly he searched the faces of the men around the table. "The future of Japan does not lie in our military. Our strength is in the people, their energy and their inventiveness. We need education, industry, and trade . . .

world trade. We cannot accomplish that with battleships. The world has just come through a blood war, and the wounds are still healing.''

"Please control yourself, my brother. Much of what you say is true, but it is not the entire story. Japan's population is growing rapidly, but we have very little usable land and a limited supply of natural resources. We need more room to grow. At one time we ruled Korea and parts of Manchuria, but we have lost all that at the hands of our weak-willed liberal politicians . . . our blood was spilled in vain. We should have kept what we won in battle. We cannot permit this to happen again!" Koji slammed his fist down on the table and papers jumped from the impact. "We need steel for ships—not freighters but battleships!"

Hiro turned to Shozo, whose thin, pale face was coldly set. He tried to assess the older man's feelings, but the eyes remained veiled. "Are you in favor of this, Shozo?" Hiro finally asked.

Shozo placed his emaciated hands on the polished table, and Hiro noted the faint tremor in his fingers. "It is the will of our people, and we must abide by it whether we agree or not."

"It is not the desire of all our people but only that of the military. Why must we spill more blood to satisfy their ambitions?"

Koji's face became suffused with anger, and he fought to control his emotions. The two officers rose to their feet. When Koji spoke again, his words fell like blows on Hiro's ears. "That is enough, my brother! There is only one course for us. Your orders are clear, and you will obey them." Except for the rasp in Shozo's breathing, the room was silent.

Finally the tallest of the two officers spoke. "I can understand your turmoil, Takezawa, but you have been away for almost a year. Changes have been wrought that you are perhaps not aware of. Believe me, we are taking the correct steps for the betterment of Japan."

Hiro closed his eyes and shook his head slowly in an effort to dispel what he hoped was only a bad dream. "What about Kato-Takaaki? He has reduced the army and eased the tension in the civil war with China, and certainly our relations with Russia are much improved. Is this not a better course for Japan?"

"Leaders like Kato-Takaaki are a detriment to the future of

Japan and they will not survive much longer," retorted the officer.

"You mean like Hara-kei?" Hiro shot back.

"Yes, like Hara-Kei, Kato-Takaaki is not fit to lead sheep."

Shozo tapped his knuckles on the table and the sound echoed around the room. "Enough! The matter is settled," the old man rasped. "You will return to Canada and carry out your duties or we will send someone else in your place. However, I am sure you will not permit that to become necessary. Should you decide to disobey these directives, there will be only one alternative for you. I am certain you will not choose seppuku."

Stunned, Hiro leaned back in his chair and stared at the stonelike faces. Slowly, the implication of Shozo's words began to dawn on him, and with chilling finality, he realized he was powerless to alter their fateful course; he was helplessly enmeshed in the inimical plan.

"What will you have me do?" he asked.

Shozo passed Hiro a heavy file. "It will probably take you some time to review the entire text. However, the main point is this: you are to encourage Richter to expand. I am sure that will be relatively easy. Richter is an exceedingly ambitious man. It will be your objective to procure as much raw materials as possible for Japan's heavy industry. Of course we still require wheat and lumber—that need will remain the same—but priorities must lie with steel and iron ore."

Hiro nodded but said nothing.

Lights still glowed invitingly through the windows of the house as Koji and Hiro turned into the driveway of the Takezawa estate. The garden was peaceful, the only sound the gentle rustling of the leaves.

Hiro walked noiselessly along the narrow path to the darkened shrine, then he sank heavily to the ground. Vividly, he recalled the premonition he had experienced before the earthquake and the terrible oppression he had felt in the days that followed. He prayed that reason would prevail and the zaibatsu would ignore the demands of the military and choose its own course, but he knew the decisions had already been made. Would another holocaust be unleashed upon Japan, one that would destroy its ancient beauty forever?

The darkness gave way to the dawn, and the sun, brilliant

and warm, touched his straight back. Finally, Hiro rose to his feet and made his way to the bench under the ancient pine trees. He thought of his grandfather, a samurai who had first planted the trees, and of his father, who had carefully transplanted and nurtured them. He sighed deeply, knowing he must indeed follow the instructions of the zaibatsu—whatever the outcome, he would fulfill his obligations.

[8]

The return passage to Canada was booked on the S.S. *Victoria*, Richter's newest and fastest freighter. The ship was besieged by violent storms, but the sturdy, oil-fired vessel, skippered by Captain Angus Taylor, stayed on course and arrived in Vancouver on schedule. Dorothea and the children were on hand to welcome the Takezawas, and their lives seemed to fall into place once again—except for Hiro. Preoccupied by the dangerous goals the zaibatsu had recently chosen, he reluctantly followed their directives and drastically altered the nature of the shipments destined for Japan.

Several days had passed after their arrival when he realized he had not truly visited with Dorothea. Suddenly the oversight weighed heavily on his conscience and he decided to stop by that evening. The lights at Drachenschlucht cast eerie shadows on the lawn, and Hiro sensed something was terribly wrong. The front door swung open even before he reached the top of the stairs.

Mrs. Lange, her face stiff with worry, motioned him in. Mrs. Richter is in the sun-room, Mr. Takezawa. She's had a nasty fall. The doctor is on his way.''

"How did she fall?" Hiro asked, looking down the hallway.

"I'm not sure, but she has been feeling dizzy lately, and I think she lost her balance at the top of the stairway. She was unconscious when we got to her . . . Karl is with her now. Please go and talk to them, Mr. Takezawa. I will keep trying to reach Mr. Richter.'' Mrs. Lange's voice trembled.

196

Karl was sitting on the edge of the large sofa where Dorothea lay, covered by a blanket. His shoulders sagged with relief when Hiro entered the room.

"Mr. Takezawa, what are you doing here?" Dorothea whispered.

"Too many days have passed since I last saw you," Hiro explained. "But what happened to you? How are feeling?"

"I will be fine by morning—I only tripped on the carpet. It was an accident."

"No, Mother, you didn't trip. You fainted and then you fell . . . all the way down the stairs."

She looked at Hiro for reassurance.

There was a sharp knock at the door, and without waiting for permission, a tall, slender man in his mid-fifties strode briskly into the room. In spite of the late hour, he was impeccably dressed. His white shirt glistened with starch, and stiff cuffs protruded from the sleeves of his suit coat. His piercing blue eyes, bright with energy and intelligence, quickly focused on Dorothea. His face was impassive, but a wave of sympathy flickered in his eyes and then disappeared.

"Dr. McAllister, thank you for coming." Dorothea tried to smile. "I hope we have not disturbed you needlessly."

"An unexplainable fall down a long flight of stairs is a good reason for investigation, Mrs. Richter," the doctor replied brusquely.

Dr. McAllister's polished British accent and blunt manners did not intimidate Dorothea, for he had been her physician when Karl and Lisl were born and had taken care of the family ever since. Although he had left general practice several years ago to specialize in internal medicine, Dorothea refused to accept anyone else as their family physician.

"Dr. McAllister, this is our dear friend and my husband's business associate, Mr. Hiro Takezawa."

Dr. McAllister acknowledged Hiro with a quick nod and turned immediately to his patient. Without diverting his attention from Dorothea, he asked, "Would you all please wait in another room? Karl, ask your housekeeper to pack a small bag for your mother. I will be taking her to the hospital." He raised his hand to stop Dorothea's protest and adjusted his stethoscope. His movements were quick and decisive, but his hands were gentle as he examined her.

"Have you had any unusual bleeding?"

"No."

"What have you been eating?"

"My appetite is poor, but I thought it was because I feel so tired all the time."

"You feel tired because you are undoubtedly anemic." Silently, he hoped that her anemia was the result of poor nutrition and not a malignancy. "How long have you been like this? Surely you must have realized you were not well. You should have come to me long ago," he said tersely.

Dorothea's eyes glistened with tears. "I know I should have, but I kept hoping I would feel better with more rest."

Dr. McAllister's abrupt manner softened, and he patted her shoulder awkwardly. "You get dressed now, and I'll take you to the hospital. In the morning we'll run some tests. Fortunately there are no broken bones, but you will have some nasty bruises."

"I don't suppose there is any point in asking if I could wait until tomorrow morning?"

"No, Mrs. Ricther, none whatsoever. You have already waited too long."

"Dr. McAllister, please reassure my family that I will be fine in a few days."

He looked into her pale face for a moment. "I will try."

Karl, Lisl and Hiro were waiting anxiously in the hallway.

"There are no broken bones, but I suspect a mild concussion," he explained. "I'm taking her to the hospital tonight for observation. I want to run some tests in the morning."

"Will she be all right?" Lisl's voice was constricted.

Lisl's deep fear was not allayed by the doctor's words. If anything serious ever happened to her mother, she would feel lost . . . devastated. The prospect of living in that cold, empty house without Dorothea's music, laughter, and constant love was too frightening to imagine. Tears glistened in her eyes, and her lip trembled as she looked to Dr. McAllister for reassurance.

The doctor placed a comforting hand on Lisl's shoulder. "I don't want you to worry. We will take good care of her and send her home as soon as possible." When he turned to Hiro, he knew instantly that he could not mask his concern from this man. He felt the keen dark eyes measuring him warily, assessing his manner and ability. As he waited in the hall, he tried to remember why the name Takezawa was familiar, and it was only when he recalled Dorothea introducing the man as Conrad's business associate that he made the connection.

"Mr. Takezawa, would you mind driving to the hospital with us? I think your presence might help ease the situation."

"Of course," Hiro replied instantly.

"Has Mr. Richter been contacted yet?" Dr. McAllister asked.

"My father's secretary has located him. He will be home by morning," Karl informed them.

"Tell him to contact me as soon as he arrives."

"Yes, sir, I will."

They drove the short distance to the hospital in silence. Dorothea seemed calm as she sat between the doctor and Hiro, and only when two nurses carefully assisted her into a wheelchair did she loose her composure. She clung to Hiro's hand before being wisked away into the sterility of the hospital.

"Dr. McAllister," Hiro said.

"There is not much more I can tell you at the present time, Mr. Takezawa, except that I will give her a blood transfusion to alleviate the probable anemia. I suspect this is more than simple anemia, and I must confess that I am concerned."

"I knew that."

"I thought perhaps you did. That is why I am being completely honest with you. I realize the relationship between Mrs. Richter and her husband is somewhat strained—I have known them for many years, and I think she will need your support for a while." Hiro nodded in reply., Dr. McAllister watched Hiro's straight back disappear through the wooden doors, and only after they had closed did he issue orders to a uniformed nurse at his elbow.

Conrad did not confer with Dr. McAllister until the second day following Dorothea's admission to the hospital.

"Mr. Richter, were you aware that your wife was experiencing dizzy spells?"

"Of course not. Had I known, I would have insisted that she see you immediately."

"You must have known that she was not well."

"Dr. McAllister, I did not come here to be cross-examined," Conrad said curtly.

"I am not cross-examining you, Mr. Richter," Dr. McAllister said sharply. "I am merely trying to ascertain when these dizzy spells began. Your wife cannot remember."

"I'm afraid I cannot answer that with certainty, but Dorothea has not looked well for several months—pale, tired, no appetite."

"I see. Well, she is extremely anemic. We are correcting that with blood transfusions, but we must also determine the cause of her anemia. She assured me that she has not had any excessive bleeding and that her diet has been adequate."

"I wouldn't be too sure about her diet. As far as I'm concerned, she doesn't eat enough red meat." Dr. McAllister recognized the disapproving tone in Conrad's voice.

"I did a sternal puncture yesterday so that we could study her bone marrow." He paused briefly, searching for the right words. "It's difficult to say definitely what's going on and it may take some time before the disorder manifests itself. I suspect we are dealing with an aplastic anemia or a myeloproliferative disorder. However, we'll keep a close watch on her and transfuse her as required."

"Then there is nothing to be alarmed about at the present time?" Conrad asked.

There was a slight hesitation in Dr. McAllister's reply, but Conrad did not notice it. "For the present time, no. I will keep you informed."

Hiro was disturbed by the sight of the thick glass bottle that fed life-giving blood into Dorothea's arm, but when he saw her radiant smile and eyes bright with color, he relaxed.

"I can't tell you how glad I am to see you." Dorothea held her hand out to him. "Have you talked to Karl and Lisl? I miss them so much."

"Yes, I have seen them often. Mrs. Lange is attending to them very admirably. You need not worry, but they miss you too."

"Dr. McAllister assured me I would be able to leave within a few days."

Hiro smiled briefly. "Yes, I spoke to him earlier."

"I thought perhaps you would. I asked him to be honest with you. I don't think he minces words with anyone though, and perhaps that is why I like and trust him."

"He is a very diligent man and dedicated to his profession. Your faith in him is well founded."

Dorothea closed her eyes for a few moments and Hiro watched her wordlessly, his gaze straying from her face to the almost empty bottle above her bed. She opened her eyes unexpectedly and caught the flicker of anguish in Hiro's face. Her hand tightened around his, and her voice was barely more than a whisper.

"If . . . if the doctor's suspicions prove correct, will you help me face the . . . will you help me tell the children . . ."

"In Japan it is common for one family to adopt another and become united for life. You and your children have become a part of my family. You will never have to face anything alone."

"I know. I just wanted to hear it."

"Even if the worst is true, with proper medical care you will have a long life ahead of you," Hiro added emphatically.

"I hope so. There is still so much I would like to do."

Patrick Fenton was most productive during the early hours of the morning, and for this reason he arrived at the office before seven. By the time Maiko joined him, he had already consumed several cups of coffee and had partially cleared his desk.

"Here. Take a break and tell me what state the world is in this morning," Maiko said as she handed him the newspaper.

Patrick smiled, emptied his cup, and watched Maiko from the corner of his eye as she organized her desk for the day's work. When she bent over, her skirt pulled tightly against her trim legs and Patrick stared appreciatively.

"From this angle it looks pretty good," he said.

Maiko straightened up, walked over to Patrick's desk, and tapped a perfectly tapered fingernail on the newspaper.

"I meant from the *Sun's* point of view." Her voice was crisp, but amusement crinkled the corners of her dark eyes.

Patrick scanned the paper quickly. "Well, same as usual— the rich get richer and the poor get poorer, but according to the promises of our government, the poor will soon become rich."

"Yes, all they have to do is find the pot of gold at the end of the rainbow," Maiko added derisively.

"No, all they have to do is have faith in our country and make the right investments."

"For which they need money that they don't have!"

"It's a vicious circle, my dear, very depressing. Hey, look at this! Mr. Takezawa's name is in the paper."

"Let me see!" Maiko said excitedly.

"Here, on the third page. According to this article, he recently had an official visit from Ambassador Suyama, who was delighted with the Takezawa gardens."

"Anything else?"

"Just a few figures in regard to the volume of trade between the Takezawa zaibatsu and Canada. Seems the reporter was impressed—called Mr. Takezawa an influential industrialist and Mr. Suyama an extraordinary diplomat."

Hiro's familiar footsteps sounded on the stairs, and a moment later he came through the door. His expression was subdued, and his voice held a tone of weariness.

"Good morning, Patrick, Maiko." He walked directly into his office and closed the door firmly behind him. Maiko raised her eyebrows and looked to Patrick for an explanation.

"Something is weighing heavily on his mind this morning," Patrick observed.

"Mrs. Richter must still be in the hospital," Maiko said softly. "Patricia said that Richter left town last night, so I assumed Mrs. Richter was getting better."

"You didn't really think something like an illness in the family would deter Richter, did you?"

They both looked up as Hiro opened his door to summon Patrick into the office. Patrick scooped the waiting files from his desk and hurried in.

"I thought you might like to see this, Mr. Takezawa," Patrick said, pointing to the article in the *Sun*.

Hiro read it carefully and shook his head with obvious amazement. "I had no idea the reporter would be so complimentary. Mr. Suyama had asked my permission to allow the reporter to come along; I thought it was for his own publicity."

"Many people have become aware of your influential position, and they hold you in high regard. Maiko tells me that the Japanese community where she lives is quite in awe of you."

Hiro stared at Patrick in disbelief. "How would they even know of my existence?"

"Word travels quickly." Patrick hesitated for a moment and then added, "You are somewhat of a celebrity here, too—there aren't many Japanese who can move into Shaughnessy, drive a Studebaker Speedster, and enroll their children in St. John's College. You have cut through many social barriers, and for that you have become . . . unique.''

"Would I have received this notoriety if I were not Oriental?" Hiro asked with resignation. Almost reluctantly, he opened the file that Patrick had placed on his desk. "Have you studied these new directives from Tokyo?"

"Yes, I have—very carefully," Patrick said. "I come to the same conclusion every time: the zaibatsu should build and operate its own ships. It could continue to utilize Richter's ships until its own fleet was large enough, but in five years the zaibatsu could be totally independent. The best course of action is obvious, and yet they refuse to take it . . . I just don't understand their motives!"

"There are two reasons. The first is the Washington Conference, which limits the number of ships that Japan can build.''

"But that law has been relaxed. The zaibatsu could proceed without too much trouble.''

Hiro stood up and walked to the window, then stood quietly staring at the street below. He clasped his hands behind his back and finally turned to look directly at Patrick. "You have a good sense for business, Patrick, and we have prospered because of your expertise, but there are political considerations that must sometimes supersede economic ones.''

"I'm not quite sure what you mean, sir.''

"The military has been steadily increasing its influence in the Diet and is slowly gaining control over Japan.''

"Including the zaibatsu?''

Hiro nodded. "They need the steel and iron ore for munitions—for their own special ships.''

"But surely the zaibatsu has enough power to resist them.'' Patrick's voice was charged with emotion.

"Unfortunately, my elder brother, Koji, sympathizes with the military, and my Uncle Shozo also feels the military is working toward the betterment of Japan. They do not consider the demands of the military to be unreasonable but rather a necessary precaution—and perhaps they are right. Japan is a very small country and is constantly under the threat of oppression. Perhaps the military should have the necessary strength to defend her shores if the need arises.''

"I cannot believe that you accept this so readily.''

Hiro smiled mirthlessly. "You know me too well, Patrick. I forsee much bloodshed on a scale that has never been seen before, but I am powerless to resist. I am bound to follow their instructions. Death is my only alternative."

"Self-inflicted death? In this day and age?" Patrick had to force himself to keep from shouting.

"I am a samurai, Patrick. My ways may seem strange to you, but nevertheless they are very real to me, as they are to all Japanese. If I did not commit seppuku, I would be put to death anyway, and I could not allow my family to bear that shame. I can only hope Japan's peace will not be threatened and the strength of her armies and navy will not be tested."

Patrick tapped the open file with his closed fist. "Will you continue to follow these directives?"

"For the time being, yes. Peace still prevails in Japan and perhaps it always will."

"I will make the necessary arrangements, sir," Patrick said finally. "I will inform Mr. Richter as soon as I've studied the directives more closely."

"I will depend on you to take care of the details." Hiro paused for a moment as Patrick gathered up the files. His face was grave but his voice steady. "Patrick, these directives and the conversation we had today—"

"Whatever transpires in this office remains here," Patrick added before Hiro could make the request.

"Good. Now, would you like to take a walk to the pier? Two of Mr. Richter's ships docked yesterday, and I would like to watch the new shorecranes unload them."

Patrick pulled a watch from his pocket and glanced at it. "Would you believe that I haven't been down to the docks since the day you hired me? Can't say I've missed them, though."

As they neared the waterfront, the smell of the sea settled around them like a fog. The longshoremen's voices, many of them Italian or Portuguese, carried easily above the noise of the cranes. Pallets of silk bales encased in huge nets swung in graceful arcs over their heads and were deposited into waiting boxcars. As Hiro and Patrick walked along the pier, the tension eased from Hiro's body. In the brilliant sunlight under a clear sky, the possibility of another war seemed remote, yet Hiro knew the threat was very real. But would Japan become the oppressor? Would they, basking in the glories of past victories, initiate the conflict? For the first time in his life, he questioned his loyalties and the integrity of his kinsmen.

• • •

Hiro instantly recognized the odor of antiseptic as he entered the main door of the hospital a few days later. He proceeded down the dark, narrow hall toward Dorothea's room. Close by, a bell sounded an emergency, and he could hear running feet answering the call, but outside Dorothea's room all was quiet. He stopped outside the open door and she motioned him in, her face no longer wan but flushed with color and her eyes full of a newfound vitality.

"Isn't this amazing!" she said breathlessly as Hiro walked in. "No more tubes, and I feel better than I have in months. When these rainbow-colored bruises disappear from my arms, I shall be as good as new and, I'm going home tomorrow! Well . . . actually Dr. McAllister said he would consider letting me, but I'm getting anxious. I miss Karl and Lisl, and it's so hard to be in here when I feel healthy and the sun is shining outside. Please, would you talk to Dr. McAllister for me?"

"Did your tests reveal anything?"

Some of the brightness faded from Dorothea's expression and she withdrew slightly, leaning against the pillows on her bed. "It's a condition that I will never be entirely free of, but with proper treatment it can be controlled. I have asked Dr. McAllister to explain it to you."

"You are concerned about it, though?" Hiro asked, his eyes searching her face as a coldness settled around his heart.

"Not nearly as concerned as I am about getting out of here tomorrow," she replied with forced lightness.

"I will see if I can locate Dr. McAllister," Hiro reassured her.

She nodded wordlessly as Hiro left the room.

After several inquiries, he found the doctor reading in a dark, stuffy room that was lined with thick medical texts and journals. His forehead was creased with concentration, and he did not notice Hiro walk in.

"Dr. McAllister?"

Without looking up, he waved the intruder away. "For God's sake, can't you see I'm busy?"

"I will wait," Hiro said quietly. As Dr. McAllister continued to read, Hiro studied him through the haze of smoke that rose from a forgotten cigarette smoldering in an ashtray at his elbow. Fatigue was evident in the sagging shoulders; unconsciously, he rubbed the back of his neck and finally closed the book with a long sigh and scowled up at Hiro, squinting to bring him into focus.

"Mr. Takezawa, I did not realize it was you! I'm sorry, please sit down." He indicated a chair. "You've come to inquire about Mrs. Richter?"

"Yes."

"Listen, why don't we get the hell out of here. It's still daylight outside, isn't it? I'm cooped up in here so much I sometimes forget what day it is."

"That is very apparent," Hiro said, following him out of the room.

Dr. McAllister shrugged apologetically. "I give good advice, but I don't follow it myself. Get lots of rest and fresh air, I tell my patients—best thing for you. But there's always so much to do and learn, and I just don't have enough time."

"And so you get impatient?" Hiro remarked.

"My bedside manner leaves a lot to be desired. I don't have time for platitudes."

"Your patients do not seem to mind," Hiro suggested. "Perhaps it is because they are confident of your ability."

"I guess that's what matters the most. Ah, feel this sunshine. Come this way, Mr. Takezawa. There's a small garden around the back."

"Could you tell me about Mrs. Richter?"

Dr. McAllister face was obscured by the flare of the sun, but Hiro sensed his concern. "Did you see Dorothea today?"

Hiro nodded. "She looks healthy again."

"The transfusions we gave her corrected the anemia but only temporarily. The cause cannot be so easily remedied. You see, normally, blood is produced in the red marrow of the bones, but in Dorothea's case, the marrow is not producing enough and anemia results. I will need to watch her very closely."

"Is there a name for this malady?"

"Well, there are several terms for this condition, but I'm still waiting for one more consultation before I can be absolutely sure."

"I have faith in your judgment. What do you think it is?"

Dr. McAllister sat down on a weathered bench in the garden, stretching his long legs out in front of him. He could feel Hiro's unwavering gaze on him. "I think she has aplastic anemia or perhaps myelofibrosis. Because the marrow is not producing enough blood, other organs like the spleen begin to help out, which explains why her spleen is enlarged. I don't see any evidence of malignancy at this time, but to be perfectly honest with you, Mr. Takezawa, it could develop into leukemia later.''

"I am unfamiliar with your medical terms, Dr. McAllister. This condition—is it fatal?"

"Yes, but perhaps not for years."

"What do you recommend?" Hiro's voice wavered slightly as his heart raced with panic and outrage.

"I would like to see her every month, more often if necessary. It will depend on how she feels. Come now, don't look so devastated, Mr. Takezawa. The disease may never manifest itself in the form of leukemia; it could even go into remission."

"But in your opinion, how long will she live?"

"I would not even venture a guess. I have not told Dorothea everything I've told you, although I have a feeling she knows more than she lets on."

"Will you release her tomorrow?"

Dr. McAllister smiled knowingly. "I suppose she told you to ask me." He stood up and straightened his shoulders. "I must be getting back." He looked at Hiro, and sympathy shone from his intense blue eyes. "Yes, she may go home tomorrow. Mr. Takezawa, encourage her to live her life to the fullest. Her children are very dear to her—see to it they spend as much time with her as possible."

The next morning Conrad was tense and agitated when he picked up Dorothea at the hospital. The doctor had not minced words when he explained her condition to him. As he watched Dorothea walk out of the hospital, a strange feeling came over him, a feeling that he had relinquished long ago and had replaced with indifference. There was a jauntiness to Dorothea's walk, and the sun enhanced the healthy glow of her skin. A breeze blew her raven hair from her face and whipped the silk dress against her trim body; a long forgotten memory stirred, and Conrad felt a twinge of tenderness toward her. He quickly dismissed it. Dorothea looked fit once again, and Conrad was sure the doctor had embellished his diagnosis with melodramatic personal opinions. By the time they reached Drachenschlucht, Conrad had decided she would survive, and after escorting her upstairs, he drove back to the office with a clear conscience.

Karl, relieved that his mother was home and well, continued his training with renewed vigor. His strength was growing each day as his body developed speed and grace, and although he and Tatsuo were still not equally matched, Karl was quickly closing the gap.

After a particularly grueling session in the dojo, Hiro examined Karl's hands. They were large hands, with broad, callused palms, heavy, solid knuckles, and strong fingers. "Karl, your thrusts and kicks have become swift and powerful. Do you think you can extinguish the candle now? It is an old but reliable test of one's speed and skill."

"I don't know, sensei. The last time I tried, I almost dislocated my arm." Karl rubbed his elbow as he recalled the humiliating experience.

"It is no disgrace to fail when you have tried your best," Hiro said, noting the expression on Karl's face. "It will not be too long before you succeed . . . perhaps it will happen today."

Hiro lit three candles and positioned them on the back of a wooden chair, anchoring them with hot wax drippings. His leathery hand closed into a fist, which he shot out over the nearest candle then retracted in a blur; the candle flickered within the vacuum and died.

"Tatsuo," Hiro said, indicating the second candle.

Tatsuo studied the candle for a moment and confidently copied his grandfather's example. The second flame disappeared without a flicker as Tatsuo stepped back.

Karl now approached the chair and assumed his stance. Fear of failure made him swallow nervously as he prepared himself for the test, his eyes remained fixed on the flame. His loud cry echoed sharply in the silent dojo as he drove his fist into the empty air above the candle and withdrew it with force and swiftness. The flame flickered resolutely for an instant and disappeared. Karl fought back the impulse to let loose a deafening cheer and, with forced humility, he accepted their congratulations.

In retrospect, Patrick Fenton recalled that the week had started quite innocently, with no indication of the tragic events that were to follow. He and Hiro had spent the morning with

Richter, examining and revising the terms for the new contract for additional shipments of steel. Patrick had arranged for representatives from the steel supplier to be present, and the meeting progressed without any undue problems. Conrad and the others were eager to expand in order to meet the growing demands of the zaibatsu. The Japanese were offering excellent prices, and all they asked for in return was speed and reliability in meeting their quotas. By midafternoon, Patrick had made the necessary revisions to the agreement and had prepared a summary for Hiro's inspection. After a perfunctory knock, he entered Hiro's office. Immediately he noticed a gap on the wall where Hiro's sword always hung. The priceless ancient weapon lay across the desk.

"Beautiful, is it not?" Hiro asked, handing the sword to Patrick.

He studied the fine engraving on the resilient blade, and after weighing it carefully in his hands, marveled at its balance.

"It is called a *tachi*," Hiro continued. "It was forged over one hundred years ago in Naro by a master swordsmith. A small block of steel was heated to more than two thousand degrees, and when it glowed exactly the right color, the master placed it on an anvil for his assistant to flatten with a heavy sledge. When the blade was flat, it was then folded lengthwise back upon itself, heated, and flattened again. This process was repeated over and over until thousands of fused layers gave it the necessary strength and flexibility."

"Why did you bring it here to the office?" Patrick asked.

"There are four other swords exactly like this one, and each has special significance to the members of our family. They serve not only to remind us of our obligations, but also to help fulfill them!" Hiro smiled and added, "It is also an extremely fine work of art and adds character to these bare walls." He replaced the sword in its scabbard and returned it to its place on the wall.

"There is a gentleman waiting to see you, sir—Mr. Nazaki. But first, here are the terms for the new agreements."

"I would like to read them over carefully. I will see our visitor first. Send him in."

Toku Nazaki was a proud man who still venerated the traditional Japanese customs even though he had spent much of his life in Canada. His face was a network of lines, but his eyes were clear and alert. Years of hard work on the sea had curved his back a little, and he walked with a slight shuffle. He bowed deeply before entering Hiro's office.

"Please accept my humble apologies, Takezawa-sama, for this intrusion."

Hiro returned the bow. "There is no need to apologize. Please come in and sit down." Hiro quickly noted the strength in the proud old face but was puzzled by the perceptible tremor in the man's voice.

"My name is Toku Nazaki, and I have come to ask for your help. I came to Canada twenty-three years ago, honorable Takezawa-sama; my three sons were born here. This country has been kind to me and I have prospered. It has not always been easy for my family, but we did not mind hard work. Several years ago my sons and I were able to purchase our own fishing boat, and even though the government decreased our fishing rights, we were still able to make a good living. Until a year ago." His voice trembled noticeably and he took a deep breath. "It is very difficult for me to talk about this, Takezawa-sama. Please forgive me for my weakness."

"Please do not hurry," Hiro reassured him.

"About a year ago we noticed that our fishing nets were being cut. We would mend them only to have them slashed again and again. My oldest son became very angry and decided to take the matter into his own hands. He discovered that the crews of the West Coast Fishing Company were responsible. He confronted them, of course, with a warning that he would go to the police. At first they seemed to take heed, but three weeks later my son was attacked and killed by unknown assailants."

"Did you go to the police?" Hiro asked, incredulous.

"Yes, of course, but they have still not found the murderers. Several weeks later the harassment began again, only this time they were not so cautious. As well as slashing our fishing nets, they rammed our boat and claimed it was an accident. The first time we were able to repair it, but the next time we had to dry-dock her, and so we lost much time and money. Money, however, is not important when you compare it to human life. Last month, my other son approached them and demanded to know why they were causing us so much trouble. They laughed and told him that the Japanese do not have any rights to fish in these waters, and then they threw him off their boat. My son could not bear this disgrace and he went back that night with two of his friends. They were brutally beaten, and my son . . . it will be a miracle if he ever walks again. He does not want to live.'' The clear eyes became moist, and his hands closed into fists until the knuckles turned white.

"And the police?''

"The police say they can do nothing offshore. I do not think they want to become involved in our affairs.''

"How can I help you?''

"I would not have come to you, Takezawa-sama, were I not desperate. Our lives depend on the fishing. You are a very important man, with considerable influence—I beg you to intervene for me with the police, or perhaps with someone who has authority, to stop them.''

"Are you the only one they have attacked?''

"No, no. I am not alone. Others have experienced similar problems. Some have given up and have turned to farming, others have suffered tragedies as grave as mine, but they are still trying to preserve their livelihood.''

"It seems the law cannot control these men—they will have to be dealt with directly,'' Hiro said calmly.

"I would be eternally grateful, Takezawa-sama. I am sorry to trouble you so.''

A heavy mist hung over the ocean, blending with the gray sky. Only the dark outlines of the trawlers preparing for the day's fishing were visible. A motor started in the distance and split the silence while voices rose, demanding to be heard. Hiro stood at the end of the pier beside a small group of men in heavy sweaters and oilskins.

"The third trawler from the end belongs to the West Coast Fishing Company,'' one of the men said nervously. "There are usually four men and the captain on board.''

"They are cruel men, Takezawa-sama,'' Toku Nazaki said in a grim voice. "We do not wish any harm to come to you. Please be careful.''

The sharp lines of Hiro's sober face were barely discernible in the predawn light, but as he turned in the direction of the trawler, a faint glimmer illuminated his eyes.

Two men stood on the deck of the trawler preparing the nets. They looked up with surprise as Hiro came on board, and then immediately their expressions became wary and guarded. Hiro felt their eyes sweep contemptuously over him before they returned to their tasks.

The older of the two men tightened a knot with a grunt and, without taking his eyes from the net, asked, "What the hell do you want?"

"Is this a West Coast trawler?"

"Yeah."

"I would like to speak to your captain."

"He ain't interested in speaking to you."

"Call him on deck, please."

Again the eyes of the older man swept over him, recognizing the firm set of Hiro's mouth and the breadth of his shoulders beneath the heavy coat. Without taking his gaze from Hiro, he yelled over his shoulder. "Hey, Captain, some Jap wants to talk to you."

"What about?"

"How the hell should I know."

"Tell him to get his ass off the boat."

"You heard the captain," the man said. "Get the fuck off this boat."

"I am not leaving until I have spoken to the captain," Hiro said menacingly.

The man looked at him with a new awareness. "Hey, Captain, I think you'd better come up and talk to this guy."

The captain, whose heavy face was made broader by a thick wool toque, came up on deck. A third man materialized from behind the wheelhouse.

"What do you want?" the captain asked.

"I have come here on behalf of the Japanese fishermen. You have caused them much grief—lives have been lost and property destroyed. This harassment must stop."

"Is that so? Who the hell are you?"

"That is not important. I am warning you to refrain from inflicting any more problems on these people."

"Get off my boat or I'll slit your yellow throat." The skipper took a step toward Hiro. With a violent shove, he pushed Hiro against a pile of partially mended nets. Hiro recoiled instantly, and before the skipper could protect himself, Hiro had the man's arm twisted high up on his back. The skipper groaned in surprised pain while the others stared in disbelief.

"Stop him, you fuckers," the skipper screamed. "Don't just stand there."

"Stand back," Hiro warned. "I want to know why you are robbing these people of their fishing territory. Surely there are enough fish in the ocean to fill all the boats."

"Tell him before he breaks my arm," the skipper gasped. "Tell him!"

The deckhand made a move toward Hiro, and the skipper screamed in agony as Hiro applied more pressure to the twisted arm.

"Stop! I'll tell you," the skipper moaned. "Whittier gives the orders. We have no choice."

"Who is Whittier?" asked Hiro.

The skipper grimaced grotesquely. His voice was little more than a hoarse whisper. "James Whittier . . . owns the fleet and wants the Japs out of here . . . wants it all for himself —canning plants, boats, everything. If we don't do what he wants, we lose our jobs." He crumpled to the deck as Hiro released his grip.

From the corner of his eye Hiro saw an ax raised and instinctively turned to avoid the lethal blow. The blade ripped across his right shoulder before lodging into the side of the trawler, blood oozed through the heavy fabric of his coat.

Something in Hiro's eyes caused fear to dawn in his assailant's face. Hiro advanced slowly toward the man, then his foot sank into the fisherman's midriff. The man doubled over, breathless. A sharp blow to the back of the neck brought him to his knees before he collapsed on the deck. The others backed away from Hiro cautiously; no one else would challenge him.

James Whittier sat behind his large desk and faced Hiro with chilling eyes. "The news of your vicious attack on my men has preceded you, Takezawa. You have made me most unhappy."

"I did not initiate the attack," Hiro replied.

"That is a matter of opinion, and right now yours will not be considered."

"I came here to discuss the trouble you have been causing the people of Steveston. This must stop immediately."

"I do not like to be threatened, Takezawa." Whittier's voice remained soft, but his tone was ominous. "As for your friends, I do not intend to stop until they are all gone. That's what the commission wants—it's the law."

"It is unfortunate you feel that way," Hiro replied.

"Don't waste your emotions. I won't change my mind." Whittier nodded to the bodyguard who opened the door. "Get out and don't come back with any more of your useless threats. Let me give you a warning, though. Don't ever interfere in my affairs again." His voice had risen only slightly, but his eyes glinted with malice.

"There will be no need to, Mr. Whittier." Hiro walked to the open door and closed it quietly.

The smug look on Whittier's face vanished. On command, his bodyguard rushed forward and flung open the door to follow Hiro. Hiro sidestepped quickly and kicked his legs out from under him; his body smashed awkwardly against the floor.

"You sonofabitch!" the bodyguard yelled.

Hiro opened his coat and adjusted the position of his sword. "My business is with Mr. Whittier. Stay where you are until we are finished."

"Get up, you bloody fool," Whittier shouted.

Enraged, the bodyguard jumped to his feet and aimed a hard punch at Hiro's face. A sharp side block easily diverted the blow, and before the man could take another breath, Hiro rendered him unconscious.

"Now, back to business, Mr. Whittier."

"You're in very serious trouble, Takezawa—get out while you still can." Whittier stood behind the heavy wooden desk; his fists were clenched.

"You will never again threaten the fishermen of Steveston. Send out the order to your crews immediately."

"You're insane, Takezawa. That fancy footwork of yours isn't worth a shit. We have laws in this country to take care of misfits like you." Leaning forward at his desk, he sneered. "What will you do now . . . break my nose?"

Whittier blinked, and before his mind could warn him to move, Hiro's sword left its scabbard and swung in a blinding arc. The blade nicked the tip of Whittier's nose; a moment later he felt the pain along with the first drops of warm blood.

"This is my final warning Mr. Whittier. Leave the fishermen alone or you will pay with your life."

"You won't get away with this. I'll sink every one of their goddamn boats and you along with them."

The sword flashed again, leaving a straight, thin incision across Whittier's forehead. Terrified, he collapsed into his chair. Again the blade cut across his head and nose with surgical precision. The blood turned Whittier's face into a crimson mask.

"Remember, this is my last warning."

Whittier pressed a handkerchief to his face. "Please . . . no more . . . it's over, I swear."

Hiro replaced the sword in its scabbard, then left quietly.

Whittier shuddered and stared at the door. He blinked rapidly, forcing the blood from his eyes. When he finally struggled to his feet, he realized his tailored pants were wet with urine.

[9]

The polished wooden floor of the dojo reflected Karl's image as it had each day for the past two years. It was clean, but he swept it carefully, enjoying the menial task. Karl recalled the first time the sensei had asked him to perform this chore; he had been confused and wondered why he should sweep an already spotless floor. He stopped for a moment to study the slightly yellowed photographs tacked to the wall. He had just earned his yellow belt that day . . . how thin he and Tatsuo looked! Karl shrugged his massive shoulders and his back muscles rippled; he had weighed in at one hundred and ninety-six pounds today and Tatsuo at one hundred and seventy-five. In the photographs Hiro loomed over them, but now they were both taller than the sensei. The countless agonizing hours spent training in the dojo had knotted the muscles in their stomachs and had thickened and strengthened their arms and legs far beyond their expectations. Karl grimaced, recalling the times he had spent holding two heavy stones at arm's length until his muscles ached and trembled.

Today Karl felt invincible and wondered if he would be a match for Tatsuo, who was now preparing for his first *dan*—degree—black belt. He would soon be visiting the temple in Tokyo to be tested by the masters of Shizen Ryu Kempo. After watching intently for a few minutes, Karl admitted that he was not yet as fast as Tatsuo; but he was improving rapidly and in time, he too, would wear the black belt. For the past three months, Tatsuo had concentrated on power moves and breaking techniques. To earn the coveted belt, he would have to break up to ten cinder tiles using his feet, hands, elbows, and even his head. The extensive training had made these contact points thick and hard. Karl marveled as Tatsuo broke fifteen tiles with a spectacular swing kick.

"Well done!" Karl shouted.

"Thanks. I've been working hard on that one and this, too . . . watch it." For an instant Tatsuo seemed to float effortlessly, and then his foot darted out, stopping just short of Karl's face. "And that's my grand finale. I hope the masters will like it."

The swing kick and leap kick impressed Karl, especially since he was having so much trouble executing them himself, even the names sounded enigmatic: *mawashi-geri*; *tobi-geri*. "You'll impress them, all right. I just hope one day I'll be able to do those as well as you."

"You will, and soon," Tatsuo reassured him. "Help me set up these tiles."

Together they carefully stacked ten tiles on top of two huge bricks which Tatsuo was expected to break with his bare hands. He positioned himself in front of the pile while Karl and Hiro looked on in hushed silence. Tatsuo concentrated on the tiles, focusing his inner forces to a point just beyond their physical barrier. Suddenly he shouted and delivered a blinding knife hand thrust; the tiles shattered and fell to the floor.

"Very good!" Hiro said. "Your *shuto-geri* was perfectly executed. You are ready to meet the masters in the temple."

Tatsuo nodded and permitted himself a narrow smile of satisfaction. "I hope so, Ojī-san. You have worked so hard with me."

"I have already booked your passage on the *Empress of Japan*. Come, let us meditate while the sun still warms our backs." Tatsuo could not help but notice the pride glowing in his grandfather's eyes.

The dry landscape garden was in perfect order and all was still as Karl and Tatsuo assumed their positions for meditation. The sensei sounded a gong four times. Its pure tone resonated in Karl's mind as he melded with his surroundings. His breathing slowed to an imperceptible rhythm while the stones in the garden fused and retreated from sight.

Karl continued his slow quiet breaths until he felt detached from his own body, and for the first time in his life he knew he could accomplish whatever he wanted simply by willing his mind to travel in the prescribed direction. Now that the door to self-mastery had been partially opened to him, he realized how turbulent his mind had been before this day. Are these the footprints of the Ox that the sensei spoke of? The Ox is me! . . . yes, it must be! I control it; but there is more, so much more. His mind became still, and darkness and total silence closed in as if he were lying on the bottom of the sea. There was no time, no joy, no grief . . . only peace. In the distance the echo of the gong could be heard . . . louder now.

Karl opened his eyes. The sun was gone and the air felt cool. He stood up and walked around the perimeter of the garden, his eyes glowed with new awareness.

"How do you feel?" Hiro asked.

"As though I have lain on the bottom of the sea and now that I have come back to the surface, everything is so beautiful—the trees, the sky, the colors are so vivid!"

"It is the same world, Karl, but you have become more beautiful. The masters say it is at this stage when 'heaven and earth come tumbling down.' "

Karl nodded thoughtfully. "Did I see the Ox, sensei?"

"Yes. You now realize there is another way, another place for your mind to dwell in solitude and to discover your true nature. Now that you have seen the Ox, you must catch it and ride it home."

"How? When?"

"Follow the footprints as you have already done, but do not hurry or become impatient."

Follow the footprints. The words haunted Karl in the months that followed. He did not glimpse the Ox for a while, but he felt himself drawing closer, reaching for a new dimension he could sense but not yet understand.

Conrad was preoccupied as he mechanically ate the carefully prepared dinner. He answered Lisl's questions with absent-minded nods while Karl and Dorothea, sensing his agitation, remained silent. Conrad had aged: his blond hair, now peppered with gray, had receded; deepening lines were etched around his eyes; and although his tailored suits hid a spreading midriff, he had obviously gained weight. Only his eyes were unchanged—cold and piercing. He had amassed a fortune; shipping was still his primary interest, but he had channeled large amounts of money into other businesses and securities. Yet he could not relax, could not enjoy his success, for his suspicious nature gave him little rest; nothing escaped his careful scrutiny. He rose from the table abruptly.

"Karl, I want to talk to you in the study."

Karl looked up, surprised. "Now?"

"Yes, now!"

In the study Conrad filled his glass with Scotch from a crystal decanter. "Your mother tells me you have had a successful year at school."

Karl nodded, waiting.

"Would you care for a drink?"

"No, thank you."

"It's time you learned to enjoy a drink."

"I would rather not. I don't like the taste too much."

Anger flashed momentarily across Conrad's face. "Still full of those high-minded ideas, are you?"

"It's my own choice, Father."

"Well, anyway, school is over for the summer. On Monday I want you to report to Walter Billick at Pier B—he's the foreman. I told him you'd be starting work there as a longshoreman. The rest of the men won't know who you are. Use the name Karl Anderson. I don't want you to get any special treatment."

"I'm not afraid of hard work, if that's what you mean."

"No, that's not what I mean. I have recently discovered that the man who kept me informed about the activities at the pier can no longer be trusted. I pay those men to produce a full day's work and I expect them to do just that. I don't give a goddamn what they do after hours, but I want them sober and productive when they're on the job. It will be up to you to report those who are not."

"I would prefer not to do that, Father."

"Prefer?" Conrad's voice rose. "I don't give a damn what you prefer. You'll do as I tell you." For an instant, Conrad thought his son would defy him.

"If you insist," Karl answered quietly.

"After you've been down there for a while, you'll work with me—get a firsthand look at the administrative end of our business too. When you've finished school and can assume some of the responsibilities, I'll have more time to spend on other ventures."

"I don't mind working hard, but I don't like the idea of spying on your men. There has to be a better way. Surely most of them can be trusted."

Conrad stood up and leaned across the desk. "Listen, the sooner you learn that no one can be trusted the better off you'll be. Those bastards will screw me every chance they get if I let them." Conrad's eyes blazed. And don't take the car. I don't want anyone recognizing you."

An early morning haze hid the sun when Karl arrived at Pier B. He turned up the collar of his jacket against the cool wind that blew off the ocean. There were several ships tied up at the Pier, two of which bore the Richter insignia on their huge funnels. A small group of men stood around a freight wagon, engrossed in conversation as smoke from their cigarettes curled above their heads. They eyed Karl suspiciously.

"Morning. Is Mr. Billick around?" Karl asked. "I'm supposed to report to him for work."

"Yeah. Walter's in the freight office," said one of the men, pointing in the direction of a wooden building.

"Thanks. I'll probably see you later."

"Big fucking deal," the man whispered under his breath.

Billick sat hunched over a cluttered desk in an office lined with shipping schedules. He was middle-aged, with a waist bigger than his barrel chest.

"I'm Karl Anderson. I was told to report to you this morning."

Billick's eyes narrowed as he noted Karl's muscular frame and powerful hands.

"Anderson, huh? Yeah, I've been expecting you." His bushy eyebrows were knit together pugnaciously. "You ready to work, kid?"

"Yes, sir," Karl answered quickly.

"Good. The men will show you the ropes, and if you can't hack it, they'll let me know. Understand?"

"I'll hack it."

"Okay, then let's get at it." Karl followed Billick toward the group of men beside the freight wagon.

"This is Karl Anderson, and he'll be on your gang. Richter wants this fucking ship unloaded by Wednesday. The insurance on this silk is running into a pile of dough, and he's beginning to sweat. Start on number-three hold."

A tall man with dark hair spoke to Karl. "My name is Gibson—you'll get to know the others soon enough. You a college kid?"

Karl nodded. "St. John's College."

"Well, let's see what you can do, college boy." The men climbed down into the hold, where naked electric bulbs glowed dimly in the dusty air.

"Think you can stand the pace, kid?" Gibson winked at the rest of the men as he rolled up the sleeves of his shirt, exposing large, sinewy arms. He grabbed a bale and swung it onto a loading net.

"Okay, college boy, just start tossing these bales." Gibson instructed. "You don't need brains here, just muscles."

"Don't let him rattle you, kid," a red-headed man whispered. "He always puts the new guys through the paces."

Karl grinned and, after watching Gibson for a few minutes, began throwing the bales onto the nets. The one hundred and thirty-three pound bales felt awkward at first; the dust coated his mouth and nostrils and stung his eyes.

Gibson increased his pace, watching Karl from beneath his bushy eyebrows as perspiration began to stain the back of his shirt.

Karl felt his muscles straining but continued measuring his speed against Gibson's.

"Nothing like good hard work to keep a man in shape, eh, kid?" Gibson taunted.

"Yes, sir," Karl answered, remembering how often his muscles ached after the grueling practice sessions in the dojo. He gave the bales a sharp twist and threw them into the nets. The task soon became easier.

"Hey, Scotty, I don't think Gibson will be able to accuse this kid of dogging it. He'll work Gibson's ass right into the ground."

"I doubt it. The kid is strong, but Gibson's been at it a long time—I'll bet he finishes him by three o'clock."

"Well, I'll put fifty cents on the kid."

"You're on," Scotty answered quickly.

When the lunch whistle shrilled, the men climbed wearily out of the hold and into the brilliant sunshine.

"Fuck, it's hot down there," Gibson complained.

"The kid's just got you working too hard," Scotty said with a chuckle.

"Up your ass," Gibson growled.

A man who looked only slightly older than Karl held out his hand. "My name is Buck. I just bet Scotty that you would wear Gibson out."

"Thanks for the vote of confidence. I hope I don't lose that bet for you."

"For a college kid, you handle those bales pretty good. Gibson can make most new guys sweat blood by lunchtime."

"Well, I have to admit I was ready for a break. Gibson is strong."

"Yeah, well, he's been doing it for a long time. It's made him strong, but it sure as hell hasn't done much for his disposition. Think you can make it to six o'clock?"

"I can make it," Karl replied with determination.

"Come on, college boy. Get off that educated ass and let's get back to work," Gibson shouted after the lunch break was over.

With a last look at the clear sky, Karl lowered himself back into the dusty hold. For the rest of the afternoon Gibson worked at a furious pace. The men watched expectantly as rivulets of sweat coursed down his face, his mouth tightened into a grimace, and the veins and muscles in his arms bulged. When the six o'clock whistle finally blew, Gibson tossed the last bale into the net and stalked off without a backward glance.

"Pay up, Scotty. You lost yourself a bet."

"Here you go, Bucko. It was worth it just to see the look on Gibson's face when that whistle blew."

Karl groaned as he climbed out of the hold. Slowly, he flexed his aching arms. "I think I've got blisters on my calluses," he remarked with a lopsided grin.

"It looks like you do more than just push a pencil with those hands," Scotty said with a curious look.

"Yeah, a bit," Karl replied matter-of-factly. "I didn't think I'd last much longer down there, though."

"You'll be okay, kid. Gibson will let up after a while. He usually does."

For two days Gibson continued to push Karl, watching closely for signs of fatigue. Karl knew he was on trial and that Gibson's reputation was at stake, but he refused to allow his weariness to show. By the end of the third day, his muscles had become accustomed to the peculiar work and the men had accepted him as part of their crew. They included him in their raucous jokes, at times making him bear the brunt of their quips and even offering to arrange a rendezvous with an accommodating barmaid. Karl sensed Gibson's growing resentment, but the men seemed to take little notice. To them Karl was just a college boy who had enough gumption to do his share of the work, and even if they made fun of his youthful inexperience, they gave him their good-natured respect.

By the end of the week, the men were ready to spend part of their wages at the tavern to compensate for the long hard hours spent in the bowels of the dirty freighter. Although he was only seventeen, Karl's rugged appearance allowed him entry into the tavern with the other men.

The Seaman's Club was a long two-storied wooden structure. A fresh coat of paint had brightened its outward appearance, but inside it still resembled an old shoe box filled with smoke and stale air. Tables, scarred by forgotten cigarettes and stained by the careless splatter of beer, covered the central area of the room. Most of them were already occupied by noisy work crews even though it was scarcely past dinnertime. Their laughter and loud voices buzzed in Karl's ears.

"Don't they ever let any fresh air in here?" Karl asked.

"Hell no, that would spoil it," Scotty answered. "This way you can't see the drunks until they fall over you."

"Ain't you ever been in a beer joint before?" Buck asked.

Karl hesitated for a moment, then opened his hands in a helpless gesture.

"And I suppose you've never been drunk either?"

Karl looked sheepish. "I've had some sake."

"Sake? Christ, that stuff will rot your guts. What you need on a Friday night is several mugs of ice cold beer. Goes down real good after a hot day in those fucking holds."

"First round always tastes the best," Scotty instructed. He saluted Karl with his mug before emptying it in several noisy gulps. "Down the hatch, kid!"

The beer was cool and refreshing, its pleasant bitterness quite unlike anything Karl had expected.

"No, no, no," Buck shouted. "You don't sip it—you swig it." He emptied his mug expertly then, with obvious pleasure, emitted a loud belch. He signaled to the waiter.

Karl took a deep breath and downed the rest of his beer, tipping the mug upside down to show it was empty. The second and third mugs disappeared in a similiar fashion, but the fourth was a little more difficult. After two hours of drinking on an empty stomach, Karl's head began to spin and he could barely feel the rim of the glass against his lips. He heard himself laughing, but he couldn't remember what the joke was. He slapped the table and the glasses rocked threateningly.

"Did you see Gibson's face by the end of the day?" Scotty laughed. "I thought he'd bust a gut trying to tire you out."

"Yeah, he was some upset when you kept up to him," Buck added.

Gibson, his face tight with anger, stood a few feet away from the table.

"Hey, Gibson," Buck said in an effort to placate him. "We're just having some fun. Nothing personal. Don't get sore."

"Well, I don't like anyone laughing at me, and that includes you three bastards." His voice rose above the din of the club; heads turned in their direction.

"Come on, Scotty, Karl, let's get the hell out of here," Buck urged.

"Sit down," Gibson roared. "You're not going anywhere until I'm finished." He reached for the collar of Buck's sweater and twisted it into a tight ring. A phalanx of people quickly gathered around them, prepared for a fight. Instantly, several waiters pushed their way through the crowd and with a few quiet words escorted the four men outside.

Karl walked unsteadily and his head spun; the street seemed to tilt at an uncomfortable angle. Someone gave him a violent shove and he fell to the ground, stunned. Slowly, he tried to lift his body to an upright position.

"For Christ's sake, Gibson, the kid's had too much to drink. Leave him alone."

"Fuck off, Scotty. If he wants to work and drink with the men, then he better learn to fight like 'em too." He shook the restraining hand off his arm, reached down, and pulled Karl to his feet by the front of his shirt. Karl could feel his hot breath, smelling of beer. Suddenly his stomach lurched and vomit shot out, spilling onto Gibson's shirt.

"You rotten bastard," Gibson screamed back.

Karl tried to control his stomach, but it seemed to have a will of its own. With one final, painful heave his stomach emptied and the spinning stopped. His head began to clear and he felt relief as the acrid smell of vomit filled his nostrils. He saw Gibson come toward him and knew that a blow was coming, but his reactions were too slow; there was nothing he could do to stop it. He felt the pain in his cheek and tasted the warm blood. Instinctively, Karl removed his boots and socks and, finally, his vomit-covered shirt. In the soft glow of the streetlight, his torso shone with sweat, the muscles in his back and arms knotted with tension. He prepared himself as Gibson advanced.

"I'll teach you to throw up on me! I'll break your goddamn neck! Go ahead, take off all the clothes you want. You smell like you've been swimming in a toilet and you look worse, turd."

Karl stepped back and Gibson mistook it for fear. He sneered and aimed a punch at Karl's face. Karl sidestepped as he had done countless times in the dojo and delivered a short powerful elbow thrust behind Gibson's ear. A stunned look crossed Gibson's face, then, with his eyes still open, he fell to the ground in a lifeless heap. Karl stared down at him, frightened.

"Hey, how did you do that?" Scotty's voice held a tone of incredulity.

"I didn't want to hurt him—just slow him down."

"Don't worry, he had it coming. I sure would like to know how the hell you did that!"

"Do you think he'll be all right?"

"Aw, he's okay," Buck said. Someone handed him a pitcher of water and he poured it slowly on Gibson's head. Gibson's eyes fluttered and he coughed as the cold water roused him.

"I think I'll go home now," Karl said quietly.

"Hell, don't go home yet. Let's have another beer."

"No, I've had enough. When Gibson comes around, tell him I'm sorry."

"You coming back to work on Monday?"

"Think I should?"

"You're goddamn right you should. Hell, kid, little skirmishes like this happen all the time—adds to the excitement. Gibson will leave you alone now. Christ, are you a mess!"

"I sure don't know how to drink beer, do I?"

"No, but you can practice again next week." He slapped

Karl on the shoulder. "See you Monday, kid."

Karl shook his head at the sage advice. He picked up his boots and shirt and began to walk unsteadily along the deserted street. In the distance he heard the deep-throated blast of a tug feeling its way through the mist. The cut on his cheek was beginning to hurt, and his stomach felt queasy again. A figure came toward him, barely discernible in the darkness. The old man clung tightly to a paper bag as they passed each other under a dim streetlight. For a moment nothing registered in the tired eyes—then something flickered: surprise first, then fear. He clutched the precious paper bag closer to his thin body and crept by Karl.

At the next streetlamp, Karl stopped and stared at himself in a window filmed with grime. He shook his head as if to clear it, but the bloodied, soiled image in the window remained, justifying the old man's fear. Slowly, Karl ran his hand over his cheek, where a crust of blood had formed, and over his hair, which was matted to his head. He could not go home in this condition. An image of his mother's alarmed, overwrought expression floated in front of him—no, he could not expose her to this. He cursed himself for his stupidity and longed for the comfort of his own bed.

Desperately, he tried to clear his sluggish mind. What if he was thrown in jail with other derelicts, trying in vain to explain to the police that he was Karl Richter and not some vagrant? He walked aimlessly until, without realizing it, he found his way to the Wilson Block, where a light still glowed in his father's office. There was no response to his light knock. He tried again, louder this time, and then stepped back into the shadows when he heard footsteps. The door opened a few inches, and Patricia Harley's worried face peered out cautiously.

"It's just me, Miss Harley," Karl said in a relieved voice. "Karl Richter. Can I come in?"

"Karl! What are you doing here at this time of the night?"

Karl stepped into the shaft of light that knifed through the partially opened door. Patricia's eyes grew wide with alarm.

"Oh my God, what happened to you?" She opened the door and helped him in, wrinkling up her nose at the smell.

"Can I clean myself up?" Karl asked.

"Yes, of course. In through the first door on your left. There are fresh towels on the shelf."

By the time he had removed the last traces of vomit and blood, Karl's head had cleared and his equilibrium returned. He looked at himself in the small mirror above the sink—his color was back, but the cut on his cheek had started to bleed again.

"Karl, are you all right?"

"Have you got any bandages?"

"Yes, let me in." She removed a small metal box from a drawer and motioned Karl to follow her. "Sit here. I'll see what I can do." Gently, she cleaned the cut and covered it with a thin bandage.

How quickly time flies, Patricia thought. She hid a smile, wondering how long he had been shaving. Caught unaware by his direct gaze, she was startled by the astonishing color of his eyes—Conrad's eyes—thick-lashed and brilliant like the ocean on a sunlit morning. But the resemblance to Conrad ended there. Karl's eyes were guileless, trusting, and she imagined they would sparkle with humor and warmth under the right circumstances. She could not help but notice the width of his shoulders and the ripple of muscles on his bare stomach.

"What will you do now, Karl?" she asked gently.

"I . . . don't know. My clothes are a mess." He tried to wipe the stains from his pants.

Patricia glanced at the tiny timepiece on her wrist. "You can't stay here, and you wouldn't exactly pass unnoticed on the street in your condition."

"I can't go home. My mother would . . ." His voice trailed off.

"No, of course not. Have you any friends close by?"

"No," Karl answered with a deep sigh.

"Well, I guess there's only one solution. You'll have to come home with me. I'll wash your clothes for you."

As they walked along the empty streets, Patricia asked, "Can you tell me what happened, or would you rather not?"

"No, it's all right. I guess I do owe you an explanation. Perhaps my father told you that I'm now working for him on the docks. The guys were going to teach me how to drink beer, but I failed the course miserably. To add to an already bad situation, I managed to get into a fight."

Patricia laughed softly. "You're a mess, all right, but nothing that can't be fixed."

They walked the rest of the way in silence. When they

stepped into Patricia's living room, for some unaccountable
reason it reminded Karl of his mother's sun-room. The furniture was different, but the same feeling was there. The room
afforded relaxing comfort with curved, overstuffed chairs and
stools for tired feet, lamps strategically placed for reading, a
radio within easy reach of the chesterfield, and a carpet thick
enough to sleep on.

"There's a blanket and a pillow in the hall closet," Patricia
said. "I'm going to change and make some coffee for us." As
an afterthought, she said, "You'd better give me your clothes.
I'll try and make them presentable."

Karl flushed, noticing the graceful sway of her body as she
disappeared into the tiny kitchen. By the time she returned
with two cups of steaming coffee, Karl had arranged his bed
on the couch and his clothes were draped over a chair.

"Here you are," Patricia said, passing him a cup. "It will
help settle your stomach."

She sat opposite Karl, sipping the steaming brew. Her light
robe did nothing to hide the supple lines of her body, and
Karl, watching her over the rim of his cup, thought even a
gunny sack could not hide her breasts. Suddenly their eyes met
and a strange warmth seeped through his body. Flustered, he
looked away. His heartbeat quickened, and he felt himself
grow hard beneath the blanket. As if in a fog, mindless of
all logic and reason, he saw her rise from the chair and hold
out her hand to him. It felt warm and small in his own; there
seemed to be a roaring in his ears, and he saw rather than
heard her say, "Come to bed, Karl."

She walked ahead of him and discarded her robe in the partial darkness of the bedroom. When she turned, Karl gasped.
Her white body seemed illuminated, almost translucent; her
breasts, free of all restraints, were erect and pink-tipped, and a
narrow waist emphasized the fullness of her hips. She was the
culmination of all his sexual fantasies, and from somewhere in
the depths of his mind he knew that she would always be the
inspiration of those same dreams.

"You're beautiful, Patricia," he whispered hoarsely.

"You are too, Karl." She reached up and ran her fingers
lightly along his cheek, over the muscles of his arm, across his
tense stomach, and finally she explored his rigid hardness. He
groaned involuntarily as her fingers became more demanding;
the urgency of passion surged through him, powerful and in

complete command. He felt the satin smoothness of her skin against his, felt himself drawn as if in a dream by the smell of her body until he was a part of her and she of him on the wide expanse of her bed. He moved against her uncertainly at first and then, encouraged by the low murmuring of her voice, his momentum increased to meet hers until his passion released in a shuddering wave of sensation. He lay back, pulling Patricia against him, burying his face in her hair.

"I love you, Patricia. I love you," he whispered.

"Hush, Karl. Lie still. Don't talk . . . not yet." She lay in his arms for a moment, then began to explore his body again. "Touch me, Karl," she said quietly.

Gently, expertly, her hands guided his over her nipples and her taut stomach. When he touched the moist warmth between her thighs, her body arched with desire and she opened herself to him again. Karl's desire surged again, more urgent than before, but this time he felt her release before his own began, felt himself floating, suspended in a sea of desire. The intensity of their passion left him weak, and he drifted into sleep, unaware that Patricia lay awake until dawn.

Music was playing faintly when he awoke, unfamiliar music that reminded him of ocean waves and billowing sails. He buried his face deeper into the pillows, drifting with the music, recalling the dream. Or was it a dream?

He opened his eyes slowly and saw that the sun's rays had formed a pattern on the carpeted floor. His pants and shirt hung on a chair beside the bed, clean and neatly pressed, and beside them, a robe—Patricia's robe. The previous night's events came rushing back: Scotty and Buck, the beer, Gibson's angry face, and finally Patricia. He remembered the way the robe had floated down to her feet. The bed was still fragrant with her perfume.

He stood up slowly, feeling a dull ache in the back of his head. The bathroom door was open, and fresh towels lay waiting on the counter. Gratefully, he allowed the water to pelt against him in the shower, driving the ache from his head and stinging his skin with its icy coldness. When he emerged, he could smell the mouth-watering aroma of coffee and sizzling bacon. He dressed quickly, closed his eyes for a moment to gather his courage, and walked out of the bedroom.

"Good morning. I thought you'd never wake up." Patricia smiled as she poured his coffee.

"Good morning. I'm sorry I slept so late . . . you should have wakened me. Thanks for looking after my clothes . . . and after me."

"You're welcome. Sit down. Breakfast is ready. You are hungry, aren't you?" She wore an apron over a crisp white blouse and dark skirt; her glossy hair was pulled into a tight knot at the back of her head.

"Patricia . . ."

"Eat your breakfast first, Karl." She smiled at him and heaped a generous portion of eggs and several strips of bacon onto his plate. She sipped her coffee while he ate.

"Patricia, about last night . . . Patricia, I love you." The words tumbled out.

"Thank you, Karl, for saying that. I will always remember last night." She looked at him, tears forming in her eyes. "I cannot explain why it happened. It wasn't something I had planned. A part of me that I never knew existed wants to keep you forever, but I know that would be foolish. I'm old enough to have a son your age."

"That doesn't matter," Karl almost shouted.

Patricia smiled sadly. "No, Karl, we both know it does. And I have commitments."

"You're not married!"

"There are other commitments even more binding than marriage, Karl. You have a long life ahead of you, and I have the feeling that you will succeed in whatever you choose to do." She walked over to him and held his face in both her hands. "You will always have a special place in my heart, my dearest, but there is no room for you in my life, now or ever."

"You won't change your mind?"

"No, Karl, I won't change my mind."

The food tasted like paper; he was no longer hungry. He pushed the plate away. Slowly, he rose and, with a straight back, walked to the door. Without turning, he said, "Patricia . . ."

"Don't stop, Karl."

The door closed behind him. She stood in the hallway long after the echo of his footsteps had died, and for a brief moment tears threatened to spill over. She did not cry often, nor was she certain why the tears were so close today. Perhaps it was a feeling of nostalgia for what might have been long ago. She flushed at the thought of her passion. It was as though her body had not been her own; it belonged to the hard-muscled youth whose eyes had reached into her heart.

For the third night in succession, Karl awoke suddenly and sat up in the darkness of his room. He could almost smell Patricia's perfume and feel the smoothness of her skin, but she remained beyond his reach. She called to him in a trembling voice, and he, running, stumbling, would cry out in frustration as she disappeared from sight. He stared into the empty darkness as the minutes ticked away at a leaden pace. He flung off the covers, reached for his clothes, and ran soundlessly down the stairs. The dogs perked up their ears as he passed them and whimpered softly before returning to their guarded sleep.

There was only one car in the garage; Conrad was away with the other. The finely tuned motor purred gently as he carefully backed out onto the street. He looked back; Drachenschlucht was in darkness; no one had heard him leave. He would be back before anyone knew he was gone—there was still two hours before dawn, just long enough for him to convince Patricia of his desperate need for her. It occurred to him that she would be asleep in bed, but he would wake her and she would understand. He opened the car window and the cool air blew on his face, ruffling his hair.

From a distance he could see a glimmer of light in Patricia's window, and he smiled. Maybe she had guessed he was coming and was waiting, or perhaps she could not sleep either.

Carefully, he eased the car against the sidewalk and stopped, his eyes riveted on the dim light in the window. Suddenly he felt himself go limp, as though his life's blood were oozing from his body. Ahead of him there was another car, and even as he recognized it, his mind rejected the implication. The car was a black Cadillac identical to the one he was driving—his father's car! What was it she had said? "Commitments more binding than marriage." Anger boiled up until it threatened to choke him. How could she? No wonder there was no room for him in her life—she already had his father! And what of his mother? Did she know? Did she care? The dim light in Patricia's window went out and he gripped the steering wheel until his hands grew numb as he pictured her naked body in his father's arms. He started the car and drove blindly through the streets, his heart bursting with anger.

Finally he stopped, aware only that he had arrived at the ocean. Tears flowed unheeded as the sun cast its first soft rays above the horizon.

All that was left of his dream was a deep concern for his mother; he would have to protect her against his father's infidelities. The image of Patricia, the beautiful goddess, was shattered forever, but the essence of the emotion he had felt for her remained. His father was another matter. Karl cringed when he pictured him returning to Drachenschlucht behind a facade of respectability and self-righteousness.

When Conrad returned home the next evening, his expression was sullen and he seemed irritable. When they all sat down to dinner, Dorothea attempted to draw him into their conversation, but drew little response.

Lisl, concerned but hesitant, said, "Father, you look upset tonight."

Dorothea smiled at her innocent appeal, but inwardly she stiffened and waited for Conrad's sharp rebuke.

"It seems you can't depend on anyone these days. Miss Harley announced that she's leaving—leaving without any notice!"

Mechanically, Karl swallowed the food that now seemed to stick in his throat. He heard his mother ask the question that was on the tip of his tongue.

"For how long?"

"Six months, possibly a year. She said she had to get away. What the hell am I supposed to do in the meantime?"

"Where is she going?" Lisl asked.

"Abroad," Conrad snapped. "England."

"Perhaps if you promised her a raise . . ." Dorothea suggested. "She has been with you a long time."

"I offered her a raise and a three-week holiday with pay, and she refused. That's as far as I'll go."

Karl searched his father's angry face for a sign of sadness or understanding—there was none. Just like that, and for him it's over, he thought. Karl excused himself and left the table abruptly. He walked through the garden and sat finally beneath a group of tall birches far from the house. Patricia was leaving because of what had happened between them, of that he was certain. Resentment against his father flared inside him. Karl could go to her now; they would leave for England, where they would be away from Conrad, and they would be happy. But the thought of her words stopped him. "You will always have a special place in my heart, my dearest, but there is no room for you in my life, now or ever." Tears welled up in Karl's eyes. The memory of Patricia would stay with him forever, but he knew he would never see her again.

The last of the silk bales had been unloaded, and the men were cleaning the holds for another cargo. They were an amiable lot, Karl decided, hard workers who needed the security of their jobs, and he knew he would miss their rough but good-natured companionship when he returned to school. Most of them had been longshoremen for many years, and they worked hard for their wages. If his father ever asked about these men, Karl could answer truthfully that he was not being cheated.

Determined that Karl should go back to school more worldly than when he left, Scotty made several attempts to include him in their weekly sessions at the Seaman's Club. Karl repeatedly refused.

"Hell, kid, you'll never learn to drink like a man!"

Karl laughed. "Sure I will, I just won't do it all in one night."

Scotty gestured to Karl to follow him out of the hold. "Come on, I need a smoke."

Karl watched as Scotty rolled a perfect cigarette. "You're pretty good at that."

"Yeah, I used to roll them for my old man ever since I was a little tyke. That's about the only time he ever noticed I was around."

"Were you born here, Scotty?"

"Sure was. My old man was a fisherman—tough as nails. The son of a bitch used to get drunk and pound me and my mother around until she just up and left him. That was the smartest thing she ever did, except she left me behind. He got real mean after that, so I left too, soon as I was old enough to get a job."

"Did you quit school?"

"Sure . . . had no choice. But I read a lot now," he added.

Karl shook his head in sympathy. "How old are you?"

"Twenty-six . . . you?"

"Seventeen."

"What's your old man like?"

Karl searched for the right words. "I don't know him too well. He's away a lot."

"But he's rich," Scotty added.

"Rich! What makes you say that?"

"I can tell just by looking at you. Don't get me wrong, you're okay, but you got class, like you're used to eating off white tablecloths and wearing clean underwear."

"Would it make any difference if I were rich?"

"Not to me it wouldn't, but it might to you one day."

"Scotty, I will never judge a man by the size of his bankroll. I do like clean underwear, though."

"Well, I hope you never change your mind. You ain't been around much yet, and you can become bitter if you get the shit kicked out of you enough times."

They climbed back down into the hold, reluctant to leave the warmth of the sun and fresh air. For the rest of the day, Karl was thoughtful as he worked. Scotty was only nine years older, but sometimes the difference seemed more like ninety years—he had experienced so much. Karl was suddenly filled with a sense of impatience and an overwhelming frustration.

"Hey, Karl, there's someone up here asking for you." Billick's voice boomed into the hold.

Even before he climbed out, Karl knew who it was. He grinned with pleasure when he saw Tatsuo. Billick stared openly at their exuberant and unrestrained greeting.

"Can I go for the day?" Karl asked.

"Yeah, sure. It's almost quitting time anyway." He watched with curiosity as Karl and Tatsuo walked away.

"Well," Karl said, "did you get it?"

Tatsuo nodded. "Yes, first dan black belt."

Karl placed a hand on Tatsuo's shoulder. "Congratulations, *kyō-dai*, I'm proud of you."

"Thank you." Tatsuo was touched by Karl's use of the word for brother.

"Was it difficult?"

"Very difficult, but you will discover that for yourself very soon. How is your family?"

"Mother seems tired these days."

"And Lisl?"

"Lisl is fine, but she missed you."

Tatsuo's face was serious. "I missed her, too."

"I've been waiting for you to come home," Karl said. "The *Cathy B* is all primed and ready for that cruise we planned."

Tatsuo's smile was wide. "Then what are we waiting for, my friend?"

[10]

It was Conrad who arranged Dorothea's meeting with Patrick Fenton. Following a visit to Dr. McAllister in early September, she told Conrad that she would like to seek professional advice in regard to her personal investments. He was surprised at first and regarded her coldly, pointing out that her assets were too meager to be overly concerned with, but she persisted until he finally suggested Patrick Fenton. He did not consider Patrick to be an authority on financial matters and often resented the advice he so readily doled out, but he did concede that Fenton was surprisingly quick with figures. He would be suitable for Dorothea's purposes.

In the solitude of her sun-room, Dorothea recalled Dr. McAllister's drawn face as he had spoken to her on the previous day. His quiet words had not been encouraging, but she had listened without flinching. She had asked that he be totally honest with her, and consequently he had given her the facts without the usual medical platitudes to soften them. Her last bone marrow samples had revealed progressive fibrosis, along with increased numbers of immature cells. She was chronically anemic and would require further supportive blood transfusions. It was only a matter of time before the disease would progress into the final stages.

"How old are Lisl and Karl now?" the doctor had asked, and despite his practiced objectivity, the tremor in his voice betrayed his emotions.

"Lisl is fifteen and Karl is seventeen."

Dr. McAllister walked slowly around his desk and took her hand in his. "It is so very difficult for me to say this, Dorothea, but I have no choice. For the past two years the disease has progressed slowly, but now it is nearing the terminal stages. It could run rampant at any time. Put your affairs in order, my dear."

Put your affairs in order. How simple and prosaic the words sounded as she mulled them over in her mind, yet there could be no mistaking their meaning. Final decisions had to be made. Karl and Lisl had to be looked after, and for the first time in many months she thought about her father, who through his farsightedness had provided financial independence for her children. Until now, the investments made so many years ago had not affected her, nor had they really interested her. She was vaguely aware that they had escalated considerably in value over the past few years—sound investments always did. The thought that she would be passing them on to Karl and Lisl comforted her. When her affairs were in order, as the doctor had so succinctly put it, she would discuss these investments with her children. Lisl was perhaps still too young to comprehend the value of her estate, but Karl, precocious, sensitive, and amazingly self-disciplined, would understand and accept the responsibility that accompanied the inheritance.

Her first meeting with Patrick Fenton had been brief; she merely emptied out her safety deposit box and delivered its contents to him. He had glanced through the papers, raised his eyebrows thoughtfully, and suggested she leave them with him for a few days. Now she sat in Hiro's office, only half-listening to a distant conversation. An ancient mask representing a lion dancer of the Kabuki theater dominated the opposite wall, its brilliant colors contrasting with the pale watercolors that hung on either side of it. A graceful porcelain sea gull with wings outstretched stood on a pedestal, where sunlight radiated through the window and caught the sheen of its smoothly polished body. In the slant of the wings and the curve of the slender body the artist had captured the instant before the sea gull's splendid flight. Dorothea admired its simple beauty as she listened absentmindedly to the conversation. Hiro came out and escorted her into his office.

"As you can see from my figures, Mr. Richter, wheat is still at the top of the list of exports, and when these total over thirty-four million dollars, I do not think you have any need for concern," Patrick said.

There was an edge to Conrad's voice. "Yes, but imports are down to just under ten million."

"I still feel you have nothing to be concerned about. Your ships will not sail empty," Patrick reassured him.

Conrad turned to Hiro. "Do you feel the same way?"

Hiro hesitated for a moment. "There is no doubt that Japan is feeling the influence of the military, but you will not be affected, Mr. Richter."

"I believe the economic climate is changing around the world. Japan is no exception," Patrick said, then abruptly turned his attention to Dorothea. "I have reviewed your investments carefully, Mrs. Richter, and although they are all basically sound, I would advise you to do some major reshuffling before it's too late."

"I'm not sure I understand, Mr. Fenton," Dorothea said.

"Well, there are definite signs that vast economic changes will be taking place in the next year or so, and I think you should be prepared for them."

"What are you talking about, Fenton?" Conrad asked. "The economy of our country has never been better!"

"I realize that, Mr. Richter, but it's the Americans I'm primarily concerned with. The course of their economy will affect us sooner or later. Even now, many large companies are reducing expenditures for capital improvements, and most investors have their eyes fixed only on the steady rise of the stock market."

"But production is continually increasing, and anyone can make a killing on the stock market," Conrad insisted.

"Certainly, but these profits are not being funneled back to the farmers, the fishermen, and the common laborers who are the backbone of the country. Who in hell is going to buy the products these large companies are producing? No one will be able to afford them! Most corporate structures are not organized to deal effectively with drastic reductions in their sales, and they will collapse totally when it happens. Even President Hoover has been trying to warn the country. He has tried to reverse the easy money policies, but it's already too late. People are too damn greedy to listen."

"What would you suggest, Mr. Fenton?" Dorothea asked.

"Convert your assets into real holdings, Mrs. Richter . . .

gold, property . . . get rid of all paper stocks!''

"Now just a minute. Let's not get all excited," Conrad pro-tested. "I realize my wife's assets do not amount to much, but there is still a great deal of money to be made on these paper holdings you talk about. I should know—I made seven thou-sand dollars on two stocks last week."

"I have no doubt that you did, but take my word for it. This boom will not last much longer," Patrick warned.

"Well, Fenton, that is only your opinion. Do what you like with my wife's assets, but I will look after mine as I see fit.'' Conrad stood up and straightened the papers in his file with quick, decisive movements. He turned to Dorothea. "Ap-parently you have already decided to follow Mr. Fenton's ad-vice, so there is no point in my being here any longer. Good day, gentlemen." He left, closing the door firmly behind him.

"Mrs. Richter, I don't think your husband is aware of the size of your assets," Patrick commented.

"No, he is not."

"Am I correct in assuming that you would prefer to keep it that way?"

"You are correct," Dorothea answered softly.

Patrick continued to make notations as they talked. "I can make the arrangements for the conversion of these assets into more tangible holdings, but the final decisions will be yours."

"I trust your judgment, Mr. Fenton. Please do what you think best."

"I see there is a copy of your will included. Are the contents of this will to remain unchanged?"

Dorothea nodded, her eyes not leaving Patrick's face. "After my . . . in the event of my death, all my personal holdings will go to the children."

Patrick looked up quickly, but the silent warning from Hiro prevented him from asking the question that had formed on his lips. Later he would ask Hiro about the seriousness of her illness.

"I will be in touch with you, Mrs. Richter, as soon as I have everything arranged."

"Thank you, Mr. Fenton. I am very grateful to you." Dorothea's face had grown pale, and there were dark circles of fatigue around her eyes, but she stood up gracefully and smiled.

Patrick stared for a moment, aware of her fragile beauty.

"I will drive you home," Hiro offered.

"Thank you. I feel tired all of a sudden. I've been concerned about these securities for some time, and I'm so relieved that my affairs are almost in order."

As Patrick watched them leave, he thoughtfully sipped the coffee that had been sitting at his elbow. He had taken several mouthfuls before he realized it was cold and tasted like dishwater. As he poured himself a fresh cup, he wondered if the wetness he had noticed in the corners of Hiro's eyes had actually been tears.

Hiro helped Dorothea into his new car, a maroon and white Packard.

"Your taste in automobiles is excellent as always," she said with a smile. "What would the sophisticates call it? Classy? Yes, definitely classy!"

Hiro laughed self-consciously. "It is a weakness of mine. My late son introduced me to my first luxury car years ago, and since then I have not been able to convince myself to buy anything that is merely practical."

They drove in comfortable silence for several blocks until coming upon an empty lot where a group of boys were playing a contentious game of baseball. Hiro slowed to a stop as a ball rolled into the street, followed predictably by an awkward boy whose outgrown trousers reached only inches below his knees.

"Karl and Tatsuo will finish school next June. What are your plans for Tatsuo?" Dorothea asked as they waited for the boy to retrieve his ball. She noted the uncertainty in Hiro's voice when he answered.

"There are no definite plans at this time, but the zaibatsu will expect him to assume his rightful position in due course."

"And you? What do you want for him?"

"Japan is undergoing dramatic change, some of which is difficult for me to accept, but I cannot escape my responsibilities. Tatsuo, however, is young and strong-willed. Perhaps for a short time the zaibatsu will make allowances for his youth. He and Karl have often talked of going to sea before they decide their futures, or, in Tatsuo's case, before he is absorbed by the zaibatsu. I would like that extra time for Tatsuo, time to allow his thoughts and philosophies to crystallize and his direction in life to become clear."

"I suppose Karl will eventually work with his father, but I'm afraid the partnership is not likely to last. Like you, I have often listened to Karl's plans about going to sea, but until now I have never considered them to be anything more than a boy's dream. I suppose I did not want to face the possibility of those dreams becoming a reality. Karl has always loved boats—while other children played with cars, Karl inevitably chose boats. Yes, he will go to sea,'' she said with a resigned sigh.

"Are you not in favor of this?"

"Yes, of course," Dorothea answered quickly. "It's just that he will be so far away, and when he returns I might not . . ." Her voice trailed away into silence.

"What did the doctor say when you last saw him?"

Dorothea stared straight ahead as she talked. "The disease is progressing. My future is very limited. But I refuse to worry about it anymore, nor will I allow it to spoil my remaining days or interfere with the lives of my children. I want to enjoy what time I have left . . . the sunshine, my garden, music, the children!"

"You are right of course," Hiro said. "But promise me that you will not try to face it alone."

For a brief moment, fear showed in Dorothea's face. "I am depending on your strength."

Hiro patted her hand. "Miyoko made me promise I would bring you back for tea today."

Dorothea settled back against the cushioned seat. "I cannot think of anything I would rather do."

Unlike the rest of the household, who carefully avoided any serious discussions with Conrad, Karl firmly refused to flinch under his father's angry and frequent tirades, although he made no attempt to openly challenge him. He refrained from drawing any unnecessary attention to his training, which he continued with the usual rigor. The observations and predictions made by Hiro began to prove correct—Karl's strength became directly proportionate to his immense size; his endurance matched Tatsuo's, and at times proved superior. His size no longer hindered the fluid, graceful footwork; his thrusts and defensive blocks were firm, his eyes sharp, and his reflexes instantaneous. It was only the more complicated and dramatic movements like the swing kicks and back kicks that still presented problems for his heavy, muscular legs.

Meanwhile, Tatsuo had reached a high degree of Zen maturity. He had discovered his true nature and had brought the Ox under control. He could reach samādhi easily now, even while he was working. He had finally attained the stage called the "great death," in which the level of consciousness is so deep that not even reflection remains; sensation and perception are gone. Tatsuo had experienced the complete purification of his thoughts and feelings, and his eyes reflected that peace. Hiro recognized the expression and shared Tatsuo's wonder in his own heart, sensing his grandson's reverence for the world and its beauty.

"It is like putting a brush to fresh, unblemished paper," Tatsuo had said. "I am at the source again, Oji-san. It is the same world but more beautiful than ever before!" Hiro had smiled in understanding.

Hiro waited until Karl had earned his first grade—*kyū* —brown belt before he broached the subject of the tea ceremony.

"It is an ancient art practiced by Zen masters and samurai warriors. It is a frugal pleasure but very rich in meaning," Hiro explained. "I will be waiting for you and Tatsuo in the tea room."

Following Tatsuo's example, Karl changed into a fresh kimono. He shook his head in disbelief. "Is the sensei serious? A tea ceremony? Look at me . . . six feet and two inches with hands like these!" He spread his large, callused hands for Tatsuo to see. "It will be like teaching an elephant to walk on eggs. I thought that stuff was just for women."

"The tea ceremony has nothing to do with your appearance. The purpose of it is to help you achieve repose of mind and tranquility of the soul. I have taken part in the tea ceremony many times, as has the sensei."

Karl faced him with a subdued expression. "I should have known." He bowed low. "Lead the way, wise one," he said with a glint of humor in his eyes.

The tea room was dimly lit with a full view of the garden. A high, narrow tokonoma contained a scroll and a slender vase with a single willow branch. Hiro knelt on a small flat cushion as he waited for Karl and Tatsuo to assume their places on the mats before him.

Watching Tatsuo from the corner of his eye, Karl followed his example and bowed to the tokonoma and then to the sensei before lowering himself onto the tatami. With slow deliberate movements, Hiro passed two paper fans to Tatsuo, who

turned and positioned them behind their feet, Karl's pointing
to the right, his own to the left. An iron pot stood on a black
lacquered brazier set into a low table. Placed neatly beside the
pot was a tea whisk made of split bamboo, a ladle made from
the same material, and a small round container.

Hiro and Tatsuo sat completely still in the silent room while
Karl fought the impulse to fidget. The water in the iron pot
began to boil and a faint hissing sound escaped.

Hiro spoke for the first time. "Does the sound of the water
boiling remind you of autumn breezes in pine needles?" He
shut his eyes and smiled while he listened to the sound. He
then lifted the ladle and examined it as though contemplating
its simplicity.

Karl watched with fascination, his discomfort forgotten.
Moving gracefully, Hiro replaced the ladle and began wiping a
rough earthenware teacup with a soft cloth. Then with the
same cloth he wiped the bamboo spatula. Without changing
his expression and unaffected by the heat, he removed the
heavy lid from the steaming iron pot and ladled water into the
cup. Ceremoniously, he opened the small round container,
which held the tea, and gravely measured exactly three
spatulas of the green powder into the cup. He whisked it carefully into a froth and bowed before presenting it to Tatsuo.

With equal gravity, Tatsuo turned the cup in his hands and
examined its texture and shape before solemnly consuming the
contents in three loud sips while Karl did his best to suppress a
smile. Tatsuo returned the cup to Hiro with a respectful bow.
Wordlessly, Tatsuo withdrew and motioned Karl to take his
place on the mat.

Patiently but firmly, Hiro guided Karl through his first attempt to conduct a tea ceremony. He made only one conces-
sion—he allowed Karl to lift the heavy lid from the pot of boiling water with a cloth to protect his hands. Later, Hiro informed him, he too would lift the lid without protection. Karl
fumbled awkwardly with the whisk and perspiration ran down
his back as he forced himself to control his clumsy hands while
he poured the water over the tea. Hiro and Tatsuo watched
without a flicker of expression on their faces as he whisked the
tea into a froth. With a sigh of relief, Karl passed the cup to
Hiro. His fingers slipped and he watched the contents seep
onto the spotless tatami.

"It does not matter. Wipe it up with the cloth and begin
again," Hiro said quietly. '

Karl nodded gratefully and began the entire ceremony again, this time receiving only three taps on his hands with the folded fan and one curt correction when he forgot to contemplate the beauty of the design on the ladle. When the ceremony was completed, Tatsuo reverently gathered up the utensils and removed them from the room.

"The tea ceremony is an exercise in self-control," Hiro explained. "The careful cleansing of the utensils is really a cleansing of the mind. The exacting movements teach spiritual discipline and self-forgetfulness. It is very important to pay strict attention to every tiny detail of the procedure. As you overcome your hesitancy and awkwardness, you will come to understand this ceremony as an expression of our philosophy—a way of achieving peace and inner light."

"It is like part of a religious service," Karl observed.

"Yes, very similar," Hiro agreed.

"Except," Tatsuo said with suppressed laughter, "you are not supposed to look like you are drinking poison when the cup is passed to you. And the look on your face when you dropped the cup!" Tatsuo burst out laughing, throwing his head back and slapping his leg. Karl laughed sheepishly at first and then with equal gusto as the tension left his body.

Hiro smiled knowingly at his two students. "Would you like me to tell you what Tatsuo did on his first attempt, Karl?"

"Please do."

"Oh no, Ojī-san!"

"I consider it my duty, Tatsuo, to teach you humility," Hiro said with an amused expression. "The first time Tatsuo took part in a tea ceremony, he spilled the entire pot of boiling water. Some of the scalding water penetrated his kimono, which he had to remove very quickly before the heat reached his tender parts. Fortunately, there were no ladies present to witness his prompt disrobing."

Their laughter echoed loudly until even Miyoko could hear them from where she sat sewing at the far end of the house.

〔 11 〕

It seemed to Lisl that she had always loved Tatsuo. Even before she met him, she had listened to Karl's stories with rapt attention and known that his Japanese friend was special. When she finally met Tatsuo, she had not been disappointed despite his strange appearance and reserved manner.

He had been impossibly shy with her, almost laughably courteous, treating her as though she were a fairy tale princess. Lisl tried to attract his attention whenever she could, yet when she received it, she was at a loss for words. Gradually their shyness toward each other lessened and they began talking, hesitantly at first, then freely and at length when their trust in each other grew. It was a gentle relationship with easy laughter at small things, an opportunity for them to reveal dreams, to share thoughts, and to express their highest ideals, each knowing the other would understand. Often they would just walk with the dogs trotting behind them or they would run with the sheer exuberance of youthful joy, jumping over imaginary obstacles, laughing at each other's nonsensical jokes, and enjoying the easy banter which is only possible between true companions.

Lisl's love for Tatsuo was not yet in full bloom, but she knew it was there. Each day she looked forward to her time with him, anticipating the exquisite joy she always felt when she saw him. Slowly, they fell into a pattern. Lisl would walk the dogs each evening after supper, knowing that Tatsuo would be waiting for her under the old maple tree. The look

on his face always reassurred her that he too experienced the
same particular thrill. She carefully avoided mentioning Tatsuo to her father, for she knew without question what his reaction would be. Conrad, however, did not pose any problems,
since he was not home often enough to interfere with any of
Lisl's activities, and when he was, his interest in her was very
limited.

Lisl did not give much thought to the distant future—it
seemed too obscure. Life for her held only the excitement of
today, and she was happy with that, content and secure in the
knowledge that she was loved and had only to ask for whatever she wanted. Real obstacles had not presented themselves,
and if they did, she was certain she could solve them easily and
that life would continue on as always. It was only when Tatsuo
and Karl neared the completion of their final year at school
that she experienced her first twinge of uneasiness and uncertainty.

It was just a few minutes past nine, and Lisl hurried through
the quiet house. The dogs, sensing her impatience, whined
softly as they padded after her, nuzzling her for attention. She
patted their smooth heads.

"Quiet, you idiots! Mother is resting. And you can't come
with me tonight either. I don't want any distractions." Both
dogs listened with their ears raised to her gentle rebuke.

"Sit here and wait for Karl," she commanded. "And don't
look at me like that because I won't change my mind." She
carelessly let the door slam behind her.

She was early, but Tatsuo was already waiting at their usual
place under the huge maple. He smiled when he saw her approach. Lisl returned the smile and slid her arm through his as
they walked along the tree-lined street.

"Tatsuo, are you really going to sea with Karl when you
finish school?" Lisl asked after they had walked several
blocks without speaking.

"Yes." Tatsuo felt her hand tighten on his arm. "It will
only be for six months or so, definitely not more than a year."

"Six months seems so long, and a year is an eternity," she
whispered.

Tatsuo stopped, his eyes level with hers. "Karl and I have
talked about this for a long time. We cannot change our minds
now. The time will pass quickly, and besides, you will be busy
in your last year of school."

"No, it won't pass quickly," she choked. "I'll miss Karl, but I will miss you most of all. And why six months or a year? Father's ships only take two months for a round trip to Japan!"

"We will not be on your father's ship."

"Why not?" Lisl stopped and looked up at Tatsuo.

"Karl and I want to go together. Your father would not allow me to sail on one of his ships."

"But that's ridiculous! Of course he would."

"No, Lisl, he would not."

Lisl began walking again. "I wish you wouldn't go."

"I have to go. Perhaps it will be a waste of time, but I must find out for myself. The zaibatsu has already given me permission."

"You mean to say they could prevent you from going but I couldn't?" Lisl's face held surprise. "But how could they do that? You will be old enough to make your own decisions!"

Tatsuo shook his head. "I will always be obligated to abide by the decisions of the zaibatsu."

"But that seems so archaic."

"It only seems that way to you because you have so much more freedom than most people." He grinned at her. "Why, young Japanese ladies are not even allowed to be alone with a man."

Lisl raised her chin defiantly. "Well then, I guess I'm not like your well-bred Japanese ladies because I will do what I want, and that is to be with you—unchaperoned!"

Stars littered the sky as they neared St. John's College, now dark except for a dim light in the rectory. Tatsuo sighed softly as his eyes absorbed the familiar sight of the school. Even in the semidarkness he could distinguish each classroom, visualize the long hallways, recall the exact position of every team photograph, and smell the stale odor of books, chalk, and oiled floors.

"You know, the first time I came here I felt more than a little frightened."

Lisl stopped and stared through the darkness at his face. "You frightened? I cannot imagine you being afraid of anything. You seem so sure of yourself."

"I was not sure of anything that day except that I was different. I am still different, but it does not frighten me anymore." Lisl's face was close to his, and in the soft light he could distinguish the curve of her mouth and feel the warmth of her breath.

"Would you be surprised if I told you that I am afraid now?" His voice was husky.

"Afraid? Of what?"

"You are so beautiful," he whispered. "I want to kiss you, and I am afraid."

"Don't be afraid," Lisl murmured as her arms slid around his neck.

Tatsuo pulled her close, and he could feel the thudding of his heart as he bent to kiss her. Lisl melted against him, her arms tightening around his neck as she returned his cautious kiss. In his arms, she felt warm and helpless, her body pliant and yielding to his. When he released her, Tatsuo realized he was trembling.

With the advent of spring, the balmy days and crystal waters lured Karl and Tatsuo to the open sea. On the *Cathy B*, with the solitude of the ocean surrounding them, they talked about their precious dreams and found in each other a reflection of themselves. Theirs was an easy friendship, demanding nothing yet giving everything. The only rivalry between them was in their tests of physical strength and skill, a rivalry which spurred them on toward the perfection each sought.

Lisl often questioned Karl about Tatsuo and pleaded to be included in their plans. At times she resented Karl for taking so much of Tatsuo's time, but she soon learned how to implement her own subtle schemes to disrupt that near monopoly. According to a carefully laid plan, she met Karl just as he was preparing for an early morning run.

"Are you going out on the *Cathy B* tomorrow?" she asked innocently.

"You mean, are Tatsuo and I going out on the *Cathy B* tomorrow," Karl corrected with a teasing smile.

"Well, are you?"

"Yes, we are. Why?"

"Would you mind if I came along?"

"No, I don't mind, but perhaps I should ask Tatsuo first," Karl said gravely.

"Oh, he won't mind," Lisl answered quickly.

"We're leaving early in the morning."

"Can I bring a friend along?" Lisl's eyes were imploring.

"Is she supposed to divert my attention so you can have Tatsuo all to yourself?"

Lisl smiled mischievously.

"Well, is she?"

"This time, Mr. Smart Ass, I think the joke is going to be on you."

"What do you mean?"

"You will just have to wait," Lisl said loftily. "See you on the *Cathy B*." She tossed her head and disappeared into the house.

Karl was already aboard the boat when Tatsuo arrived with Lisl and her friend. He heard Tatsuo's familiar whistle and climbed up to the deck to motion them aboard while he stored the last of the supplies.

"Karl," Lisl said, "I want you to meet my friend, Janice Chandler."

"I'll be right with you. I just want to put this last carton away." He turned toward Lisl and Janice. Had he been less disciplined he might have let his mouth fall open in a gape. She was the most beautiful girl he had ever seen. "Hello, Janice," he stammered, "I'm glad you could come along."

"I'm pleased to meet you, Karl," Janice replied.

It took a moment for Karl to realize that she was waiting for him to take her outstretched hand. He was surprised at how small and delicate it felt in his. Her smile spread and deepened the dimples in her cheeks. Karl guessed that the top of her blond head would just reach his shoulders, but her legs looked long and slender beneath the white slacks she wore; her bulky sweater did nothing to conceal the full curve of her breasts.

"Don't you think we should be on our way, Karl?" Lisl asked sweetly.

Karl glanced at his sister, ignoring the devilish gleam in her eyes. "Everything is set. We can leave anytime."

As Lisl passed Karl, she leaned over and whispered, "Glue yourself together and put your eyeballs back in your head. I told you you were in for a surprise."

They cruised the ocean at a leisurely pace, fishing half-heartedly for salmon and relaxing in the warm sun. They anchored in a deserted cove and walked along the white sandy beach, jumping to avoid the crashing waves. A family of sea otters, sunning on the rocks, slid gracefully into the water. Further out in the water the otters turned on their backs and floated, their stubby paws and bristled whiskers just above the water.

Janice stumbled upon an injured sea gull helplessly gasping for its last breath. Karl was surprised to see tears fill her eyes and run down her sun-flushed cheeks as they carried the dying bird to a less exposed spot.

"Isn't there anything we can do?" she asked through her tears.

"Nothing except leave him where the other animals can't get at him. Don't cry," Karl said gently. "We've done all we can."

"I hate to see it suffer."

"I think his suffering is over," Karl said after a few minutes.

As they walked along the beach again, Karl reached for Janice's hand and she, conscious of his closeness, felt her heartbeat quicken. Trying not to be obvious, she stole glances at him. He had a lean face with a straight nose and a square jaw, a strong face, but when he smiled, the cleft in his chin deepened and he looked disarmingly boyish.

"Do you come here often?" Janice asked.

"Not as often as I would like to."

"Lisl told me that you and Tatsuo are planning to join the merchant marine."

"Yes, as soon as school is over."

"That's too bad. We've just met and you're planning to go away." Janice smiled, but there was genuine disappointment in her voice.

"I'll only be gone six months or so. Then we'll come back here and celebrate."

"I'd like that," Janice said softly.

Karl looked at her upturned face and their eyes met and held. Slowly he bent down and kissed her, drawing her to him.

"Six months is such a long time," she whispered as Karl released her.

Before he could reach for her again, she turned and walked away; Karl followed. She had removed her sandals and rolled up her slacks to reveal long, smooth legs. The breeze from the ocean molded her sweater and slacks to the rounded, pliant curves of her body, and Karl found himself wishing that his sea voyage was over and they were alone on the deserted island.

When they rounded a huge rock that jutted out of the sand, they found Lisl and Tatsuo sitting in its shade.

"I fell," Lisl said apologetically. Blood seeped from a jagged cut on her leg.

"You two go ahead," Tatsuo said. "I'll take Lisl back to the boat and clean this up. The saltwater should take care of any infection."

"Can you walk?" Karl asked with concern.

"Of course, I can walk," Lisl answered. She stood up and winced with pain. She leaned against Tatsuo for support as they started toward the *Cathy B*.

"Do you think we should go with them?" Janice asked.

"No, she'll be all right. Knowing my sister, she probably staged the whole event."

"By the look on Tatsuo's face, her audience of one appreciated the performance," Janice said, laughing.

Aboard the *Cathy B*, Tatsuo gently cleaned the cut and applied a clumsy makeshift bandage, apologizing for his ineptness.

"Well, I wouldn't want you to perform major surgery on me, but as a first aid attendant you'll do just fine."

"Just don't go wandering around the beach alone," Tatsuo said firmly.

"Perhaps I should ask Will Stanton to accompany me while you're away," Lisl teased.

There was a look of pain on Tatsuo's face.

"Oh, Tatsuo, I didn't mean that. I'm sorry," Lisl cried instantly.

"I have no right to tell you what to do," Tatsuo said.

"Sure you do." She ran in front of him, forcing him to stop. "Damn you, Tatsuo, I wish I could figure you out. Why should caring for me be a problem?"

"Lisl, I have tried to explain to you so many times. I am not entirely free to make my own decisions about my future."

"I just can't believe that you would allow some tired old men in a foreign country to tell you how to live your life."

"Japan is not a foreign country to me, Lisl, and those tired old men will not tell me how to live my life. I already know how I must live it."

"And I suppose that life does not include me." Tears of anger were gathering in her eyes. "Tatsuo, I love you. Doesn't that mean anything to you?'' she shouted.

"Lisl, please. You know how I feel about you, but I cannot make any promises to you now, and I cannot ask you to make any to me. I just do not know what is going to happen.''

"You mean your zaibatsu and all those obligations are more important than me?''

Tatsuo stared, wordlessly begging her to stop.

"Well, are they?'' she demanded.

Tatsuo took her by the shoulders. "It is not a matter of who is more important or what is more important. I have no choice. Please understand!''

"No, I don't understand. Everybody has a choice. Are you going to tell me that you don't love me?'' The tears coursed down her cheeks.

"Please do not cry, Lisl. One day I will show you how I feel.''

"Show me now. Tell them to go to hell!''

Tatsuo's shoulders sagged. His eyes were dark with anguish. Lisl's face had grown pale and her mouth was set with defiance.

"We'll just see who's more important—right now!'' she challenged. Deliberately, she began to undo the buttons on her shirt, her slacks were next. In one swift movement she slipped the shirt and slacks off and threw them down. She was barefoot and her long legs glistened in the sun. Tatsuo caught his breath as she began to remove her undergarments.

"Lisl, wait . . .''

She stood facing him, legs apart, breasts rising and falling with each angry breath.

"Here I am, Tatsuo. Now make your choice,'' she said harshly.

Tatsuo's voice was choked, barely more than a whisper. "Lisl, you are more beautiful than I ever imagined.''

She moved closer to him, pressing against him, kissing him lightly. She felt his arms close around her, heard him moan softly as she began to undo his shirt.

"Tell me that you love me, Tatsuo. Tell me that you will stay with me. You belong to me, not to the zaibatsu.''

Her kisses became more demanding, and he trembled. "I love you, Lisl, but I do not want you like this. Please, not like this.''

"They can't have you. I'm going to keep you, and I'll do

whatever I have to, to make you mine.'' She felt the urgency in him, despite his protests, and the hardness of his body against hers. For an instant she hesitated, frightened, until she heard him whisper her name. Then her body arched against him as he drew her gently down on the deck. The world receded and disappeared; only they remained, locked in the intensity of their emotions, searching, exploring, demanding, giving. Suddenly Lisl heard Tatsuo groan, the sound almost a sob.

"Lisl, I cannot do this to you. I want you so badly, but not like this. I will still be Japanese, I will still be a Takezawa, and I will still have to do the things that must be done.'' He slammed down his clenched fist over and over until Lisl stilled him.

"Don't,'' she said quietly. "It's all right. It's all right.''

Slowly, she gathered up her clothes and began to dress. "Well, you can't say I didn't try.'' Her eyes shone with unshed tears. "But I love you, Tatsuo, with all my heart.''

Tatsuo reached for her and held her close. "I know.'' He placed his own wet cheek against hers while she cried. "And I love you.''

In the early evening, the room was quiet except for the rhythmic scratching of Dorothea's pen. Her fingers were cramped, but she continued to write and to carefully fold each letter precisely below her signature and directly above the date, May 25, 1928. The letters were brief, announcing the cancellation of the annual spring party at Drachenschlucht. She did not give any reason for the cancellation but merely alluded to Conrad's pressing business affairs. She had considered admitting that her illness had worsened until she was no longer able to attend a party let alone arrange one, but that would undoubtedly evoke sympathy or, worse, curiosity. She could not face that, at least not yet. Cancelling the party did not distress her; in fact, she felt a great sense of relief despite Conrad's annoyance.

Through the open window a breeze, cool and scented with the fertile fragrance of spring, gently lifted the papers on her desk. She closed her eyes, and the memories of other spring days came flooding back: she was a young girl, her legs already brown from the warm sun, running with the glorious release of energy after several hours at the piano. The music would still ring inside her, vibrant and beautiful, and the world would join in the chorus as she ran. But that was a long time ago.

She rose wearily and walked out into the gathering dusk. Unconsciously, she slipped off her shoes and blissfully curled her toes around the moist, freshly cut grass. She was alone in the near darkness of the garden, and yet she could feel the presence of God. She prayed often now, asking for courage and strength and a secure future for her children, but there was no need for prayer tonight. She felt safe, protected by the silent communication, and she knew she would no longer question why she had to die. The desire to live still burned intensely within her, but perhaps in time that too would disappear.

The moon rose in brilliant splendor, tinting the edges of every leaf, petal, and blade of grass with shimmering light. Somewhere close by a night bird trilled softly, a lonely and beautful sound. Familiar words formed in her mind: "One generation passeth away, and another generation cometh: but the earth abideth forever." She looked back at the house, up to where a light glowed in Lisl's window and another in Karl's room. Her heart ached. One thought still haunted her—that she would never see her children mature and reach out to find their place in the world.

All heads were bowed while Father O'Brien recited the opening prayer, his deep voice echoing hollowly through the gymnasium. Thirty-four young men, the graduating class of 1928, sat on the elevated stage facing their parents and guests. Karl, forcing himself to concentrate, caught only a few words here and there. His own thoughts intruded on the prayer.

Father O'Brien's voice vibrated with emotion. "We are thankful for the privilege of having guided these boys, most of whom have been with us for twelve years . . ."

Twelve years! Karl thought. They had gone by so quickly, and yet at times they had seemed endless.

Karl opened his eyes and looked at his mother, sitting between his father and Lisl. Next to Lisl sat Janice. Their heads were bent in prayer as Father O'Brien's resonant voice flowed over them, but Karl had no doubt that Lisl's foot was swinging restlessly beneath her long dress. He saw her glance up, and Karl followed her gaze to Tatsuo, who sat at the far end of the stage.

The ceremonies proceeded on schedule, and parents glowed with pride as the graduates stepped forward to receive their diplomas.

Father O'Brien again addressed the audience. "Ladies and gentlemen, I would now like to introduce the young man whom the graduates have chosen to deliver the valedictory address. I believe they have made an excellent choice. This student has proven himself both academically and physically and has earned the respect and admiration of all of us. He has been instrumental in our overwhelming victories on the baseball field—we won the city championship four years ago and have kept it ever since. He came here a stranger, but we've learned from him as he has learned from us. Ladies and gentlemen, this year's valedictorian, Tatsuo Takezawa."

The applause from the audience was hesitant and sporadic, but as Tatsuo walked to the podium, the graduating class stood up and their ovation was resounding. Unaware of the whispers around them, Hiro and Miyoko were on their feet along with the graduates.

Tatsuo stood before the podium, and an uncomfortable hush spread across the huge auditorium and finally settled into an expectant stillness. Tatsuo's form was rigidly erect, his face composed, and his eyes steady as he looked down at the audience. He smiled first at his grandparents, then at Lisl and Dorothea. He noted Dorothea's wave of encouragement.

"Parents, friends, teachers, and fellow graduates," he began in a voice that was rich and distinct. "It has been my privilege to attend St. John's College for the past five years. During these years, my classmates and I have shared many good times and experiences, and we have reached this milestone together. We are sad, my fellow graduates and I, for we have grown close over the years and now we must travel along different paths, paths that may separate us forever. But that is the nature of life. It flows like a mighty river, and although we may alter its course, we cannot stop its flow, nor do we want to. Our futures lie before us and we are ready. The fathers and brothers here at St. John's have not only instilled in us a valuable education, they have taught us the value of fellowship and sacrifice, and we shall carry these lessons with us for the rest of our lives. They have guided and molded us as we in turn will guide and mold the world of tomorrow. We do not know what effect the passage of time will have on us, but we will always remember the friendships we have shared, the battles we have won on the playing fields, and the hardships we have overcome with the help of our teachers. We will go forward well armed with knowledge and fortified with glorious memories.'' Tatsuo spoke slowly, his voice gathering strength with each word until the entire audience was captivated.

". . . in closing, I would like to recite an ancient poem my grandfather taught me. I hope you will carry its message with you.

> Sow a thought and reap an act;
> Sow an act and reap a habit;
> Sow a habit and reap a character;
> Sow a character and reap a destiny.''

Tatsuo bowed respectfully and returned to his seat as the applause from the audience and the graduates rose to a deafening crescendo.

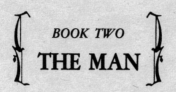

BOOK TWO

THE MAN

[12]

The name *Liverpool* was barely legible on the rusted hull, where grime and salt had accumulated in unsightly ridges. Up top, the decks and machinery had also lost their battle against the sea and they too bore the signs of age and neglect. Karl and Tatsuo approached the freighter cautiously.

"It's the *Liverpool*, all right, but do you think it's safe to go aboard? She might sink!" Karl said.

"Lots of good years left in her," Tatsuo said heartily.

The gangway creaked under their feet and swung gently on corroded chains. A seaman with sleepy eyes and a pock-marked face watched them approach.

"Is the captain aboard?" Tatsuo shouted.

The seaman finished lighting his cigarette before flicking the match over the rail. "He's up on the bridge. Why?" he asked with a Cockney accent.

"I'm Karl Richter, and this is Tatsuo Takezawa. We heard the skipper is looking for extra crew, and we would like to sign on."

"That's what I was afraid of. You been to sea before?"

"Sure," Karl answered quickly.

There was a sardonic gleam in the seaman's eyes as he pointed in the direction of the forward deckhouse. "Up there."

Captain Ferguson's flint gray eyes peered out from beneath shaggy brows. He studied Karl and Tatsuo only for a moment and then returned to the logbook in which he was writing.

When he had completed the entry, he closed the book loudly and stood up.

In stark contrast to the neglected ship, the captain's uniform was spotless, and the creases in his pants were straight and sharp. The clean-shaven face was weather-beaten and etched with distinct lines around his mouth and eyes. He looked to be about fifty-five.

"So you're the two men the shipping agent sent over?"

"Yes, sir."

"May I see your papers?"

Tatsuo and Karl handed him their seaman's identification cards and certificates of discharge. He turned the pages quickly. "There are no entries in here!"

"No, sir, there aren't. You see, we're fresh out of school, but we're willing to work hard," Karl explained quickly.

"We're used to hard work, sir," Tatsuo added.

"Are you, now?" Captain Ferguson's shaggy eyebrows rose slightly. The boys shifted uncomfortably under his direct gaze. "I need a couple of trimmers. Do you know what that means?"

"No, sir," they replied in unison.

"Well, it doesn't matter. The *Liverpool* is a coal burner and we need a couple of mules like you two in the bunkers. It's bloody hard work, but you look like you can handle it with a little practice."

"Yes, sir. I know we can," Karl said.

"We're prepared to work hard, Captain," Tatsuo added. "We enjoy hard work."

Captain Ferguson smiled faintly. "We'll see how much you enjoy it after a few days in the bunkers. When you sign on articles with me, you do so for the entire voyage, and that's all the way back to Vancouver. Think you can shovel coal for half a year?"

Karl's heart raced; he did not trust himself to speak, but he nodded quickly.

"We can shovel coal for a whole year," Tatsuo said firmly.

"Good. We sail in three days. You be here in two." He held out his hand. Karl grinned widely as he pumped the captain's hand, but Tatsuo's face was without expression.

"Well, we did it," Karl said as they walked along the dirty steel deck. "Do you think we'll really like shoveling coal for the next six months?"

"No, but we have to start somewhere," Tatsuo answered.

"I don't know why I'm so excited! I don't think this is going to be any picnic."

"Well, it's too late to change our minds now."

As they approached the gangway, they were again met by the seaman with the Cockney accent. "Well what's the good word, mates? Are you to be sailors?"

"We're sailors. Trimmers to be exact," Karl said.

The seaman grinned, exposing his tobacco-stained teeth. "Hah! The captain could always spot a good mule. We'll find out what you're made of, all right. Where are you blokes headed now?"

"We have two days before we report," Tatsuo announced.

"Well, you better drain your balls, before then 'cause you're not going to get any aboard this old tub." He slapped his leg with a loud whack, and his laugh came out in a wheeze.

"What? You mean to tell me the *Liverpool* doesn't carry dames?" Karl asked in mock surprise.

The seaman stopped his wheezing long enough to catch the laughter forming on Karl's face. "You're on the ball, matey. Dames on the *Liverpool*! Shit, that's a laugh!" He cuffed Karl on the shoulder.

"Can we bring anything back for you?" Karl asked.

The seaman's eyes were instantly alert. "Hey, matey, good of you to offer. I could use a carton of fags—Players, Navy Cut. I don't get wages for a while 'cause I've been logged, but I'll pay you back soon enough. My word's good as money in the bank."

"Sure, we'll get some for you."

The seaman watched them bounce down the gangway and then called after them. "I won't forget you mates, I owe you one. The name's Gilhooly—Jack Gilhooly."

"Good, I have a feeling we're going to need a few favors before this voyage is over," Tatsuo said under his breath.

Karl turned to look at the *Liverpool* once more and was reminded of the repugnant odor that seemed to permeate the entire ship. There was a hollowness in the pit of his stomach as he thought of the green lawns surrounding Drachenschlucht, the dogs waiting patiently by the door, and the morning sunlight streaking through his bedroom window. In a few days his bed would be a narrow berth on an aged freighter, Harras and Prinz would be many miles away, and the sun would never penetrate his dingy quarters.

"Hey, are you having second thoughts?" Tatsuo asked,

noticing Karl's grave expression.

"No . . . just doing some comparing. I don't think the *Liverpool* will have many of the comforts of home."

"No, but you can't see the world from your bedroom window," Tatsuo said cheerfully.

That evening at the dinner table, Conrad questioned his son. "Why the hell didn't you sign on one of my ships?"

"I wanted the challenge, Father."

"Challenge! Damnit, I work like a horse to make life easy for you and you want challenge. What ship did you sign on?"

"The *Liverpool*."

"The *Liverpool*!" Conrad shook his head. "I know her—British—part of the Imperial Line. Nothing but a rusty old tub."

"Well, she's old, but she looks okay."

"She's a junk heap, and you're a bloody fool for signing on."

Karl stared down at his plate and clenched his teeth.

"Conrad, please, there's nothing we can do about it now," Dorothea said.

Conrad ignored her. "What did you sign on as?"

"Trimmer."

"Trimmer! That's the worst job there is. Just be ready to work your ass off. If you had signed on one of my ships, you could at least have been in the fresh air."

"Your ships only go as far as Japan, and we want to see more of the world," Karl explained quietly.

"What do you mean—we?"

"Tatsuo and I."

"So that's it. The *Liverpool* isn't fussy about who it takes on."

Anger flashed in Karl's eyes, but he forced his voice to remain calm. "I think they are very particular, Father. They're just not narrow-minded."

"We'll see who's narrow-minded when you get home. I think you might have a change of heart after you've worked on that tub."

Dorothea noticed an angry retort beginning to form on Karl's lips. "Oh, please. Karl will be leaving in two days. We won't all be together again for a long time." Dorothea's face was pale and drawn.

"I'm sorry," Karl apologized.

"I have some work to do," Conrad muttered. "Tell Mrs.

Lange to bring my coffee into the study." He left the dining room without looking at his son.

Lisl toyed with the food on her plate. "I'll help you pack," she said finally.

"Are you that anxious to get rid of me?" Karl asked, forcing a smile.

Lisl shook her head silently; there were tears behind her lowered lashes.

"Thanks, Lisl," Karl said soberly. "I'd really appreciate the help. You know, Mother, I think she might even miss me."

"We're both going to miss you, son. Promise that you'll write often and take good care of yourself."

"I promise."

"And, Karl, should anything happen to me while you're away, my will is with Mr. Takezawa. There is also a copy at the Federal Bank."

"What are you talking about? Why a will?"

"Just a precaution," she answered quickly.

"Mother, I have a strange feeling that you're not telling me everything. Is anything wrong?"

"No, darling, everything is fine."

Later that night, Lisl knocked gently on Karl's door. "Mother is asleep. If she wakes up and is looking for me, tell her I'll be back soon and don't let her worry," she whispered to Karl.

"Tatsuo?"

Lisl nodded and closed the door before Karl could say another word. She ran down the stairs, knowing she would not be able to control her tears if Tatsuo was not waiting at their usual meeting place.

"Lisl, I was beginning to think I would have to come looking for you." Tatsuo held out his hand and she clung to it tightly. "Please don't cry."

"Oh, Tatsuo, I love you so much and I don't want you to go."

"I know, but we won't be gone forever."

"It will seem like forever. Tell me we'll be married when you get back so I'll have something to look forward to."

"I can't tell you that, Lisl," Tatsuo whispered.

"But you love me. People who love each other get married."

"Lisl, how can I make you understand?" He released a

deep ragged sigh. "Lisl, you know that I am a member of the Takezawa zaibatsu and I must assume certain responsibilities. If my father had not been killed in the Kanto earthquake, perhaps my life would have been different . . . but he *was* killed, and I am the next in line."

"But that's like being a prisoner," Lisl choked. "You have no more freedom than a common prisoner."

"Perhaps it seems that way to you. In fact, at times it seems that way to me too, but I must still meet my obligations. To do otherwise would bring great dishonor to my grandfather and to the zaibatsu."

"Dishonor!" Lisl's voice broke and tears streamed down her face. "You're going away for months and all you talk about is that damn zaibatsu." Her sobs were muffled as she pressed her face against Tatsuo's chest. "Tatsuo, make love to me now, please, before you go. Then I'll know for certain that you're coming back . . . please, Tatsuo."

"Lisl . . . I . . ."

"Please, Tatsuo." Her eyes were bright and her fingers dug into his arms.

"Lisl, I love you. I promise I will come back."

They lay in the soft grass concealed by the surrounding trees; the moon sent slivers of light filtering through the branches. Lisl shivered and Tatsuo drew her closer. She felt small and helpless in his naked arms, her skin smooth against his.

"I love you," she whispered. "I belong to you now and you to me—forever."

A deck officer followed their ascent up the gangplank.

"Morning, sir. We're supposed to report for duty today."

"Your names?"

"Karl Richter."

"Tatsuo Takezawa. We're your new trimmers."

"From the look of you, you'll need some practice before we sail. I'm Mr. Falkner," he said emphasizing the "Mister." "The cap'n is topside. Report to him before you do anything else."

As they walked toward the forward deckhouse, Karl noticed that the holds were filled and ready to be closed off. Some of the hatches had already been battened down. "No wonder she's sitting so low. They've loaded her to the hilt."

"Is that good or bad?" Tatsuo asked.

Karl grinned. "Hell, that's good. This rusty old tub should float for a while. Otherwise, who would take the chance with all this cargo?"

"Well, I'm glad someone else has faith in her besides us."

Captain Ferguson welcomed them aboard, dated their certificates of discharge, and told them in no uncertain terms what he expected from every member of his crew. "You lads just follow orders, do your jobs, and it will be a pleasant voyage. The bos'n will take you to your quarters."

Below, Tatsuo's nostrils flared in distaste at the stale air, and he did not need to look at Karl to read his thoughts. Bunks lined the cramped quarters, each with a small shelf and a metal box which served as a night table. Remnants of paint clung to the walls, but most of it had peeled away long ago. Several small vents near the ceiling did nothing to alleviate the odor of perspiration and dirty laundry.

"What the hell did you expect . . . a state-room?" the bos'n said gruffly.

"Do the officers live down here too?" Karl asked.

The bos'n laughed. "That'll be the bloody day! Ain't you never been on a tramp before?"

"Not like this one."

"Well now, don't tell me you don't like it here," the bos'n drawled.

Karl hesitated, recognizing the taunt in the officer's voice. "It's perfect."

"Yes, perfect," Tatsuo echoed. "Which bunks are ours?"

"You can take the two at the end. The chief engineer will be here to take you under his motherly breast, so sit tight until he comes."

"Yes, sir! Anything you say, sir!" Karl said loudly. Tatsuo shot him a warning look. Flinging the duffel bag over his shoulder, Karl started toward the bunks.

The bos'n followed close behind. "Listen, snot nose, this here is a ship and we run it on discipline. You'd better learn real quick that you do your fucking work and watch your manners with your superiors."

Karl's mouth was tight and his eyes flicked over the bos'n with disdain.

"Which bunk do you want?" Tatsuo asked, stepping between them.

"It doesn't matter to me. Take you pick," Karl said.

"Make up your mind, pinhead," the bos'n sneered. "The Jappo is giving you first choice."

"His name is Tatsuo Takezawa, and I want him to have first choice."

The bos'n sidestepped Tatsuo and twisted Karl's sweater into a tight knot under his chin. "I said, make up your mind, pinhead."

"Take your hands off me or I'll break your arm," Karl warned softly.

The bos'n snarled and twisted the sweater tighter. Karl grabbed his wrist and slowly began to squeeze, bending the arm until the bos'n grimaced and released his grip. Karl kept bending the arm back until the stocky man was on his knees.

"Let go, you bastard!" The bos'n's lips were drawn back in pain.

"Yes, sir!" Karl straightened his sweater and looked calmly at the bos'n. "Nothing personal, but you see, my mother made this sweater for me."

Rage contorted the bos'n's face. "You son of a bitch."

Karl braced himself for an attack.

"What the hell's going on in here, Gilman? Can't a day go by without you causing trouble?" A huge man, whose bulk filled the doorway, stepped into the cabin, his voice deep and authoritative.

"Sorry, Chief, but this pinhead is giving me some bad mouth. You'd better teach him proper manners or I'll have to."

"Yeah, yeah, Gilman. Get the fuck out of here and tend to your own business."

The bos'n stared at Karl through narrowed eyes for a moment before leaving the cabin.

The huge man shook his head. "That bastard is always asking for trouble. I advise you to stay clear of him or he could make things rough for you."

"I'll bet," Karl replied. "Thanks for the advice."

"I'm the chief engineer—Ray DeJong, but the men call me Chief."

"I'm Karl Richter, and this is Tatsuo Takezawa. We're your new trimmers.

"I hope you stay longer than the last two we had. Jumped ship right here in Vancouver, just like I figured they would.

Leave your gear, and I'll take you below and show you what you'll be doing on watch."

As they left, Karl heard the deep-throated chuckle of a sailor lying on his bunk at the far end of the cabin.

"Well, well, well, looks like we're going to have an interesting trip this time," the sailor muttered under his breath.

The engine room was hot and noisy, but in contrast to the rest of the ship, it was meticulously tidy. The polished instruments glistened, and the walls and pipes were all carefully painted.

"These are the bunkers where we store our coal. The firemen shovel it from here into the boilers. Your job will be to move the coal to where they can reach it easily. As the coal gets used up, your job gets tougher. By the time you get to the bulkheads, you should be in good shape . . . or dead." The chief engineer was obviously proud of his domain. "Well, lads, that's the way it will be for the next seventeen days until we reach Yokohama. Since you won't be on regular watch until tomorrow, you'll work with the donkeyman today."

"Donkeyman?"

"Yeah, he's like a bos'n. Look after the day workers . . . painting, general maintenance, and whatever else comes up. From the look of the ship you might think we never clean her up, and you're right, but the engine room is different. I won't stand for any bloody mess down here. Understand?"

"Yes, sir!"

"Now I'll give you a few words of fatherly advice. The skipper is a good man, so do your job, keep your noses clean, and we'll make sailors out of you. If you get into any trouble, come and see me right away—don't try to fix things by yourself."

"Yes, sir!"

"Now go up and report to the donkeyman. You can't miss him. He's got red hair and he's thin enough to shove into a wormhole."

Karl and Tatsuo spent their first day cleaning steam winches and battening down hatches. By suppertime their stomachs were painfully empty and the simple food, served hot and in large quantities, tasted surprisingly good.

"Hey, kid, remember me? Jack Gilhooly . . . the bloke you were going to buy the cigarettes for." He slid in beside Karl.

"Yeah, I got them for you. They're in my duffel bag."

Gilhooly raised his eyebrows in surprise. "You did?"

"Sure. I'll get them for you after supper."

"Thanks, laddie, you're one fine gentleman."

Karl's first watch began the next morning at 0800 hours. The coal was heavy and the dust soon penetrated every pore, encrusting his clothes and turning his blond hair a streaky gray. His blue eyes glowed like beacons from his black face. In spite of the suffocating dust, he found the work exhilarating and the steady pull on his muscles pleasurable. Ignoring the suspicious glances, he moved in to help the fireman when his own job slackened temporarily.

Except for cold stares and innocuous threats from the bos'n and his friend Cookie, the ship's cook, life aboard the old freighter settled into a routine for Karl and Tatsuo. The members of the "blackgang" became familiar to them, and their free evenings were spent playing cards late into the night or listening to stories that stretched even their willing imaginations. Out of necessity, Karl and Tatsuo modified their training schedules to accommodate the duty roster but continued to exercise vigorously each day. The crew, who initially had watched these sessions with curious fascination, now simply ignored them or attempted halfheartedly to join in. No one denied the new trimmers respect for the self-discipline they displayed in the rigidity of their training.

Karl found meditation on board the *Liverpool* exceedingly difficult, and although he sought desperately to still his mind as he had done in the sensei's dry landscape garden, he could not catch a glimpse of the Ox. He longed for Hiro's quiet encouragement and admitted only to himself that he sorely missed the solitude and comfort of his room at Drachenschlucht. Janice, too, was often on his mind and in his dreams. The memory of their brief times together on the *Cathy B*, on the deserted beach, and at the commencement ceremony became more vivid with each passing day. He recalled how she had looked the night before he boarded the *Liverpool*, her eyes bright with tears even though she had smiled and wished him well. Her kisses had been tender but held a promise of passion, and even now, remembering those moments, excitement surged through him—quickly followed by frustration. Eventually, though, Karl grew accustomed to the loneliness, and his appetite, which had waned briefly, returned.

The sea, with its endless, changing beauty, held a special fascination for him. Even on days when the wind whirled the clouds in wraiths and sent the waves crashing against the *Liverpool*, Karl felt no fear, only respect for the power and consuming depth of the ocean. In the presence of the vast ocean and under the limitless sky, he tried to recapture a sense of harmony of the universe. It was on the *Liverpool* that he and Tatsuo performed their first tea ceremony at sea, kneeling on a new tatami mat. They prepared the tea and drank ceremoniously while the amazed crew members looked on, some with bemused curiosity, others making loud remarks about what they considered to be a childish game. Neither activity prevented Karl and Tatsuo from completing the ceremony with proper decorum, as Hiro had taught them. But when the cook came to stand with both feet on the edge of the tatami mat, Karl considered pouring scalding water into his unlaced shoes. Sensing the threat, the cook hastily retreated to a safe distance, but from there he acted out an exaggerated imitation of the ceremonious movements, punctuated by guffaws of laughter.

"Ignore him," Tatsuo warned, seeing the anger in Karl's eyes. "He's got the mind of a jackass and a face to match."

When Karl stood up and moved toward the cook, the fat man turned abruptly and walked away.

"Bastard. One day I'll put my foot up his arse."

On the morning of the seventeenth day, the *Liverpool* steamed along the rugged coastline of Honshu Island and into Tokyo Bay. The engine room was hot as usual, but Tatsuo hardly noticed as he walked quickly to the bunkers to relieve Karl. The voice of the third engineer stopped him.

"Hey, before you go in there, we got a call for you from the skipper. He wants to see you topside."

A puzzled look on his face, Tatsuo hurried to the bridge, where he found the skipper peering through his binoculars.

"You wanted to see me, sir?" Tatsuo asked.

"Yes . . . yes, I did," Captain Ferguson replied without lowering the binoculars. "Do you see all those ships out there waiting to tie up at the docks?"

"Yes, sir."

"Well, I'm just a little curious. Usually I have to sit out here for several days, sometimes even a week, waiting for my turn, but today an unusual thing happened."

Tatsuo waited for the captain to continue.

"Our radio operator just received word from the harbor master that we can tie up within the hour. Just like that! No request on our part, no explanation on their's. Can you explain that?"

"No, sir, I can't." Tatsuo's mind raced now. Unless . . . no, how could the zaibatsu know he was on board? Surely the harbor master wouldn't give the *Liverpool* preferential treatment just because of him.

Captain Ferguson lowered the binoculars and looked at Tatsuo. "You are a member of the Takezawa zaibatsu?"

"Yes, sir."

"Then that's probably the reason we're getting in so quickly. It's my guess there will be a delegation waiting for you as soon as we tie up."

"But I don't think they even knew I was part of the crew on this freighter."

"Don't look so worried, lad. I'm damn happy. We'll save at least a week, and that's money in the bank."

"Will that be all, sir?"

The captain nodded. "That's all."

By midday a powerful tug was pulling the *Liverpool* into port, and just as Captain Ferguson had predicted, a delegation was waiting for Tatsuo. With the captain's permission, he was the first one off the ship, and it was evening before Karl realized that his friend was no longer on board.

"Talk about VIP treatment," the steward remarked as he passed Karl in the mess hall.

"What do you mean?" Karl asked.

"Well, ain't you heard? Your friend is part of some big organization, and they got the *Liverpool* through the harbor without waiting around. He's already gone."

"You mean Tatsuo's not on board?"

"Nope. Left before the hawsers were even over the bollards."

"I didn't know he was gone," Karl said incredulously.

"Well, laddie, I don't really think he had time to come and tell you. It was kinda suddenlike."

Karl found a note from Tatsuo on his bunk: "Sorry I don't have time to explain. I'll be waiting for you on the dock when you get shore leave."

Karl spent the next four days on general maintenance with

the day crew. Finally he was summoned to the bridge.

"You sent for me, Captain?" Karl asked after he had come to attention.

"Yes I did, Karl." Captain Ferguson looked up from the papers he was studying. "We will be sailing on August twenty-eighth, which is well ahead of schedule. You're off duty until then."

"Thank you, sir!" Karl said, wondering what had prompted the captain's decision.

With a duffel bag slung over his shoulder, Karl bounced down the gangplank to the pier below. The waterfront, teeming with activity, was exciting in its unfamiliarity. Suddenly realizing he was alone in a maze of strange faces, he stopped, uncertain of which way to turn until a jinrickisha runner drew in front of him, his naked back glistening with perspiration. He gestured to Karl, holding up his fingers to indicate the price, while he chattered. Nodding in approval, Karl threw in the heavy duffel bag and started to climb on.

"Karl, wait! Karl!" A familiar voice called out, and he turned to search the crowd. Clad in a gray yukata, Tatsuo pushed his way toward Karl. "Where do you think you're going? Don't you know you can get lost in Yokohama?" Tatsuo demanded, his face wreathed in smiles.

"Tatsuo! How the hell did you know I would be leaving the ship today?" Karl asked as he stepped out of the jinrickisha.

"The harbor master is an old friend of my uncle's, and I asked him to keep in touch with Captain Ferguson. Follow me, I've brought my uncle's car." He dropped several coins into the jinrickisha driver's hand while Karl retrieved his duffel bag.

The driver bobbed gratefully. "Arigato, Takezawa-sama, arigato."

"He knows you!" Karl exclaimed.

Tatsuo shrugged self-consciously. "Well, the family crest is on the car, and it's bold enough to knock your eyes out. My uncle is not as modest as my grandfather."

Tatsuo drove slowly through Yokohama, then raced through the countryside toward Kawasaki. The fields, once covered with lush vegetation, were now the site of warehouses and factories. Dark smoke billowed from the stacks, partially obscuring the Takezawa emblem which identified most of them. Karl searched for familiar landmarks from his trip five years before, but they had been swallowed up in the industrial expansion.

"Notice any changes?" Tatsuo asked.

"I thought my memory was bad. I can hardly recognize anything," Karl answered.

"Japan has changed so much. I'm glad Grandfather is not here now. It would be difficult for him." He glanced at Karl with sad eyes, and when he finally spoke, his voice had a forced lightness. "I want to take you to Kyoto. At least there time stands still—the temples and shrines are the most beautiful in the world. I will show you the temple where you will go to receive your black belt."

"I would like to see some nightlife too," Karl said with a grin.

"I thought you would get around to asking about that. Don't worry, I have already made all the necessary arrangements with a very beautiful and talented lady at the House of Many Lanterns."

"You have?"

"I also took the liberty of warning her about you."

Karl raised his eyebrows. "You did! What did you say?"

"I told her your feet match your pecker—both oversized and uncontrollable!"

The picture-book beauty of Honshu Island unfolded for Karl in the days that followed as he and Tatsuo explored the rugged mountains and followed the cold, swift streams that flowed from the high peaks into the ocean. With typical graciousness, they were accepted as honored guests in the tiny fishing villages by the poor but happy people who eked out their livelihood from the sea. Karl and Tatsuo ate their lunch and watched the pearl divers search the ocean floor for the tiny treasures. Karl was amazed at how long the divers could hold their breath, especially the women, but he was appalled by the disfigured bodies whose limbs had been ripped off by marauding sharks.

"Why do they keep going back when they know how dangerous it is?" Karl asked. "God, if a shark took my arm off, I'd never go back in."

"But then how would you live? These people have been pearl diving for generations, and they know of no other way to support themselves," Tatsuo replied matter-of-factly. "Besides, they do have a way of getting revenge."

"Against a shark? How?"

"Whenever they catch a killer shark, they shove prickly urchins down its throat with a stick before releasing him. The shark dies an agonizing death because he is unable to eat with the urchins stuck in his throat."

"I can understand how they feel, but it seems cruel. The sharks are just acting on instinct."

"It is difficult to understand the ways of the villagers and even more difficult to change them. Let's go home. Tonight the ladies at the House of Many Lanterns will be waiting for us."

Karl was fascinated by the tiny geisha and her two dancing girls, called *maikos*. Skilled in music and dance and trained in subtle sensuality, they entertained, cooked seasoned morsels of food, and gently enticed in a manner that Karl had never experienced. Their movements were suggestive but graceful, almost ethereal, and yet he found himself tremendously aroused. Later in the evening, one of the two maikos knelt beside him, eyes downcast.

Karl looked at Tatsuo for an explanation.

"She is yours for the rest of the night."

"What do you mean?" Karl stammered.

"She will entertain you for the rest of the evening—privately."

"I don't know . . ."

Tatsuo grinned. "You look as though someone has just given you a blow on the side of the head. She is my gift to you. Do not deny me the pleasure. Go with her and don't worry, she will do the rest."

"But how do you know?"

"I spent a month in Japan last year, if you'll remember, and my uncle very graciously introduced me to a very lovely geisha," Tatsuo explained.

"You bastard, you never cease to amaze me! But what if she doesn't like me?"

"If she didn't like you, she wouldn't have consented to spend the night with you."

"Did you have to pay her?"

"I gave her a gift, and now I am giving you a gift through her."

"Aren't you staying?"

"No, but I will be here to pick you up in the morning. Enjoy yourself." With a formal bow, Tatsuo left quietly on slippered feet.

When Karl looked around, the geishas and their maikos had disappeared. The brazier had been removed and only the mats and soft pillows remained. Karl waited in silence, expectant and a little afraid until the maiko returned. Bathed in moonlight from an open window, she stood before him, completely naked. Karl's heart began to race and she knelt behind him on the mat. Slowly she began to rub the muscles around his neck and down his back, opening the kimono and letting it fall to his waist. She murmured appreciatively at his muscled torso and continued to massage him, gently pushing him back against the pillows. With skillful fingers, she explored his body. When she removed his kimono, she gasped softly, but her fingers continued their search, approaching sensitive spots but not quite touching them until Karl groaned with anticipation and his body arched toward her. Trained in the sensual arts, she gave pleasure without reservation, bringing him to the brink of his release and then retreating over and over again until only a light flick of her moist tongue against his flesh sent shudders through his body. Slowly her response became attuned to Karl's, her arousal matching his, until they were both caught up in the ecstasy of their desire. Karl heard himself cry out as she knelt over him for a moment. Only when the surge of his passion was near its peak did she lie back and allow him to move inside her, then she met his powerful thrusts with a fervor that matched his. The final thought Karl had before sleep came was that Tatsuo had given him a truly unique gift.

The road to Kyoto was narrow and dusty, but their intrepid driver casually ignored all potential hazards and continued along at a dangerous speed. The ancient meditation hall they had come to visit was surrounded by simple, immaculate gardens and enclosed by leafy oaks and towering pines. Water splashed over moss-covered rocks and trickled into a crystal clear pool. They ascended the steps quietly and were met by a young priest dressed in black robes.

"May we see the master of the temple?" Tatsuo asked in Japanese.

The priest returned Tatsuo's bow. "The *roshi* is presently occupied, but if you would like to wait, I will tell him you are here."

"Thank you. We will wait."

"The master of this *zendo* is very old. Oji-san trained under him," Tatsuo explained almost in a whisper.

Karl only nodded, conscious of the serenity of the temple, its timeless architecture, and the incredible silence that was broken only by a faint tinkle of a bell in the distance.

The young priest returned. "The roshi will see you presently. Please follow me."

The ancient master sat perfectly still as Karl and Tatsuo approached, his angular face intricately lined with age but his eyes clear and surprisingly youthful. Karl addressed him in Japanese, and the roshi replied in carefully accented English.

"Please speak in your own tongue, for I do not have this opportunity very often," the roshi explained.

"I am Tatsuo Takezawa, and this is my friend Karl Richter. We are both students of zazen."

"Ah, yes, under your grandfather. I remember him well, and I am delighted to meet his pupils. Please allow me to serve you o-cha."

As they drank the hot, bitter tea, they talked. The roshi answered their questions with infinite patience and subtle wisdom until a temple bell indicated it was time for them to leave.

"May I ask one more question, master?" Karl asked.

The roshi nodded.

"I have been struggling but cannot find the answer to one of the sensei's questions."

The master smiled. "But that is the only way to enlightenment—through struggle. When you look for Buddha there is a Buddha, but when you find him there is no Buddha."

More confused than ever, Karl asked, "What is the purpose of life?"

The roshi smiled knowingly. "That is the basic question. After much study, many Zen masters will answer, 'no purpose.' I too, have felt the logic of that simple answer, but there is more." His eyes closed for a moment. "Can you imagine a universe without intelligent life . . . an unfeeling void in which countless suns pour out their warmth for no purpose? No, there is so much more, but my limited knowledge ties me to the earth. The only answer I can give you is that life seems to have no other purpose than to allow the universe to become aware of its own divine essence."

"I am not sure I understand," Karl whispered.

"We and the universe are one. When you return, perhaps you will add to my simple explanation."

A young priest arrived to escort them out of the temple. The roshi became still, his eyes closed; he had dismissed them.

On the day of their scheduled departure, Karl and Tatsuo rode in silence as their car bounced over the dusty road to Yokohama.

Finally Karl turned to his friend. "You have a greal deal on your mind today."

Tatsuo sighed deeply. "It is as my grandfather feared," he said in a low voice. "Japan has chosen a dangerous course, and it is already too late to turn back. There are five sacred swords in our family, and soon one of them will be placed in my hands. My fate is sealed."

"And your grandfather? What about him?" Karl asked.

"His duties are drawing to a close, but how can I carry out the instructions of the zaibatsu when I do not agree with them?"

"Tell them to go to hell!"

"I wish it were that easy," Tatsuo replied.

"Then what will you do?"

A resigned look crossed Tatsuo's face. "When the time comes, I will do what must be done, but for the next few months I am going to forget about it and enjoy life."

"I don't think there will be much time to think about anything except shoveling coal," Karl said lightly.

Tatsuo deftly changed the subject. "There is a box on the front seat beside the driver. My uncle asked me to give it to you."

Karl reached over and carefully unwrapped its contents—an iron pot, smooth with age, two ladles, a bamboo whisk, and four porcelain cups. Inside the pot was a container of tea. "But why didn't your uncle give me this himself?" asked Karl.

"My uncle is not one to show emotion, but he wanted you to have the proper implements for the tea ceremony. He hoped you would be pleased."

"I wish I could have thanked him personally." Karl said simply. "Perhaps now the ceremony will take on added meaning."

The driver finally stopped the black limousine at the waterfront, just out of sight of the *Liverpool*.

"I thought it best to walk the rest of the way. The docks are not so crowded today, and I have the feeling a few eyes will be peeled in our direction when we come on board," Tatsuo explained.

"I understand," Karl replied, hoisting the duffel bag over his shoulder. The box containing Koji's gift was secured under his arm.

"Well, lads, I notice you ain't walking bowlegged. You couldn't have had any fun." Jack Gilhooly laughed in his familiar wheeze and nudged Spence, the chief steward, with his elbow.

"Your sense of humor hasn't improved, Gilhooly, but it's good to see you guys," Karl said.

"Are you two the official welcoming committee?" Tatsuo asked cautiously.

"That's right," Spence announced with a grin. "We're here to examine you for crabs. We got the kerosene ready just in case you got the little critters. Can't have you infesting the whole ship!"

"Go to hell, Spence! I'm showing you nothing." Karl shouldered his way past him.

"So what the hell did you do with your time?" Spence asked as he followed Karl and Tatsuo to their quarters.

"We toured Honshu Island, hiked in the mountains. Visited temples," Karl added with a wide grin.

"Visited temples! What the hell for?"

"To talk to the master about the purpose of life."

"Yeah?" Spence shook his head and looked at Gilhooly, who just shrugged.

"You guys got any ideas, any pearls of wisdom you want to share with us about life?" Karl teased.

"Sure, I got one for you," Gilhooly answered. "Life is a shit sandwich. The more bread you have, the less shit you have to eat."

"Very profound," Tatsuo said, laughing.

"Just ask me, I've got dozens more."

Spence and Gilhooly were genuinely pleased to have their cabinmates back on board. Gilhooly continued his questioning, for he was sure they had spent at least one night in a geisha house.

Karl stowed his duffel bag and sat on the edge of the bunk. "Well, nothing has changed here while we were away. The same stink, dirty clothes, garbage on the floor . . . but it's good to be back. Anything exciting happen?"

Spence shrugged. "Not much . . . except—"

"Except what?" Tatsuo urged.

"Except I heard from the steward that Cookie, our fat cook, has a rubber lady hidden in his foot locker." Spence cackled loudly.

"What the hell does he have a rubber lady for?" Karl asked.

The cackling stopped. "He blows it up and makes love to it."

Karl and Tatsuo looked at each other and then back at Spence and Gilhooly. "You're crazy!"

A wide grin softened Spence's sharp features and his black eyes sparkled with humor. "From what I understand, the damn thing looks real when she's all blown up. Besides, Cookie would screw a rock pile if he thought there was a snake in it."

"Maybe so, but a hunk of rubber!" Tatsuo exclaimed.

The idea struck Karl like a thunderbolt. "What if we steal her and—"

"Hold it right here, mate," Gilhooly said. "If you get caught, the skipper will have you in irons."

"What do want it for?" Spence piped in quickly. "Thinking of trying her yourself?"

Karl grinned. "No, you idiot, but Cookie has been giving us all a hard time and maybe this is our chance to get even."

"Yeah, then we can rent her out to the officers," Gilhooly added with a chuckle. "But knowing them, they'd probably bite her tit and she'd fly out the door."

In spite of Gilhooly's reservations, their plans began to take shape, and the preliminary reconnaissance was started. Execution of the plan took place two days later.

As expected, the cook's cabin was unoccupied.

"Are you sure he's in the galley?" Gilhooly whispered.

"Yeah, he's up to his balls in pie dough," Spence answered.

"Gilhooly, you and Spence keep watch while Tatsuo and I find the box."

"If you guys get caught, your certificates of discharge will be black as coal," Spence cautioned.

"We're not stealing the damn thing, we're only going to borrow it for a few minutes," Karl assured them.

"What the hell are you going to do with it when you find it?" Spence persisted.

"Just alter her a bit so Cookie will know that his love life isn't private anymore. That should drive him crazy," Karl laughed softly.

"For Christ's sake, let's find the goddamn thing and get out of here," Gilhooly urged.

The metal box, complete with a huge brass padlock, was partially hidden under the bunk.

"Gilhooly, get in here. I can't pick this lock," Karl called over his shoulder.

In moments the lock was opened. Inside the box, rolled up and covered with a cloth, was the deflated rubber doll.

"Goddamn!" Gilhooly whispered hoarsely. "The steward was right."

The doll began to take shape as Karl and Tatsuo took turns blowing it up. It soon became life-size, revealing a pink fleshy body, and coarse black hair on its head and between its protruding legs. The cone-shaped breasts stood firmly at right angles to its body and the eyes stared glassily from a painted face.

"Holy Mother of God! She looks good enough to take to dinner!" Gilhooly was peering over Karl's shoulder.

"You couldn't afford a classy dame like this," Tatsuo whispered.

"The goddamn thing feels great!" Gilhooly noted as he felt a soft lifeless breast. "No wonder Cookie hides her under his bed."

"Gilhooly, stop drooling," Karl said.

While the others watched, Karl quickly cut away the hair between the doll's legs and glued it to her upper lip. "Sorry to do this, miss, we really don't mean any offense to you personally."

"She sure doesn't look as charming with a moustache and a bald snatch," Spence said between laughs.

"Okay, let's get her deflated and back into the box before someone comes," Tatsuo warned.

Safely in their cabin several minutes later, Spence let out a long sigh. "I was sure we would get caught. Think Cookie will know who did it?"

"He'll have a damn good idea after all the trouble he and the bosn'n have been causing us, but he won't dare tell anyone about it." Karl stretched out on his bunk and smiled contentedly.

"I sure would like to see the bastard's face when he finds his rubber snatch has been to the barber shop." Gilhooly wheezed with laughter.

The *Liverpool* steamed due south for the Philippines, her holds filled with fragrant tea and bales of fine silk. Except for one occasion, and then only by chance, the cook's angry face was not to be seen. In the dim light of an early dawn, Cookie stepped out onto the cold rusty deck and looked around furtively. With no one in sight, he hurried to the guardrail and heaved a weighted burlap bag into the sea below. It sank quickly and he seemed relieved—until he turned and stood face-to-face with Firpo, the blackgang peggy.

"What the fuck you sneaking up on me like that?" Cookie roared.

Firpo smiled and pointed to the ship's wake. "I hope that wasn't our breakfast?"

"No, it wasn't your breakfast. Now get the hell out of my way."

"Hey, Cookie," Firpo called after him, "don't take it so hard. I know it was more than a lover's quarrel, but at least there weren't any children involved."

The cook froze in his tracks and turned quickly, his face a mixture of anger, hatred, and fear. "Name your price," he said finally.

"Price! What price?" Firpo asked innocently.

"Cut the bullshit, Firpo. Name your price."

"Okay, Cookie. The game's over and your friend is gone. Price, eh? Well, I don't want to be too hard on you, you being bereaved and all, so I'll keep my mouth shut and you lay off the new trimmers. Let the bos'n fight his own battles. And I want you to serve the blackgang the same grub as what the officers get—no more fucking leftovers. Got that?"

Cookie nodded. "I'll cut you up for stew if you ever breathe a word of this."

Firpo shrugged his shoulders. "Might improve it."

The door slammed shut behind Cookie as Firpo laughed aloud.

As the ship approached Luzon Island in the Philippines, the humidity increased along with the intensity of the tropical sun. Small fishing boats plied the coastal waters of the island,

where the lush vegetation and turquoise waters provided a
scenic backdrop for the small vessels. The *Liverpool* steamed
sluggishly into Manila Bay, a natural harbor, thirty-five miles
wide and deep enough to accommodate the world's largest
ships. The *Liverpool* waited for three days before she was
allowed to tie up at the busy pier. Despite the size of the harbor, the shore facilities were minimal and the unloading of
cargo was a long, tedious process. Stripped to their trousers,
the crew worked long hours to complete the ship's maintenance in time to have a few day's shore leave in Manila.

Freshly shaved and attired in their best clothes, Tatsuo and
Karl descended the gangway followed by Gilhooly and
Spence. Karl was unaware that curious people turned to watch
him as he strode along the pier. His sun-bleached hair and
startling blue eyes were an attraction among the short, dark-
haired Filipinos.

"Hey, Karl," Gilhooly whispered, "Stick close. I think that
white hair of yours is going to flush out a few birds for us."

Karl grinned self-consciously. "Hell, Gilhooly, you're the
ladies' man around here. I'll expect you to set the example."

The streets of downtown Manila were crowded with a variety of people: sailors, Malaysians, Chinese, blacks, and resi-
dent Europeans, each group contributing to the clamorous
bustle of the sprawling city. The noise increased as night fell,
and it seemed to Karl that an endless flow of people appeared,
filling the streets and spilling into the countless bars and dance
halls. Sloe-eyed women with soft languid faces vied for the attention of the foreign sailors.

The evening was the beginning of three memorable days in
Manila, days spent on white sandy beaches with cool tropical
water lapping their naked bodies and food cooked in traditional native fashion. Their nights were spent in the arms of
willing native girls who shared their charms with the generous
sailors from the *Liverpool*. Exhausted, penniless, and happy,
they returned to the ship just before she was due to sail for
Singapore with a cargo of copra.

Large brown bugs came aboard with the tons of coconut
meat, and Karl yelped in pain the first time he was bitten. He
leaped from his bunk and stook naked in the middle of the
floor.

"Where the hell did that thing come from? It bit me!" Karl
shouted.

"Ah, calm down, lad," Gilhooly said brusquely. "It's just

a copra bug. They'll leave when we drop this cargo in Singapore.''

Karl shivered in disgust as Gilhooly swatted the bug from his bunk and crushed it under his heel.

"You might as well get used to them. They'll be all over the ship by tomorrow," Gilhooly advised.

The bugs seemed to attack Karl's fair skin with particular zeal, leaving large red welts. Unable to trust the security of his bunk any longer, he spent several sleepless nights sitting on the deck under the beauty of the tropic skies. Often Tatsuo would keep him company, talking until the early hours of the morning.

In Singapore, the *Liverpool* refilled its bunkers, and by mid-October she steamed through the Andaman Sea into the Bay of Bengal and then up the Hooghly River toward Calcutta. For Karl, the world of Rudyard Kipling came alive, a world that spelled magic in his mind. In the distance, heat rose in waves above the golden mosques and temples. Small boats scurried about the congested harbor, selling every form of merchandise, the traders calling out in high-pitched voices above the plaintive music of the snake charmers' flutes.

The unloading of the copra was a slow, dirty process. Hundreds of natives, naked to the waist, formed a human chain and carried out the cargo in baskets balanced on their heads.

"Hey, Gilhooly, how come their gums are all red? Are they sick?" Karl asked.

"No, it's them friggin' beetle nuts. They chew them all the time. Stains their gums red."

Karl's initial excitement was short-lived. The humidity became unbearable; his clothes were continually damp and sleep was impossible. The high temperatures warmed the water in the ship's tanks so that cold showers were only a memory, and the crew became increasingly irritable. Reprieve from the oppresive heat finally came with the torrential rains that began to fall during the third week after their arrival. The crew stayed below listening to the violent rain.

"God, I can't stand this any longer," Karl said. "Who wants a shower?"

"In hot water? No thanks," Spence grumbled.

"No, in the rain right out on the poop deck."

"You're crazy!"

"No he's not. It sounds like a good idea. Let's go," Tatsuo shouted.

On deck, they stripped naked and soaped themselves while the rain pelted their bodies with driving force. One by one the other crew members joined Karl and Tatsuo and soon the soap suds were ankle-deep around them as they whooped with abandon in the cool rain.

When permission for shore leave was finally granted, Karl and Tatsuo rode into the heart of the city on rickishas with Gilhooly acting as their travel guide. Karl was appalled by the emaciated beggars who lined the roadside, some with faces grotesquely disfigured by leprosy, reaching out to them with hands bound in dirty rags. Holy men and worshipers crouched quietly in the marketplaces, waiting patiently for charity. The poverty was overwhelming.

"I heard this existed," Karl said, "but now that I see it, I can't believe how bad it really is."

Tatsuo stared wordlessly, his eyes mirroring sympathy for the wretched despair around him. They stopped in an open marketplace, where the air was filled with strange odors and where traders hawked their wares from makeshift stands.

"Follow me," Gilhooly said. "I want to show you something interesting."

A long row of cages lined a narrow winding street. Some were curtained; all resembled jail cells.

"I'm almost afraid to ask, but what the hell is this, Gilhooly?"

"Surprise! Sidewalk whorehouses. You can pick anyone you want . . . I'll even pay."

Karl and Tatsuo peered hesitantly into the cells. Each one contained a cot and a woman. Most of the women were old, and all were dirty. Several called out to them as they passed, displaying their bodies with cold indifference. At the last cage, an old man pointed to the coins in the palm of his hand while the woman in the cell shook her head in refusal. With a look of resignation he added two coins to the small pile and the door opened. He grinned lasciviously before the curtain was drawn.

"By the sound of it, he's not wasting any time," Tatsuo observed.

"That old bastard must be eighty," Gilhooly laughed. "You blokes want to have a go at it?"

"Let's get out of here," Karl said quickly.

By the end of the sixth week, the *Liverpool* had been unloaded and left Calcutta with empty holds. Rubber from

Ceylon would be picked up and delivered to England.

December was a particularly lonely time for Karl, and although the crew celebrated Christmas, Karl sorely missed Lisl and his mother. For the first time in his life, he was glad when the holiday season was over.

In February, the *Liverpool* had reached Athens via the Suez, and an uneasiness began to grip Karl, an uneasiness which he attributed to a combination of homesickness and cabin fever. Somehow he sensed the tragic news he was about to receive.

The captain faced him with sympathetic eyes the day they reached Athens. "I'm afraid I have some bad news for you, lad."

Karl's stomach tightened. "Sir?"

"I was contacted by the shipping agent in Athens. He had a message for you from Mr. Takezawa. Your mother is seriously ill, and you are to go home as soon as possible. I'm very sorry."

Karl's face was rigid. "What is the fastest way, Captain?"

"I think you'd better stay with the *Liverpool* until we reach London. I'll book you on the fastest liner for Halifax or New York, then you can catch a train for Vancouver."

"Thank you, Captain."

When Karl returned to his quarters, Tatsuo was waiting. "I should have known she was not well. I know now what it must have cost her to watch me leave."

"She wanted you to go, Karl. Don't blame yourself."

"I only hope I make it home in time."

"Do you think it's that serious?" Tatsuo asked.

"Your grandfather would not have called if it weren't."

[13]

London lay concealed beneath a blanket of fog. The melancholy blasts of foghorns dissipated into faint echoes around the *Liverpool* as she sat idle, waiting for daybreak.

Tatsuo walked with Karl across the empty deck to the gangway. "You'll be home soon."

"I hope it's soon enough," Karl replied.

"Take care of yourself." Tatsuo's voice was tight.

"Yeah, I will . . . you do the same."

"You're sure you won't change your mind and let me come with you?"

"No," Karl said softly. "It's better if I go by myself." He touched Tatsuo's shoulder and walked down the gangplank. Tatsuo stood alone in the darkness until the sound of Karl's footsteps faded away.

The *Mauritania* was due to leave Liverpool on March 23. Karl had two days to reach the liner before the scheduled departure. He boarded the night train in London, which took him to Birmingham and then on to Liverpool, where the luxury liner was already taking on passengers. As usual, the *Mauritania* would be filled to capacity—2,335 passengers and 812 crew members, plus tons of food and supplies. Holder of the blue ribbon for many years, she was the fastest, most lavish ship on the Atlantic. Karl was grateful for the effort Captain Ferguson had made on his behalf; a booking on the *Mauritania* assured him that he would be in New York within five days.

Karl purposely avoided the clamorous gaiety aboard the luxury liner. He picked at the elaborately prepared meals with little appetite and tactfully ignored the overt advances of several of the ship's eligible young ladies. The seas were rough, and March winds blew with vengeful bitterness, giving Karl the opportunity to be alone on the open deck with only an occasional stalwart fresh-air buff to keep him company. Despite the *Mauritania*'s respectable progress across the North Atlantic, the days seemed to stretch endlessly for Karl. He felt an overwhelming relief when he saw the welcoming torch of liberty in New York harbor. As soon as the ship had been secured to her moorings, Karl disembarked and telephoned home. Even with an entire continent between them, he recognized the fear and sadness in Lisl's voice.

"She's waiting for you, Karl. Please hurry."

"I'll be there as soon as I can—four or five days."

Karl heard the tremor in her voice. "She's very weak."

"I'm catching the train tonight. Look after her until I get there, please!" Lisl was crying when he hung up.

From his cramped quarters, lulled by the monotonous rattle of the train, Karl watched the countryside slip by through drowsy eyes. In a state of partial wakefulness, dreams mingled with memories and became nightmares, starkly real and frightening. He knew that his mother was dying, and yet he refused to accept it. Death was only a word, not a reality; it was something that happened to strangers and to old, tired men—not to vibrant, loving people like his mother. Fearful that she might not be there when he arrived, he felt cold in spite of the over-heated closeness of the berth.

Wind had blown the layers of snow into mounds across the empty prairies, and the moon, partially hidden behind a gauzy ribbon of clouds, cast dark shadows on the gravelike heaps. When the flatlands became rolling hills, Karl felt some of the tension leave, and when the hills became mountains, he slept.

It was past midnight when the train reached Vancouver. In the dim light, the station was unfamiliar to Karl, populated by a handful of watchful faces, furtive and suspicious because of the late hour. His legs, weakened by inactivity and weariness, trembled as he stepped from the train, and he groaned under the weight of his duffel bag. He squinted across the platform at a huge clock.

Twelve thirty-five, not exactly a convenient time to arrive, he thought.

"Welcome home, Karl-san."

Karl's shoulders sagged with relief, and he turned in the direction of the familiar voice. "Kon-nichi-wa, Takezawa-sama. Am I glad to see you!"

Hiro smiled as his eyes searched Karl's drawn face. "It has been a long journey for you."

Karl nodded wearily. "How did you know I would be on this train?"

"Lisl informed me of your telephone call from New York. I did some calculations and then met every train that has arrived in the past twelve hours."

Karl smiled thinly. "How is my mother?"

Hiro's expression became strained. "She is very weak but anxious to see you." He picked up Karl's duffel bag and led him across the platform.

As they drove through the ever-wakeful city, Karl asked, "How long have you known my mother was dying?"

"Her illness was first discovered when she fell down the stairs several years ago. The disease apparently is not a predictable one, or at least it was not predictable at that time. The doctors could not tell for certain how long she would live."

"But why didn't she tell me? She should have told me! I wouldn't have gone if I had known."

"That would not have stopped the disease, Karl. She knew how long you had planned this trip, and she also knew it was an important part of your growing up. It was her decision to let you go."

"She should have told me. No . . . I should have known myself, recognized the signs." Karl's voice was ragged.

"The last few months have been very difficult for her, but she could not have been content had you abandoned your plans."

"Lisl? How is she taking this?" Karl asked.

Hiro shook his head with concern. "Not well." He glanced at Karl. "She will cling to you, Karl, and you will have to be strong."

Drachenschlucht was a welcome sight, with its familiar narrow windows, the expansive veranda, and the four doric pillars, but as Karl stepped out of the car, he had an uncomfortable feeling that something was missing. Perhaps it was the lateness of the hour that made him uneasy.

Suddenly the front door flew open, and Lisl was in his arms. "Karl, I'm so glad you're home!"

"Hey, don't cry." Karl lifted her off the ground. "It's good to see you." Still holding her arms, he stepped back and looked at her. "Hasn't Mrs. Lange been feeding you?"

"It's just the poor light out here. Besides, I've grown an inch."

"I noticed. But that doesn't explain the bony ribs and hollow cheeks." He tapped her lightly under the chin with his closed fist.

Conrad met them in the foyer, his face puffy; Karl's arrival had awakened him. Behind him, they heard Hiro's car pull away.

"You're home." Conrad's lips stretched into a smile. "Your mother is waiting for you."

"Hello, father," Karl said as he held out his hand.

Conrad shook his hand, but he avoided looking directly into Karl's eyes.

"Is Mother awake?"

"Yes. Go on in."

Karl tapped lightly on the bedroom door.

"Come in, Karl."

The light from the bedside lamp cast harsh shadows over Dorothea's face. Karl, unprepared, felt his stomach constrict when he saw her. The glistening eyes, enormous in her pale face, shone with happiness. "Karl, I'm so happy to see you."

Karl knelt by the bed and kissed her. "Why didn't you tell me sooner?" He rested his head against her, hiding the tears. Through the heavy blankets he could feel how frail she had become.

"Where did you leave Tatsuo?" She stroked his hair gently.

"In London. He'll be home in a few months."

"When you have rested, I want to hear about everything you did." Karl looked up to see her smiling at him. Her gums were swollen and tinged with blood.

"Mother, you waited too long," he whispered with anguish.

"There was nothing anyone could have done. The disease could not be stopped, and I was happier knowing you were doing what you have always dreamed of." She closed her eyes wearily.

"Would you like me to go? Are you tired?"

"Oh no, please stay." Dorothea opened her eyes again.

Karl moved a chair beside the bed and held her dry warm hand.

"You close your eyes, and I'll tell you all about the *Liverpool* and its crew, then tomorrow I'll tell you about the countries we visited." He talked, describing the freighter in vivid detail, bringing to life each member of the crew for Dorothea until her lips formed a smile; she slept peacefully for the first time in several weeks.

Lisl and Conrad were waiting when Karl came down the stairs.

"Would you like some coffee, Karl?" Lisl asked, indicating the silver pot on the table. "Mrs. Lange said she would make you a sandwich if you wanted one."

Karl helped himself to the coffee but said he was not hungry.

"Is Mother asleep?" Lisl asked.

"Yes, she's asleep, finally. She hasn't much time left, has she?"

Conrad spoke up. "No. Dr. McAllister said there is nothing more that can be done. We just have to wait now."

"We can't just sit around waiting for her to die," Karl said in a strangled voice.

"What else would you suggest?" Conrad asked harshly. "The doctor has done all he can."

"I'd like to talk to him anyway."

"Do whatever you like, but it won't change matters a damn bit."

Resentment welled up in Karl's throat. "Did you try to do anything?"

"Of course I tried. Your mother is . . . I did not give her the disease, and I cannot miraculously make her well either. Face facts, Karl."

Karl stood up and clenched his fists. "You added to her grief!"

Conrad stared at Karl for a moment. "Your mother had everything she wanted. Look around you." He waved his hand around the opulent room, with its velvet draperies, intricately carved furniture, and paintings housed in ornate gold frames. "Do you think she could have done without these things?"

"Yes, very easily. They weren't important to her."

Conrad laughed dryly. "Only because she has always had them." His expression hardened, and his voice rose in anger. "And you? How long would you last without all the comforts?" He stood up and walked toward Karl. "Hell, every time you raised your little finger, Mrs. Lange was shoving food under your nose. You don't even know what it's like to go hungry!"

Surprised by his father's vehemence, Karl hesitated for a moment. It was true; he didn't know the feeling of constant hunger or the fear of poverty, but despite his father's wealth, his mother was dying and they were powerless to prevent her death. What did it matter now that she had lived in a splendid home filled with elaborate trappings? She had lived with a man who dominated her life, deprived her of the love she craved, and kept her shut away from the world. No, she had not experienced any physical privation, but he had sometimes heard her weeping in utter despair after Conrad had cut her with words that shattered her spirit.

"I don't know what is worse, Father," Karl said, "having a hungry stomach or a hungry spirit."

"Six months at sea hasn't taught you a bloody thing. If you had spent your time grubbing out a living from a worthless hunk of land or lying awake nights trying to figure out how to make ends meet, you wouldn't have the time or the energy to think about whether or not your spirit was hungry."

"This is pointless, Father. My mind doesn't run along the same track as yours, and I don't think Mother's did either."

"Please, Karl, stop this," Lisl begged. "You've just come home. I don't want Mother to hear any of this. That's not what she needs now."

"You're right, Lisl. I'm sorry." He knew his father expected an apology, but the words stuck in Karl's throat. They would be spurious words and were better left unsaid. For a moment he looked at Conrad, hating him with an intensity that almost choked him. "I'm going out to get some air," he announced finally.

"I'll go with you," Lisl said. "I don't think I can sleep anyway."

The sun was just coming up as they stepped outside, and the warm air was heavy with the smell of honeysuckle. As they started down the stairs, Karl stopped abruptly.

"I knew something was different when I got home. It's the dogs! Where are Harras and Prinz?" He grinned boyishly and let out a sharp whistle. "I've missed those two mutts." He looked around and whistled again.

"Karl, they're not here."

Karl's grin dissolved as he looked at Lisl's stricken face. "What do you mean they're not here? Where are they?"

"They're dead."

"Dead?" Karl's face registered disbelief. "They can't be dead."

"Well, they are. Father shot them."

"Why? For God's sake, why?"

Lisl looked away as the tears started to roll down her cheeks. "Who knows why Father does these things? He was angry so he shot the dogs."

"Lisl, I want to know what happened!" Karl grabbed her shoulders, forcing her to look at him.

"He came home in a foul mood one day just as the doctor was leaving. Father started yelling about Mother always being sick, saying that he was tired of her complaining, that the house smelled like a hospital, and on and on. He said if she was going to die, why didn't she get it over with so that the rest of us could start living again." Lisl swallowed back a sob and continued. "He said he was going out. Harras and Prinz were lying just outside the door, but I guess they were a little closer than usual. When father stormed out, he tripped over them. He must have really hurt Harras or surprised him, because he snapped at Father's ankle. Father went back into the house, loaded his gun, and shot them right on the porch. The porch has been painted, but if you look closely, the stains are still there."

"The bastard!" Karl said through clenched teeth. "Did Mother see it happen?"

Lisl nodded. "She never said a word, but the look she gave him was one that I never want to see on anyone's face again. She loved those dogs, and she knew how much they meant to you. We took her to the hospital the next day, and she was there for two weeks. I think that was the beginning of the end for her."

"Lisl, would you mind if I went for a walk by myself?"

Karl said gently. "I'd like to be alone for a while."

"No, I don't mind. But would you do me a favor tomorrow?"

"Anything at all."

"I want to hear about Tatsuo."

Karl saw her lip begin to tremble. "Sure, I'll tell you," he said.

In the daylight, the ravages of the disease were even more evident on Dorothea's face and body, but her voice was strong and her smile radiant.

"Ready for breakfast, Mother?" Karl asked with forced cheerfulness.

"Ready."

"Here or in the dining room?"

"The dining room," Dorothea said firmly. "But you'll have to help me."

Karl tried to keep his hands from shaking as he lifted her weightless body into the wheelchair, and he hoped his face did not reveal his anxiety.

"Your mother hasn't been out of the house for weeks, Karl," Mrs. Lange said as she placed an enormous helping of eggs in front of him. "Why don't you take her out for a drive?"

"Mother, would you like to go?" Karl asked brightly.

Dorothea's eyes lit up. "There is nothing I would like better." She turned to Lisl. "Will you come too?"

"I'm ready whenever you are," Lisl agreed quickly.

Billowing clouds floated in the sky, cooling the day and providing a lazy backdrop for the city. As they drove, Karl made picturesque comparisons between Vancouver and the cities he had visited. Later, they stopped in Stanley Park to listen to a brass band performing in the shade of a giant oak tree. The novice group struck several discordant notes in every song, but their appreciative audience clapped with gusto after each number.

"This reminds me of the times I used to bring you here when you were babies," Dorothea said fondly. "All we need now is some ice cream to complete the memory."

"One memory coming up," Karl replied instantly.

They ate their ice cream to the strains of a Sousa march and threw the cones to the pigeons. At Dorothea's request, Karl and Lisl took turns pushing her wheelchair around the flower gardens and beaver ponds.

"I think we should take Mother home," Lisl whispered, noticing Dorothea's strained face.

"We'll take another drive tomorrow," Karl promised.

"I would like that," Dorothea said weakly.

At home, Karl lifted his mother back into bed; she moaned, helpless with pain.

"I'll call the doctor," Karl said. "He will give you something for the pain."

"Please," Dorothea gasped. Her teeth were pressed against her bottom lip and her hands were clenched tightly.

Karl was pacing the floor when Dr. McAllister arrived in the driveway. "Please hurry. She's in a lot of pain."

Dr. McAllister nodded and rushed inside. He closed the bedroom door behind him, leaving Karl and Lisl alone in the hall. Karl didn't resist when Lisl guided him into the sunroom.

"Oh God, Lisl, I can't stand to see her suffering like that. Can't the doctor do something?" Lisl shook her head. "But she's in so much pain! Does she have to die like that?" He looked up just as Dr. McAllister walked in.

"I've eased the pain somewhat. There's not much else that anyone can do for her now. I'm sorry."

"How long is she going to suffer?"

Dr. McAllister shoulders slumped. "She won't suffer much longer."

"What's wrong with her? What is this thing that's eating her up?"

"It's a form of cancer. Myeloplastic leukemia. There is no cure for it. It's times like this when I wish I were a truck driver instead of a doctor!"

"Why *her*, damnit? She doesn't deserve to die like this!" Karl cried.

"Disease doesn't play favorites. If she needs me, please do not hesitate to call—day or night."

"Thank you, Doctor."

The front door slammed.

"Father is home." There was alarm in Lisl's voice.

Conrad stopped the doctor in the hallway. "How sick is she this time?" he demanded.

"She was in considerable pain, but I've given her a sedative and she is resting comfortably. I've told your son to call if she needs me during the night. The next few days will probably be very difficult for her.''

"She belongs in the hospital, goddamnit. Why don't you do as I ask and put her there? It will be better for her and a hell of a lot easier on us.''

"It was her choice to stay home, Mr. Richter. I suggested it, but she begged me to leave her at home. She wants to die here, and I think you should abide by her wishes for the little time she has left.''

Conrad stepped closer to Dr. McAllister. "How the hell does she know what she wants? I don't even think she knows where she is half the time. I want her out of here and in the hospital right now!''

"She is not going to the hospital," Karl said ominously.

The words didn't register in Conrad's mind for a few moments, only the threatening tone in his son's voice. "What?'' he finally said.

"Mother will remain here.''

"Who do you think you are, telling me what is to be done in my own house?'' Conrad shouted.

"Mother has a right to stay here, and I'm going to protect that right. I don't want to hear any more about her going to the hospital. We are going to do the best we can for her in the little time she has left.''

Karl opened the door for Dr. McAllister. "I'm sorry you have been subjected to our constant family battles," he said bitterly.

"Karl, I have known your mother and father for many years. I'm well aware of the situation. But don't be too harsh with him. He is a complex man with many fears which I'm sure he hides behind his temper.''

"Fears that have made my mother's life miserable.''

Dr. McAllister sighed. "I'm glad you're home, Karl. For your mother's sake, of course, but also for Lisl's.''

After Dr. McAllister had left, Karl put his arm around Lisl and led her into the sun-room.

She clung to him tightly. "Oh, Karl, how can Father be so stupid and cruel?''

He stroked her hair and placed his cheek gently on her head. "I don't know, Lisl . . . maybe it's like Dr. McAllister said. The bad temper hides his fears.''

"That's no excuse!" Lisl said. "For as long as I can remember he's treated her like that. He's never been decent to any of us—never a hug or a kind word. It's only because of your strength that he hasn't hurt you too. I hate him—I hate him!" Her hacking sobs were muffled against Karl's sweater.

"I know, Lisl, I know. Let's just try to keep everything calm for a bit longer."

As the days passed, Dorothea's condition deteriorated rapidly. What little appetite she had had disappeared until mealtimes became a trial. When she was awake, she was confused, wandering back to her childhood and crying out in pain. When the drugs took effect, she would smile and talk as though nothing were wrong. During the day, Karl closed the draperies to prevent the brilliant sunlight from revealing the cruel devastation of the disease, but at night he would pull them open, and he and Lisl would sit with her while the moon cast slivers of light through the open windows.

Late one evening, Dorothea asked to be wheeled outside.

Lisl shook her head. "It's late, Mother. I think you should rest."

"Karl, please put me in my wheelchair," Dorothea said with surprising strength in her voice. "I want to go outside and sit in the garden." Her face was flushed with unnatural color, and a look of alarm passed between Lisl and Karl.

As gently as he could, Karl lifted her into the wheelchair and covered her with a heavy blanket. It had rained during the day, but the night air was clear and fresh. The sound of the wheelchair echoed through the stillness as Karl pushed her along the path.

Dorothea's breathing was labored and uneven. "Stop here, Karl, and turn me around so I can see the moon over the mountain." Lisl knelt and laid her head on Dorothea's lap. Dorothea stroked her hair gently. "Karl, promise me you will look after your sister. I love you both so much."

Karl nodded mutely, unable to trust his voice.

"You are the strong one, Karl," Dorothea said softly. Her head sank slowly and rested on her chest. An unnatural stillness settled around them.

"Lisl, she's gone."

Lisl stood up slowly and, sobbing, leaned against her brother for support.

〔14〕

"Close the window!"

Conrad's voice shattered Karl's thoughts. Only when he began to roll up the window did Karl realize that the arm of his jacket was drenched from the unrelenting rain. In the mirror he could see his sister and Mrs. Lange huddled in the back seat, the older woman's face obscured by a black veil. The church had been filled to capacity, and now, as they proceeded slowly to the cemetery, Karl tried to recall the faces of the people who had attended the service. Janice had been there, and he had recognized a few others; the rest were strangers who had come to share their grief and to pay their last respects. Some had wept openly, others wore masks for the occasion, masks that were a perfect balance of grief and dignified composure—the most perfect had been worn by his father.

The procession wound its way through the cemetery to the grave site, where the anonymous crowd began to regroup. In spite of Conrad's displeasure, Karl had insisted that Hiro be one of the pallbearers; the other five were only vaguely familiar. As Karl had instructed, the coffin remained closed. Even in death Dorothea's face was peaceful, but only those who knew and loved his mother could have recognized the serenity; in spite of the ravages of the disease. The simple graveside ceremony was completed swiftly, as Karl had requested, and the mourners soon began to disperse.

Lisl stepped forward to place a single white rose on the casket. "Good-bye, Mama," she said softly.

Karl caught her by the arm as she stumbled. His heart ached for Lisl and his mother; tears threatened to break forth, and his words were caught in a painful lump in his throat. He felt as though he were sleepwalking and could not force himself into wakefulness; his voice sounded hollow. "Let's go home, Lisl."

Karl helped Lisl into the car as she wept, wrenching sobs that no one could stop. What had his mother said? "Karl, you are the strong one." He didn't feel any of that strength now, only numb despair, but Drachenschlucht would be their home even without her. That was her wish.

The day after the funeral, Conrad ordered Mrs. Lange to remove all traces of Dorothea's illness from the room she had occupied during the last months of her life. "Throw out the bedding and disinfect the room completely. I don't want the smell of death lingering in this house any longer. Throw the bed out, too. And Karl move the rest of the furniture into the basement."

"But the desk—it was her favorite piece!"

Conrad's eyes froze on Mrs. Lange. "She is not here anymore. Move it downstairs!"

"Yes, sir."

The room was empty by the time Conrad returned home that evening. The desk was now in Lisl's room, a room Conrad never entered. Dorothea's books had been placed on the shelves in the library, and her other personal effects were stored in the basement along with the rest of the furniture, except for the bed. It had been disposed of as Conrad had ordered. The scent of lemon oil and wax permeated the entire house for several days, a grim reminder that Dorothea was gone forever.

"Your training is not suffering, tomodachi, but your spirit is," Hiro said after a long session in the dojo.

Karl sighed deeply. "Life seems so lonely and empty without Mother. And Lisl can't stop clinging to me. Maybe I should take her and move away from here."

"Do not be too hasty," Hiro cautioned. "This is a difficult time for you both, and the decision you make now will affect the course of your future."

"I know, but I have a feeling that my father will try to pull me into his business."

"Do you want to work for him?"

Karl looked at Hiro for a moment and shrugged. "I guess you know me better than anyone else. Do you think I could work with him?"

Hiro's knitted his eyebrows thoughtfully. "I do know you well, but you are a man now, Karl. Whether you can work with your father or not is a decision you will have to make."

"I know, but I would appreciate your opinion."

Hiro stared at Karl for a moment. "My first thought is that you would find it very difficult, but then I know you have tremendous strength and determination. Your father could use your quick mind, and you would have the opportunity to work with ships, which is what you have always wanted."

"I would rather be a trimmer on the *Liverpool* than work by my father's standards," Karl answered bluntly.

Although Hiro did not speak, Karl knew instinctively that the sensei approved of his decision.

Within a month of Dorothea's death, the family was summoned to the offices of Pittman, Drake and McAuly for the reading of her will. Mrs. Lange, at the request of the lawyers, was also asked to be present. After a short wait, they were directed into the spacious but cluttered office of Richard Drake.

"Good morning. Please sit down," Drake said. "Before I begin, I must offer my sincerest sympathy in your tragic loss."

"Thank you," Conrad murmured.

Drake opened a folder on his desk and adjusted his narrow glasses on his nose. "In an estate of this size, we usually advise our clients to seek professional financial advice before allocating its disposition. Mrs. Richter assured me this had been done."

Drake read the document slowly, unaware of the shock that registered on Conrad's face as he listed the various holdings in Dorothea's estate, the majority of which were bequeathed to Lisl and Karl. Conrad gripped his chair tightly when Drake estimated the value of the estate at two million dollars.

"What the hell are you talking about?" Conrad exploded. "Where would she get that kind of money?"

Drake looked up at Conrad with disapproval at the sudden interruption. "Why, I thought you knew, Mr. Richter! Your wife had some very sizable holdings that her father had left her. Judging from the portfolio she presented to us, he must have been a financial genius. Recently your wife had some of these investments converted into more tangible holdings and they, too, have increased in value. Now if you will permit me to carry on, Mr. Richter . . ."

Conrad sat back and cursed himself for being such a fool. He had carelessly assumed that Dorothea's accounts were insignificant and had allowed a fortune to slip through his fingers. He stiffened when he heard Drake mention Drachenschlucht.

"Wait a minute. Read that again," he ordered.

"As you wish, Mr. Richter." Drake followed along with his finger as he read. "I do hereby bequeath Drachenschlucht to my children . . ."

Conrad leaped from his chair and smashed his fist on the desk. "What the hell do you mean, Drachenschlucht? That house belongs to me!"

Drake looked up at Conrad. "According to the official documents we have on file, Drachenschlucht belongs to Mrs. Richter." He removed a long sheet of paper from the file and passed it to Conrad.

"This was only a temporary arrangement—she knew that! I had the house transferred to her to avoid any unnecessary risks while I was establishing my business. She had no right to do this to me!" His voice had risen to a shout.

"She had every right, Mr. Richter. According to this deed, the house was legally hers. She was free to dispose of it as she saw fit. Now, may we proceed?"

Conrad sank back into his chair, his face drained of color.

". . . to my children Lisl and Karl. It is my wish that they reside in Drachenschlucht and that they retain Mrs. Lange for as long as she wishes to live with them. She is to receive her salary each month from a special account I have established for that purpose. Should she decide to leave their employ, she is to be paid twenty-five thousand dollars or the balance of that account, whichever is greater."

Conrad's eyes darkened in his pale face as Drake completed the reading of the will. "Now, are there any questions?" Drake asked.

Conrad stood up slowly, as if in a daze, and walked out of the office.

Karl shook the lawyer's hand. "Thank you, sir. No doubt we will have to consult with you again."

"Your mother has left you and Lisl with enough money to

sustain you for the rest of your lives, if you handle it well. She had great faith in you, Karl, and I know that you will live up to her every expectation.''

They drove home in silence. Conrad's face was dark with anger while Karl struggled with his own thoughts. He had just been handed a fortune, and he had no idea what to do with it. First Mother, then Mr. Takezawa, and now Richard Drake— all three felt he had the strength and wisdom to make the right decisions. Then why did he feel such terrible uncertainty? He looked over at his father, sensing the anger smoldering within, the resentment against Dorothea and against his own children. Karl braced himself for the confrontation that was sure to come.

The issue was raised almost as soon as they entered the house. Conrad quickly downed two glasses of Scotch, then faced Karl.

"You and your mother had no right to do this," he said coldly. "You have taken what is rightfully mine. I want it back and damn soon."

"I cannot give it to you, Father. From what I understand, Mother provided you with collateral on many occasions. What she had left she wanted to give to Lisl and me, and I do not intend to go against her final wishes. I'm sorry, Father, but that's the way it has to be."

"This house is mine! I had it built."

"With her money," Karl added pointedly.

"It is none of your goddamn business whose money it was."

"It is now, Father. The house belongs to Lisl and me."

Conrad threw his glass on the floor and it shattered, sending tiny pieces of crystal flying. He stepped closer to Karl, mindless of the glass that crunched under his feet. "I will throw you out of here bodily if I have to. You and those slant-eyed bastards planned this whole thing!"

Karl took a deep breath, suddenly feeling very tired. "Father, the Takezawas had nothing to do with it, and Mother and I have not swindled you out of anything. You don't even need that money. As for the house . . . it was her way of providing security for us, Lisl in particular. I think if you had to, you would trade Drachenschlucht for a new freighter without a second thought. I could fend for myself very easily, but what would happen to Lisl and Mrs. Lange? I am sure Mother thought about these things for a long time before she made her decision. Had you loved her, you would understand why she did it, but I don't think you are capable of love." Karl knew Conrad was going to strike him, but he made no move to protect himself against the blow that struck the side of his face. He looked at his father with clear unflinching eyes. "We cannot live in this house together any longer, Father. Take whatever you want and leave. If you want any of the furniture, leave a list with Mrs. Lange, and I'll see that it's delivered to you," Karl announced calmly.

Conrad's face became livid with rage; his voice was menacing. "You will pay for this, Karl. Others have tried to stand in my way but they did not succeed, and neither will you!"

"If you're trying to frighten me, you are wasting your time."

"Julius Forsythe probably said the same thing," snarled Conrad. "You remember Julius Forsythe, don't you?"

Karl remembered the Forsythes well.

"That bastard hired thugs to attack me in Tokyo. It took a while, but I got even with him." A mirthless smile stretched across his face. "Do you want to know how?"

"Not really, Father."

"Well, I'll tell you anyway. His business depended on silk shipments from Japan. I made sure he didn't get them." Conrad laughed aloud. "His business went bankrupt, and he blew his fucking brains out."

"I don't want to hear any more. Get out!"

"Don't underestimate me, Karl. You've taken what belongs to me, and I will get it back!"

Lisl met Karl in the hallway. "Father sounded furious." She looked at him with frightened eyes.

"I've told him to leave the house," Karl said flatly.

Lisl caught her breath. "Is he going?"

"Yes. Stay out of his way until he leaves."

In the morning Conrad was gone. With a hollow feeling in his stomach, Karl watched him drive away. It had been a long time since he had felt any love for his father; resentment, anger, and, sometimes, fear had taken it away. What he felt now was a sense of loss for what might have been.

"Karl, this is the third time I've called you!" Lisl said impatiently.

"Sorry, I was thinking of something else."

"That much I guessed," Lisl sniffed. "I'm bringing Janice home with me this afternoon. She wants to see you."

"Janice? I should have gotten in touch with her. I haven't seen her since the funeral. How is she?"

"She missed you, Karl."

"I've been thinking about her."

"She should be grateful for small favors, I suppose."

"Lisl, what's this all about?" Karl asked impatiently.

"Oh, nothing."

Karl looked at her knowingly. "No letter from Tatsuo this week?"

Lisl shook her head.

"He'll be home in six weeks, then your wait will be over."

Left alone in the living room, Lisl sat beside the draped window, an unopened book on her lap. Karl was right: Tatsuo would be home in six weeks, but would he be home to stay? Her heart told her he would not again deny her the promises she needed to hear, but instinct threatened to destroy what hope she had. She remembered lying in his arms and praying that the moment would last forever. Her prayers had not been answered then, and she wondered now if they ever would be. The specter of the zaibatsu loomed over them, larger than ever. Familiar helpless anger welled up and she flung the unread book across the room viciously. With determination on her face, she filled a slender glass with her father's favorite Scotch and quickly downed it. For a moment she could not breathe; the alcohol burned in her throat and an involuntary shudder ran down her spine. Slowly, she replaced the decanter, feeling the tight knot of tension leave her body.

When Janice walked in, Karl experienced the same heady reaction as when they had first met. Karl knew he was staring.

"Hello, Karl," Janice said softly.

"You've cut your hair," Karl stammered.

She smiled, and Karl realized he had forgotten how white and even her teeth were.

"It was becoming a nuisance," she said, patting the curls that barely covered her ears.

"I liked it better long."

"Then I shall let it grow again," she replied simply, and laughed.

Karl smiled tentatively and then joined her laughter. Their awkwardness disappeared, and conversation flowed between them as easily as it had a year ago. When Karl finally took her home, he kissed her tenderly.

"Do you remember the promise we made before I left on the *Liverpool*?"

"That we would go back to that island and the deserted beach when you returned. Yes, I remember."

"I'll pick you up on Saturday morning."

"I'll be ready," Janice replied.

In preparation for the cruise, Karl had refueled the *Cathy B*, restocked the tiny galley, and cleaned the boat from the wheelhouse to the white dingy secured at the stern. The engine started easily and its dull throaty rumble quieted as the boat cut through the First Narrows and into the waters of the Georgia Strait. By noon they had crossed the strait, toured the shoreline of Salt Spring Island, and finally anchored in a small cove between a group of little islands.

"Would the lady like a swim before lunch?" Karl asked.

"The lady would love it."

The sun had warmed their skin and the ocean seemed painfully cold in comparison. To Karl's surprise, Janice endured the cold water far better than he did. She floated on the waves long after he had scrambled back on board, where, wrapped in a thick towel, he watched with open admiration as she swam with long easy strokes. They ate their lunch on the open deck and threw the remains of their sandwiches to hungry sea gulls.

When they lay back on their towels to enjoy the warmth of the May afternoon, Janice wondered if Karl could hear the drumming of her heart whenever he touched her, or if he ever guessed how she felt when he looked at her. One day she would tell him how much she had missed him when he was away and how eagerly she had read the few letters he had written. The intensity of her feelings for him surprised her, for she had always considered herself to be levelheaded, in total control of her emotions. But Karl was the culmination of all her dreams, and it took every bit of her willpower not to tell him that she loved him.

"You're beautiful, Janice," she heard him whisper.

Janice smiled, afraid to trust her voice. She felt Karl's fingertips caress her lips and brush the hair back from her forehead. He drew her against him, and she returned his kisses with an urgency that equaled his. His hands roamed her body, and when he moved to kiss her neck and the curve of her breast, a growing desire threatened to consume her. She arched against him, feeling his hardness against her thighs. She did not let herself think as she got to her knees and slipped off her bathing suit, and she barely heard his sharp intake of breath when she opened herself to him. There was an excruciating stab of pain when he entered her, gradually assuaged by the throb of desire as her body rose to meet his.

Later they lay quietly, Karl holding her close to still the trembling of her body.

"I've never made love before," Janice whispered.

"I know."

"Have you?"

"Yes, but not often," Karl answered.

"When you were at sea?"

"In Japan. It was a gift from Tatsuo."

"A gift from Tatsuo? I don't understand."

"He arranged for me to have a geisha for an evening." He saw Janice's eyes widen and explained, "It's an accepted custom in Japan."

"Was she very beautiful?"

"Not as beautiful as you." Karl drew her close again and kissed her gently. "Not nearly as beautiful as you."

On the day the *Liverpool* was due to arrive in Vancouver, Lisl, Karl, and the Takezawas were on the pier by midmorning, anticipating an early arrival; they were not disappointed.

"There she is—just past the marker!" Karl announced.

Two hours later the rusty, aging freighter tied up at Pier B. Tatsuo's face, bronzed by the sun, was among the other familiar faces that lined the guardrail. He waved and called out to Karl, but his eyes lingered on Lisl.

"Hey, Karl, the captain is looking for a trimmer. Get up here and sign on." Spence's voice was unmistakable.

"Not this trip," Karl said, shaking his head.

"What did you do—get yourself an ol' lady?" That was Gilhooly. Karl smiled, wondering what Gilhooly would say if he knew how close he had come to the truth.

Tatsuo was the first one down the gangplank. He bowed ceremoniously to Hiro and Miyoko, carefully observing protocol, but then, unable to contain himself any longer, he drew his grandmother into his arms and lifted her off the ground.

"Obā-san, I am so glad to see you!"

He desposited his grandmother on the ground and turned to Karl.

"Good to have you back, old friend," Karl said.

"It's good to be back. The *Liverpool* was a lonely place after you left." His face became serious. "I wish I could have been here sooner, but the happy memories of your mother will stay with me forever."

"You meant a great deal to her," Karl said quietly.

"I received a letter from her shortly after you left London. It was a beautiful expression of her faith and acceptance but also of her yearning for life."

Finally, Tatsuo turned to Lisl. He seemed ill at ease until he noticed tears playing at the corners of her eyes. He held out his arms, and she was in them instantly. He kissed her gently as the tears spilled down her cheeks.

"You've been away too long," she whispered.

Looking at them, Karl realized he had never seen Lisl so blissfully happy.

During the first few weeks of October 1929, the brokerage houses in Vancouver and New York showed intense activity. As usual, the trend was forever upward until Wednesday the twenty-third, when the price of several major stocks dropped significantly. On the following day the trend continued but at an accelerated pace, alarming many investors—including Patrick Fenton and Cyrus Wilson. In the offices of Pacific Far Eastern Trading, Karl discussed the feverish turn of events with Hiro, Patrick, and Cyrus. He studied their faces with concern. "What is happening? Everyone seems to be panicking."

"It's just what we've feared for some time. The country isn't prepared to ride out the storm this time," Patrick answered solemnly.

Cyrus Wilson, who had been sitting glumly in his chair, finally spoke up. "The goddamn country is running blind . . . has been for some time. Coolidge and Hoover never did a bloody thing to stop this lunacy, and now we're all in the pickle barrel, you mark my words . . . damn fools!"

"Exactly what is going on in New York?" Karl asked.

"The market is sliding drastically. There's going to be hell to pay," Patrick announced.

"How can this be happening?" Karl demanded.

"Because so many of the securities are overpriced and people are buying on margin . . . buying bloody paper as if it were gold! Our economies are not geared to handle this crisis. You could see the signs over a year ago, even longer."

Karl nodded. "I remember your warnings to Mother."

"Did you get rid of the rest of those securities?" Patrick asked.

"Yes, we did, long ago," Karl assured him.

"It's greed, that's all it is," Cyrus said. "We're all guilty. Everyone's trying to make a fast buck, and nobody in government has done a bloody thing to regulate the market."

"I wonder if my father realizes what's going on," Karl thought aloud.

"If he does, he's not admitting it. I spoke to him yesterday and tried to warn him, but he told me I was crazy," Patrick answered. "Maybe you should talk to him, Karl."

"He wouldn't listen to anything I have to say, either. I think he's been speculating heavily."

"I can't understand him," Cyrus said, drawing on his huge cigar. "He's always been so careful, but in the last year or so he's gone crazy. It's just not like him."

"Your father has made a fortune on paper stocks, and the easy pickings have whetted his appetite and made him careless—just like a lot of other people," Patrick said.

The following day, Thursday, October 24, was even worse; the market dropped tremendously, then staggered like a wounded bull through the Friday and Saturday sessions. On Sunday, Wall Street was overrun by tourists who had come to see where all that money had been lost. The market plunged further on Monday, causing brokers to work late into the night, demanding that customers put up more cash and pay off their loans. It was then that Conrad came to visit Karl at Drachenschlucht.

"Your father is here to see you," Mrs. Lange announced. "He doesn't look well."

"Tell him to come in, and don't look so worried. There won't be any trouble."

"I'll bring some coffee," she said before leaving the study.

Conrad did not waste time on preliminaries; his voice shook as he spoke. "I need your help. I must have the money from your mother's estate."

"How much?"

"All of it. I bought stocks on margin, and I need that money now, before it's too late. It will just be until this crazy market straightens itself out. In a few days I'll sell everything and get my money back plus some. I'll make it worth your while."

"It's too late, Father. You should have done that months ago when Mr. Fenton told you to. The market won't level out until it hits rock bottom."

Conrad's voice rose, and he gripped the chair in an effort to control his temper. "You don't know what you're talking about. You must help me, or I'll lose everything."

"You'll lose anyway, and if I give you the money, you'll be throwing good money after bad. Just try to salvage what you can now without taking any more risks."

"You're denying your own father! Don't you realize what you're doing to me?"

"I'm not denying you, I'm trying to be sensible," Karl said as gently as he could.

"Damn you . . . I'll get it all back. You'll see."

When Mrs. Lange brought the coffee tray into the study, she found Karl sitting alone with his face buried in his broad hands.

"Are you all right, Karl?" she asked.

"I suppose so. I know I did the right thing, but I still feel as if I've been beaten with a club."

The selling panic continued into Tuesday, when the dam broke wide open. News came over the wires that Radio Corporation of America's first sale was down ten and a quarter from forty and a quarter, ITT down 17 from 88, Allegheny down 4 and 7/8 from 20 and 1/8 on a single block of 50,000 shares. People began selling stocks for whatever they would bring, and by ten-thirty a record of 3,259,000 shares had been sold on the New York Stock Exchange. The ticker tapes ran behind schedule, and the subsequent uncertainty brought on even more distress-selling and -dumping.

By midmorning a small brokerage house had failed, bringing on another burst of selling; hysteria swept the country. Telephone lines and all forms of communication became clogged; even transatlantic calls from London had to be rationed. Telegraph companies hired entire fleets of taxis to help with telegram deliveries, crowds gathered in mute fascination, staring at the Stock Exchange Building. In nearby churches people prayed for the madness to end, but it didn't—it became worse. By 1:20 P.M. more than 12 million shares had been sold on Wall Street and there was still two hours of trading left. At 5:23 eastern time the final quotation came through on the Translux screen, after which the operator ticked off: "Total Sales Today . . . 16,388,700 . . . Good night!"

Hiro was at his desk when Patrick brought in the latest reports. "You have advised us well, Patrick, and we will undoubtedly ride out the financial storm, but there are other far-reaching consequences that we cannot prevent. Not only will the whole world feel the effects of the financial collapse, but Japan will now wear its other face."

Fenton listened in silence, hypnotized by Hiro's ominous words. "Today Japan has lost its last chance to develop by peaceful means. The military will waste no time in offering alternatives."

Patrick and Hiro stared at each other grimly, with despair in their hearts.

[15]

The offices of Pacific Far Eastern Trading were quiet and dark except for a lamp which glowed dimly on Hiro's desk. He shifted in his chair, attempting to ease the tension he felt, and stared bleakly out the window. A wet snow had started to fall, covering the streets with slush. The winter had been harsh, and Christmas had offered only a brief respite from the grim realities of the depression, the holiday seeming only to accentuate the growing despair. In Japan and Canada and around the world, factories were being closed, banks failed, prices sank to rock bottom, and the buying power of every nation was drastically reduced. Trade between Japan and Canada slowed to a mere trickle; silk bales gathered dust in warehouses, and Japan's imports of Canadian wheat and lumber were negligible.

Hiro closed his eyes wearily. The economic collapse had marked the end of a peaceful trade era for Japan; the big buyers were gone, and new international tariff laws further hampered all rehabilitative efforts. Japan was now forced to follow the dictates of the military, whose power had increased immeasurably. Even the zaibatsu's influence receded as the military, acting in the name of the emperor, seized control.

Hiro reread the zaibatsu's latest directive: "Expansion into Asia will provide needed raw materials and will alleviate the problems brought about by the worldwide depression." There was no mistaking the implications. The floodgates had been thrust open—there would be no stopping the tide. The military would eventually lead Japan into war. Hiro sat erect in his chair. His premonition—the bloodied faces of his people and their cries of anguish came flooding back to him.

Hiro heard heavy footsteps outside his office. The door opened, and Conrad Richter stood silhouetted in the dim light. Hiro looked at him blankly for a moment before speaking. "Richter-sama! Please come in."

"You're still here. I must talk to you," Conrad said.

"Of course. Sit down, please." Hiro indicated a chair beside his desk.

"Do you have any Scotch?" Conrad asked.

Hiro moved to a wood cabinet by the window and returned with an unopened bottle bearing a label that Conrad recognized.

"I see you still have the best in stock. You're one of the fortunate few," Conrad said as he sat down heavily. His skin had a grayish hue, and the desk lamp revealed the lines that crisscrossed his face. He had lost weight, but his body sagged around the middle. His pants had been worn until their crease disappeared, a button was missing from his coat, and his tie hung in a loose knot.

"What do you wish to talk about?" Hiro asked, passing him a half-filled tumbler of Scotch.

Conrad emptied the glass before answering. "I want to know if you have received instructions from the zaibatsu about further shipments. My freighters are lying idle in the harbor, and I have to know what the hell you and the zaibatsu are going to do about it."

Hiro refilled the glass. "I am afraid I have not received any good news. We will have to maintain limited shipments until the economic situation resolves itself," he answered wearily.

"Resolves itself? For Christ's sake, that may take years! In fact, it may never happen. I can't wait much longer. Out of fourteen freighters, I've had to give up six to pay off loans, another four are tied up doing nothing, and only three are sailing!" His voice rose loudly in the empty room.

"That is only thirteen, Richter-sama. What happened to the last freighter?"

Conrad's face tightened with anger. "Federal agents confiscated it last month in Seattle."

"Were you transporting alcohol?"

"What the hell else could I do?" Conrad demanded.

"There is a prohibition law. You committed a criminal offense."

"Spare me the lectures," Conrad said, waving his hand. "It's a stupid law passed by idiots."

"Nevertheless, it is the law and you have broken it."

Conrad leaned forward in his chair. "You sit there and condemn me for trying to survive. What the hell do you really know about it? You still have a vault half-full of gold. I'm the one who's losing his shirt because the goddamn zaibatsu hasn't followed through with our contract! I would be happy to carry shipments solely for the zaibatsu if they could provide me with the cargo."

"The zaibatsu is facing the same problems as everyone else, Richter-sama. The whole world is feeling the effects of the economic collapse. I know this is no consolation to you, but I am as helpless as you are. There is nothing more I can do." Hiro longed to add his own thoughts—that he would make any sacrifice that could free Japan from the dictates of the military and give his grandson freedom.

Conrad formed a tight fist and slammed it down on the arm of the chair. "If I could only convince Karl to give me enough money to see me through this! Christ, I could get half of Vancouver harbor if I played my cards right." He pushed himself from his chair and leaned over the desk to look directly at Hiro. "That money is rightfully mine! Dorothea cheated me out of it, gave it away behind my back—and you helped her do it." There was a fierceness in his eyes. "You've got to convince Karl to give it back to me!"

Hiro sat motionless, aware that Conrad's face was only inches away, his breath sour from the alcohol.

"My son threw me out of my house," Conrad continued. "She turned them against me. She planned it all—stealing the money, the house—but I want that money back, goddamnit, I want it back." Once again his fist slammed down on the desk.

The light from the desk lamp did not reach Hiro's face. He sat in the shadows, but his voice cut through the stillness. "The legacy Dorothea left for Karl and Lisl belongs to them. You have no right to it. Make no mistake, Richter, I will protect them and the legacy, not only because it is my legal responsibility, but because I promised Dorothea on the honor of our friendship.''

"Honor! What the hell does honor matter now? The whole fucking world is sinking, I'm going down with it, and you're talking about honor! Don't you understand! I need that money!''

"The zaibatsu will not abandon you. Of course there has been a sharp reduction in trade, and under the circumstances this cannot be avoided, but there will be enough activity to keep you solvent until the economy stabilizes.''

"Well, they had better get off their asses right now and do something before it's too late.''

"I am expecting new orders soon,'' Hiro said.

"Yes, I'll bet you are.''

"What do you mean, Richter-sama?'' Hiro asked, suddenly alert.

"I've been to Japan recently. I'm not blind and I'm not deaf. There's something in the wind, and you and I both know how ambitious Japan's military has become. They will be needing raw materials—and I don't want the zaibatsu to forget that they have a contract with me.''

"That is merely conjecture on your part, Richter-sama. I find your implications distasteful.''

For the first time since he arrived in Hiro's office, a smile appeared on Conrad's lips. "Unlike you, I have no particular loyalties except to myself.''

"If you will excuse me, I am very tired.'' Hiro stood up to leave.

"Do you mind if I take this with me?'' Conrad asked, pointing to the whiskey bottle.

"Take it.''

The door closed quietly behind Conrad, and as the echo of his footsteps receded down the stairway, Hiro sank back into his chair. That night, for the first time, he did not join Karl and Tatsuo in the dojo.

The next directive from the zaibatsu was very specific. Tatsuo was ordered to report to the Tokyo office. In the weeks that followed, the zaibatsu gave evasive answers to Hiro's questions, stating only that Tatsuo must now meet his obligations. In an effort to determine the extent of these obligations, Hiro appealed directly to Shozo and Koji, but they too were reticent. Hiro now felt separated from his country and from the people with whom he had always shared the same ideals and principles. He began to have grave suspicions that Tatsuo would be sent to Korea or Manchuria.

As a last resort, Hiro sought out Ambassador Suyama. They had not seen each other for several months, and Hiro was disturbed by the weariness evident in his friend's eyes and sagging shoulders. Warmed sake was served in ornate porcelain cups.

"I am afraid that hostilities may soon erupt, my friend," the ambassador admitted sadly. "The zaibatsu has ordered my grandson back to Japan."

"I know."

"Do you know what their intentions are?"

Ambassador Suyama studied his slender hands for a moment. "If I knew, I would certainly tell you, Takezawa-san. Let us pray that the final outcome will be for the betterment of everyone concerned."

"Your words sound hollow," Hiro answered. "A country led by its military is in a very vulnerable and dangerous position. No, if the final outcome is war, it will not be for the betterment of anyone."

"As ambassador, it has always been my duty to promote peaceful relations. The thought of war is abhorrent to me." Ambassador Suyama walked to an open window. Below him, surrounded by green lawns, several ornamental cherry trees were in bloom. It reminded him of a tapestry that had hung in his father's house. "I have lived in this country for many years and have grown to love it, but I cannot forsake my loyalty to Japan. I must follow whatever course the emperor chooses to set, and serve as best I can."

Hiro stood up and bowed. "I admire you for the strength of your convictions, Suyama-san."

The ambassador stopped him before he reached the door. "Takezawa-san! It is my sincere hope that your grandson will not be forced to abandon his freedom or his principles in these difficult and uncertain times."

Tatsuo's departure for his first official visit to the zaibatsu headquarters was accompanied by deep concern and sadness.

Karl stayed close to Lisl in the days that followed, sharing mealtimes and speculating about the future. She convinced Karl that she expected Tatsuo to return within two months and that she would hold on until then.

"You know, I'm finally meeting Janice's parents," Karl told Lisl one day. "She invited me for dinner tomorrow," Karl announced. "What are they like?"

"You'll like her father, but her mother is a social climber. She and Janice aren't very close."

"Thank God Janice didn't take after her."

The family resemblance between David Chandler and his daughter was evident—the same candid brown eyes, engaging smile, and easy manner. A onetime seaman himself, he showed obvious interest in Karl's stint on the *Liverpool* and laughed uproariously when he related some of his experiences. In spite of his casualness, Karl had the feeling that David Chandler was carefully scrutinizing him, measuring him against the standards he had preset for the man who might one day marry his daughter. Karl understood; Chandler obviously loved his daughter very much, and it was only natural that he would want to protect her. Janice smiled confidently at Karl as she poured sherry from a sparkling crystal decanter. Karl sipped the drink, knowing that he wanted to meet David Chandler's standards; in fact, he wanted to win ¡.im over completely.

"And what do you plan to do with your future, Karl?" Mr. Chandler asked directly.

"I'm not quite sure yet, but I do have some plans."

"What sort of plans?"

"I want to build ships—cargo ships!" Karl said, suddenly, almost blurting out his ideas. "In order for a country to be strong, they need a viable merchant marine. I've been reading about new designs for freighters, ships that will cruise the oceans at eighteen knots and carry twice as much cargo as the *Liverpool*."

For the first time that evening, Janice's mother looked up and gave her full attention to Karl. "That's quite a plan! Do you know anything about shipbuilding?" she asked.

"Only what I've read and a bit that I learned from my trip on the *Liverpool*."

"And you feel that's sufficient?" Helen Chandler asked.

"No, but I'm prepared to work hard, and I'll hire the right people."

David Chandler detected an obstinate purposefulness in Karl's manner, yet his instincts told him that beneath that strong exterior was a vulnerable sensitivity . . . perhaps it had been the way Karl sat on the edge of the chair, or perhaps the way his fingers shook slightly when he accepted the glass of sherry.

"I wish you luck, Karl," he said, "but I have the feeling you won't need luck. I think you will realize your ambitions on your own initiative." He accepted a kiss from Janice and left the room, accompanied by his wife.

Karl had surprised himself even more than he had Janice's parents by announcing his intention to build ships. Although the idea had been taking shape in his mind, it had been more in the form of dreams than realities. But suddenly the dreams became tangible as evidenced by the simple statement he had made to them: "I want to build ships—cargo ships." He was filled with excitement, and he spun Janice around the room.

"I've been dreaming about building ships ever since my mother bought me my first model, but that's all it was, a dream. But today when your father asked me what I planned to do with my life, I realized that the time for dreaming was over. I felt like I did the day I completed my first bottle ship. I had worked for three months putting all those little pieces together through the neck of the bottle, and all that was left was to pull the string and the ship would come to life. That's what I feel like now. I have plans, I know where I could get the men, I have the money from my mother's estate—all I have to do is pull the string."

"I think my father was right," Janice said. "You'll get what you want."

The next morning, Karl arrived several minutes early for his appointment with Patrick Fenton. Karl talked quickly, revealing his plans for building the new cargo ship. When he was finished, he looked up expectantly at Patrick. "Well, what do you think?"

"Your ideas sound good, Karl," Patrick said thoughtfully, and I think you're financially capable of swinging it, but you're going to need professional help from someone who can tie the whole operation together."

"I know. But I'm not sure who to contact first."

"I think I know just the man—Vernon Buick. He's a marine engineer and has more energy than you and I and fourteen kids put together."

"What makes you think he'd want to work with me?"

"The company he worked for went down the drain a couple of months ago. He's looking for something to do, and I have the feeling you two would be compatible."

"How soon can I meet him?" Karl asked, his excitement mounting.

"I'll contact him, and then you two can take over from there."

The day before Vernon's arrival in Vancouver, Karl was charged with enthusiasm as he spoke to his sister.

"Don't get your hopes up too high," Lisl warned. "He's probably old and has a potbelly and a wet cigar."

"If he knows shipbuilding, I don't care if he has two heads."

Lisl snickered. "How long do you think he'll stay with us? Why didn't you find out more about him before you invited him here?"

"Lisl, will you please relax? We have a big house, Mrs. Lange is here to help out, and you'll make a perfect hostess."

"How long is he staying?" Lisl repeated.

"Lisl, stop asking questions! All I know is that he's a brilliant engineer and knows all about shipbuilding."

"Vernon Buick. What kind of a name is that?"

"He's Scandinavian, Finnish to be exact. Patrick says his ancestors were all boatbuilders. Oh, one more thing—apparently he likes to eat. Patrick claims he has a bigger appetite than mine."

"That I'll have to see to believe."

"Just tell Mrs. Lange to prepare more than usual."

"It's times like this when I really miss Mother," Lisl sighed.

"So do I. Anything from Tatsuo yet?"

Lisl shook her head and looked away.

"I'm taking Janice out for dinner tonight. Please come with us."

"Thanks for asking, Karl, but I would rather not. I'll be all right."

Karl walked out the door feeling helpless and a little guilty.

Lisl ate alone in the sun-room. After Mrs. Lange had

removed her tray, she opened the cabinet and took out a crystal decanter of Scotch. Hesitantly, she filled a glass, raised it to her lips, and took a deep swallow. She held her breath for a moment so that the first taste wouldn't make her shudder. Her throat and stomach felt warm, and she began to relax. Lisl filled the glass again and sat down heavily in Dorothea's padded chair. No wonder her father drank so much Scotch, she thought. But this was not the first time a lonely evening had sent her to the liquor cabinet; the ritual was becoming comfortably familiar.

It had been three hours since Mrs. Lange had seen her, and she came into the sun-room to check if Lisl had fallen asleep. "Lisl . . . are you in there?" Mrs. Lange asked softly.

Lisl thought of hiding the partially filled glass but didn't care enough to try.

Mrs. Lange turned on all the lights. "What on earth! Oh dear child, what are you doing?"

Lisl grinned crookedly and waved up at Mrs. Lange. "Doing? I'm having a little drink and relaxing."

"I think you've had enough."

"And I think you should mind your own business." Lisl turned away from the hurt look on Mrs. Lange's face.

"Oh, Lisl, what will I do with you?"

"Just leave me alone, please," Lisl replied sullenly.

"I can't. If you don't stop your drinking, Lisl, I will be forced to tell Karl."

Anger replaced the sullen look on Lisl's face. She stood up, gripping the chair for support. "He can't tell me what to do any more than you can! Now get the hell out of here!"

"Lisl, you are very dear to me. I cannot let you do this to yourself," Mrs. Lange said gently.

"What does it matter? What does anything matter anymore?" Lisl sank back into the chair. "Mother is gone, Tatsuo is somewhere on the other side of the world, and Karl . . . he's too busy to give a damn." Tears flooded her eyes and she hid her face in her hands while Mrs. Lange gently stroked her hair.

Vernon Buick arrived precisely on schedule. His immense bulk filled the doorway, and a cloud of smoke from a smoldering cigar hovered over his head.

"Karl Richter?"

"Yes, I'm Karl Richter."

"Good! I'm Vernon Buick."

"Come in, Mr. Buick. This is my sister, Lisl."

Vernon grasped Lisl's hand gently in his. "Good evening, Miss Richter."

"Welcome to Drachenschlucht. Dinner will be served soon."

"Good, I'm starved. Haven't eaten since four o'clock."

Lisl looked surprised. "Four o'clock yesterday?"

"Hell no, ma'am. Four o'clock today."

"But it's only six now."

"I know. That's why I'm starved."

Lisl laughed, and all her apprehension about having a forbidding houseguest vanished. "Please make yourself at home while I tell Mrs. Lange to hurry."

Over dinner, Karl learned that Vernon had a degree in marine engineering and had worked as a designer and chief engineer for two large shipyards in the San Diego area.

"My father and grandfather were shipbuilders in Finland, and I guess it's inbred in me. I don't ever want to do anything else." He nodded with approval as he bit into a large slab of apple pie. "Mrs. Lange, I have to tell you that this is the finest dinner I have eaten in a long, long time. Good plain food without all those sloppy sauces—that's exactly the way I like it."

Mrs. Lange smiled with pleasure and retreated to the kitchen for more coffee.

Vernon patted his expansive stomach. "Well—enough about food! Let's take a look at these plans you have, Karl."

"Come with me. I have everything laid out for you."

Karl led the way into the sun-room, where the designs and maps had been carefully arranged. Vernon glanced around the room approvingly and then focused his attention on the papers that were spread out on the desk. For the first time since his arrival, Vernon was silent, intent on Karl's blueprints and sketches.

"Well?" Karl asked after several minutes.

Vernon ran his broad fingers through his hair. "There is a lot of potential here, Karl."

"I sense some hesitation in your voice. What's wrong?"

Vernon looked back at the plans for a few moments. "This is no small undertaking. It's going to take a lot of bucks."

"I have the money," Karl said simply.

"There're shipyards sitting idle all over the world and harbors are lined with empty ships."

"I know. I've thought about that, but this can't last forever, and when it's over I want to be ready."

"Christ, do you realize how much this is going to cost? It may be a long time before you get any of it back."

"I told you, I have the money." Karl stood up and walked over to the desk. "I've done a lot of looking around. Property is cheap, cheaper than it has ever been, and machinery is available at bargain prices. And you know how many people are desperate for jobs at any price."

"Yes, I know," Vernon said grimly.

Excitement mounted in Karl's voice. "I'm not saying we should go overboard and buy up everything in sight, but we can look things over carefully and buy with an eye for the future."

"All right, where do you want to go from here?" Vernon asked.

"You tell me. What do you think I brought you here for?"

Vernon's grin widened. "I'm hired?"

"That's right. Now start earning your keep."

Vernon reached for the bowl of peanuts on the side table and unconsciously began dropping them into his mouth as he talked.

"We'll need a boat tomorrow. I want to take a close look at the harbor, see what property is available."

"I have a boat. She's not the *Queen Mary*, but she's good and sturdy."

"Fine, we'll start looking here." Vernon pointed his finger at the map, indicating the north shore of Burrard Inlet.

"Why there and not False Creek?" Karl asked.

"Too congested and probably very expensive. You want room to expand. Right here, opposite Ballantyne Pier, might be a good possibility." He looked over at the empty bowl. "Nervous habit," he said apologetically. "I eat when I'm excited."

Karl laughed. "I can see that."

"Then again, I eat whether I'm excited or not. I'll have to do something about it one of these days." He turned back to the map. "How early can we get started?"

"As early as you want."

"Good. We should be out there by six. You're not a late sleeper, are you?"

"No, I'll be ready," Karl said, mentally rescheduling his training session.

During the following week, Karl and Vernon explored the Vancouver waterfront from the deck of the *Cathy B* and on foot. After the first two days, Karl realized that Vernon was seldom still; his energy never wavered and his enthusiasm matched Karl's own. He was shrewd and aggressive without being overbearing, and his sense of humor did not hinder his ability to make quick and accurate decisions. Karl knew he had found the right man. Evidence of the economic crisis was everywhere. The waterfront, once a hive of clamorous activity, was now quiet and empty; Karl began to have misgivings about his project.

"You can't get scared now, Karl. Not with all these opportunities under our noses. God, this property is worth five times what they're asking for it, and they're practically giving away the machinery. Like you said—the situation has to change. It sure as hell can't get any worse."

"It's just that it's so damn quiet. When I hear about people leaping off buildings or blowing their brains out because they can't face the future, I begin to wonder what the hell I'm doing."

"There's a difference between you and those guys that are blowing their brains out, Karl. You're not gambling with someone else's money, you're not guilty of stock manipulation, you're not investing in worthless paper, and you're not going in blind. Sure you're taking a chance, a bloody big chance, but if nothing else, you'll end up with a piece of land that should sell for a whole lot more than you're going to pay for it. And let's face it, there's only so much land—nobody is going to make more!"

"You're right. Vern, we're going to build the biggest, fastest freighters that ever crossed the ocean, and we're going to have the best damn refitting yards on the west coast! We can't lose."

"Now you're talking."

By the end of the week, Vernon decided the best parcel of land was on the north shore, directly across from the Ballantyne Pier.

"But it's not for sale," Karl observed.

"Everything is for sale for the right price, especially now. Let's search the title and go after the owner."

"What if he won't sell?" Karl asked.

"He'll sell!"

Vernon was correct. The property was owned by a man who was no longer rich but was still proud and somewhat arrogant. He had allowed himself to be influenced by his eldest son, who had convinced him that idle money was wasted money. Together, they had invested the bulk of his fortune in several steadily rising stocks, and after the first spectacular gains, they became overly confident. Now, reeling from the market crash, they were unable to accept the fact that they would never regain their lost fortunes or live in the style to which they had become accustomed. The waterfront property was one of his last assets, but to keep it he would have to move from his fine home. Karl offered five thousand dollars and he accepted readily. The following week, they purchased a floating drydock from an idle shipyard in False Creek.

"It's a little big—sixteen thousand tons is twice what we'll need for any freighter afloat," Vernon said.

"At the present time," Karl reminded him.

With the help of Patrick Fenton, Karl completed the paperwork for his transactions while Vernon planned to return home to settle his own affairs.

"I'll be back in two weeks, and then we can get to work," he announced.

"We haven't exactly been loafing these last few weeks. Don't you ever get tired?" Karl asked.

"Hell no! This is the first time I've been involved in the birth of a real company, and I think you and I are going to make this baby grow."

It was late when Karl drove into the driveway at Drachenschlucht. He was surprised to find Mrs. Lange waiting for him, her face anxious and her manner agitated. His sense of elation vanished instantly. "What's wrong?"

"It's Lisl. She's been drinking . . . steadily for several days."

"Oh no. I shouldn't have left her alone for so long. I thought she was past that."

"She wasn't really drunk—just sort of . . . well, not herself last night. She went out for a while and then—oh, Karl, I think someone has beaten her up. She's locked the door to her room.''

Karl brushed past Mrs. Lange and ran up the stairs. "Lisl, open the door or I'll break it down!" He heard her switch on the lamp, and a shaft of light appeared under the door.

"All right, Karl, wait a minute."

The lock clicked and the door swung open. Lisl went back to her bed and sat huddled with her knees drawn up under her chin, her face hidden in the ruffles of Dorothea's favorite robe.

Karl opened both windows as far as they would go.

"Let's get some fresh air in here!" He sat down beside her on the bed. "What's wrong, Lisl?" She cringed from the hand he placed on her shoulder. "Lisl, look at me. Tell me what's wrong. I'll fix it."

"You can't fix it. Nobody can." Her body began to shake as the tears came.

"Lisl, you've been drinking. Why?"

"It helps me to forget that Tatsuo's been gone for two months and he hasn't even written me. I don't think he wants me anymore, and I love him so much." Her last words came in a gasp.

"Lisl, Lisl. Tatsuo loves you as much as you love him, maybe more, but he can't do anything about it right now. You know that."

"No, I don't believe that any more."

"Did he ever tell you what would happen if he disobeyed the orders of the zaibatsu?"

Lisl shook her head, waiting for Karl to speak.

"Lisl, if he disobeys the zaibatsu, he would have to commit suicide. If he does not do it himself, they would do it for him."

Lisl looked up with tear-swollen eyes.

Karl caught his breath. "Someone did beat you up!" He held her by the shoulders. "What happened?" Lisl tried to look away, but he held her firmly.

"I had too much to drink and I fell."

"Stop it, Lisl! I don't doubt that you had too much to drink—but I don't think you just fell. Now, for God's sake, tell me what happened!"

Lisl's shoulders sagged and she gave a ragged sigh. "My

whole life is pointless. Who needs me? Tatsuo is gone and I don't know if I'll ever see him again. Mother is dead, and Father doesn't need anyone. And you—you've got your big business venture with Vernon and you have Janice. And don't peddle that same lecture about a big rosy future."

"That shit in a bottle isn't going to solve anything, and you do have a rosy future. And as far as the business goes, once the preliminaries are completed, I will need your help. The money we invested is yours, too."

"I'll try and remember that," Lisl said sarcastically.

"Look, Lisl, I'm sorry I left you by yourself so much. I never thought . . . I mean, I figured things had settled down for you."

"Oh, Karl, you don't have to baby-sit me."

"Where were you last night?"

"I went to a party."

"Is that where you got roughed up?"

Lisl nodded.

"Where was the party?"

"They were old school friends."

"It was Tully Salton, wasn't it?" Karl asked, his face tight with anger. "You've been to his place before."

"Yes, but it's over. I won't go back there again."

"What happened?"

"I was bored and they were having a party. Tully and his sister are always having parties—their parents are in New York. Tully and his friend Barry had too much to drink, just like everyone else." She looked at Karl and added ruefully, "Including me. When Tully ripped my blouse, I started to fight back and that was when Barry got in the act. I wasn't quite as drunk as they were, and I managed to get away with only a couple of bruises and a blouse and a skirt that I threw in the garbage." She walked unsteadily to the open window and took several deep breaths before turning back to face Karl. "There now, you have the whole unsavory little story. I want to forget it."

"He won't bother you anymore, Lisl. That much I can promise you," Karl said calmly.

Lisl looked at him, the scratches vivid on her face. "Karl, please don't do anything. I don't care about Tully and his friends."

"But I care about you, Lisl, and I won't risk Tully bothering you again. Get back into bed, and I'll have Mrs. Lange bring you something hot to drink." Before Lisl could protest, Karl was gone.

The Salton residence sat well back from the street on a wide expanse of lawns and gardens, but the stillness of the night carried the sounds of laughter and music from the house to the street. As Karl drove slowly up the driveway, he noticed the grounds were beginning to show signs of neglect. Like many others in the exclusive Shaughnessy district, the Saltons were surprised victims of the stock market crash, but their indulged children did not yet fully comprehend its consequences.

A shattered bottle crunched under Karl's feet as he walked to the front door. It opened before he could knock. An inebriated young lady with a flawless complexion stood just inside.

"Come in, handsome. You're exactly what this party needs. The rest of them are so drunk they've become utter bores."

Karl disengaged her arms from his neck and stepped into the room. "Is Tully here?" he asked.

"What do you want with Tully when you can have me?" the girl whined.

"I want to talk to him. Now."

"Well, you don't have to get huffy about it. I'll get him for you. Just remember, though—after you talk to him, you belong to me." She giggled and ran a long fingernail along his cheek.

In a few minutes she returned with Tully following close behind her. He looked at Karl with a mixture of contempt and curiosity. He was taller than Karl and wore his well-cut clothes with casual indifference. "Who are you and what do you want?"

"I'm Karl Richter. Lisl's brother."

"Oh yeah! Nice girl, Lisl. Well, come on in and join the party. Can I get you a drink?"

The young woman held Karl's arm and led him into the crowded room.

"Make yourself at home." Tully grinned broadly. "Lots of nice little ladies to pick from."

"I'd like to talk to you privately," Karl said.

For a moment Tully looked surprised. "Me and you? With

all these dames to choose from?'' Then he shrugged and turned down a hallway.

Karl followed him into a huge bedroom, where coats and jackets were piled on the bed.

"Well, what can I do for you?'' Tully asked.

"I don't like what you and Barry did to Lisl.''

Tully's grin vanished. "What the hell are you talking about? We were having a good time, grabbed a little bit of tit, then she started acting crazy and screaming at me. I told her to quiet down. I finally had to slap her.''

A young man that Karl assumed was Barry stepped in from the doorway and stood beside Tully. "She had it coming. No one can expect to come here, strut their ass around like she did, and not get touched.''

Karl clenched his fists. "Maybe so, but I'm warning you—never touch her again.''

"You're just like her,'' Barry sneered. "Think you're better than everyone else. Get the fuck out of here while you can still walk.''

The last thought Karl had before Barry's inconsequential blow hit him in the stomach was that he must exercise control. He knew that if he allowed his anger to take over, he might kill them. All he wanted to do was remove their insolent smiles and prevent them from ever taking advantage of Lisl's vulnerability again. But as soon as he saw Barry double up his fist, his body reacted instinctively. There was a look of utter amazement on Tully's face as he watched Karl lift Barry overhead, hold him suspended for a split second, then send him crashing across the room. Tully raised his clenched fists to guard his face. The air left his lungs in a loud whoosh as Karl's foot sank into his stomach; Tully hit the floor beside Barry. In the next room someone raised the volume of the music.

"Get up,'' Karl said roughly.

"You prick,'' Tully choked. "I'll get you for this, and your fucking sister, too.''

All of Karl's pent-up anger went behind the blow that smashed Tully's perfect nose. Bright red blood splattered in an arc around his face. Fear replaced Barry's dumbfounded look as he backed up against the wall.

"If either of you ever lays a hand on my sister again, I'll break your legs and arms.'' He advanced toward Barry, who cowered against the wall and whimpered.

"No, please, don't," he squealed.

Karl turned to Tully. "And you, you useless prick, get off your ass and do something worthwhile."

A blast of noise hit Karl as he walked through the boisterous group outside. The girl who had met him at the door was immediately by his side.

"Come on, big boy, dance with me." She welded her ample body against his.

"Thanks, but I think your friend Tully needs you more than I do. He's in there."

"Ah, Tully's a beast. I like you better." Her breath smelled of strawberries, the exact color of her freshly applied lipstick. "Hey, you've got blood on you! What did you do to Tully?"

"He's all right, but you'd better check on him."

The girl giggled as she started off in the direction of the bedroom. "It's about time somebody made Tully bleed a little. He deserves it." She staggered slightly on her stiletto heels. "God knows he's made a few of us girls bleed." She giggled again at her own joke before disappearing into the bedroom.

During the next few days Karl spent most of his time with Lisl, but her lethargy did not lift, nor would she leave Drachenschlucht despite his repeated efforts.

"Lisl, you can't just shut yourself away in this house. You're making yourself ill," Karl said. "You used to take long walks. At least try to do that. I'll go with you."

Lisl shook her head mutely. How could she explain to him why she did not go for walks anymore? Tatsuo would not be waiting for her by the old tree. There was no more laughter in her life, no excitement, no anticipation. She wanted to feel her hand in Tatsuo's when she walked, she wanted to hear his voice.

It was Vernon who finally made a breakthrough by convincing her that they desperately needed her help at the shipyards. By that time, the Burrard Shipyards had come into being, and mounds of paperwork had piled up on all three desks in their makeshift office. A secretary was yet to be hired. Lisl came to the office with them and surveyed the scene with a disapproving eye.

"You're right, you do need me!"

Two months were needed to prepare the yards for limited operations, during which time Vernon was able to secure three refitting contracts.

"It isn't much, but it's a start. We've got to make sure we do the best damn job possible," he told Karl and Lisl.

"That's for sure," Karl agreed. "I've hired on some shipwrights, steelworkers, and a handful of dayworkers. Some of them are Japanese from Steveston. I think they're all as anxious as we are to get started."

"I'll bet," Vernon replied. "I turned away about twenty men in the last few days. They look so desperate, the poor bastards."

The refitting contracts were completed quickly and to the complete satisfaction of the customers, and within the month, Burrard Shipyards received an order for two small custom-built barges. Karl and Vernon were ecstatic.

"God, I think I might be able to breathe again. Would you believe I haven't even had an appetite lately?" Vernon asked innocently.

"No!" Karl answered quickly. "Business will never be that bad."

Vernon shrugged his shoulders. "Well, maybe I did exaggerate a bit, but I think the order for these two barges just might get us rolling toward bigger things."

"You've worked damn hard, Vern, and I'm grateful," Karl said. "That last shipwright you hired is a genius."

"There are a lot of good men out of work these days, but I agree—we were lucky to find Larson. He's the best builder there is, even if he is a temperamental bastard."

At that moment Lisl walked into the room.

"You two are smiling at each other like a couple of tomcats after a busy night. Something I should know about, or do you think it will singe my delicate ears?"

Vern smiled indulgently. "Karl, if this baby sister of yours wasn't doing such a fine job in this office, I'd tell you to send her away to a private school. She's beginning to sound like one of the yard workers."

Lisl had shaken loose from the grips of her depression, and today she seemed to radiate from within.

Karl read her expression easily. "You've heard from Tatsuo?"

Lisl nodded and waved a cablegram. "He's been in Korea and Manchuria, just what we were afraid of. But he'll be home in a few weeks! Mr. Takezawa thinks it might even be sooner."

"This fellow must be very special," Vernon said.

"He is special," Lisl replied. "Now what is your good news?"

Unable to conceal his excitement, Karl showed her the order for the two barges.

"Well, just don't sit there, get to work!" she said.

The orders continued to come in slowly. Soon it became commonplace for Karl and Vernon to work through the night, hovering over their plans and blueprints. Vernon would carefully explain the technical details that were second nature to him, and Karl would listen with intense concentration, occasionally adding his own ideas. Karl's confidence grew with the successful completion of each contract.

In spite of their full days at the shipyards, Janice Chandler continued to occupy Karl's thoughts, and the idea of spending his life without her became intolerable. For the first time he began to seriously entertain thoughts of marriage, of having Janice by his side and and in his life forever. There was the possibility that her parents might refuse to give their permission, but he doubted it. The shipyard was beginning to enjoy modest success, and in comparison to the crashing blows the rest of the business world was suffering, that success was phenomenal. The only one he would have to convince was Janice. It was with this purpose in mind that he began to spend as much time as he could with her, and he found to his surprise that the more time they spent together, the more anxious he was to see her again.

"It's beautiful, isn't it?" Janice said as she and Karl sat on a park bench one afternoon and watched a sailboat float lazily toward shore just as the sun was setting.

"Almost as beautiful as you," Karl answered in a teasing voice. Janice edged closer to him, and he draped his arm around her shoulders, rubbing his nose in her faintly scented hair. He leaned down and kissed her softly on the lips and she responded hungrily.

"Janice darling, I love you," he whispered.

"Oh, Karl, I never thought I would hear you say that. I love you so." Her eyes were moist with tears.

"Janice, I know I'm not the easiest person in the world to live with, but I'll do my very best to make you happy."

"Are you asking me to marry you, Karl?" she said softly.

He nodded, not trusting his voice. The last rays of the sun glinted on his blond hair, and Janice looked at him with complete adoration.

"I will marry you, my darling. Just say when."

Karl released the breath he had unconsciously been holding. "First I have to go to Japan for my black belt. It's something I've been working toward for so many years, and I can't postpone it any longer. Can we be married as soon as I return?"

For an answer, Janice threw both arms around his neck and kissed him, as curious onlookers smiled with understanding.

[16]

Many years of physical and mental training are required before one attempts to earn the rank of *Sho-dan*, first degree black belt. In the final stages of preparation, Karl intensified his grueling regimen under Hiro's strict tutelage. His fighting skills were exemplified and sharpened by repeatedly performing the *kata*, a mock battle against four imaginary opponents. In the battle sequence, Karl demonstated his proficiency by executing the required blocks, kicks, thrusts, and foot movements. The sensei was pleased. An hour of sparring and breaking techniques followed before master and pupil were ready to soothe their tied muscles in the steaming o-furo. With grateful sighs, they lowered themselves into the near-scalding water.

Karl splashed water onto his face. "Do you think I am ready to go to Japan?" he asked.

"You are ready, tomodachi, and you will be successful," Hiro answered. "I will make the necessary arrangements."

"Will Tatsuo be home before I leave?"

"No, but he will be here when you return."

Karl grinned boyishly. "Should I tell Lisl?"

"Yes. You will not be raising false hopes."

They sat luxuriating in the comfort of the o-furo as the fire beneath them crackled musically. When the steam settled, Karl studied Hiro's face above the water. The lines around his eyes had deepened; the strain of the last few months had taken its toll. His body, though still taut and thickly muscled, showed the evidence of his concern. He had lost weight. The black penetrating eyes were closed now, but Karl had seen the sadness behind the disciplined veil. It seemed as though several decades had passed since he had first seen the sensei in his garden and had been awed by the silent warrior. Karl still felt that awe, but he was also moved by the depth of his love for Hiro, who was his friend, his teacher, and something akin to a parent. Karl wondered what he would have become had he not met this man. If nothing else, he would be eternally grateful to his father for that meeting.

"Have you seen your father lately?" Hiro asked.

Hiro's uncanny perception never ceased to amaze Karl. "No, I haven't. I've been so busy that I haven't given him much thought." He felt a twinge of guilt.

"His life is no longer following the pattern he drew out so carefully. He is having difficulty adjusting."

"Should I be concerned, sensei?" Karl asked.

"I cannot answer for you."

Karl sighed heavily as he emerged from the warmth of the o-furo. "All right, I'll go and see him as soon as I can." His face brightened again as he thought of Tatsuo's homecoming. "So much has happened since Tatsuo left. I hope it will be like old times."

"Yes," Hiro agreed. "Much has happened. I am afraid it will never be quite the same. However, we will have a festival anyway, even if the homecoming is only temporary."

The next few weeks passed quickly for Karl. Hiro gave him some last minute instructions. "In Yokohama you will be met by a representative from the zaibatsu and taken directly to the temple. There you will be given two days to enjoy the peace and solitude of your surroundings, time in which to prepare yourself. There will be no language barrier—English is not completely foreign to many of the occupants of the temple, including the master. He and I have often debated the merits of several English writers—his favorite is Wordsworth."

"I'm afraid I wouldn't be much help to him in that area, but if he were to discuss Chopin or Beethoven, I would be more in my element, thanks to my mother."

The trip across the Pacific proved to be totally unsettling for Karl. His body was geared now to an accelerated pace, and relaxation did not come easily. Thoughts whirled through his mind: his love for Janice and their plans for marriage; the shipyard; Lisl with happiness in her eyes because of Tatsuo's anticipated return; and his own impending challenge in Japan.

• • •

"Richter-sama, Richter-sama."

A young man gestured excitedly above the heads of the crowd. Karl wormed his way toward the man, and they exchanged polite bows. It was not difficult to tell who had sent the car that waited at the edge of the pier; it bore a large Takezawa emblem on the door. As they drove, the driver whistled and occasionally glanced at Karl through his rearview mirror, but since he did not speak more than a smattering of English, communication between them was limited during the ride to Tokyo. Karl was grateful for the respite, for it gave him an opportunity to enjoy the countryside in peace.

The narrow approach to the temple was almost hidden by low-hanging shrubs, which brushed the sides of the car when they drove in. As Karl stepped out of the car, he was struck by the stillness surrounding the temple; here, the outside world ceased to exist. He drew in a deep breath and held it for a moment as if by doing so, he would absorb the serenity which the temple exuded.

A man dressed in a black keiko-gi tied with a silver cord welcomed Karl. His voice was accented but clear. "Richter-sama, we have been expecting you. Please come with me."

Karl followed the black-robed figure, who walked on soundless feet over the gravel walkway. The man's feline grace was familiar to Karl as they scaled the stairs leading up to the temple. They passed a statue of an omnipotent but jovial Buddha who guarded the entrance of the dojo, where a group of adept students were practicing in unison. Silently, the guide motioned Karl into a room, empty except for a mat and a low table. Alone, he stared out the open window at the minature garden and waited.

The master of the temple arrived shortly and greeted Karl with utmost formality. "Your friend and mentor, Takezawa-sama, is a very dear friend of mine. It is therefore with the greatest pleasure that I welcome you here, Richter-sama."

"Thank you, master. I am pleased and honored to be here."

"May I inquire as to his health?"

"He is as able-bodied as ever, master, but he has a great deal on his mind these days. I think he is very concerned about Japan's future and that of his grandson, Tatsuo," Karl replied.

"The whole world seems to be undergoing great upheavals. Even we, who are sheltered here, cannot help but feel the unrest and sense the imminent danger. I have great sympathy for my friend. He does not suffer alone, even though he is so many miles away."

"I will tell him that when I return."

"Yes, perhaps it will comfort him."

The door opened. An apprentice bearing the implements for the tea ceremony padded in on slippered feet. Karl prepared himself mentally for the well-practiced ceremony. The tranquility of the temple calmed him, and while he readied the utensils they talked. By the time he began to serve the green tea, the ceremony seemed as natural and simple as breathing.

"You will have two days in which to prepare yourself for the task ahead. Use the time wisely. You are free to enjoy the garden—we often meditate there. Someone will fetch you at mealtimes, but otherwise you will be left alone. You will be excused from our usual duties to allow you time for contemplation. On the third day we will determine if you will be Shodan."

Inside the temple walls, time was meaningless to Karl. He was able to control his mind and to separate himself completely from the outside world. The master returned at regular intervals to talk with him; his subjects varied, thought-provoking and at times amusing. He encouraged Karl to speak openly, to express his opinions, which he considered gravely with either a nod of approval or a subtle comment to the contrary.

On the third day, Karl was awake as soon as the first glimmer of light struck his curtainless window. There was a soft knock on his door.

"Please come with me," a young man instructed. He led the way to the dojo.

The floor of the practice hall was covered with a spotless white canvas around which eight men sat. Each was dressed in the traditional keiko-gi; all wore the coveted black belt. Karl proceeded to the center of the hall, where he kneeled and bowed to the master. He searched the faces of the eight men who sat around him, and like a novice actor on stage for the first time, he felt panic. Eight pairs of somber penetrating eyes flicked dispassionately over him, and his muscles grew rigid. For an instant he gave serious consideration to running away.

He pictured himself bolting down the pebbled walk, past over-grown shrubbery, and into the street with his immaculate keiko-gi flapping unceremoniously in the wind. The thought brought a smile to his face and released the tension. He noted that no one acknowledged his smile; their stonelike faces did not soften.

The master's voice thundered through the silent dojo. "What is *shin-ki-yoku?*"

Karl swallowed before answering. "Shin-ki-yoku expresses the purpose and ideals of Shizen Ryu Kempo. It means mind, spirit, and strength." The faces remained impassive through-out the balance of the questioning. Karl was then asked to demonstrate his skill.

He began the kata slowly until he felt his muscles swell and begin to work effortlessly. Gaining momentum, he forgot the faces around him and concentrated only on the execution of the intricate moves until perspiration beaded on his forehead. He stopped at the master's sharp command.

One of the men stood up and walked toward him. His black belt swung ominously as he bowed and assumed the stance for combat. They sparred cautiously for the first few minutes, each testing the other's skill: thrust, attack, block, move. Karl would have prepared for the blow to his stomach had he seen it coming, but it happened too fast. The force of it stunned him, but it also sharpened his senses. In the next few moves he discovered that although his opponent was extremely fast, he was not as clever as the sensei. Silently, he thanked Hiro as he anticipated the next move. Karl spotted the opening and delivered a blinding side kick followed by a swing kick. The blows dazed his opponent momentarily. Karl faked another kick and followed it with a bearpaw thrust, again bringing his adversary to his knees.

Karl heard the master's next command, and two combat-ants stepped forward to replace the first opponent. Despera-tion increased Karl's strength; he felt his body grow taut as he braced himself for their attack, and from somewhere in the depths of his mind came the enigmatic sense of happomoku: he must see with more than his eyes.

The two men were quick and powerful, and Karl felt their stinging blows. He retaliated with equal force, hearing their grunts with satisfaction. He began to tire, but his mind refused to acknowledge the weariness and he forced himself to con-

tinue moving with the fluid grace that Hiro had instilled in
him. In both pairs of inscrutable dark eyes he saw a glint of
respect, which spurred him on to deliver the deciding blows.
He leaped into the air and aimed a powerful kick at the neck
of one of his opponents, one that would have snapped it had
he purposely connected. With a sidestep, Karl avoided a blow
from his second adversary, and it was here that the master intervened again. The men bowed to Karl and returned to their
places.

"You have fought well and you have exhibited exceptional
self-discipline. The men with whom you have just tested your
abilities are all fourth dan. They were testing not only your
physical skills, but also your spirit and self-discipline."

Karl stared at him. He did not need a formal speech to
know that his opponents, either together or singly, could have
defeated him easily had they been instructed to do so.

The final test was familiar to Karl, that of breaking stacks
of cinder tiles with various parts of his body. Karl approached
the table with confidence, even though he knew it would not
be a painless effort. To his utter surprise he failed on the first
attempt, and some of his confidence ebbed. Determined not to
fail again, he summoned all his strength and, with a loud yell,
brought his hand down with all the force he could muster. The
tiles shattered easily. Karl was asked to use his other hand,
elbows, feet, and, finally, his head. He knew the ensuing
headache would be with him for several hours, but in his elation he hardly noticed it. The corners of the master's mouth
lifted into a narrow smile to which Karl replied with a wide
grin.

"Congratulations, Richter-sama. You have performed well.
Your sensei will be proud of you."

"Thank you, master."

An ancient *bushido* ceremony followed and Karl, over-
whelmed, felt a lump rise in his throat as the black belt was
tied around his waist. The years of arduous training, pain, and
sacrifice were worthwhile—he now belonged to a most honorable society of men and warriors, descendants of the samurai.
Like Hiro and Tatsuo, he, too, wore the black belt.

Karl's return to Vancouver was celebrated with a magnificent
Japanese dinner at the Takezawas' home. Janice was there,
her face proud as Karl was escorted to the seat of honor by

Tatsuo. A feeling of warmth and love drew the small group together, like a family long separated, reunited for a happy occasion.

Within a week of his return, Karl was once again immersed in the mainstream of activity at the shipyard. In his absence, Vernon Buick had managed to secure another refitting contract—no small deed considering the number of ships lying idle in the harbor. It seemed to Karl that while he was away the lines of people waiting despondently for food at the soup kitchens had lengthened drastically. Hobo jungles had sprung up everywhere, especially along False Creek, where the decrepit shanties and tin-roofed shacks dotted the shoreline. Vancouver had become a catch basin for thousands of men who had left the desolate prairies in search of work, riding the rails into a city that was equally destitute. Feeling pity for the beggars who occasionally came to Drachenschlucht, Karl instructed Mrs. Lange to give them food. The word spread quickly, and before long there was a constant stream to their kitchen.

"You'll soon be feeding the entire country if you don't put a stop to this," Mrs. Lange said.

Karl tried to discourage them, but they continued to come.

"I can't understand it," Karl said to a thin man who sat sipping the cup of hot soup Mrs. Lange had given him. "Why are they all coming here? Surely there are other homes they can go to as well."

The man raised his head and hesitated for a moment. Finally, he said, "There are marks on your fence that say you're an easy touch."

"I'll give you five dollars if you'll show me where they are," Karl offered.

"You've got yourself a deal, mister."

When the tiny code marks were pointed out to Karl, he said with amazement, "I never even noticed them."

"You weren't supposed to. They're just for hobos like me. For another five dollars I'll change them so that folks won't come this way."

The removal of the marks did not discourage everyone. People came in a slow but steady stream, and Mrs. Lange continued to give them her nourishing soup and homemade bread in the months that followed.

In September, Lisl decided to return to school. She had lost weight again and there were circles under her eyes, yet she seemed calm and self-assured. "I like working here at the shipyard, Karl. I've learned so much. But I have to do something else with my life," Lisl explained.

"What are your plans with Tatsuo?"

"We have no plans, at least none that I can count on," she replied quietly. "If you like, I'll help you find someone to replace me."

"We'll find someone, Lisl. Just relax and get ready for school," Karl said gently.

Finding a replacement was not as easy as Karl had anticipated, not because there was a shortage of applicants but because there was an overabundance. It was difficult for Karl to make what he hoped would be the best choice.

"I always use the process of elimination," Vernon said, sensing Karl's quandary. "Just disregard the ones with obvious inadequacies and before long you come up with one that measures up to your expectations."

In the end, it was Rose Thornton, a thirty-two-year-old widow with three small children, who filled the position. With efficiency gained from years of experience, Rose assumed her duties, and before long Karl and Venon came to rely on her.

"That lady," Vernon observed, "is giving this place some class."

"She's attractive, all right." Karl shuffled the papers on his desk into a neat stack. He did not mention that Rose also reminded him of Patricia Harley and a night he would always remember in spite of his love for Janice. Karl was not blind to Rose's attractiveness, but he did not consider her to be particularly beautiful. He did appreciate her competence and was grateful when she readily accepted more and more responsibility. Yet there were moments when he would catch himself staring at her, wondering what it was about her that reminded him of Patricia. When Janice stopped by to pick him up one afternoon, he introduced her to Mrs. Thornton.

"I'm pleased to meet you, Mrs. Thornton." Karl was surprised by the note of coolness in Janice's voice.

"Please call me Rose. I'm not a matron yet," she replied, laughing.

Janice did not smile. "Karl, let's get going, if you don't mind."

"Would you please sign these letters for me, Karl, before

you go? They should go out today," Rose said. Her perfume wafted toward Janice as she bent over the desk.

Karl quickly signed the letters and then, hooking his hand under Janice's elbow, escorted her out of the office. Several times, Janice's feet barely touched the ground. In the car, he turned to her. "Now, do you want to tell me what's bothering you?"

Janice's eyes snapped with anger and she stared straight ahead.

"Look, I'm in no mood for guessing games. I want to know why the hell you're so mad," Karl demanded.

"Then I'll tell you," Janice yelled. "That sweet little bundle of efficiency you have in your office is no wilted rose. She's in full bloom, and she's hot after your pants."

"Now how would you know that, for God's sake? You just met her!"

"Because a woman knows. I can see the way she looks at you, and I can sense it. And besides, that perfume she wears would knock over a cement wall."

"Janice, you are being absolutely childish. Rose Thornton is my secretary and nothing more. I love you with all my heart and I always will. Now please stop this stupid routine, it doesn't suit you."

"Oh, Karl, I'm sorry. It's just that I love you so much and I guess I didn't expect your secretary to be so pretty. I'm so possessive . . . I'd fight the world for you."

Karl smiled and kissed her. "And I hope that will never change."

They drove to Drachenschlucht, Janice comfortable in the crook of Karl's arm.

"Karl, can I ask you something?"

"Ask away."

"Are you planning to invite your father to the wedding?"

"No." He had paid his father a brief visit before his departure for Japan, and had quickly learned that nothing had changed between them.

"Karl, he's your father! Don't shut out of your life completely."

"Janice, the less I see of him, the happier I am. Things have happened in the past that I would rather forget. But if it would make you feel better, then invite him."

The wedding ceremony took place in the small chapel of St. Anne's Cathedral with only the immediate family, the Takezawas, Vernon Buick, and Mrs. Lange present; Tatsuo and Lisl attended the bride and groom.

Karl held his breath as he watched Janice walk toward him on her father's arm in a cloud of white tulle and lace; he had never seen her look so beautiful.

During the ceremony, tears streamed unchecked down Lisl's cheeks, and afterward she clung to Karl for a moment. "If you had asked me to choose a wife for you, Karl, I would have chosen Janice. I wish you both a lifetime of happiness."

"Thank you, sis," Karl replied in a husky voice.

"They truly do look happy," Tatsuo said with a wistful note in his voice.

Lisl slipped her arm through his and leaned her head against his shoulder. "Yes, they do. Do you think there will ever be a time for us?"

"I want that so badly, Lisl," Tatsuo replied raggedly. He held her close, his voice muffled in her hair as he said, "We will know soon, and after that I don't ever want to see such pain in your face again."

The reception held in the Chandler home was not the formal affair Janice's mother would have preferred, but she conceded to her daughter's wishes. Helen Chandler had never entertained Japanese guests in her home, nor did she intend to; however, Janice was her only child, and when she threatened to hold the reception at Drachenschlucht, her mother gave in. Helen Chandler was not quite sure whether she was in awe of the Takezawas or whether she resented them. They were unlike anyone she had ever encountered—definitely not the typical Orientals one hired as servants. There was something commanding in their manner, not overbearing; they seemed to possess the same casual confidence that people with very old money exude, and surprisingly enough, they did not seem out of place in her home.

Conrad arrived just as the guests were preparing to sit down to dinner. After a few polite nods to the other guests, he came directly to Karl and Janice. "Congratulations, Karl. You have chosen a beautiful bride. May you both get everything you want out of life."

"Thank you, Father," Karl replied stiffly. He shook his father's hand briefly.

"Thank you for inviting me. It's not every day that a man's only son gets married."

"I'm glad you could come," Janice said warmly. No one

commented on his having skipped the ceremony.

Later as they sat down to dinner, Janice searched Karl's face anxiously. "I shouldn't have asked him to come. You look upset."

"No, I'm fine. It's just that when I see him I want to feel good things for him because he's my father, but I can't, and I end up feeling only pity. I picture myself being an unwanted guest at my own son's wedding, and the thought makes me sick."

"Karl, you and I are going to be the best parents a child ever had, just you wait and see."

"And I can't wait to get started on the 'child,'" Karl said, faking a leer.

After a brief honeymoon, Janice settled in at Drachen-schlucht as though she had always belonged there. Lisl grate-fully relinquished some of her duties, and Mrs. Lange quietly accepted Janice as the new mistress of the house. A routine developed naturally. Janice claimed exclusive rights to Karl every evening after nine o'clock, and apart from an occasional late night at the shipyard, she held fast to her claim.

"Lisl had a visitor today," she informed Karl as they sat one night in front of a crackling fire.

Karl nodded absently. His eyes were half-closed with drowsiness; his mornings still began at five o'clock. "Who?"

"The same fellow who was here before—James Ellesworth. He wouldn't win an award in Hollywood with that nose of his, but he seems nice, and he certainly has it bad for Lisl."

"What does Lisl think of him?" Karl asked, his interest picking up.

"Well, she's polite to him, and I think she looks on him as a good friend, but she loves Tatsuo and makes no bones about it to him or anyone else."

"She's loved Tatsuo since she was a little girl. It's no wonder she won't consider James Ellesworth or anyone else."

"Well, I wish she would. Tatsuo is a fine person, but I don't think he will ever marry Lisl."

"Why?" Karl looked at her with surprise.

"Because he will never be free of his commitments, and he loves Lisl too much to expose her to the heartache they may bring."

On September 18, 1931, Japan attacked Manchuria. The reverberations of that attack were felt around the world. The military power of Japan was not to be taken lightly. With the news of the attack still ringing in his ears, Karl went to the Takezawa home.

"Why, damnit, why?" he asked Hiro.

"The military has gained control of the country! The emperor is powerless to resist. I knew it was only a matter of time after Prime Minister Hamaguchi was assasinated for signing the London Naval Treaty, and when the world markets collapsed."

"What does this mean for you?" Karl asked Tatsuo with a calmness he did not feel.

"I must return to Japan immediately. I have no choice."

"What about Lisl?"

There was naked emotion on Tatsuo's face. "Help me tell her. And look after her until . . . until I get back."

After Karl had left, even more grim-faced than when he had arrived, Hiro wandered through the empty dojo. The silence that usually welcomed him seemed hollow now, reminding him that he would never again hear the sound of two boys' laughter in the dojo.

17

"Good morning!" Karl's voice boomed unexpectedly in the quietness of the office.

Startled, Rose turned quickly. "Oh, I didn't hear you come in. You're early today!"

"I thought I would get a head start," Karl explained, returning her smile. "I see you have everything ready for me." He pointed to the neat stack of files on his desk.

"You also have two appointments today—one at eleven with Mr. Reid of the Gerrard Shipping Company, and a luncheon meeting with the bank manager."

"Would you remind Vern about the luncheon meeting? I want him there too."

"I already have, and I've made reservations at the Captain's Table for one o'clock."

"Rose, what would I ever do without you?"

The color in her face heightened visibly, but her voice remained briskly efficient. "One more thing, Karl. Your father called this morning."

"I suppose he wants to know why his ship isn't ready!" Karl snapped.

"That's right."

"Damn! Did he mention anything about when he plans to pay for the other refits we've done for him this year?"

"Not a word."

Anger crossed Karl's face. "I should never have agreed to

do business with him in the first place! Rose, get him on the line for me.''

"What if he refuses to talk to you again? He'll know why you're calling."

Karl's words were slow and deliberate. "Tell that alligator who intercepts his calls that I intend to take his beat-up freighter out into the bay and sink it."

Normally Rose would have laughed, but the tone in Karl's voice warned her that his last statement was not just an empty threat. She spoke quickly into the telephone and in a few moments handed the receiver to Karl. "He's on the line."

As usual, tension knotted Karl's stomach at the thought of a confrontation with his father. "Hello, Father," he said evenly.

"What the hell is this crap about taking my freighter out into the bay and sinking it?"

"I thought that might get your attention," Karl replied.

"Don't play games with me. Do you realize how much it's costing me to have that freighter tied up in your yard?"

"I have a good idea."

"Well then, why don't you do something about it? You've had it sitting in dry dock for a month."

"Father, I have been in this business for four years now, and I am far from being in a position where I can refit ships for nothing. And you, goddamnit, still have not paid for the last two jobs we've done for you." Karl could feel his control slipping. He caught Rose's anxious look.

"I'll pay. Just get that bloody shaft replaced on my freighter. I've got shipments waiting to go out."

"It will be ready in two weeks, but it's not leaving this yard until you pay for the repairs on it as well as the other two jobs!"

"Good Christ!" Conrad exploded. "Do you know what this will do to me? It will empty my—"

"Father," Karl interrupted, "you are not as poverty-stricken as you pretend to be, nor am I managing a benevolent society. Just pay your bills and you'll get your ship. It's as simple as that."

"I'll mail you a check this afternoon," Conrad said stiffly. "Just get that freighter fixed by the end of the week." He hung up with a sharp click.

Karl replaced the receiver quietly and sat staring at the telephone until Rose placed a steaming cup of coffee in front of him.

"Don't be upset, Karl. You have a company to protect as well as the livelihood of over a hundred men."

"And one woman," Karl added absently as he sipped his coffee. It was scalding hot and laced with exactly the right amount of sugar and cream. "I don't know how he does it, but he always manages to make me feel guilty. With him, I lose my temper just like that." He snapped his fingers. "And that makes me feel doubly guilty. Hell, I've spent years training myself to be disciplined, and he can make me feel like I've wasted my time, which is precisely what he thinks I've done anyway."

"You have more self-control than anyone I know," Rose protested. "Sometimes, I think . . ." She caught herself before she could say more, but she was momentarily flustered. If Karl noticed her loss of composure, he did not let on.

"Rose, I can always count on you to be my staunchest ally. I only hope I will always be deserving of that loyalty."

This time Rose could not stop the words that escaped from her mouth. "You'll always have it anyway."

Karl looked up from the letter he was reading and met her eyes. Both looked away quickly as an abrupt knock sounded on the door.

"Look at this, Karl! Just look at this!" Vernon dropped a roll of blueprints on the desk. "I think we have the problem licked on that ship of Gerrard's. That last guy you hired from Steveston is a bloody genius when it comes to repairing boilers."

Karl studied the diagrams. "I think this will work. Reid should be pleased. I have a meeting with him today."

"This job will be our ace in the hole with Gerrard Shipping," Vern boasted, thumping his fist on the desk. "I really think they figured we'd be dumping the damn thing back in their laps."

"You're right. Reid isn't an easy man to deal with, but if we can complete this job, we'll have him as a permanent customer."

"And that," Vern added, "is what we're in business for! Now, where is that sweet secretary of yours?"

"She's right behind you," Karl replied.

"Rose, my love, how about dinner tonight?" Before she could answer, he added, "I'm not taking no for an answer. I know your mother is staying with you and can look after that trio of yours. I want to show you a place I found—candlelight, soft music, and the fattest, juiciest steaks you've ever seen! I'll pick you up at seven." He strode out of the office, leaving Rose to stare blankly after him.

"Well, I guess that's that," she said without emotion. "Tonight I eat steak by candlelight."

Karl felt a stab of envy as he watched Rose return to her desk. It had been a long time since he and Janice had eaten by candlelight—not since the twins were born. For a moment he felt disoriented; the world was rushing by. Where had the time gone? The first eighteen years of his life had seemed so leisurely, so full of excitement, but now the days, the months, and even the years seemed a blur. The realization disturbed him, and he realized that his time with Janice and the boys was also a blur, devoid of detailed memories, precious memories that make life worthwhile. But what could he do? Vernon, the men, the shipyard—they all needed his constant attention. Just a few more months, then perhaps he could leave them on their own, but not yet.

He thought of the hurt on Janice's face each time he was called away. The hurt was eventually replaced by emotional outbursts and tears of anger, and finally by silence. For Karl, the silence was deafening and far more difficult to deal with than tears. He had tried explaining to her that it was a crucial time for the business, that families depended on him for their livelihood and even a small error in judgement could result in financial disaster. Janice had tried to understand and be patient, but the resentment remained until it became a barrier between them. He returned to the work on his desk, wondering what it would be like to have a quiet candlelight dinner with Rose. She knew how important the shipyard was; she understood.

That evening when Karl drove home, he was aware that he was late again. He cursed under his breath at the car ahead of him; its snaillike pace forced him to slow down. When he finally opened the front door of the house, he could hear Janice shouting above the wailing of Andrew, the more stubborn of the two boys. He walked into the dining room just as Janice finished scooping up from the floor what remained of Andrew's supper.

"Hey, what is all this hollering and noise about?" Karl asked with a smile. He picked up Andrew, and the boy's sobs stopped immediately. "What's the matter, son? Are you having a bad day?"

"We're all having a bad day," Janice snapped.

Karl put Andrew back in his chair and tousled John's hair. He was rewarded with one of his son's rare smiles. Unlike his garrulous, active brother, John was quiet and undemanding. The boys were very similar in appearance except for their eyes; Andrew's were a striking blue beneath a mass of blond curls, while John's were gray. It was always Andrew who created the disturbance while John looked on with an expression of disconcerted seriousness. Karl loved them both with an intensity he had never thought possible.

"Well, let's have some supper. Maybe we'll all feel better."

"Supper was served an hour ago. Yours is probably cold by now."

As if on cue, Mrs. Lange came into the dining room. "I've kept your supper warm, Karl. I'll dish it up for you."

Janice glared at her receding back.

"Do I detect an atmosphere of dissension in this room?" Lisl asked lightly from the doorway. "Andrew, are you to blame again?" She laughed and kissed his chubby cheek before sitting down. The tension between Karl and Janice hung uncomfortably in the air despite Lisl's attempt to make light of it.

"How close are you and Vernon to completing that supership of yours?" She was relieved to see the anger disappear from Karl's face.

"We dropped the boilers in last week. She should be ready to launch right on schedule." Pride and excitement glowed in his face. "She'll be the first turboelectric ship made in Vancouver. Hell, we might even become famous!"

"I think it's a marvelous achievement. I know the problems you've had and yet you've managed to keep on schedule."

"It's meant a lot of hard work, but she'll be worth it," Karl added.

Janice grew angrier as she listened to Karl and Lisl discussing the freighter again. She knew that Lisl was only trying to ease the tension, but it seemed there was nothing more to their life than business and money. How often had she heard Karl denounce his father for neglecting his own family? Now he seemed to be doing exactly the same thing. She loved Karl so much, and yet he seemed totally insensitive to her feelings. Suddenly the dam burst. "Is that all we can talk about in this family? Ships, ships, and more ships! I'm sick and tired of listening to it! Isn't it bad enough that you work on them sixteen hours a day? Do you have to bring your work home with you, too?"

Karl looked at Janice with surprise, then held up his hands as if to stop the sudden tirade. "I'm sorry. You're right. Let's talk about something else." His voice was tight.

Janice looked relieved when Karl changed the subject, but all her vitality seemed to disappear. She played listlessly with the twins and added little to the conversation. Before long, she collected the reluctant boys and directed them up the stairs to their bedroom.

"I'll help," Lisl offered.

Karl watched Lisl walk up the stars behind Janice and the twins. As a woman, Lisl had acquired a graceful elegance that was enhanced by her own natural warmth. After leaving the shipyard, she had completed her final year of school and gone to work as a model for an exclusive clothing store. A month ago, she had been promoted to assistant buyer, a position in which she was already proving her worth. On occasion, Karl would notice a distant look in her eyes, though, and he would remember that it had been almost a year since she had heard from Tatsuo. He wondered if Lisl had finally accepted the futility of waiting for him or whether some hope still glimmered in her heart. Lately she did nothing to discourage James Ellesworth, who was now James Ellesworth attorney-at-law, but she did nothing to encourage him either. "He's a fine person and dedicated to his profession," was the most personal remark she would make about him.

After a brief "Good night," to Mrs. Lange, Karl walked slowly up the stairs, conscious of his weariness. In the boys' bedroom, he sank heavily into the rocking chair that had been his mother's. In the semidarkness, he listened quietly to the soft breathing of his two sons. At two years of age, the twins were already forming such distinct personalities . . . he longed to hold on to their infancy and their innocent dependence on him, but he knew that time would soon disappear. With a sigh, he rose and walked across the hall to the bedroom he and Janice shared.

"Your father sent birthday gifts for the boys today," she said, watching Karl in the mirror as she methodically brushed her hair.

"Already? Their birthday isn't until next week."

Janice shrugged. "Well, they arrived today by special courier. I think he's lonely, and he's ensuring an invitation to the party."

"I don't want him here," Karl said more vehemently than he had intended.

"You can't exclude him from our lives completely."

"Yes I can! I don't want him influencing Andrew and John in any way."

"The way he influenced your life?"

Karl stripped off his shirt and threw it on the bed. "What the hell do you mean by that remark?"

"When was the last time you stopped to consider how much time you're spending with the boys and with me? You're so involved in that damn business of yours that we haven't had you to ourselves for months, and when we do see you, your mind is back at the shipyard anyway. Why don't you move your bed down there?"

"That's not true! I want it to succeed for you and the boys, too. Besides that, there are over a hundred men who depend on me for their survival."

"The boys and I don't need that kind of success, Karl—we don't need all that money. And the men who work for you would eventually find jobs somewhere else. Admit it, Karl, you want that success for yourself, just as your father did."

"Don't ever say that again," Karl said coldly. "I'm not like my father now, nor will I ever be."

They finished undressing in silence. Karl slept fitfully, unable to shake his sense of foreboding. He woke before dawn, exhausted. Grateful for the physical exertion, which seemed to clear his mind, he ran his regular route with more effort than he had put forth in a long time. At the finish line, the air burst from his lungs in labored gasps. He was not surprised to find he had beaten his average time by a full minute.

Janice was still asleep when he returned. He looked down at her, and an unexplainable sadness came over him. He knew her accusations were not entirely without substance; the shipyard had become a big part of his life. He loved the ocean, and as for the ships—they had been in his dreams for as long as he could remember. But they were his dreams, and his alone! He would never believe that they were secondhand dreams, inherited from his father.

As usual, the shipyard with its familiar sounds was a welcome sight for Karl. Vern, in his oversized coveralls, was supervising the installation of the telegraph system on the new freighter. He looked up and waved when he saw Karl approaching.

"Vern, could I see you in my office later this morning?" Karl said.

"Sure thing."

Immaculate in a crisp navy and white jumper, Rose was already at her desk when Karl walked in. She brought him coffee as soon as he sat down; her smiled faded when she saw his face.

"You look tired this morning." Her eyes mirrored her concern.

"I guess I am tired. I didn't sleep well last night." He turned his head slowly from side to side and rubbed his neck in an effort to loosen the tight muscles.

Rose stepped quickly behind his chair. "Here, let me do that. I used to be pretty good at it." Deftly, her fingers sought out the knotted muscles.

"That feels good," Karl murmured with relief. "Where did you learn to do this?"

"It's all part of the package deal," she answered lightly.

"You're just what the doctor ordered."

"Am I, Karl?" There was a catch in her voice, and her hands rested on his shoulders. Karl turned and stood up; she reached for him and moved her lips against his. As though his body was detached from his mind, he saw himself draw her into the circle of his arms. He felt her clinging to him, submitting to his urgent caresses as her fingers dug into his back. Through the barrier of their clothes, he could feel her warm body, pliant against his. In the distance, someone was approaching with quick, heavy footsteps. Karl's mind suddenly jerked back to reality and he released Rose abruptly.

"Tell him to go away, Karl," she whispered in a husky voice.

Reading the refusal in his eyes, Rose hurried out of the office brushing past Vernon. Karl tried to still the wild pounding of his heart.

"Come in," he said in a strangersounding voice.

Vern raised one eyebrow quizzically but made no comment as he walked in.

"How do those gauges fit?" Karl asked, shuffling the papers on his desk.

"Perfect. We should be ready for the next phase in another week. I'm not bragging when I say this, but our ship is going to be a monument to our engineering genius and a credit to this shipyard."

Karl smiled. "And I'm not fool enough to think I could have done it without you."

"Money and brains are a great combination—your money and my brains," Vern said with a deep-throated chuckle.

"That's one of the things I like about you, Vern—you're subtle as hell." The banter gave Karl the extra time he needed to collect himself. "Vern," he began, "what do you foresee for this company?"

"With proper management, hard work, and a smattering of luck, you'll have a winner," Vern answered without hesitation.

"I want you to have twenty-five percent of the company."

"I appreciate the gesture very much, but what do you propose I use for money?"

"I'm not asking you to buy it. I'm giving it to you."

"You're giving it to me?" Vern's mouth dropped open.

"That's right."

"But why? . . ."

"There are several reasons," Karl continued. "The first is that I consider you to be the most valuable asset this company has, and I know it won't be long before someone tries to entice you away from me. A share in the company will give me a safeguard against that eventuality."

"I have no intention of leaving. I have everything I want here."

"Sure, right now you do, but I'm looking into the future.

This country isn't going to stay in a slump forever. Second, if you have part ownership in the company, you'll work that much harder—impossible though that seems, since your energy overwhelms me now. And most important, I need someone to share the administrative duties so I can spend more time with my family. I've been neglecting them. The twins are two years old now, and sometimes I feel like a visitor in their lives. My offer is not as generous as it sounds, though—there will be some strings attached. You will not be able to sell your shares to anyone other than me or, in the event of my death, to the members of my immediate family. The shares will not be transferable, and when you die, they will revert back to me for their assessed value, payable to your beneficiaries. You will, of course, be entitled to twenty-five percent of the profits when and if this company makes a profit. I trust your judgment, Vern, and your integrity. If I didn't, I wouldn't be making this offer."

"I understand. I don't trust too many people either."

"Then you are willing to accept with all the strings attached?"

"Of course I accept. I have nothing to lose, and I stand to gain a great deal. Thank you very much," he said solemnly.

"Then I'll have the lawyers draw up the necessary papers.

There was a soft knock at the door, and Rose walked in. "There's a Mr. Bob Brown to see you. He's a reporter from the *Vancouver Sun*."

"Thank you, Rose. I was expecting him." He looked at Vern with a half smile. "Mr. Buick, your executive duties are about to begin. Let's see what the two of us can do to impress this guy. We need all the free publicity we can get."

The *Sun*'s chief reporter, not quite five feet tall, with an ageless gamin face and ears that protruded like fans, had a mind as sharp as a saber. When Karl opened the door for him, he sauntered in without bothering to remove the hat that was balanced at a precarious angle on his head.

"Thanks for giving me some of your time, Mr. Richter. It's a real pleasure to be here," he said. He stole a quick glance at Rose before Karl closed the door.

"Glad to have you," Karl said. "I'd like you to meet Vernon Buick, our chief engineer."

"Oh, I thought from those coveralls that you were the janitor," Brown said. "But then, I didn't make the list for the ten best-dressed men this year either." The grin was so unexpected and sincere that the remark lost its barb, and Vernon laughed.

"Well now, what can we tell you that will astound your readers?" Karl asked as he motioned him to a chair.

Sitting down made little difference to the reporter's height. He studied Karl with friendly curiosity from his low vantage point.

"You're something of an enigma, Mr. Richter. You have managed, during these very trying times, to build a successful business. I know our readers would like to know the secret of your success, and I can't say that I blame them."

"The secret is hard work, I guess. Not the kind that builds muscles in your back, but the kind that leaves ulcers in your stomach. You get an idea, you make plans around that idea, and then you keep working on them until all the flaws are taken out. You have to produce something that people are willing to pay for." Brown scribbled hastily in a little book that he held in the palm of his hand. "I've also been fortunate to have Mr. Buick with me. He's set up some unique processes on the production line, much as Henry Ford did in Detroit. We can show you if you're interested."

"I'm interested."

"Vern, will come along with us and explain the line set-up?"

"Thanks, but can I ask you a few more questions, Mr. Richter, before we start the tour? Personal interest for our readers, you know."

"Sure, go ahead."

"You look surprisingly fit for a white-collar executive. Any explanation?"

"I've been practicing martial arts and zazen for several years," Karl replied.

"With that big shot from Pacific Far Eastern?"

"How did you know that?"

"It's my business to know, Mr. Richter," the reporter replied with a quicksilver smile. "Your father has some connection with him too, doesn't he?"

"Yes, he has a contract with the Takezawa zaibatsu, if that's what you're referring to," Karl answered carefully.

Karl was not prepared for Brown's next statement.

"Rumor has it that your mother outmaneuvered your father and left you with a fortune when she died." Brown moistened his pencil with the tip of his tongue before he looked up at Karl through narrowed eyes. Karl stared back at him and felt his anger rise.

Brown did not waver. "It's my job to get a story, Mr. Richter. Deny it, and I won't print it."

Karl stood up and leaned over the desk toward Brown. "You bastard! Of course I'll deny it. My sister and I inherited only what had been left to my mother by her father."

"Relax, relax, Mr. Richter. I figured it wasn't true. Sorry if I upset you." He shrugged his shoulders and added, "Some aspects of my job build ulcers too."

Karl hesitated for a moment, staring into the guileless face until his anger subsided. He knew well enough where the rumor had started, but there was nothing he could do except deny his father's allegations.

"Now let's take a look at this shipyard of yours," Brown suggested.

As they walked, the reporter took pictures and directed countless questions at Karl and Vern. "That ship in dry dock —is it Japanese?"

"Yes, it's a Maru ship," Vern replied. "We get quite a few of them. That one has a bent prop."

"What's the capacity of your dry dock?"

Again Vern answered. "Sixteen thousand tons. Most freighters are about eight thousand, so we have room to spare."

"Why Japanese ships?" Brown asked with only his eyes visible above the camera.

"Because we have the best damn shipyard on the west coast," Vern said firmly.

The eyes above the camera narrowed again. "Does your connection with Mr. Takezawa have some bearing on it as well?"

Vern glanced quickly at Karl, not quite certain how to answer the pointed question.

"It did to begin with," Karl answered easily. "But Mr. Buick is right. We have the best dry dock on the west coast, and the Japanese know it."

"From the look on your face, Mr. Buick, you have something else to show me."

Vern nodded and started in the direction of the new freighter. "I've saved the best for last," he said, pointing to the ship. Even in its state of partial completion, it demonstrated a certain majesty. There was a strength and beauty in her blunt lines that even an untutored eye such as Brown's recognized immediately. He whistled softly to reveal his appreciation.

"This is our baby," Vern said proudly. "She's five hundred and twenty-six feet long and will be propelled by turboelectric drive. When we finish, she'll carry twice as much cargo as the tramps and cruise easily at eighteen knots. Our men have named her *Titan*."

"Who designed her?"

"Karl and I began with an idea four years ago, and this is the result."

As they climbed aboard the freighter, Karl explained the reason for building a ship like *Titan*. "The basic design of the tramp hasn't changed for twenty-five years, and although it's still a good design, it's not efficient enough for today's requirements. *Titan*, with its speed, larger cargo capacity, and reduced fuel consumption, may not revolutionize the merchant marine, but it sure as hell will improve it."

They descended into the engine room and for the first time since his arrival Brown was silent, pursing his lips and nodding as Vern explained the construction and innovative design of the ship. With growing respect he listened to Vern, recognizing in him glimpses of genius. The fact that he seemed so totally unimpressed with his own intelligence surprised Brown. To the seasoned reporter, it was like a drink of cool spring water after a long drought. When they finally stepped outside again, a light drizzle had started. Brown pulled up the collar of his overcoat and continued with his questions.

"Mr. Richter, I noticed you have quite a few Japanese employees. I am not paid to be prejudiced or opinionated, just curious, so if you don't mind my asking . . . are there not enough qualified Caucasians around to fill the jobs?"

"These men are loyal and they work hard. Right now, we have a narrow margin of profit and we need men we can depend on."

"Off the record, do you pay them less than the other employees?" Brown asked, completely without malice.

Karl felt the muscles in his face tighten, and he fought the urge to give an angry retort. "My employees are paid fairly, according to their abilities. These men are from Steveston, born and raised near the sea. They know ships like the back of their hands. It's been their livelihood for generations.''

''I gather you don't have any union problems yet.''

''No, and I don't expect any,'' Karl said, aware of the skeptical look in the reporter's eyes.

''What are your plans for the future?'' Brown asked as they headed back toward the office.

''We have a contract to build four barges for a pulp-and-paper mill, and of course we'll continue with our refitting operation. When the market improves, we're anticipating a demand for our new cargo ship, and we'll be ready for it. *Titan* is just a start. As for the more distant future—who knows? Vern and I just might build a luxury liner that will astonish the world.''

''I'd like to book a first-class deluxe suite on the maiden voyage with press privileges, of course,'' Brown said with a chuckle. ''Thank you, gentlemen, for your time. It's been enlightening.''

Hiro and Karl faced each other in the dojo, each aware of the other's strength and skill. They were, however, still master and student, and Karl bowed in deference to the sensei's rank. Their thrusts were quick and powerful, but they stopped just short of full contact. Occasionally a blow would reach beyond its intended mark, but neither man showed evidence of pain. Karl appeared to be moving a half step behind Hiro until his swing kick, executed with savage speed, caught the master in the solar plexus. Hiro's expression did not alter except for the flicker of his eyes. Karl understood; he had faced the sensei often enough to recognize the compliment. In a few more minutes, Karl realized he was able to anticipate the sensei's moves and counter them successfully. In that instant he lost his concentration; Hiro's attack was swift and deadly, and Karl was on the canvas from two rapid thrusts and a swing kick which struck his ankles. Instantly he jumped back to his feet with renewed strength and determination. Hiro sensed the change in his student and knew Karl had become a master. To win now, Hiro realized he would have to use every ounce of his strength together with five decades of experience. With a final powerful thrust to Karl's upper thigh and an equally swift blow against his neck, he managed to gain the advantage. He signaled to end the practice session and stepped back.

"You have progressed beyond my expectations, Karl. I believe you are ready for your second dan."

"Thank you, sensei."

"You have come a long way since Tatsuo first threw you over his back in Tokyo."

"All that seems so far away, as though it happened to someone else. So much has changed since then," Karl mused.

Later, while they soaked in the o-furo, Karl asked about Tatsuo.

"He is still in Manchukuo."

"Did he say when he would be home?"

"Home? Where is home for Tatsuo?" Hiro asked. The strain showed in his face at the mention of his grandson's name.

Karl knew the facts—Tatsuo was in Manchukuo, Japan's new title for defeated Manchuria, building railroads that would bring iron ore to the coast for shipment to Japan.

"I fear for my country now, more than ever," Hiro confessed. "When a powerful governing force like the military begins to fight among themselves, it is like a festering wound that will never heal. The two opposing groups, the Imperial Way and the Control Group, are in disagreement over the extent of Japan's expansion. The Imperial Way wants only to develop Manchukuo, but the Control Group, which consists mainly of senior military officers, wants to march into China."

"China? Why China?" Karl asked.

"They want to expand Japan's frontiers and stop the spread of communism. I shudder to think what will happen when they reach China."

Karl was thoughtful for a moment. "Europe is also threatened by great upheavals, especially since Adolf Hitler has come to power. Do you think Germany will ever pose a similar threat to the world?"

"Their chancellor has some very definite plans, and I don't think the world is even aware of the implications of his evil designs."

"I suppose we are all too concerned with countering the effects of the depression . . . the prohibition is over, gold is selling for thirty-five dollars an ounce. Maybe the worst is over,'' Karl suggested.

Hiro smiled briefly. "Perhaps I will indulge myself with a new car—a Cord with smooth leather seats."

They left the o-furo discussing the merits of owning a Cord, each conscious of the other's unrest but unwilling to relinquish the precious happiness he found in the other's company.

Later in the week, a Norwegian ship, crippled in a sudden gale, limped into the dry dock at the Burrard Shipyard. Karl promised to accommodate the captain, who offered three times the amount they would normally receive for the same repairs. Shipwrights, laborers, and engineers worked around the clock to make the ship seaworthy while Karl and Vernon often stayed behind to supervise the work.

"Couldn't your men handle this themselves?" Janice demanded. "I've hardly seen you in two weeks, and the boys haven't seen you at all!"

"We'll be finished soon. I can't very well ask the men to work double and triple shifts unless I'm ready to do the same," Karl explained.

"How long is this job going to last?" Janice asked.

"About four more days."

"Do you really think you can last that long? You've hardly slept all week."

Karl sighed. "I know. But I have to make sure the job is done right. It could open the door to some major contracts for us."

"That's what I'm afraid of."

"Just bear with me for a few more days, Janice. I promise I'll take some time off just as soon as this is finished."

She looked at him with accusing eyes but remained silent. When Karl bent to kiss her, she suddenly became very absorbed in the delicate rose she was embroidering on a white tablecloth.

The day the Norwegian ship was ready, the sense of satisfaction Karl had expected to feel was missing. The job had been completed a day ahead of schedule, and the grateful captain presented Karl with an envelope containing the promised payment. From his office window, Karl watched the ship until she disappeared from view. In a way he was envious of the captain and his crew, who would soon feel the sway of the deck beneath their feet and the caress of ocean breezes on their faces. He returned to his desk with a feeling of despondency.

"Karl, I'm sorry to have to bother you, but I had to stay and finish some work. Could you drive me home?" Rose asked.

"Has Vern left?"

"Yes, he couldn't wait tonight."

"But he—"

"I asked him not to wait," Rose explained.

Karl nodded silently. They drove in silence for several minutes. "Vern wants to marry me," Rose said finally.

"And what did you tell him?"

"I told him I would need some time to think about it."

Karl hoped his voice would not betray the emotions he felt. "Vern is a fine person. You would have a good life with him."

"I know." Rose was silent for a few moments. "I loved my husband very much. I don't know if I could marry again for anything less."

When Karl stopped to let her off, she turned to him. "Would you like to come in? The children are with my mother for the weekend, and I hate coming home to an empty house."

The house was small and simply furnished, but it reflected Rose's personality. As Karl followed her into the kitchen, he noted the brightly upholstered furniture, the soft lighting, and the smell of wax liberally applied to the hardwood floors. Rose moved quickly, and the aroma of coffee soon filled the room. She fixed a tray of thick sandwiches and handed it to Karl to carry into the sitting room.

Karl leaned back lazily in his chair. "I don't know how you do it, Rose, but you always manage to make me feel comfortable. I haven't felt this relaxed since we secured our first contract." He sighed with contentment. "I'm grateful to you, Rose. You're an exceptional secretary and a good friend."

Rose stood up slowly. "Karl . . . I want to be more than just an efficient secretary and a friend." Her voice was husky and her eyes glistened with emotion.

"You know that's impossible," Karl replied unevenly as he rose to meet her. He watched, mesmerized, as she undid the buttons of her blouse, revealing lacy undergarments that strained aginst her body.

"Let's forget who we are tonight, Karl. Stay with me,

please. Tomorrow I will probably tell Vern that I will marry him, but tonight I want to experience love for the last time.''

"Oh, Rose, Rose." Karl groaned as the lace fell to her feet and her breasts spilled out against him. His mind went blank to all else but the urgency that gripped him as she gently caressed him with her hands and lips. She helped him remove his clothes and gasped when she saw him naked.

"Karl, you're magnificent! Even more than I imagined!"

Slowly, Karl lifted her and carried her to the bedroom. They floated on waves of desire, cresting again and again until the overpowering demands of their passion were spent and they fell asleep.

The sun had risen just enough to cast a warm glow over the city as Karl drove home through the empty streets. He tried not to think of Rose or of what Janice would do if she discovered where he had spent the night. The unfamiliar discomfort of guilt made him squirm in the seat as feelings of remorse washed over him. He loosened his tie. The smell of Rose's perfume was still present even though he had showered until his skin burned.

In retrospect, he knew last night had been inevitable. He could not deny the attraction he felt for Rose any more than he could erase his memories of Patricia. Perhaps Rose offered an escape from the reality of his daily turmoil and a way to bring back the poignant memories of his youth. But whatever the reason, he knew it was not enough to justify what had happened. He felt trapped in a web of guilt, pity, and regret.

Karl walked through the front door of Drachenschlucht and waited for the excited voices of John and Andrew. But the house was quiet. He called out but heard only the echo of his own voice. In the living room, he called again.

"They're not here." Lisl's voice startled Karl.

"Where are Janice and the boys?" he asked.

"They spent the night with Janice's parents. It was their thirtieth anniversary last night. You were to give the toast. I assume you forgot."

"Oh God! I did forget!"

Lisl's eyes raked over him. "And I suppose you're going to tell me that with all the trouble you've been having at the shipyard, it completely slipped your mind," she said with a mocking voice.

"That's right."

"Cut the bullshit with me, Karl! You know damn well you weren't at the shipyard last night, because I checked. You left with Rose Thornton."

Karl turned away from the open accusation in her eyes. "You're jumping to conclusions, Lisl. Mind your own business."

Lisl's nostrils flared with anger. "You are my business whether you like it or not. So is Janice, and so are the boys. You were screwing around with that Thornton bitch last night while your wife and children were sitting here worrying about you!"

Before Karl could stop himself, his hand shot out, and Lisl's head snapped back as he slapped her across the face. The blood seemed to drain from her, and she stared at him in disbelief. An angry red welt appeared on her cheek.

"Lisl, I'm sorry. I didn't mean to do that." He reached out for her, but she stepped back.

Her voice was cold as she spoke. "You're becoming more and more like Father every day. Why don't you take a good look at yourself before it's too late?" Her expression softened slightly at the despair on his face. "Do something about it now, Karl, or you'll lose everything—just as Father did." She turned and walked quickly out of the room.

Karl sank heavily into a chair and buried his face in his hands. He did not know how long he sat there as his conscience tore at him; when he stood up, his limbs felt stiff and tired. Partly from habit and partly because he did not know what else to do, he walked through the quiet streets to the Takezawa residence, to the peacefulness of the sensei's garden. It was cool there, shaded by the cedars that had grown tall over the years. Hiro was in the middle of the dry landscape garden, raking the white pebbles into delicate patterns. His back was to Karl, and he did not turn as Karl approached.

"Welcome, Karl," he said.

"How did you know it was me, sensei?"

"We have been together for many years and I have seen your feet grow larger. I know when you are near." Hiro turned around, and although he smiled Karl could see he was disturbed.

"What else do you know, sensei?"

"I know you are troubled. It is written all over your face. Can I help?"

"This time I must help myself," Karl replied softly.

They sat down on the wooden bench at the edge of the garden, and as always, these surroundings reflected a mood of timeless peace.

"Too many weeks have slipped by since we last sat here. I can sense the turmoil within you. Have you been meditating?"

"I cannot find the peace I have experienced in the past. I have tried praying, but it eludes me. I can ride the Ox, but I always emerge into a world that is tormented with problems."

"That peace you speak of is elusive. Even zen masters often lose it. But you must continue to search," Hiro said.

"I feel so far removed from it now. Life seems hopeless. I have failed in so many ways. Have I wasted all these years looking for something that I will never find?"

"Nothing is ever wasted, Karl. Wisdom has its roots in experience."

I seem to be following in my father's footsteps, and that thought is abhorrent to me. I don't ever want to be like him, and yet that seems to be my destiny."

"No!" Hiro said sharply. "You are yourself. You shape your own destiny."

"My *karma* is my own?"

Hiro nodded emphatically. "Let us meditate together."

In the familiar lotus position, Karl felt himself relaxing. He slowed his breathing until it was controlled and deliberate and only the muscles of his abdomen moved. His body seemed detached from the ground, removed from the garden, separated until there was no feeling. His mind was emptied of all thought, and he hovered in silence before descending further into a void where only the vestiges of mood remained. Several hours later, he opened his eyes and looked about the garden.

Hiro recognized the serene expression. "Where have you been, Karl?"

"I . . . I don't know. Everything is alive again, the air is scented. It is like the first time I rode the Ox home."

"You have returned to the source. Enjoy your world as it really is, in harmony."

"I hope it's not too late for me to undo my mistakes."

"It is never too late as long as you have life. Start at the top, do the important things first, and then work down, like a pyramid."

They walked slowly through the garden.

"Where will you go now, Karl?"

"To the top of the pyramid, sensei."

When Karl returned to Drachenschlucht, he was relieved to see Janice's car in the driveway, and although the rest of the house was dark, there was a light in their bedroom window. As he walked up the stairs, he felt his confidence ebb.

Janice sat in the chair by the window, her hair gleaming from a recent brushing. She looked up when Karl walked in, her face closed.

"Janice," Karl said softly. "Janice, I have to talk to you."

"Where have you been? You look different. Are you all right?"

"I feel different, Janice. I've done a great deal of thinking today, sorting things out in my mind." Karl walked toward Janice's chair and knelt down in front of her. "Please look at me. Do you know that you and the boys are at the top of my pyramid?"

"I don't think I know what you mean."

"You and the boys are more important to me than anything else in the world. Without the three of you nothing would be worthwhile."

"But I thought the shipyard, your men, and your contracts were so important. Why have you suddenly changed your mind?"

"Because today I realized what was happening, the kind of person I was becoming. Perhaps you were right, Janice—I was following in my father's footsteps. I swore I would never do that, never lead the kind of life he did, never neglect my family and become obsessed by success, and yet there I was on the verge of doing just that."

Janice's expression softened. "Even though I accused you of it, you're not really like your father, Karl."

"I love you, Janice, and I'm sorry for so many things. I want to try and undo my mistakes."

"I'm sorry for many things too, Karl, but I don't think we can undo our mistakes." She looked at him with eyes that were filled with tears. "But maybe we can try not to make the same mistakes again."

"Do you want to try?"

Janice's voice was barely above a whisper. "I don't know, Karl. I've been afraid for so long, afraid that I had lost you to the shipyard and to the world. I almost convinced myself I didn't care anymore, that I had the boys and that was enough. I've been so lonely. We've become like strangers."

"There's no need for you to be afraid anymore. I can't promise there won't be times when I'll have to spend an evening at the shipyard or that I won't have problems with my men. But I promise you it won't happen very often. I will not allow any more days to go by without spending time with you and the boys. I want to store up a lifetime of memories. I want to watch them blow out their birthday candles, teach them to throw a ball, I want to show them how to build a snowman, and I want to make love to you on the *Cathy B*."

"But how can you do that without neglecting your work? Isn't *Titan* almost ready for launching?"

"I've given part of the business to Vernon. He's very capable, and more than willing to assume the responsibilities." Karl stood up and pulled Janice to her feet. "Let me try to make up for time I've lost."

You know I love you, Karl. I always have."

"I won't make the same mistakes again, my darling."

"Karl, are you sure? Please don't make any promises you won't be able to keep. I don't think I could stand that again."

"I've never been more sure of anything in my life." He pulled her close to him and buried his face in her fragrant hair.

"I've missed you so," she whispered as she felt his arms tighten around her.

〔18〕

The launching of *Titan* came at an opportune time. The world was slowly wrenching free from the bog of the depression, and several major shipping companies were waiting hopefully for the new workhorse to prove herself on the open seas. *Titan* had never been on official display, but Bob Brown had whetted many people's curiosity by following his first long story with short, articles in the *Vancouver Sun* on the progress of the new ship. He was among the first to arrive for the ceremony.

Attendance at the launching was impressive. Invited guests included influential ship owners from the United States and Europe, a delegation from Japan led by Ambassador Suyama, the president of the Bank of Canada, the mayor of Vancouver, and several of his council members. Hiro and Patrick Fenton stood well back of the crowd, but when Karl caught their attention, he recognized the look of pride on their faces. Janice, who would christen the ship, arrived a few moments before the ceremony was to begin. Her blond hair was long again, framing her face in soft waves. The red suit she wore accentuated her slightly fuller curves and the whiteness of her skin.

"Karl, I didn't think there would be so many people here!" She sounded apprehensive.

He grinned. "Neither did I. *Titan*'s received a lot of publicity, though, and I guess people are curious. Don't worry, you look beautiful." He turned to the reporter. "Bob, this is my wife, Janice."

"You sure know how to pick 'em, buddy." He grinned and extended his hand to Janice. "I'm pleased to meet you."

"I've heard so much about you, Mr. Brown," Janice said warmly.

"All bad, I hope. I love notoriety."

"Sorry to disappoint you, but it's all been good."

"Ah well, that's the story of my life. With this angelic face, everybody thinks I can do no wrong. Very dull, very dull indeed."

"I have to disagree with you on that," Karl said. "You can be an absolute bastard when you want to be."

They stood quietly for a few minutes watching the people milling around the ship.

"Excuse me," Janice said. "I want to talk to Mr. Takezawa for a minute."

Karl and the reporter started to walk toward the ship. In the distance, Vern waved, motioning them toward him.

"Say, didn't I hear your partner was getting married. What happened?" Brown asked.

"Damn! Do you ever stop being a reporter?"

"Nope. I've tried, but my curiosity always gets the best of me. Now what about Vern? Wasn't he going to marry that gorgeous secretary of yours?"

Karl shrugged. "Rose and Vern had plans to be married, but they fell through a couple of weeks before the wedding."

"Is that when she quit her job?"

Karl nodded.

"I'll bet she was difficult to replace."

"She was an excellent secretary," Karl said.

"She looked like the type who knew how to look after her man," Bob said with a wistful sigh. "I gave her the opportunity, but she turned me down." His face creased into a grin, but the shrewd eyes that met Karl's were sympathetic.

The ceremony was impressive and when Janice, smiling brilliantly for the cameras, broke the champagne bottle against *Titan*'s hull, there was an excited roar of applause. The huge ship slid easily into the water with a mighty splash, heaved over, then righted herself.

"There she is," Vern said. "I'm so goddamn proud, I could cry."

Karl nodded in agreement, unable to speak because of the lump that had formed in his throat. Sitting high in the water, *Titan* was no longer dependent on them; she belonged to the sea. With the launching of the supership, a chapter had closed in Karl's life. In retrospect, the last five years had flown by, leaving only sporadic memories of people and events: Tatsuo's sad eyes in an expressionless face as he prepared to leave for Japan, the birth of John and Andrew and his overwhelming pride and love as he stared at them for the first time, the endless hours spent planning and building *Titan*. But what lay ahead?

"Hey, guy, where are you?" Vern waved a hand in front of Karl's face. "I've been trying to get your attention, and you're a million miles away."

"Sorry, I was just thinking about everything that's happened since we first drew up our plans for *Titan*."

"You'll have lots of time to think about that later. Right now our adoring public needs us to pop the champagne corks. You can give the speeches while I sign the contracts."

Karl laughed. "Are you sure we're going to get contracts?"

"Hell, yes! *Titan*'s a winner, Karl. I have the feeling we're going to get more business than we can handle."

"We'll handle it. Just get the contracts signed."

It was well past the supper hour when Karl arrived at Drachenschlucht. He was delighted to find Hiro and Miyoko drinking tea with Janice. John and Andrew raced to meet him with exuberant shouts and then returned to their places at Hiro's feet, where they were building a Japanese temple with colorful wooden blocks.

"I've never seen them this quiet," Karl observed as he accepted a cup of tea.

"It's Mr. Takezawa," Janice said. "He seems to have a calming effect on them. They totally monopolize his time." It saddened her that Karl had spent too little time at home to have witnessed this relationship grow.

"When do you think they should start training in the dojo?" Karl asked while he watched Hiro fit a difficult block for Andrew.

"They are not even five years old, Karl-san. Let them enjoy their childhood for a while yet. Duty will bear down on them soon enough."

"Tatsuo is coming home at the end of the week," Janice announced.

Karl looked at Hiro with surprise.

"That is correct," Hiro said. "I received a cablegram this

morning. Perhaps you would like to come with us to meet him."

"I'll bring John and Andrew with me. What time does the ship dock?"

"He is not coming by ship this time. He is flying into Vancouver airport."

"You weren't expecting him this soon, were you?" Karl asked.

"No. I suspect that his return has something to do with recent events in China."

"Japan seems to be living up to its national slogan: bring the eight corners of the world under one roof," Karl said.

"It is an undeclared war, but Japan has already captured Peking, Tientsin, and much of northern China. They have also set up a naval blockade along the Chinese coast. The latest incident is bound to cause even more trouble."

"Incident?"

"Chinese soldiers fired on a Japanese unit in Peking. I am familiar with the ways of the military, and I suspect it was a planned incident to allow the Japanese government to take even further punitive action against the Chinese."

"But what has this to do with Tatsuo's return to Canada?"

"The world refuses to recognize Japan's conquests in China, and most nations, including Canada, are continuing to sell war materials to Japan. Her might is increasing and so are her demands. I am not certain, but I believe Tatsuo will be bringing confidential directives from Tokyo. There is also the possibility his return has something to do with the sinking of an American gunboat in the Yangtze River. Tatsuo is well-versed in American customs. He could be useful in a diplomatic role."

"Do you think he has been asked to be an arbitrator?"

"I do not think Japan is prepared to apologize for the incident."

Karl sighed. "I don't envy his position."

Hiro's face was grim. "Tatsuo feels as I do. War and conquest are not honorable goals in today's world, and to aid those who are promoting war is unacceptable to us."

Lisl walked between John and Andrew as Karl directed them to the gate where Tatsuo's plane would land. She wondered why she had consented to go along to meet him. Old habits were hard to break, she admitted silently. Certainly her life no longer included plans for Tatsuo, plans that could never have materialized. She had accepted the futility of their relationship and had filled her life with her work. Her friendship with James Ellesworth had long ago settled into a comfortable courtship. She had also convinced herself that she no longer loved Tatsuo.

Tatsuo appeared older and gaunt-faced as he stepped down from the trimotor aircraft, but the smile that crossed his face when he saw his welcoming committee was the one she remembered. He wore a light blue shirt, open at the neck, and dark pants; Lisl thought she had never seen him look so handsome. For a moment she wished with all her heart that he would run to her with open arms, forgetting formality and protocol, and declare his love for her for all the world to hear. She held her breath as he began to run toward them. Then, as if remembering who he was, he stopped before he reached them and walked toward his grandparents. There were formal bows and exchanges of excited greetings before he turned to Lisl.

Nothing has changed after all, Lisl thought as she returned his warm embrace. But that was not really true. She felt only comfort and relief in his arms, not the breathless ecstasy she had always known.

"It is good to see you again, Lisl," Tatsuo said softly.

Lisl met his eyes and smiled. "It is good to have you home."

"It is not like old times, though, is it?"

Lisl shook her head wordlessly. She saw the sadness in his eyes and looked away.

"How are you, kyō-dai?" Karl asked as he stepped forward.

"I am well, or as well as can be expected. It is good to be home among family and friends."

"What's it like to fly in one of those contraptions?"

"Well, twenty-two hours in the air as compared to a week on the *Empress* . . . but if I were not in such a hurry, I would still prefer the ocean."

"Will you have time to look through my new ship? Her owners will be claiming her next week."

"You have sold her already?"

Karl was unable to suppress the pride in his voice. "We already have a contract to build two more. And if I sound like

I'm bragging, it's because I am." He laughed self-consciously.

"It is not wrong to be proud of something like that. I would be honored if you would give me a tour tomorrow."

"Right after our session in the dojo?" Karl said.

Tatsuo looked surprised and then laughed aloud. "You have a date, kyō-dai, before the sun comes up. Now, where are those two blond warriors of yours?"

John and Andrew stood back and eyed Tatsuo suspiciously. He was a stranger in their small familiar world, yet because he reminded them of their beloved Oji-san, as they had been taught to call Hiro, they accepted him, though not without some reservation.

"Come on, you two. I have not changed as much as you have. The last time I saw you, you still had baby fat and a thumb in your mouths."

Both boys smiled tentatively and advanced toward Tatsuo. With a glance at Hiro, they bowed—crookedly, but with as much formality as they could muster. Hiding a smile, Tatsuo returned their bows and then knelt down and hugged them.

"I have something for each of you, but you will have to wait until you come to Oji-san's house tonight." He was not surprised when their arms tightened around his neck. "Amazing," he observed, "what a little bribery will do."

As on the occasion of so many other homecomings, there was a traditional Japanese feast. Miyoko glowed with pleasure while her guests ate the carefully prepared dishes with relish.

Lisl watched Tatsuo's subdued expression, noting the pallor of his skin and the thin smile that did not spark laughter in his eyes. She longed to reach out for his hand, to curl his fingers tightly around his, to rest her head on his shoulder. She ached both to comfort him and to feel the tenderness of his own caress, but she willed herself to sit still. Mentally, she had prepared for this reunion, knowing her strength would depend on her ability to convince herself of the futility of loving him. An image of James's gentle, intelligent face flashed before her and some of the pain receded. When dinner was finished, she rose from the table.

"I'm sorry but I have to leave . . . an engagement I cannot break." Seeing the disappointed look on Tatsuo's face, Lisl knew she could not tell him where she was going.

Tatsuo escorted her to the door. "Thank you for coming, Lisl," he said quietly as he helped her with her coat. "Can I see you tomorrow by the old tree?"

"The old tree isn't there anymore," Lisl replied sadly. "It has given way to progress."

"Ah yes, progress, the eternal malady of the world. May I come to your house, then?"

"I would like that."

"So many things have changed. You have changed, Lisl."

"I had no choice."

"I know, and I understand."

"Oh, Tatsuo, what do I see in your face?" she cried suddenly, clutching at his shirt. "I'm so frightened for you."

Tatsuo covered her hands with his, holding them tightly against his chest. "Please don't be frightened. There is nothing for you to worry about."

Lisl reached up and kissed him lightly on the cheek. "Come tomorrow when you can. I will be waiting."

Tatsuo stood by the door until he could no longer hear her retreating footsteps, but when he walked back to the dining room, the sound of her voice still rang in his ears.

While the twins played with their new toys from Japan, Tatsuo related with chilling clarity the stories of political assassinations and intrigue so familiar now in Japan. "Our armies have made rapid advances into China."

Hiro's eyes narrowed with anger. "But what of our people? Do they not question the motives of the military? We are a peaceloving people—farmers, merchants, and fishermen. What is happening to them?"

"They, too, are caught up in the cause," Tatsuo explained sadly.

It was past midnight when Karl and Janice finally left, each carrying a sleeping child. Karl knew that sleep was still hours away for Tatsuo and Hiro; they had much to discuss, and he could not be a part of it.

"I have brought new orders from the zaibatsu," Tatsuo said when the house was quiet.

"But why the secrecy?"

"Our factories are now turning out fighter planes, battleships, carriers, and tanks. They need vast amounts of raw materials. They have gone so far as to dismantle lampposts and confiscate radiators from private homes because our factories need the steel. Your new directive is to stop all shipments of grain and lumber and to replace them with steel and iron ore.''

"But how will our people live? Japan is not self-sufficient. Will the military allow the nation to starve?''

"The military claims there is enough food in Manchuria to feed all of Japan.''

"You and I know that is not so. Manchuria cannot feed itself and Japan as well!''

Our government does not foresee that as a problem.''

Hiro shook his head in disbelief.

"Our job is to arrange for the extra steel shipments,'' Tatsuo continued.

"On Richter's ships?''

Tatsuo nodded gravely. "He has already consented to this.''

"Of course, and he has doubled his price.''

"Conrad Richter is a mercenary. He will do whatever is necessary for the money.''

A change came over Hiro's face, and he straightened his back defiantly. "I will not be a part of this any longer. I cannot stop what has already been started, but I will not contribute my energies or my life to the perpetration of war.''

Tatsuo stared at his grandfather with shock and disbelief. "Will you openly disobey the zaibatsu?''

Hiro nodded. "I will inform them of my decision.''

"But you know what that means, Oji-san!''

"There was a time in my life when I would have committed seppuku for even harboring such thoughts, but not now—not for the sake of the military! They are ruthless and ambitious, and I will not be influenced by them any longer! I will relinquish my position and all the privileges that accompany it, then I will wait for their reaction. There is nothing more I can do.''

"You have devoted your life to the zaibatsu. Surely they will allow you to live out the remainder of your life in peace.''

"I have made my decision. The rest is up to them.''

"I will not allow any harm to come to you or my grandmother.''

"I am of no consequence, Tatsuo. It is you who must decide which path to follow.''

"I now hold one of the five sacred swords,'' Tatsuo said grimly. "It was given to me along with my latest orders. I have always felt that I had no choice but to do whatever they asked even if my conscience told me otherwise."

"You must do what you feel is honorable and right. You have been taught the significance of these swords. I want you to make your own decision and not be influenced by anything I have said or done."

"How can I not be influenced, Ojī-san? I have spent all my life with you. Your wisdom has given me direction; the book you wrote for me years ago has been my guide. We think as one!"

"What else does the zaibatsu demand of you?"

When Tatsuo answered, his voice rang with emotion. "I am expected to act as an observer and report to the war office in Tokyo if there are any developments in western naval strength. Ojī-san, how can I do that? I am not even sure where my loyalties lie anymore!"

"They ask too much. You came here when you were only thirteen. Your loyalties cannot help but be divided." Hiro placed a hand on Tatsuo's shoulder. "Perhaps some rest will erase the shadows from your face. Your mind will be clearer in the morning."

Tatsuo's shoulders sagged. "It is like a nightmare, Ojī-san. Where is that peace and harmony we have always talked about? I am torn between duty and conscience."

"I have lived three times as long as you have, Tatsuo, and yet I cannot give you any definite answers," Hiro said. "I can only tell you that I will pray for this madness to end and for you to have the wisdom and strength to make the right decisions."

The sun was just beginning to envelop the city in its warmth when Karl arrived at the Takezawa residence for the scheduled practice session in the dojo. He was not surprised to find Hiro sitting in quiet meditation and Tatsuo sweeping the well-worn floor.

When Tatsuo and Karl faced each other, the months and years of separation fell away. They were no longer worlds apart. As Hiro had predicted, they seemed evenly matched; where Karl had gained in size and strength, Tatsuo countered with skill and speed. Their session ended in a draw, with both of them exhilarated and wet from exertion.

"You have progressed, Karl. Your feet no longer stick to the floor as they used to," Tatsuo said as he wiped the perspiration from his forehead with the sleeve of his keiko-gi.

"You're not exactly lagging behind either, my friend," Karl replied between breaths. "It's been too long since we've done this."

"I wish we had time for the o-furo, but today the shower will have to suffice. I want to see your *Titan*."

"You're seeing Lisl later today, aren't you?"

Tatsuo nodded, searching Karl's face for some sign of disapproval.

"Be gentle with her, Tatsuo. She's had a difficult time, and I don't want to see her hurt again. I never thought I would be telling you that . . . I know how much you care for her." Karl shook his head sadly. "Where the hell is that harmony we struggled for? Somehow I had this picture in my mind of peaceful gardens, happy homes, you and Lisl together, ocean voyages . . . hell, I haven't had the *Cathy B* out for months. What's happening, Tatsuo?"

"I guess we were dreamers, kyō-dai. Nothing is like we thought it would be. You know what kept me going in Manchuria? I kept thinking about my grandfather's peaceful garden and I told myself that whatever happened, I would come back and you would be here with Lisl and my grandparents."

"When you came back before, it was always like old times, but now something is different and I can't figure it out."

Tatsuo's face lost all its expression. His eyes turned cold. Karl felt a chill course through him; the face he was staring at was not Tatsuo's but the face of a stranger.

"I am Japanese, and I have awesome duties and obligations to live up to, duties and obligations that are choking the life out of me. Japan is planning to go to war, Karl, and the world is ignoring all the signs."

"But it will always be the same here! This is your home. Nothing can ever change that."

Tatsuo sighed deeply and his shoulders sagged. "You are not a fool, and I know you do not really believe that. Look at yourself. Are you the same person you were two years ago? Even I can see that you are not. And Grandfather—who is to say what will happen to him now?"

"Your grandfather? What are you talking about?"

"My grandfather has followed the dictates of the zaibatsu all his life. He has bowed to Japanese tradition for sixty-five years, and he did it willingly. This morning he is sending a cable to the directors of the zaibatsu informing them he will not accept their latest orders. What they are proposing to do is against his principles, and he has had enough. My grandfather is a samurai, and what he has done is unthinkable, yet he did it! Do you realize what that means?''

It was a few moments before Karl could answer. ''Yes, I think so,'' he answered slowly. ''I know how he felt about the military and the zaibatsu's involvement, but I didn't think he would openly oppose them.''

''Neither did I. I was dumbfounded at first, but now . . . my grandfather is a brave man, and he would die for what he believes in.''

''Surely they wouldn't . . .'' Karl could not bring himself to finish the question.

Tatsuo shrugged. ''He has made his decision. Now he will have to wait for theirs. He is a very important man and highly respected by many people. He can still exert considerable influence, and I have no idea how they will deal with him.''

After a long silence, Karl said, ''You know if there is anything I can do . . .''

Tatsuo smiled, the gentle sincere smile that Karl remembered. ''Thank you, kyō-dai. I appreciate that. Now let's shower and change. I want to see that ship of yours.''

Tatsuo's heart quickened with excitement as he slid behind the wheel of the yellow Cord. He ran his fingers along the smooth leather upholstery and examined the numerous gauges on the dashboard. His grandfather had obviously not lost his passion for cars. This one, Tatsuo concluded, was the finest yet. At the touch of the starter, the engine sprang to life, gave a low throaty response to the pressure on the accelerator, then settled down to a quiet hum as Tatsuo swung out onto the street.

Shaughnessy, with its stately homes and well-tended gardens, was as serenely beautiful as always, set apart from the madness that gripped the rest of the world. He drove slowly through the shaded streets, past wide expanses of lawns closeted behind high fences, past cascading willows and oak trees colored by recent frosts. Would the threat of war alarm the people who lived here, or would they stay hidden behind their draped windows, untouched by the terror that was spreading across Europe and by the miasmal nightmare that already had Japan firmly by the throat? But now, with the sun shining from a cloudless sky, the air just cool enough to be refreshing and the thought of Lisl waiting for him, Japan, the zaibatsu, and the threat of war seemed far removed. Tatsuo opened the window and let the cool air blow against his face as he turned the Cord toward Drachenschlucht.

"Would you mind if we went for a drive?" he asked as he and Lisl stood together on the veranda. "It is a beautiful day, and I have my grandfather's car."

There was a flash of indecision on her face, but it disappeared as quickly as it came. "Why not?" She threw a sweater over her shoulders and tied the sleeves jauntily around her neck. As they walked to the car, the wind caught her hair and whipped it around her face.

"Well, so much for my carefully coiffed hair." Lisl pulled the hairpins out and let it fall to her shoulders.

"I like it better that way," Tatsuo said. He touched her lightly on the cheek with the back of his hand. "You are the most beautiful woman in the world."

"And you, sir, are a flatterer." Lisl kept her voice jaunty.

"I am not flattering you. I am only saying what I know is true."

"Thank you," Lisl whispered.

"Where would you like to go?" Tatsuo asked.

"Anywhere. Just drive until you get tired."

"One does not get tired driving a machine like this. You may end up on the other side of the world."

There was a semblance of a giggle from Lisl. "A few years ago I would have been egging you on. Now I am properly horrified but secretly delighted by the suggestion. But your grandfather would not be too pleased. He loves this car."

"He loves me more."

Lisl glanced at him with one eyebrow raised. "Well then, the ends of the earth, here we come," she said gaily.

They drove until the city disappeared, replaced by sparsely populated farmland on one side and an expanse of ocean on the other. They stopped to watch a fleet of fishing boats pulling their long nets behind them, followed by gulls waiting for their usual handout. When they got out of the car to walk along the white sandy beach, Tatsuo's hand closed around Lisl's.

"Do you remember the trip we took with Janice and Karl on the *Cathy B*?" Tatsuo asked.

"I remember it well, but it seems part of another world, another time."

"Are you happy now, Lisl?"

"I have a great deal to be grateful for. I guess I am happy."

"Lisl, I—"

"Are you happy, Tatsuo?"

"I am not even sure I know how to define happiness anymore. I suppose I would be happy if my obligations ran parallel to the dictates of my heart and conscience. My grandfather says that with such harmony, a man could conquer whatever world he chose."

"I could have made you happy, Tatsuo, had you chosen my world," Lisl said softly.

Tatsuo looked at her, pain naked in his eyes.

"I'm sorry, Tatsuo," Lisl cried. "I shouldn't have said that."

"No, you are right. These past few years have been wasted; I have been fighting for a cause I do not even believe in. But I had to do it, Lisl, otherwise I would have despised myself for the rest of my life."

"I know and I understand. I didn't at first, but I do now."

They walked in silence for a long time. The sun began to set and the air became cool. In the distance, the fishing boats were black shadows on the water.

"Is James Ellesworth still a part of your life?" Tatsuo asked, breaking the silence.

"Yes, very much so."

Tatsuo felt his stomach constrict, but he forced himself to keep walking, conscious that Lisl's hand was still in his. "Is he practicing law?"

Lisl nodded. "He chose the right profession. He's a brilliant lawyer. Karl hired him to do some work about a year ago, and now James handles all the legal affairs of the shipyard. Vern and Karl both sing his praises constantly."

"And you, Lisl, what do you think of him?"

"He's one of the most intelligent people I have ever known. He runs circles around me. Apart from his brains, though, he is gentle and sincere, and if he had to, I think he would move heaven and earth for me."

"Are you planning to marry him?" Tatsuo's voice sounded hollow.

For a moment Lisl did not answer. "Yes," she whispered finally.

The ache in Tatsuo's heart became almost unbearable. "Do you love him, Lisl?"

She whirled around to face him. "Dear God, what do you

want me to say? I'm twenty-five years old and I've loved you since I was eleven. I've never loved anyone else. But I want a home and children, and I want someone who will be there when I need him. Can you give me that? You're too busy fighting somebody else's senseless war.'' The words were torn from her heart, and they fell on Tatsuo like whiplashes. ''I went through hell waiting for you, hoping, praying, but it didn't help. If you had said, 'Come with me,' I would have followed you to the other side of the world, but you didn't.''

''I wanted to.''

Tears welled up in Lisl's eyes. ''You're asking me if I love James. Well, I do! Maybe not the way I loved you, but I love him enough to know I'll be secure and content with him.'' She was crying now with deep harsh sobs.

Gently, Tatsuo drew her into his arms and held her until she was quiet again. ''I am sorry, my darling, for all the pain I have caused you. Forgive me,'' he whispered against her hair.

''Oh, Tatsuo, there isn't anything to forgive. You didn't make any promises to me even though I wanted you to. But until I realized that we truly are from different worlds, I went through it all . . . rebellion, resentment, depression. You couldn't commit yourself to me because you were already committed from the day you were born into the Takezawa family. When I finally got that through my head, I understood what you were going through. I found out something else, too. Even though I missed you terribly and even though I love you, I can still go on living and enjoying life. I can make it in this world without you. I've learned how.'' She disengaged herself from Tatsuo's arms and stood back so she could see his face.

Tatsuo brushed a final tear from her cheek. ''You are a beautiful person, Lisl. I love you as much as any man can love a woman.'' He stopped and took a deep ragged breath. ''I cannot tell you how difficult it is for me to say this, how much it hurts to let you go, but I know I must. Marry him, Lisl. I know you will be safe and your children will grow up in a world you are familiar with. I will always pray for your happiness.''

''And I will pray for you too, my dearest.''

''Will you make me one promise, please?'' Tatsuo asked. ''Promise you will always be my friend. The world is in a state of turmoil and the outcome will not be solved peaceably, but whatever happens, I want to be sure our friendship will remain intact.''

"Of course! I promise I will never allow anything to change that."

The corners of Tatsuo's mouth lifted into a sad smile. "James Ellesworth is a most fortunate man."

They walked in silence for several minutes. When Lisl shivered, Tatsuo asked with concern, "Are you cold?"

"No, I was just thinking that James feels as you do. That there's going to be a war soon. He thinks it will involve the entire world. I really cannot imagine it, but then, James is not often wrong."

Tatsuo did not reply. He could not bring himself to tell Lisl that James was not wrong this time either.

As they neared Drachenschlucht Lisl felt an overwhelming sense of loss. "A part of me will always belong to you, Tatsuo," she said softly.

Tatsuo's voice was choked. "The selfish part of me wants to hold on to you. Be happy, my dearest Lisl. I know we will not meet like this again."

Lisl ran from the car and up the steps. When she reached the top, she stopped, and Tatsuo waited for her to turn around. She hesitated momentarily but did not turn. Tatsuo did not see her open the door for his eyes were filled with tears.

The news of Hiro's decision had an electrifying effect on the zaibatsu. A delegation was swiftly drawn up and dispatched to Canada to dispel the lunacy that had overcome one of their most loyal and revered members. Since Shozo, the eldest member of the zaibatsu, was far to feeble to travel, Koji was asked to accompany the delegation along with two staff officers of the imperial navy. Once in Canada, their mission would be aided by Suyama, the consul general.

The two officers who arrived with Koji, although not in uniform, were introduced as Vice Admiral Tokugawa and Commander Fukuzawa. Hiro noted they were approximately the age his son would have been.

Koji's greeting was polite but stilted; the stern-faced naval officers did not smile.

"You have never had the opporutnity to see my home of the last fifteen years, Koji. Allow me the honor of escorting you through my garden. Although it is late in the season, it is still very pleasant," Hiro said.

"Your brother's garden is a masterpiece and a loving work of art. It would be tragic if you did not take this opportunity to enjoy it," Suyama urged.

"An hour in the garden will not alter the nature of our business," Koji announced. The two officers nodded in agreement.

They walked slowly along the footpaths, stopping often to admire Hiro's work and nature's beauty. The naval officers did not really understand the intricacies and subtle architecture of the well-planned garden, but it was intrinsic to their nature to recognize the touch of a master's hand. The dry landscape garden received the highest praise and had the most satsifying effect on the visitors.

"I have spent a great deal of time here," Hiro explained, "as have my grandson and his friend. We have all learned many lessons in this garden."

Koji thoughtfully studied his brother's composed face. He did not, even remotely, look like a man who had lost his senses. In fact, Koji had never seen him look as much at peace with himself as he did now. Perhaps the zaibatsu had left him in this foreign country too long after all, a situation which would have to be remedied as quickly as possible.

"It is late. I think we should proceed with our business," Vice Admiral Tokugawa suggested, his eyes defying contradiction.

"As you wish," Hiro answered. "We can talk in my study."

Hiro sat behind his desk and faced Koji and the members of the delegation.

There were a few moments of uncomfortable silence before Koji finally spoke. "I am sure the purpose of this visit is no mystery to you."

"I know why you are here," Hiro replied.

Again, there was an uncomfortable silence. This time Vice Admiral Tokugawa spoke. "Your decision to disobey the direct orders of your zaibatsu has shocked all of us. Of course, we cannot allow you to carry out that decision." Tokugawa's words were delivered without emotion; he merely stated an irrefutable fact.

"I will not change my mind." Hiro looked directly at the officer. The vice admiral's face turned pale with anger and he began to rise from his chair.

"Wait, please," Koji cried, holding up his hand. "I want to know why my brother has made this decision!"

The vice admiral sat down, but his expression did not

change. In his opinion, orders issued by the government through the zaibatsu were to be obeyed without question. Whatever explanation Hiro Takezawa gave would make no difference.

Hiro's words were slow and deliberate, like those of a teacher addressing a class of bright but disobedient children. "My decision was not made lightly. I have seen the direction in which the government is steering our country, and I have watched as Japan's prepares to expand its borders through war. Japan is a peaceful country, populated by industrious people. We are farmers and merchants, not warmongers. You demand that I send iron ore and steel instead of grain and lumber to my people—people who do not have enough to eat!" Hiro's voice rose, and his hands tightened into fists. "I cannot honor your directives! I cannot send the materials to help propagate destruction when my own people will starve because of it, nor can I condone another senseless war!"

"There is enough food in Manchuria to feed our people," Vice Admiral Tokugawa interrupted sharply.

"Food stolen from a country that can ill afford to part with it."

"You have been away too long!" Tokugawa shot back. "If you were to speak to our people now, they would tell you to ship exactly what we have ordered. Japan is united, and we will go forward. We are the leaders of the Greater East Asian Co-Prosperity Sphere, and you, old man, are foolish to go against the wishes of your own people and of the emperor."

Hiro stared at the vice admiral in disbelief. He turned to Ambassador Suyama and then to Koji.

"He is correct, my brother," Koji said. "The people of East Asia look to Japan for leadership. We will prosper together. Our invasion of Manchuria was simple and justified. Now the imperial armies are advancing through China just as the German divisions in Europe are preparing to take what is legally theirs."

Hiro stood up and leaned over his desk toward Koji. "I am appalled! You are comparing Japan with Nazi Germany. I know that you have read *Mein Kampf*. You understand what Hitler's objectives are!"

The vice admiral spoke again, this time with a smile. "We have signed treaties with Germany and Italy. Together we can easily stop the advances of the communists."

Hiro shook his head, not really believing what he had just heard.

"Of course you now realize why we consider your decision to halt the shipments of steel completely inconsistent with our plans," the vice admiral continued.

The commander began speaking where the vice admiral left off. "We have an additional duty for you to perform. You are familiar with the people and customs of this country, and they are familiar with you. Because of this, you are able to travel freely in Canada and in the United States. The naval office would like you to act as a civilian observer—casually, that is—and to report any developments in naval strength or changes in the general feeling of the North American governments. We do not wish to come into direct conflict with the United States at this time."

"But these are my friends. You cannot expect me to spy on them!" Hiro protested.

"Your duty to Japan comes before all else," the commander replied.

"You are bound by duty and honor, Hiro," Koji warned. "You are a samurai. You will continue to use Richter's ships along with the Maru ships, which we will contract. Richter has already consented to refit some of his freighters to accommodate shipments of oil as well. It will be your duty to arrange for these shipments."

Hiro stood up to his full height. He could feel the eyes of the four men boring into him. "I have made my decision, and nothing you have said or can say will change my mind. You are right, Koji. I am a samurai and I must live according to my own conscience but not that of Vice Admiral Tokugawa or Commander Fukuzawa. I will not contribute to the needless death of my countrymen, nor will I betray the people who have befriended me for the past fifteen years."

"You are a fool and a coward," the commander screamed. "You are afraid to die for what you believe in."

"No, I am not afraid to die for what I believe in, but I refuse to die for what you believe in."

"Then we have nothing further to discuss," the vice admiral said. "It is time to leave."

"Koji, will you stay?" Hiro asked.

"No, I cannot stay in this house. It reeks of treason."

Consul General Suyama was the last to leave. He turned to

Hiro and said, "Good-bye, my friend. May I commend you on your bravery?"

Hiro sat in his study until his eyes ached from staring into the darkness. He was truly alone now, separated from his country, a victim of the unbending traditions that he had sought to uphold for so long.

A persistent knock at the door roused him from his thoughts.

"Come in."

"I have brought you some tea." Miyoko peered into the darkness.

"Come in, please. I have something to tell you."

"I can see by your face that you are troubled," she said.

"A stone wall has been raised between me and the members of my family. I cannot follow their orders any longer, nor can they concede to my wishes. I have chosen the only course of action that will allow me to live in peace, but it means we can never return to Japan."

Miyoko seemed to crumple into a chair as she buried her face in her hands. Hiro walked around his desk and took her hands, gently pulling her to her feet.

"I love you very deeply, and it grieves me to see your tears. You have been more than just a good wife. You have been a faithful companion, and now you are suffering because of a choice I have made." Carefully, he explained to Miyoko what he had done and what had prompted his fateful decision.

"I have not been blind to your fears or your agonies," Miyoko whispered. "You have done the right thing. But what of our grandson?" she asked, suddenly afraid.

"I know Tatsuo thinks and feels as I do but he is younger and more zealous. I cannot make his decisions for him."

Informing Conrad Richter that he would no longer be engaging his ships was not a task Hiro relished. He realized Conrad could bypass him and deal directly with the suppliers, but that would involve a huge personal investment and Hiro doubted that Conrad was in a position to pursue that option. The depression and Richter's own gross errors in business judgment had placed his shipping company in a precarious position from which he had only partially recovered.

At their meeting, Hiro observed Conrad and felt a mixture of pity and disgust for the man with whom he had reluctantly dealt over the past fifteen years. Conrad's appearance had deteriorated. He carried far too much unhealthy weight, his once gleaming blond hair was almost gone, and what remained was gray and unkempt. He had long ago given up his tailor-made suits. Only his eyes were the same; they had not lost their incredible piercing color, although overindulgence in Scotch had given them a watery vagueness. Today, he had obviously made an attempt to improve his careless appearance; his shirt was freshly starched, and he wore a tie. There was an expectant look on his face.

"I'm early, but I'm anxious to find out what the new schedules are. I guess you know I've talked to your people in Japan."

"Yes, I know," Hiro answered.

"I don't mind admitting that the new shipments are going to save my neck."

"Are you aware that the cargos you have agreed to carry will be used for armaments?"

"I just haul the stuff. What they do with it afterwards is their own damn business," Conrad retorted.

"There has been a change in plans."

"A change in plans? What the hell do you mean?"

Hiro leaned back against the high, straight chair. "I will no longer be arranging shipments for Japan or anywhere else. You are released from your contract with the zaibatsu."

A look of disbelief passed over Conrad's face. "You're out of your goddamn mind! Your own brother informed me that I would be hauling more cargo than ever before. You can't release me from my contract!"

"The last shipment of wheat is scheduled for two weeks hence. After that you are free to conduct business wherever you wish."

"You're crazy! You can't do this to me. They made the deal with me, and you can't just throw it out the window like this."

"Our contract lasted fifteen years, Mr. Richter," Hiro said calmly. "I think I have more than fulfilled all my obligations to you."

"If you think I am going to sit back and let you do this to me, you had better think again." Conrad's voice was low and measured. "You have tried to ruin me before—in fact, you nearly succeeded—but I won't give you a chance to do it again."

"Whatever was ruined in your life, you brought about all by yourself," Hiro said as he rose from his chair.

"I'll go over your head this time, Takezawa. I'll set up new contracts and deal directly with your brother," Conrad shouted, his face flushed with rage.

"That is entirely your prerogative, but I still wield a great deal of power, and I will use it to prevent those shipments from reaching Japan. That I promise you on my life!"

"Then it may well mean your life."

[19]

Tatsuo sat on the bench in his grandfather's garden. The evening had turned cold, and he pulled his coat closer up around his ears. A vague restlessness had plagued him since the meeting between his grandfather and the delegation sent by the zaibatsu. They had heard nothing since that meeting, but Tatsuo knew the silence would be short-lived. He rose and stalked Hiro's garden like a wary animal. Should he, too, rebel and take a firm stand against the zaibatsu? Tatsuo knew that he was not afraid to die, but, like his grandfather, he would not give his life for an empty or unjust cause.

Somewhere in the distance he could hear a car racing wildly down the street. Within moments it careened into the driveway, the glare of its lights cutting through the darkness like two brilliant sabers. Tatsuo rushed toward it, the headlights blinding him as he ran, his fatigue forgotten in the terrible urgency. He could not see anyone, but a voice edged with panic called out to him.

"Are you Tatsuo Takezawa?"

"I am Tatsuo," he answered breathlessly.

"There has been trouble. You must come immediately!"

"What is it? Tell me!" Tatsuo grabbed the arm of the man who materialized from the darkness.

"It is your grandfather. We will take you to him." He almost pushed Tatsuo into the car where two more men waited. Tatsuo could sense their agitation and fear.

"What has happened to my grandfather?" Tatsuo demanded.

In the darkness Tatsuo could not see the driver's face clearly, but he recognized the pity in his voice. "We are fishermen from Steveston, and your grandfather has often helped us. We had an appointment with him this evening. We arrived later than expected, but we were pleased to see the lights were still on in your grandfather's office. When we walked in, the office looked empty. We thought your grandfather had just stepped out and would return, but then we heard a noise in the back. There was water boiling on the stove as though he were preparing to make tea." The driver's voice became thick with emotion, and he swallowed painfully. "We found your grandfather on the floor. He had been shot."

"Shot? Is he . . . is he dead?"

The fisherman nodded. "Yes. We did not call the police or anyone else. We thought it best to tell you first and let you decide what to do."

"You did the right thing," Tatsuo whispered as a paralyzing numbness spread through him.

The fisherman spoke again. "You must prepare yourself, Tatsuo. He was brutally murdered."

Tatsuo heard the words but could not connect them with his grandfather. Brutally murdered? That was not possible! And yet why were these men here?"

At the office building, Tatsuo willed his feet to climb the stairs. The first thing he noticed was the sword, which had been removed from the wall and now lay on the richly burnished surface of the desk. The wall where it had hung was stained with blood; fragments of bone and lifeless flesh clung to the wood. Steam rose from the kettle on the small stove; two cups stood beside the sword. With leaden steps, Tatsuo walked behind the desk. Hiro lay face down on the floor in a pool of blood, his arms awkwardly askew. Tatsuo knelt down and touched the lifeless body.

"Ojī-san, Ojī-san," he whispered. Gently, he turned Hiro's body over. His stomach rose into his throat and a groan escaped from his lips. The right side of Hiro's face, just above the cheekbone, had been blown away, and the blood had gushed in torrents from the grotesque wound. With fingers that were surprisingly steady, Tatsuo closed the remaining eye.

"We would consider it an honor if you would allow us to

prepare your grandfather's body for burial," the fisherman said as he placed a gentle hand on Tatsuo's shoulder.

Tatsuo nodded. Wordlessly, he indicated the fragments of tissue and tufts of hair that clung to the wall.

"We will take care of everything."

Tatsuo watched silently as the men carefully removed the body. Someone shook him, and he stared vaguely into the concerned face of one of the fishermen.

"Shall we drive you home, Tatsuo?"

"No, I want to stay here for a while longer."

"I understand."

A look of realization crossed Tatsuo's face. "I do not even know your names or where you live!"

"My name is Nazaki. Many years ago, when your grandfather came to Canada, he helped us keep our fishing rights. He has been a true and honored friend. When you come to Steveston for the body, just ask for me. Someone will show you the way."

"Thank you, Nazaki-sama."

Tatsuo waited only until the sound of the car died away, then dialed Patrick Fenton's number. "I'm sorry to bother you at this late hour," he said when Patrick answered.

"It's no bother." Patrick recognized Tatsuo's voice. "But is something wrong?"

"Yes. Could you come down to the office? I must talk to you, and it cannot wait until morning."

"Certainly, but please tell me what's wrong."

"My grandfather was murdered tonight," Tatsuo said flatly.

There was a moment of silence until Patrick regained his voice. "I will be there in ten minutes." The line went dead.

While he waited, Tatsuo sat in Hiro's chair, his eyes riveted to the bloodstain on the floor. His grandfather's last visitor was apparently someone he knew well, which would explain the two teacups. But the sword—why would he have removed the sword from the wall and placed it on the desk between them? Was he being threatened? The reality of Hiro's death finally gripped Tatsuo, clearing his mind of all else but retribution. When Patrick arrived, Tatsuo was ready for him.

Patrick's knees buckled at the sight of the bloodstain on the floor, and he fell into the chair. His face paled when he saw the wall behind the desk. He looked at Tatsuo with eyes filled with horror. "Dear God, why would anyone do this?"

"That is what I want to find out," Tatsuo replied coldly.

"How . . . how was he killed? It looks like he was blown apart," Patrick whispered without looking up from the huge stain.

"He was shot by someone who must have been aiming for his head, but was a little off target and succeeded in blowing away the right side of his face."

"He must have been insane!"

"Perhaps, but I doubt it. The killer was either frightened or angry. He might also have been acting under the guise of duty."

"Duty?"

"My grandfather often confided in you, Patrick, so I assume he told you of his decision to oppose the military even though it meant defying the zaibatsu."

Patrick nodded. "He was preparing a formal report which would sever his ties with the zaibatsu, and I was in the process of finding alternate trade commissions for Pacific Far Eastern Trading."

"Then you were aware that the zaibatsu and the Japanese government were very displeased with his decision?"

Again Patrick nodded. "But surely they would not resort to this—to come here and shoot him in cold blood?"

"I intend to find out."

"Have you notified the police?"

"No!" Tatsuo said sharply. "And I do not intend to. I will look after this matter myself. The body is being prepared in Steveston, and I will take my grandfather to Japan for burial."

"But the police can help . . ."

"No! I do not need their help. If my grandfather was assassinated by our own people, then the police will only complicate the situation. This is not their affair. By the time they find out what has happened, we will be in Japan. In the meantime, if anyone asks, tell them he is away on business."

Tatsuo wondered if Patrick was aware of the brutal political assassinations that had taken place in Japan over the last few years. The job of an assassin was not to consider the character or rank of his victim, his job was to kill, and this he had done.

Patrick seemed to regain some of his composure, and even

though his color did not return, his voice was steady. "What would you like me to do?"

"You have been with my grandfather for many years, and I know you have been an invaluable associate. Pacific Far Eastern Trading is an independent company. It belonged to my grandfather. He alone was answerable to the zaibatsu; the company was not. If you can find alternate trade commissions, you are free to carry on with them. I do not know what provisions my grandfather has made, but I do know that other than my grandmother, I am his only heir. I would like this company to carry on with business as usual."

Patrick looked relieved. "I will do that." There was respect in Patrick's eyes as he listened to Tatsuo. The grandson had inherited Hiro's quicksilver mind and had added to it the confidence of youth and the deadly precision of a well-trained soldier. "What about your grandmother? And Karl. Do they know what has happened?"

Tatsuo closed his eyes for a moment. "No, not yet. I will tell them in the morning. Will you explain to Maiko?"

"Of course. She loved Mr. Takezawa very much."

There was a flash of emotion on Tatsuo's face, but it disappeared as quickly as it had come. He knew he could not allow himself the luxury of grief if he was to face the tasks ahead.

"He was the best friend I had," Patrick added.

"I know. Please go now. I will contact you later."

After Patrick left, Tatsuo paced about the room, searching. He stopped in front of Hiro's desk and picked up the sword. It was identical to his own, a symbol of power within the Takezawa zaibatsu. He strapped it carefully to his side, then stepped back to the center of the room. In the semidarkness, he stood still for a moment, then in one swift electrifying motion, he drew the sword, swung it in a perfect arc, and dropped it back into its scabbard. A faint smile appeared on his lips.

The darkness lifted, giving way to the cool light of the morning. Tatsuo drove toward the residence of Consul General Suyama, where he knew Koji and the two naval officers were staying. He parked the Cord opposite the house, settled back into the comfort of the leather seat, and waited until the sun rose above the mountaintops.

The man who answered the door was Suyama's secretary.

He admitted Tatsuo immediately, and bowed politely. "I will tell Mr. Suyama you are here, Mr. Takezawa. Within a few minutes he was back. "The consul general is in the study with your uncle, the commander, and the vice admiral. They will see you now."

"Thank you." Tatsuo proceeded to the study, aware that the secretary's eyes were following him. Under normal circumstances Tatsuo would have removed the sword, but today circumstances were not normal, and he had no intention of leaving it behind.

Mr. Suyama stood up when Tatsuo entered. He indicated an empty chair beside Koji, who, along with the officers, sat facing the consul general. Tatsuo declined the invitation and walked around the room. The eyes of the four men followed him.

"Tatsuo, is something wrong?" the consul general asked.

"Please sit down, Mr. Suyama," Tatsuo commanded. "My business is not with you. I have come to see my uncle and these officers." He stopped and appraised them coldly, his hand tight on the hilt of the sword.

Koji glared at Tatsuo. "Did your grandfather send you?"

"My grandfather is dead!"

Koji rose partway from his chair, then fell back again. Beside him, the two naval officers tensed but remained seated.

"What are you saying? Hiro cannot be dead!"

"He was murdered last night . . . shot in the head while he served tea to his assailant."

"Oh, no!" the consul general gasped in a strangled voice. "Who would do such a terrible thing?"

Tatsuo looked directly at the commander and the vice admiral. "Someone who considered him a threat and felt he was not acting in the best interests of Japan. Someone who could kill my grandfather and not have to atone for it."

The commander jumped up, his face suffused with color. "Are you suggesting that we did it?"

Tatsuo's gaze did not leave the commander's face. "Political assassinations by the military are not uncommon."

"Stop this immediately," Koji shouted, his voice harsh with anger and grief.

The vice admiral raised his hand. "No, let him continue."

"My grandfather represented a threat to you, to your plans, and now he is dead. He was brutally murdered because he refused to do what was contrary to all his principles, because he refused to follow your orders even though they were directed through the zaibatsu.''

The vice admiral was not a tall man, but his years of service in the Japanese imperial navy had given him a look of distinction and power. His gaze flicked quickly over the sword and back to Tatsuo's face; his voice was firm. "I am deeply grieved to hear of your grandfather's death. It is, indeed, a tragedy. Hiro Takezawa was an honorable man and highly respected by everyone who knew him. His decision to disobey the orders of the zaibatsu did not come as a complete surprise to us; we were aware of his feelings. However, we firmly believed his common sense would prevail and that he would put aside personal opinions for the betterment of Japan.''

"In my opinion, admiral, that is exactly what my grandfather did.''

"Perhaps. In my opinion, however, his decision to sever his ties with the zaibatsu and to openly oppose our orders constituted a breach of allegiance toward the government of Japan and a breach of faith to his family. But it did not earn him his death. We did not kill your grandfather. Whether you choose to believe that or not is entirely up to you, but I assure you that despite our differences, our respect never wavered. You have come to the wrong place to seek retribution for his death.''

Tatsuo looked from one face to the next for a hint of deception—there was none. He sighed and released his grip on the sword. There was visible relief on the faces of the four other men.

Koji stepped forward. "Where is my brother's body now?" he asked, his voice betraying the sadness that his rigid features hid.

"It is being prepared for burial," Tatsuo replied.

"Will you bring him to Japan for burial?"

Tatsuo nodded. "His final resting place should be beside my parents in Tokyo. That is where he would want to be.''

Koji nodded in agreement. "Our council has requested your immediate return. I will advise them today of Hiro's death, and they will understand that your return will be delayed.''

"Thank you," Tatsuo answered. "I cannot leave until I have dealt with my grandfather's murderer.''

After Tatsuo had left, the vice admiral walked to the window, from where he watched Tatsuo walk to the gate. "I would not like to be that man's enemy," he said finally.

"Life has not been easy for Tatsuo," the consul general said. "I think his grandfather's death is more of a blow to him than we realize, perhaps more than even he realizes."

"He would make a fine soldier," the commander said. "Perhaps without his grandfather to influence him, he will be easier for us to mold."

"Do not underestimate him," Koji warned. "Like his grandfather, he will not bend easily, if at all."

Tatsuo found his grandmother in her favorite place in the house, the room where Hiro's books lined the shelves and where the huge expanse of windows was never covered by draperies. She sat by the window, intent on her sewing. Her eyesight was still sharp and her fingers as nimble as they had always been. She rose when Tatsuo entered the room, and her sewing fell to the floor.

"You have come to tell me about Hiro," she said quietly.

"Yes, Obā-san, I have. How did you know?"

"He has been the center of my life for forty-five years. Last night I sensed that he was not with me any longer. I have been praying since then that I am wrong, but I can see by your face that my prayers have not been answered."

"He is dead, Obā-san."

Miyoko stood very still for a few moments, and then she began to tremble. "Where is he?"

"In Steveston. His body is being prepared for burial."

"We will go back to Japan now," she said calmly. We will bury him beside our son and Yuri. When the time comes, I will be buried beside him." Tears began to spill down her cheeks, and Tatsuo reached out to hold her, suddenly realizing how small and frail she had become. Hiro had been her strength, the source of her happiness and vitality.

"We will pray that his spirit will have a safe journey," she said with a firm voice, although she was still trembling. She did not ask how he had died, and Tatsuo was relieved.

"Yes, Obā-san, we will pray," Tatsuo said. Inwardly, he thought, My grandfather's spirit will not rest until I have found his murderer.

"What will you do now?" Miyoko asked.

"I must tell Karl what has happened."

Tatsuo went directly to the shipyard and found Karl in his office. Karl dropped the report he was reading and stood up when Tatsuo walked in.

"Tatsuo, what's wrong?"

"It is my grandfather. He has been killed."

There was horror on Karl's face. "Killed? When?"

"He was shot to death last night. The villagers of Steveston are preparing his body. We will bury him in Japan."

"Have you called the police?"

"They can do nothing except cause unnecessary delays—it is not their affair. But I will need your help."

"Of course. What can I do?"

"Can you arrange passage for us on a fast freighter? We must get home as quickly as possible. Once we are gone, the matter will be forgotten."

"I'll make the arrangements immediately."

"Thank you."

Tatsuo slept fitfully. In his mind, he carefully tried to reconstruct the events which had taken place. If the murder was not carried out for political reasons, then who could have committed it, and why? He had to find the answers quickly; their return to Japan could not be delayed. He dressed without turning on the lights and returned to his grandfather's office.

The room was as he had left it. The teacups were still on the desk, but the bloodstain was dry, and it had darkened the floor where his grandfather had lain. He sat in Hiro's chair and stared at the cups. It was some time before he heard the soft but persistent knocking at the door.

"Takezawa-sama, are you in there?" a voice called.

Tatsuo opened the door and recognized Nazaki. "I am sorry, I did not hear your knock. Come in."

Nazaki closed the door behind him. "I am glad I found you." The older man seemed hesitant and uncertain. "I discovered this when I was preparing your grandfather's body." He held out a miniature hand carved from ivory. "I thought you should see it. I think your grandfather may have purposely concealed it."

"Where did you find it?"

"It was clenched in his hand. Perhaps he grabbed it just before he was shot. His fingers were grasping it so tightly, it was almost impossible to remove."

"Thank you, Nazaki-sama. "Thank you very much."

Tatsuo let the older man out and then leaned back against the door, the ivory miniature gripped tightly in his hand. Realization came slowly at first. A severed hand . . . why would his grandfather have the miniature clenched in his fist? He walked toward the desk again. There it was: the samurai statue with its right hand missing! The clue could mean only one thing. It was Conrad Richter who had killed his grandfather.

He should have guessed, Tatsuo told himself. It was Conrad who stood to lose the most because of Hiro's decision to cancel their contract; he must have come here to try to change his grandfather's mind. In the moments before his death, Hiro must have suspected the extent of Conrad's rage and had searched desperately for a way to leave a message. My grandfather knew me well, Tatsuo thought. Hiro had guessed he would immediately assume that the commander and vice admiral had been instructed to kill him, and he wanted to absolve them from blame. Perhaps Conrad had also counted on his leaping to that conclusion.

The following few days were a test of endurance for Tatsuo. To move a household after fifteen years was not an easy task with the myriad details that had to be taken care of. Tatsuo relied heavily on Karl. On the day prior to the scheduled departure, Tatsuo drove to Hiro's office for a final meeting with Cyrus Wilson and Patrick Fenton. Except for the desk, the straight-backed chair, and a sofa, his private office was bare. Tatsuo sat down at the desk and opened a folder.

"In the morning," he began, "I will be leaving for Japan with my grandmother. I will not be back. My grandfather left specific instructions which I would like to pass along to you today." He stared at the papers thoughtfully, without reading the words. He did not need to; he had already read them several times. "The bulk of my grandfather's estate will revert back to our family and to the zaibatsu, except for the company known as Pacific Far Eastern Trading. He has left instructions that it be transferred into your name, Patrick."

Patrick gripped the arm of the sofa, but his face did not show surprise. "Mr. Takezawa and I discussed the prospect of my taking over the company, but I figured it was too far in the future to even think about." Patrick swallowed and tried to clear his throat. "I will do my best to continue the same traditions Mr. Takezawa established." His voice broke, and he looked away.

"This building belongs to you, Mr. Wilson," Tatsuo continued. "What do you wish to do about the lease for this office?"

Cyrus lit his pipe and looked around the office for a few moments before answering. "It won't be the same without Hiro. I'm seventy-four years old, and I'm too tired to climb these stairs anymore. I don't want to lease it to anyone else. I would rather sell it."

"Would you consider selling the building to me?" Patrick asked.

"Why not? If you have the money, I'll give you a good deal. I've got a piece of property in Tofino. I think I'll buy a boat and catch those fish I've always talked about."

"I have the money," Patrick said.

"Well then, it's settled. You know what the building is worth. Make me an offer, and I'll have my lawyer fix up the papers."

"There is one more thing that concerned my grandfather," Tatsuo added. "He wanted Maiko's security to be ensured. Her family depends on her more than ever since her father died. I have made some provision for her, but I want to be sure she will be guaranteed a job for as long as she needs one."

"Maiko will have all the security she will ever need. She has finally agreed to marry me." Patrick smiled shyly. "We were planning to tell Mr. Takezawa the day he was . . ."

"My grandfather would have been very happy for you both, Patrick. You are a fortunate man." Tatsuo rose and walked around the desk. "It has been a privilege and a pleasure to know both of you. Thank you for what you have done for my grandfather and for me."

"Like I said before, it just won't be the same around here without Hiro." Tatsuo saw a glint of tears in Cyrus Wilson's eyes as they shook hands. For an instant Cyrus hesitated, then he quickly embraced Tatsuo. "Take care of yourself, young Takezawa." He released him abruptly and strode from the room.

"He is right," Patrick said. "It won't be the same here for anyone. But I will miss him most of all." He walked over to the window and looked out at the waterfront. "He altered the course of my life, and I never regretted it for one day."

"Ojī-san depended a great deal on you."

"Not nearly as much as I depended on him." Patrick smiled wanly. "I never did get used to drinking that green tea of his, though."

"Ojī-san said you drank too much coffee."

Patrick turned and looked at Tatsuo, his face somber and drawn. "What will you do now, Tatsuo?"

"I have some unfinished business with Conrad Richter, and then I will go home to Japan. What happens after that will depend on the zaibatsu."

"You won't be able to finish your business with Conrad here. He left for Japan two days ago."

Tatsuo stared at Patrick with disbelief. "He has gone to Japan?"

"Yes. Is there something I could do for you?"

"No, it is something I must take care of myself. I will find him without too much difficulty when I reach Tokyo. I think I know why he is there."

"So do I," Patrick replied. "One day that man's avarice will cost him more than he is prepared to pay."

"It already has." Tatsuo picked up the folder from the desk and then extended his hand to Patrick. "Good-bye. May you and Maiko live together in peace and harmony."

"Thank you. I shall think of you often."

At Drachenschlucht, Janice opened the door in answer to Tatsuo's knock. She kissed him and pointed to the study door. "Karl is waiting for you."

Karl heard Tatsuo's footsteps and opened the door. "Come in, kyō-dai."

"I cannot stay long, Karl. I have come to ask another favor of you."

"Name it," Karl said instantly.

"I would like you to come to Japan with me. You will only need to stay a few days."

"Of course. When?"

"Tomorrow."

"I'll be ready."

Tatsuo's lips curved into a grateful smile. "I knew I could depend on you."

"Can you tell me why?"

"I must face the zaibatsu as my grandfather did, and I will

need your strength and understanding for what I am forced to do.''

''I am not sure I understand.''

''In time you will. Is Lisl home?''

''No, she won't be back until the weekend.''

''Perhaps it is better this way,'' Tatsuo said. ''Give her my love, Karl, please.''

Janice held on to Karl's arm as they watched Tatsuo drive away. ''I feel as though I will never see him again. Tell me I'm being foolish, and then maybe I can stop crying.''

Karl looked at her tear-stained face and said nothing.

BOOK THREE
THE MASTER

⟦ 20 ⟧

Tatsuo gazed at the bold character imprinted on a rising sun, emblem of the Takezawa empire. Wealth, power, family, the legacy of fierce samurai warriors whose code of honor was still venerated as it had been centuries ago—all this was represented in the simple black strokes surrounded by a red circle. Tatsuo's muscles tensed, but he gave no outward sign of his agitation.

A uniformed doorman bowed as he held the door open for him. "Your uncle is expecting you, Takezawa-sama," he said gravely.

"Thank you. Have the rest of the council members arrived?"

"Yes, Takezawa-sama."

Tatsuo entered the council room. "Welcome, Tatsuo," Koji said. "Please sit down." He indicated the chair at the head of the table beside his own.

Tatsuo bowed and moved toward the chair, aware of the silence. When he turned to sit down, his breath stopped in his throat . . . Conrad Richter was sitting at the opposite end of the table! Tatsuo steadied himself, clutching the chair as he forced his breathing back to normal. He met Conrad's eyes and held them. The man who was responsible for his grandfather's death looked back without flinching, but Tatsuo recognized the uncertainty in the blue eyes, and then the hint of fear.

"You seem surprised to see me, Tatsuo," Conrad said boldly.

"On the contrary, Richter-sama, I would have been surprised had you not been here."

"May I offer my condolences to you in the death of your grandfather. His absence will certainly be felt by many." Conrad straightened the papers in front of him into a neat stack.

"Your concern is noted, Richter-sama."

"May we begin the meeting, please," Koji interjected. Behind him, the interpreter's voice quickly translated for the benefit of the council members who did not speak Japanese. "Mr. Richter has offered us a proposition. He will continue to procure and ship iron ore, steel, and other such materials without the aid of our Canadian office, for an additional five percent."

"How do you plan to do this? You no longer have the financial backing of Pacific Far Eastern Trading," Tatsuo said.

"I have already made the necessary arrangements, and I have secured adequate financial backing. I will make my own contacts and deal directly with this office." Heads nodded in agreement. "However, I would like to have written contract with the zaibatsu, if that is agreeable to you."

"Are you intimating that these men are not as honorable as my grandfather was?" Tatsuo asked.

Conrad knew he was being baited. "Certainly not, but I feel they would prefer to have the protection of a binding contract."

"Are you saying then that you are not trustworthy?"

Anger sparked in Conrad's eyes. "I am saying that under the circumstances, a contract would be desirable for both parties. The world situation is not as stable today as it was fifteen years ago when we first started, and the fact that I would like to have a written contract has absolutely nothing to do with anybody's character. I am investing a great deal of money, and I want to avoid any unnecessary risks."

"I certainly would not want you to take any more unnecessary risks," Tatsuo said politely.

"Gentleman," Koji intervened. "Let us get on with the business at hand."

"My apologies, Uncle. Mr. Richter, you and I have some

unfinished business, but I do not want to waste any more of the council's precious time. Perhaps we could arrange to meet after the burial of my grandfather?"

Only Tatsuo noticed Conrad's hesitation before he nodded. For the rest of the meeting he avoided looking at Tatsuo.

A tentative agreement was reached, and Conrad consented to remain in Japan until the contracts were drawn up and signed. He convinced the zaibatsu that a five-percent margin of profit was the minimum he could accept, and the zaibatsu finally agreed to it. For Tatsuo, it took enormous effort to remain dispassionate during the negotiations and to conceal his revulsion for Conrad Richter. He felt intense relief when the meeting was over; he excused himself and left quickly.

Outwardly, nothing had changed at the Takezawa estate. It was exactly as Tatsuo remembered, serenely beautiful, quiet, and untouched by the outside world.

Karl met him at the door. "You look exhausted!"

"That is an understatement. I feel as though I have been tied to the mast in a storm."

"Then it went badly this afternoon?"

"Actually, it went very well, but I am weary of negotiations." He sighed heavily. "How is my grandmother?"

"We spent the afternoon in the garden, reminiscing. Like you, she is tired but cannot sleep. It is as though she has no life left in her."

"You are right, Karl. She told me on the trip over here that her heart cannot accept Oji-san's death. Except for me, she has nothing else to live for. Her dream of enjoying a house full of grandchildren will never come true, and if one has nothing to live for, then one must die."

Karl looked at Tatsuo with sympathy in his eyes. "What can I say at a time like this?"

"There is no need to say anything. Your presence here when I need you more than ever before says enough." Tatsuo studied Karl's anxious face and wondered if Karl would still feel the same after the next few days. Would their friendship survive the ultimate test? It made Tatsuo sad to consider that it might not, but his decision had been made; there was no turning back. "At dawn, we will bury my grandfather near the shrine beside my parents. I have made the final arrangements with the priest." Tatsuo was talking more to himself than to Karl. "It will be a simple ceremony in accordance with the shibui spirit of the samurai."

As he listened, Karl realized it had been a very long time since he had heard Tatsuo laugh, as he had so often when they were young. Perhaps when the aching loss of his grandfather passed, he would make him laugh again, long and heartily from the bottom of his stomach.

The Buddhist priest arrived at dawn to begin the burial ceremony; the family was already assembled in front of the small shrine. The coffin bearing Hiro's body stood on a low pedestal. It was closed, but Tatsuo knew that Hiro would be draped in white silk, resting on a simple tatami mat and pallets of rice straw. Earlier, Tatsuo had opened the coffin for Miyoko, who placed several copper coins inside to ensure a safe journey for her husband across the Sanzu River. The priest rang a tiny bell and began his prayers. When the ceremony was completed, he nodded to Tatsuo.

"My grandfather wrote a haiku years ago after the death of my mother and father," Tatsuo said slowly, his voice steady. "It meant a great deal to me, and over the years it has helped me through difficult times. My grandfather was awed by the mysteries and infinite expanse of the universe. He preferred simplicity and strived to know himself, so that harmony with all things would be the result. In his final days, certain events brought him unbearable anguish, and he was forced to make decisions that disrupted his entire life. Yet I firmly believe he found that inner peace and harmony before he died. His words are recorded in my book:

> 'How black the night without its stars,
> Gulls are happy
> In the morning sun.'

I hope you understand his message and that you will forgive me for the things I must do."

After a lengthy pause, Shozo hobbled forward with great difficulty and placed a single flower on the coffin. His voice was frail and grating. "Although we mourn, we can still appreciate the fleeting and fragile beauty of a flower, and we appreciate it all the more because of its brief life, its unrepeatable individuality. The words are Buddha's, but never have they seemed more appropriate to me than now.'' Koji helped him back to his chair beneath the willow tree.

Miyoko did not weep. She stood beside Tatsuo, barely breathing, her face waxen as though a part of her had been buried with Hiro, wrapped up in the gossamer silk inside the coffin. The marks of grief that had been drawn on her face when Hitoshi and Yuri had died were now etched into deep crevices that could never be erased. Tatsuo placed his arm around her shoulders and comforted her.

Karl and Tatsuo were together later in the glassed-in veranda. ''I did not understand everything that was said, but I could sense the grief your family felt. Your words, especially, seemed to penetrate.''

''I spoke about the way my grandfather lived,'' Tatsuo explained.

''When this is all over, come back to Canada with me, Tatsuo. I need help with the shipyard.''

''No, I cannot go back with you.''

''But why? Japan's military leaders have bastardized the ideals and purpose of your zaibatsu. You've already told me you have no intention of beating their war drums, so what's to keep you here?''

Tatsuo searched for an answer. ''I must complete my duties.'' He looked directly at Karl. ''I need your understanding now, Karl, and your support.''

''You're not telling me everything, Tatsuo, and maybe that's why I'm scared. I have this feeling you're planning to do something . . . something that's going to drastically change our lives. You've been my friend for fifteen years, but sometimes I can't quite figure you out. It's as though part of you still lives in sixteenth-century Japan.''

''Karl, listen! Tomorrow I must face the council for the last time and carry out my grandfather's final wishes, which will be to officially sever all ties with our 'bastardized zaibatsu.' Then I will need your help. Give me your word that you will try to understand what I have to do.''

''You have my word that I will try, but I can't promise any more until I find out what the hell you are planning to do.''

''That is enough. Please stay here until I come for you.''

''Would you allow me to come with you now?''

"No. There is something I must do alone."

Karl had asked about his father only once since their arrival in Japan. He had been informed that Conrad was ensconced in a palatial residence reserved for visiting military and political dignitaries. It was there that Tatsuo had arranged to meet him.

Hidefumi, without his traditional loose-fitting kimono, his face only partially visible in the dark dojo, did not resemble the affable family servant who had adopted the Takezawa family many years ago. As he waited for Tatsuo with his arms folded, clad in black trousers and matching shirt, he easily could have passed for a stone carving.

"Are you certain that you wish to go through with this, Hidefumi?" Tatsuo asked the moment he entered the dojo.

Hidefumi nodded.

"You do not have to come with me. You have already done enough."

"You and your grandmother are all that is left of my family. I know what you are planning to do. Please afford me the honor of helping you in my small way."

"Thank you, Hidefumi." Tatsuo removed the sword and its silver scabbard from the wall and strapped it to his waist. "I am ready."

Hidefumi maneuvered the car with surprising dexterity through the city, where crowds streamed along the streets under a kaleidoscope of neon lights. Aware that Tatsuo was preparing himself for his meeting with Conrad, Hidefumi did not speak until he stopped the car in front of the elaborately porticoed building. "There are no guards, just servants and guests. I will go with you as far as the door. Richter is in suite number seventeen. I will see that you are not bothered during your meeting."

Heavy carpets muffled their footsteps as they climbed the stairs to the second floor. In the wide hallway, the lighting was subdued, the colors muted to enhance the magnificent decor. At the door to Conrad's suite, Hidefumi stopped and nodded to Tatsuo.

Tatsuo knocked once, opened the door, and entered. Conrad did not move from the richly embroidered armchair at the opposite end of the sitting room. For a moment, his eyes betrayed surprise as they flicked over Tatsuo's black robes and sword, but his hand was steady when he reached over to refill his glass from a crystal decanter.

"Will you join me?" Conrad asked calmly. He leaned back in his chair and smiled. "Let's see. The last time I had Scotch that tasted like this was when I secured my first contract with your grandfather. I stayed in that bamboo fortress of yours, but you probably don't remember."

"I remember it well, Richter-sama," Tatsuo replied. With a quick shake of his head, he refused the glass Conrad held out to him.

"Suit yourself." In one short gulp, Conrad downed what he had poured for Tatsuo. He crossed his legs with exaggerated ease and observed Tatsuo through half-closed eyes. "Well, what is all this urgency about?"

Tatsuo's hand moved instinctively to the hilt of the sword, and Conrad's eyes were instantly alert. "My grandfather's murder," he said flatly.

"Your grandfather's murder? What the hell has that got to do with me? He disobeyed the orders of your government and they assassinated him!"

"No, Richter-sama. It was you who killed him."

Conrad bolted up from his chair, knocking over the crystal decanter. It shattered, and the liquid flowed unnoticed onto the carpet. "And just how do you think you're going to prove that?"

"I do not have to prove it. I know, and that is enough."

Panic edged into Conrad's voice. "What the hell do you know? You weren't there."

"That is correct, but this was in my grandfather's hand. It explains a great deal." From his robe, Tatsuo produced the tiny ivory hand and threw it across the room. It landed at Conrad's feet.

Conrad picked it up and examined it; comprehension dawned on his face. "He deserved it, the bastard! He took everything I had—my wife, Lisl and Karl, even Drachenschlucht. I had nothing left, and it was his doing." Conrad's voice began to rise. "And then he was going to take the last thing I had—my contract with the zaibatsu. Sure I shot him, and there isn't a goddamn thing you can do about it!" He leered defiantly at Tatsuo, who drew back in revulsion. "You threaten me, and your military will have you strung up by the balls. They need me to haul that steel and oil so they can make their guns and run their tanks. They won't let you or anybody else stand in the way.''

"I am not afraid of them, Richter-sama. Taking your life holds no risks for me,'' Tatsuo said quietly.

"You're crazy!'' Conrad shouted. "You're bloody crazy. Your grandfather was an old man and he's dead. Why the hell do you want to die too?''

"I do not want to die, but there is no other way. Prepare yourself to pass honorably from this world.''

He advanced slowly toward Conrad, who momentarily seemed rooted to the floor. Like a cornered animal, he drew his lips back from his teeth and his breath came in harsh gasps. Tatsuo saw the glint of a silver muzzle an instant before Conrad fired the revolver. He moved instinctively and the bullet missed its fatal mark, but he felt the jarring explosion in his left shoulder. Conrad's eyes darted wildly. Tatsuo swung the sword in a wide arc above his head and through Conrad's neck.

When the spinal column is severed and the arteries and veins are cut, death occurs, but not instantaneously. For a few moments the brain continues to send its vital messages, fighting desperately for life, and the heart continues to pump its life-giving blood—and so it was with Conrad. He stood motionless for several seconds, his eyes distended with horror and his mouth open in a long, silent scream. He seemed to hang there suspended, refusing the inevitable, his hand still pointing the gun at Tatsuo. He toppled finally, his head first and then his body, which jerked spasmodically as blood gushed in violent spurts from the neck.

Tatsuo shuddered and stepped back from the lifeless head that had fallen at his feet. The blue eyes that stared vacantly were even more vivid in death.

Hidefumi touched Tatsuo on the shoulder. "We must leave quickly.'' Tatsuo felt himself begin to sway dizzily as he turned toward Hidefumi. "You are injured!'' Hidefumi steadied him. "We must get help for you immediately.''

"Just take me home, please,'' Tatsuo whispered.

"But you are bleeding.''

"I must go home, Hidefumi. I have to see Karl and tell him what I have done. Please take me home.''

The look on Tatsuo's face stopped further protestation

from Hidefumi. With his shoulder under Tatsuo's right arm, they hurried from the building, aware that behind them lights were flicking on in darkened rooms and raised voices announced that the body had been discovered.

"We've left a trail of blood!" Hidefumi helped Tatsuo into the car.

"It does not matter."

Under the artificial lights of Tokyo, Tatsuo appeared totally without color as he slumped against the seat. When he spoke, Hidefumi was startled. "Have you ever had a friend whose life you valued more than your own?"

"No, I never have."

Tatsuo shook his head as if his pain was too intense to bear. "I have such a friend, and I have just killed his father."

"You had no choice."

Tatsuo shifted his position to relieve the pain in his shoulder; blood seeped through the sleeve of his robe and trickled into his hand.

Hidefumi watched anxiously, fearful Tatsuo would bleed to death before they reached their destination.

"Do not look so alarmed, Hidefumi," Tatsuo said when they reached the outskirts of the city. "The wound is not fatal. The bullet tore the flesh, but I do not think it damaged the bone. When we get home, do not alarm my grandmother or wake anyone except Karl."

"You must get medical attention. You will bleed to death if nothing else."

"You can bandage it for me as soon as we get home."

"Your face is the color of parchment. You will need more than a bandage," Hidefumi insisted.

The house was in darkness when they drove into the driveway. A figure emerged from the dimly lit doorway the instant the car came to a halt. Hidefumi recognized him immediately.

"Karl! Quick, help me with Tatsuo."

"I can walk." Tatsuo stood up, swayed unsteadily, then leaned against Karl.

"Good Lord," Karl cried. "You're bleeding . . . you need a doctor."

"No! Hidefumi will tend to it, then you and I must talk."

"Talk? What is there to talk about except getting medical attention for you?"

"Please, Karl. You must do as I ask."

There was an urgency in Tatsuo's voice that Karl could not ignore. He waited helplessly while Hidefumi assuaged the bleeding, disinfected the wound, and bandaged it. Only then did a semblance of color return to Tatsuo's face.

"I will go now," Hidefumi said. "If the bleeding begins during the night, call me. I will sleep outside your door."

"Thank you, Hidefumi," Tatsuo whispered. "Thank you for everything."

Karl waited only until the door was closed, "Now, will you tell me what happened?"

"I was shot, shot by the same weapon that killed my grandfather."

"The same assassin who killed your grandfather? But why does the military want to kill you?"

"The military is not responsible for my grandfather's death, nor did they try to kill me tonight."

"Then who did, for God's sake?"

"My grandfather was shot by . . . by your father, Karl. He was the one who put the bullet through my shoulder tonight."

"My father?" Karl gasped.

Tatsuo nodded wordlessly.

"But why? How did you know he killed your grandfather?"

"I discovered it by accident. The fishermen from Steveston found a small ivory hand from a statue clutched in my grandfather's hand. They did not know the significance of the message, but I did."

"The bloody battle that saved my father's life years ago! How ironic! Hiro saved my father's life, and in return my father took his." Karl clenched his fists as he fought to control himself.

"I am sorry, Karl. I am truly sorry."

"What kind of man do I have for a father? Is he so hungry for power and money that he has turned into a monster?" Karl asked desperately.

"I do not know, Karl, I only know that he is dead."

"My father is dead too?" Karl asked incredulously.

"Yes. I took his life." The agony that Karl felt was mirrored in Tatsuo's eyes. "Forgive me, please."

Karl buried his head in his hands. "Forgive you? What is there to forgive? He was my father, and now that he is dead, I feel nothing—no love, no pity, no hate, nothing! He didn't care about anyone but himself, and he destroyed whatever feelings I had for him when he told my mother to leave home and die in the hospital. I never loved him, Tatsuo, but I loved your grandfather. Why should you ask for my forgiveness? He meant to kill you when he fired at you. It was self-defense."

"No, my friend, you are wrong. I would have killed him anyway."

"To avenge your grandfather's death?"

"Yes and more. My grandfather could not bring himself to send shiploads of iron ore and steel to Japan, nor could he allow your father to circumvent our office and continue these shipments. So you see, Karl, your father's death was inevitable. Now can you still say there is nothing to forgive?"

"Maybe his death was inevitable, but he killed Hiro and he made an attempt on your life, and you ask me if I can forgive you for killing him!" Karl paced the small room, trying to understand his own feelings. Was he himself a monster for not feeling anything but a sense of relief? Suddenly he slammed his fist into his hand, and the sound echoed in the enclosure of the room. "I'm glad he's dead! Do you know that? I'm glad he's dead! He made life intolerable for my mother, he almost turned my sister into an emotional cripple, and he would have wrung me dry for my mother's inheritance if he could have found a way. He used people and discarded them when they were no longer useful to him. He hated everyone and everything that would not bend to his will." Karl sank down onto the mat. "The sins of the father are visited upon his children."

"You are not like your father, Karl. You never have been and never will be," Tatsuo said firmly.

"I'm not so sure I never have been. Janice has accused me of it more than once."

"Then she does not know you as well as she should."

"At the time, her accusations were justified—but never again! Never again!" Karl repeated fervently. "I used to wonder if my father ever felt love or anything close to love. There were times, long ago, when I thought he loved me, but he was using me too. He thought he could mold me into an image of himself. When his plan didn't work, he tried to make me a victim, too." Karl breathed deeply. "What a fool he was—he could have had it all, and he threw it away. He had money but he wanted more, he had success but it wasn't enough, he could have had our love but he didn't value it. I guess what I really feel now is pity, pity for my mother and for the life he forced her to live and pity for the tragic waste of your grandfather's life." Karl was quiet for a few moments, then added, "And I suppose I feel pity for myself because I never had a father who loved me for what I am."

Tatsuo nodded with understanding. They sat in silence for a long time before Karl asked, "What will happen now?"

"In the morning I will go before the council, Uncle Koji, Great-uncle Shozo, and the members of the military. I will tell them that I will not follow their orders any longer. I feel the military has no place on the council of the zaibatsu and that Japan is being led needlessly into another war. I will also tell them that I killed your father."

"Do you think they will release you from your obligations?"

"No, but that does not matter now."

"What do you mean?"

"They cannot decide my fate any longer. They cannot release me from my obligations. It is not within their power. Only I can do that."

"I don't understand," Karl said hesitantly. Fear began to dawn in his eyes as he looked at Tatsuo's calm face.

"I want you to be my second, Karl, when I commit seppuku."

The feeling that coursed through Karl was smothering in its intensity. "No! No! I won't let you do it. You can't!" he shouted.

"It is the only way for me, Karl."

"Why? Why do you want to die?"

"I do not have to explain the meaning of honor to you. I am my own master, and I will decide my fate."

"To hell with fate! You're talking about killing yourself." Karl was on his feet. "You're talking about sticking a knife into your guts! You're asking me to help you kill yourself!"

"I am not afraid to die," Tatsuo answered.

"I'm not going to let you do it. For Christ's sake, Tatsuo, do you know how final death is?"

"I know. I have thought about it for a long time. I knew it would come to this from the first time the zaibatsu sent me to Manchuria."

"How am I going to make you change your mind?" The

terrible weight of Tatsuo's decision had sent him reeling under its force. He lashed out with words. "The bastards, the rotten bastards—your uncles, my father, the military—they drove you to this. I'll kill them! I'll kill them all." His voice rose into a shout and he paced the room. "What will you gain by killing yourself for those bastards?"

"My honor," Tatsuo said quietly.

His anger spent, Karl sank down on the mat beside Tatsuo. "Your honor is more important than your life?"

Tatsuo nodded.

"Is this why you asked me to come to Japan with you?"

Again Tatsuo nodded.

"I'm not going to change your mind, am I? You're really going to do it."

"Will you be my second, Karl?"

Nothing Karl had ever experienced, nothing he had ever seen or felt, could have prepared him for this moment. Every nerve in his body screamed denial, every thought and feeling wanted life to continue for this man who looked at him with eyes as clear as a summer sky and as old as life itself. Memories from their past flashed before him: the two of them in the dojo, perspiration glistening on their foreheads, their bodies in tune with Hiro's commands; Tatsuo with his arm around Lisl on board the *Cathy B*, his face reflecting love and happiness; the *Liverpool* and the adventures they had shared. Memories to last a lifetime were not enough; Tatsuo's death would leave a terrible void that he could never fill or even want to fill.

"Will you?" Tatsuo asked again.

"Yes," Karl replied in a hoarse voice. "Yes, I'll be your second, kyō-dai. It is my place."

During the long night Karl could not sleep; he lay with his eyes wide open, staring into the darkness. In his mind, he knew that he must come to terms with Tatsuo's decision and accept it fully, without reservation, or he would surely fail him. He longed for Janice and the comfort of her warm body against his; he longed for John and Andrew and their rough-and-tumble smell, and then he felt the dawn of understanding.

Understanding did not come like a thunderbolt; rather, it evolved slowly, releasing his heart from its cage of pain. He had planned his life, had willingly obligated himself to Janice;

he had accepted the full measure of her love, and together they had given life to John and Andrew. His blood flowed in their bodies; they were his claim to immortality, and the center of his life. Whatever goals he would aspire to, whatever happiness he achieved, the final analysis would always reveal the real core of his existence to be his love for John, Andrew, and Janice. How much was he willing to give up for them? If their lives were threatened, would he willingly forfeit his life to save them? The answer came simply. He would offer his life, for to do anything less would not be enough.

Karl recalled the look on Tatsuo's face when he had stepped from the airplane after his first trip to Manchuria. Valiantly, Tatsuo had attempted to follow the course someone else had chosen for him, and the results were painfully evident: his face infinitely older, his eyes afflicted with something more than sorrow. To live contrary to one's own conscience was, to Tatsuo, worse than death. How far had they pushed him before he made this final decision?

Karl slept finally, with the knowledge that when he held the ceremonial sword above Tatsuo's head, he would not fail.

The meeting of the zaibatsu council was held in the morning, and as Koji had forewarned, it was dominated by the military. A senior naval officer, whose penetrating glance and brusque voice commanded instant attention, rose to speak. "In recent months we have signed nonaggression pacts with the Soviets as well as with Germany and Italy. They guarantee Japanese supremacy in Southeast Asia. However, the United States, Great Britain, and the Netherlands are marshalled against the empire. The Americans are threatening to put an embargo on our supplies of oil and rubber—we are using twelve thousand tons of oil each day, and at that rate our supplies will be depleted in two years. We must either bow to the demands of these nations or . . . conquer the whole of Southeast Asia and take what is rightfully ours." He sat down stiffly; the room crackled with tension.

A second officer addressed the council. "I must agree with Admiral Mayada. Although some sources intimate that the United States would lift its embargo and allow us a free hand in Manchukuo and Korea if we retreat from China, we have no assurance that this would be honored. It is true that our supplies of oil are being rapidly depleted and we must consider this in our planning, but we must also consider that the Americans have ten times the industrial might of Japan and they will surely win a protracted war. But . . ." and here he stopped for emphasis, "but if we unleash a series of stunning attacks and consolidate our empire before the United States war machine can get into full production, we will have a fortress of Pacific bases extending from the Kurile Islands in the north down through Wake Island to the Bismark Archipelago and to New Guinea." The room was deathly still.

"Sit down, please, Admiral," Tatsuo commanded. "It has become painfully obvious to me that you have already planted the seeds of destruction, and they will surely yield a plentiful harvest. The peaceful efforts of our ambassadors and those of other nations are not being heeded. This is unfortunate, because our empire is extensive enough with Manchukuo and Korea."

Koji stood up, his face flushed with anger, while the rest of the council stared at Tatsuo with amazement. "How dare you! How dare you show such cowardly disrespect? Leave this room immediately!"

"I will leave presently, Uncle. We have all been taught to revere and serve our emperor. A few years ago, Emperor Meiji revealed his concern in a poem:

> 'All the seas everywhere
> are brothers to each other,
> Why then do the winds and waves of strife
> rage so throughout the world?'

That is exactly what I feel, and I will not carry out your orders any longer. You will not need the contract which you have drawn up for the Richter Shipping Line. Conrad Richter is dead. I killed him." There were several audible gasps, but no one moved. "He killed my grandfather." Tatsuo saw Koji clench his fists. "Tomorrow morning, I will commit seppuku in accordance with the ancient code of the samurai." Slowly, Tatsuo looked from one face to the next until his gaze rested on his Uncle Koji.

"Who is to be your second?" Koji whispered in a choked voice.

"Karl Richter."

Tatsuo bowed respectfully to the members of his family before leaving the room. The silence resounded from the walls.

[21]

How could one prepare for the death of a cherished companion and lifelong friend? If death is quick, there is a numbing shock to soften the blow; if death offers a merciful escape from unrelenting pain, there is a sense of relief; but for Karl to prepare for Tatsuo's death was a brutal assault on all his emotions, a desperate battle with himself to let go. He understood Tatsuo's reasons, yet inwardly he clung to the fading hope that somehow it would not happen, that ultimately Tatsuo would choose life over death. Karl paced through the house and garden waiting for the hours to creep by, yet when Tatsuo returned, he wondered how the day had passed so quickly.

"The day was long for you," Tatsuo said, noticing the dark shadows beneath his eyes.

Karl shrugged, not trusting himself to speak.

"After the meeting with the council, I spent several hours in a monastery."

"Did you tell the monks what you are planning to do?" Karl asked.

"They knew without my telling them."

"They didn't try to change your mind?" Karl asked, his dim hope fading.

"No. To them, death is a continuation of life. I used to think that the monks, isolated the way they are, had withdrawn from life and from reality, but this is not true. It is just that they have no worldly attachments. They live each day as it comes, totally free and at peace. Death is not a tragedy for them, yet they consider life very precious." Tatsuo's face was calm, the taut lines smoothed. "I must talk to my grandmother now. Will you join me later in the o-furo?"

Karl managed a smile. "I would like that." He marveled at Tatsuo's strength and tried not to think of what lay ahead.

Later, in the steaming water, Karl tried to speak, but the words seemed to stick in his throat.

Tatsuo prompted him. "Say what is on your mind, kyō-dai."

Karl leaned his head back against the rim of the wooden tub. "I know your decision is the right one for you. I understand your reasons. But damnit, Tatsuo, I'm going to miss you. I guess our lives have been fused together for so long, I feel as though a part of me will die with you." Karl's throat constricted and his eyes burned.

"Your friendship has been one of the finest aspects of my life, Karl."

The corners of Karl's mouth lifted into a smile. "Did you know I made a promise to your grandfather the first time I came to Japan that I would always protect you and be your friend?"

"No, my grandfather never told me. You have kept your promise, and I am grateful."

"I guess tomorrow will be the greatest test of all." Karl's voice trembled.

"You are a sensei, Karl; you will not fail." Tatsuo winced with pain as he stood up. The heat had opened the wound in his shoulder, and blood seeped through the bandages.

"Do not look so concerned—I have suffered more in training. I will have Hidefumi change the dressings."

Despite his exhaustion Karl did not sleep, and at midnight, when Hidefumi knocked on his door, he answered immediately.

"Please come now, Richter-sama. Tatsuo is ready."

Hidefumi led Karl to the dojo, where Tatsuo was waiting, his black robe tied with a silver cord. An ivory-handled knife hung from his waist.

"Uncle Koji will be going with us. He will bring my body back for burial." Tatsuo removed a sword from the wall and passed it to Karl. "I have returned my grandfather's sword. This one belongs to me. It is the fifth sword. When we are done, please give it to Koji."

They drove to the ocean without speaking. The sound and smell of the sea reached them long before Hidefumi eased the car to the side of the narrow rutted roadway that ran parallel to the shore. The moon had risen in a clear, star-ridden sky, and from the road, the ocean appeared green and luminous.

In the moonlight, Hidefumi's face was impassive; only the faint workings of his mouth revealed his emotions. He bowed to Tatsuo, then stood rigidly erect. "I will wait here, Tatsuo-sama," he said in a strange voice. Tatsuo touched his shoulder lightly before starting toward the beach. Karl and Koji followed.

In the light of the moon, the three figures walked along the narrow beach, ignoring the spray from the crashing waves. Gradually, the beach began to widen into an expanse of fine white sand above which rose the craggy, unscalable cliffs.

Here Tatsuo stopped and waited for Koji. They regarded each other for a moment without speaking, and whatever was left to say passed between them in silence. Tatsuo reached into the folds of his robe and brought out a book, which he passed to Koji.

"Ojī-san wrote this book and gave it to me many years ago. It has brought me comfort and understanding. Perhaps it will do the same for you."

Koji accepted the book and ran his fingers slowly over the cover. "I know of this book, Tatsuo. It will be treasured by the Takezawas."

Tatsuo bowed. "When the sun rises, you will be able to see me from here." He did not mention that it was from this very spot that his grandfather had kept his silent vigil over him in the aftermath of the Kanto earthquake.

Koji, lines of sadness on his face, bowed deeply to Tatsuo. "You are samurai, Takezawa-sama."

Tatsuo chose a place on the beach where the rush of waves did not wet the sand. He faced the east and spread his mat carefully. "I will meditate and pray until the sun rises."

Karl sat beside him and, like Tatsuo, he willed his body to relax and his mind to become quiet until the crashing of the waves faded and the wild hammering of his heart slowed to an even rhythm. With heads slightly bowed, they sat motionless, oblivious to the night—sentinels awaiting the last sunrise.

Karl heard the gulls, first only one and then, in the distance, several more. He opened his eyes and realized the night had passed; the first hint of dawn had already brushed the sky.

"The gulls are back," Tatsuo whispered, his eyes following the graceful swoop of the birds. Finally his gaze rested on the sun, now fully risen above the horizon. "It is time." He turned and looked directly at Karl. "May God always be with you to guide your footsteps."

"And you, my friend," Karl replied.

Tatsuo removed the knife from its scabbard and opened his robe to expose his chest and stomach. Karl stood behind him, withdrew the sword, and held it high above Tatsuo's head, his knuckles white from the force of his grip.

"We are both masters, Karl, do not let me fail."

Karl's grip loosened, for he knew Tatsuo would not falter; there would be no need to use the sword. The ocean seemed to grow still, and an unusual calm enveloped them.

Tatsuo took a deep breath and held it, then pushed the knife deep into the left side of his stomach and drew it effortlessly across his body. He removed the blade only to plunge it in again above his groin. His eyes glazed and blood rushed freely as he pulled the knife upward until his lacerated bowels slid into his lap. He looked up at Karl, and a faint smile appeared on his face.

"Look, Tatsuo," Karl whispered. "There are hundreds of gulls above you. You are free now just as they are." He dropped to his knees and caught Tatsuo as his body crumpled.